Betty McInnes was born in Aberdeen and trained as an architect in Dundee. She worked as an architectural assistant, after qualifying in 1953, and took up writing in 1974 in order to spend more time at home with her two children.

Betty McInnes lives in Dundee with her husband, and her hobbies include delving into local history, gardening, and travelling around Scotland and England.

The River Calls Us Home

Betty McInnes

HEADLINE

First published in 1992
by HEADLINE BOOK PUBLISHING PLC

First published in paperback in 1993
by HEADLINE BOOK PUBLISHING PLC

10 9 8 7 6 5 4 3

ISBN 0 7472 3992 4

Printed and bound in Great Britain by
HarperCollins Manufacturing, Glasgow

HEADLINE BOOK PUBLISHING PLC
Headline House
79 Great Titchfield Street
London W1P 7FN

To Anna and Malcolm

Chapter 1

Christina Kennedy was born in April 1890, as a clamour of bells summoned the jute workers of Dundee to another day's labour in the mills. The healthy, wailing lass was treated with scant ceremony. Bessie McCutcheon wiped the baby's nose and mouth, wrapped her in a blanket and popped her hastily into the carved, wooden crib that had rocked Christina's three stalwart brothers before her. Then Bessie and Dr Alexander concentrated all their efforts on the middle-aged mother, until presently the doctor shook his head gravely.

'Aye, William Kennedy will be a sad man, I fear, when his whaler berths in King William dock and he finds himself the father of the lassie he hoped for, and a widower forbye.'

But that was four years ago, ample time for a baby to grow into a little lass whose winsome ways had captivated her three brothers, and gone a long way towards mending William Kennedy's grieving heart.

It was a fine, spring morning, the sky hazy blue, the Tay estuary shining silver, on Christina's fourth birthday. Christina stood with her father at the window of the house her grandfather had built close by the river, in the flush of the family's fortune. They'd owned a fleet of whalers once, years before she was born, but the cruel, Arctic ice had crushed many of William Kennedy's brave ships. Poor yields of whale oil, and a scarcity of whalebone required for the corsets of fashionable ladies, had put paid to all but two of the rest.

William had his hopes pinned upon one last venture. He tugged nervously at his neat beard, his gaze, like Christina's, fastened eagerly westwards. He fished out a watch on the end of a gold albert, and frowned at it.

She was late. What could be hindering her? Some mischance in the dock? Oh, he should have been there himself, to oversee, and not left it to his two older sons and Albert Dickson, a good enough old veteran of the ice, but—

'Papa! She's coming!' Christina flattened her nose against the glass, then became quite still, mouth open, scarcely breathing with excitement.

The ship came slowly and majestically from the yard that built her. She was graceful, yet sturdy, with tall masts, and furled creamy sails square rigged on the mizzen-mast, a tall funnel with a drift of smoke dark against the light sky. A sight for a little girl to remember all her life, a sight to bring moisture to a man's eyes.

'Oh, Papa! There's my ship!' Christina breathed.

William laid a hand gently on her golden head. Now he knew why he'd chosen to stay at home when his new ship set out on her trials. He'd wanted to be with his beloved daughter, to watch the pleasure on the child's face as the ship, named for herself and the mother she'd never known, sailed from the Tay.

The *Christina K*.

'Aye, my wee lass, it's your very own ship,' William said gruffly.

Christina had been still for at least three minutes, which was a record for her. Now she whirled on her toes, eyes dancing.

'Ernest, Ernest! Come and see the *Christina K*. You're missing it all, you silly!'

Her brother Ernest had drifted back to his books, wearied with waiting and watching by the window. Good-naturedly, he rose from the desk in answer to the imperious summons. Skipping across, his little sister tugged his hand, looking up at him.

'Hurry! George promised he'd dip the flag as she passes, and I want to be sure he does it.'

Ernest seemed immensely tall and adult to Christina, though he was barely fourteen. He'd been judged too young to join his brothers, George and Arthur, on the bridge of the *Christina K* and was secretly thankful for the reprieve. Ernest was an uneasy sailor, and had no love of the sea. Books and a serious study of mathematics took up most of his time.

Smiling, he allowed the little imp to drag him to the window. His eyes widened in awe as he saw the ship.

'Papa, she's beautiful.'

'And she's mine! My big, bonnie ship!' sang Christina blithely, making the young lad and the older man laugh tolerantly at her antics.

Her father fished in his pocket and drew out a red leather box. 'Aye, and this is yours too, Chrissie, a keepsake for your fourth birthday, to mind you of the birthday of your ship.'

Christina fumbled with the little box, its catch defeating her small fingers. Ernest stooped and opened it for her, and her mouth dropped open in wonder.

'Oh, Papa!'

'A brooch, Bessie? Never!' the cook said.

Bessie McCutcheon took a thick wad of flannel to lift the smoothing iron, heating on the range. She held the iron a short distance from her red cheek, gauging its heat.

'Aye, Martha. Her pa gave Chrissie a brooch to mark her birthday. A bonnie brooch he'd had made special

3

in solid silver. It's made just like the ship, with a pearl at the masthead, an emerald to port, and a ruby to starboard. Fancy giving a four-year-old a pricey thing like thon!' Bessie declared.

Martha, the cook, dourly thumped a lump of bread dough with the heel of her hand. 'Some folk have more siller than sense!'

Bessie smoothed Christina's lace-trimmed petticoat with loving fingers, then applied the iron energetically. 'Mind you, Martha, she's a bonnie wee lass, a charmer to steal your heart. But a brooch! Did you ever hear the like? The wean will lose it, she's so flighty.'

'Aye, she can twist her pa round her wee finger, when the man comes home from the whaling. And she knows it. She's a spoiled, wee madam!' nodded Martha grimly.

Chrissie roamed freely on the stoney beach in front of the house. She was left in Bessie McCutcheon's tender care while her father and two older brothers voyaged to Antarctica, to test the mettle of the *Christina K* in its icy wastes. Bessie had her own lenient theories concerning the benefits of cold, fresh air in the toughening up of bairns, and allowed Chrissie to venture out in all weathers. She learned to relish cold rain on her skin, and salt spray on her lips, and she was there in all weathers, standing on the shore watching with a lift of the heart and shining eyes, when the *Christina K* came sailing home across the bar, at the end of her father's trips.

Her own, bonnie ship that held within it all that was dear to her.

It was a balmy day, and the ship not due for some months, when Chrissie met the mill girl. Chrissie was clad in a sparkling-white, starched pinafore over a pale blue linen dress intricately smocked, with a peep of lace

4

petticoat below the knee, and long, deep-blue knitted stockings. Bessie had polished her charge's buttoned boots vigorously that morning until they shone, but she needn't have bothered. They already had a white line of salt and sand along the uppers, caused by jumping gleefully on wet seaweed, to make the bladders pop.

The mill girl was sitting so still, huddled beneath the shadow of a rock, Chrissie almost jumped on her instead of the seaweed. She stopped just in time, and smiled her wide, friendly smile.

'I'm so sorry. I didn't see you. Nobody comes here usually, you see, and the Broughty Ferry fisherfolk keep their boats further east. Are you one of them?' Chrissie asked curiously.

'Naw. I'm a half-timer at the mill, learning the spinning,' the girl admitted grudgingly.

There was an awkward silence, during which Chrissie examined her newfound friend frankly. Chrissie felt sorry for her. She didn't look much older than Chrissie herself, but her lank hair was scraped back and tied so fiercely on top of her head with twine, it looked as if she might have difficulty smiling. She clutched at a black shawl covered in wisps of golden strands, and wore a nondescript blouse and skirt. Her feet were wrapped clumsily in jute cloth, like small sacks. Chrissie's keen interest was aroused.

'Is it pleasant, working in the mill?' she enquired politely.

'Pleasant!' The girl gaped incredulously for a moment, then to Chrissie's distress, fat tears welled up and rolled down her cheeks.

'Ooohhh! I canna keep my ends up. I tried an' tried, but the mill runs so fast I canna keep my ends up. The foreman came roaring at me again, so I ran away, out the mill. I never stopped running till now, and I'll no' go back!'

5

The mill girl's words made no sense to Chrissie, and she was mystified and worried. She didn't know why it should be so difficult to keep your end up in the mill, but she supposed they were very proud and haughty people in there, who looked down upon a poor girl. Chrissie's sympathetic heart ached for her.

'Oh, dear me! Where will you go?'

The mill lass wiped her eyes on her shawl and stood up. 'I've an auntie that's a fishwife in Broughty. She'll maybe let me do the gutting for her. I'd rather gut fish than go back to the mill.'

Chrissie longed to help. She suddenly remembered the two farthings she had in her pinafore pocket, all that was left of her Saturday penny. She took them out and offered them generously to the girl.

'Here, this is for you. Take it.'

The mill lass stood stock still, staring at the farthings. Then her expression slowly darkened until her eyes looked angrily black, and she suddenly lifted a fist and struck Chrissie's hand away. The two farthings went flying, to be lost forever amongst the shingle.

'Keep your dirty money!' the girl shouted in Chrissie's face, then ran off clumsily in her shapeless footwear.

Chrissie went weeping indignantly home to Bessie.

'She was horrid, Bessie! A rough, ill-mannered working girl in ugly clothes. I'm glad I'm not like that. Why, the nasty creature wouldn't even accept the farthings I gave her.' Chrissie wept.

'No, she wouldn't. That was charity, Chrissie. The lassie had her pride, if nothing else.'

Bessie made no further comment on the incident. Her mouth tightened grimly, that was all.

Chrissie was wakened rudely in the pitch dark next morning by a popping hiss as the gaslight lit. Bessie blew out the taper.

'Come, lassie. Up you get!' she ordered in a tone that brooked no argument.

'But . . . but—' Chrissie rubbed the sleep out of her eyes. The window frames rattled. It was raining and windy outside, as well as being dark. It must still be the middle of the night!

'What . . . what time is it?' she yawned, while Bessie helped her dress.

'Half past four. Come eat your brose.'

Chrissie was too sleepy and confused to argue. Besides, Bessie wore a grim look that subdued her. She supped the hot brose obediently, without appetite.

'Fetch your cape, Chrissie. We're going out,' Bessie said.

Out!

Huddled in the cape, with the hood pulled well over her head, Chrissie could hardly believe it when Bessie took her hand firmly, and they set off into the teeth of a westerly wind and driving rain, along the Dundee Road. It was like a bad dream.

'Where are we going, Bessie?'

'You'll see.'

Early though it was, there were plenty of people about. Fishwives with creels of fresh fish walked from Broughty towards the town. Vegetable carts and milk carts from the farms loomed out of the dark and clip-clopped away ahead, their drivers huddled beneath makeshift shelter.

Bessie walked along the Dundee Road, then climbed the hill when they reached the first dark mass of tenements at Blackscroft. Chrissie trotted along valiantly by her side, too cold, wet and miserable to complain. They stopped on the cobbles outside a large, arched gateway. The ground seemed to shake under Chrissie's feet, and she drew closer to her nurse, frightened.

'Bessie, where are we?' she whispered.

7

'Outside the mill.'

Bessie's face looked stern in the dawn light. Chrissie wiped her nose unhappily on the back of her hand, and decided to keep a host of questions till later. They stood in silence.

Suddenly there was a raucous din that made the little girl cling to Bessie and whimper with terror. Bessie laughed, and touched her face.

'Wheest, lamb. It's only the hooters for the beginning of the shift.'

When the noise ceased, even the thunder of the mill seemed quiet. Chrissie found she was holding her breath, waiting.

'Look!' ordered Bessie, pointing.

In the grey light, Chrissie could see that doors were opening up and down the street. She could hear the clatter of hundreds of pairs of boots on the tenement platforms and stairs, and the soft, swishing sound of just as many jute-clad feet shuffling along. Down the street from all sides came pouring a vast army of men and women, so many that Chrissie's jaw dropped. Their number was beyond her imagination.

For the most part, they were chaffing and cheery, despite the wind and rain and the early hour, and the street echoed to shouts and loud laughter. Bessie appeared to be well known.

'Aye, Bessie! Have you lost your soft job?' someone cried.

Bessie smiled, but tightened her lips. Some of the younger men greeted Bessie with a wink and a squeeze of the waist, which made Chrissie open her eyes wider. She'd always thought of Bessie as old, but now she examined her in a different light, she saw that her nurse was buxom and bonnie, with clear, unlined skin. She wondered why Bessie hadn't gone courting, and been married. It was a puzzle, like this endless mass of people. Her head was spinning. The brose had long since ceased to warm her, and she was hungry and ready to cry. Only a stubborn pride stopped her.

There were only a few stragglers now, hurrying into the factory as if Old Nick himself was after them, as Bessie remarked. She bent down to her small charge and spoke quietly.

'This is the life your mill lassie was running from. Do you blame her for her roughness and rudeness? Don't judge folk too hasty, my lass. Think on it, Chrissie, and mind it.'

Chrissie nodded solemnly, not really understanding, but she was to mind Bessie's words in years to come, and wish that she'd acted on the sound advice.

Bessie smiled more cheerfully and put an arm round her shoulders.

'Come away, my wee lambie. My sister's place is not far. Biddy's just had another wean, so she'll be in.'

Biddy Murphy was in her tenement flat, when they clambered up the outside stairs on to the stone platform that ran along outside the doors. She gave a loud squeal of delight when she saw Bessie, tucked the tiny baby she'd been feeding into a drawer of the dresser, left open for the purpose, and hugged her sister fondly. Then she clasped Chrissie to her ample bosom.

'Ah, the wee motherless hen! And her so bonnie!' Biddy wiped tears from her eyes, then bellowed so fiercely it made Chrissie jump, 'Get away ben, you lot!'

The three small, curious faces that had appeared in the doorway of an adjoining room, hastily disappeared. Another urchin, older and taller than Chrissie, stood his ground, watching.

Biddy bent down to Chrissie. 'Would you like a piece, dear?'

Chrissie was baffled. 'A piece of what?'

9

The big boy doubled up, laughing noisily. 'Ma, she's a gowk!'

Biddy aimed a swipe at his ear, which he dodged neatly. 'You mind your manners, Danny Murphy. Miss Christina's a little lady. She's not in the habit of dining off bread and dripping like us, nor a jelly piece, neither.'

'She'll take a jelly piece, Biddy. If you have a scrape o' jam to spare,' intervened Bessie.

While her sister hastened to do the honours, Bessie cooed to the baby, then smiled at the young lad.

'Not at the mill today, Danny?'

'I've had the mill-hoast. I've been bad with it, but I'm not coughing so much now, and Ma says I'll be back the morn.'

Biddy dealt out bread and jam recklessly to all the children, then settled down by the grate for a blether with Bessie. Chrissie and the boy bit into thick slabs of bread and eyed one another cautiously. He was a well-built lad, with sturdy legs. His thick, curly hair was very black, his eyes the deepest blue Chrissie had ever seen, apart from the deep blue of the sea far out beyond the estuary. There was a dimpled cleft in his square chin which hinted at mischief.

'What do you do, in the mill?' she asked him.

'I'm a shifter. I shift the empty bobbins.' Chrissie was none the wiser. He took another bite of bread and jam and munched, studying her. 'Are you the whaler's lassie?'

'My papa owns three whaling ships. One of them's named for me,' Chrissie told him proudly.

There was a glint in his eye. 'We use whale oil in the mill, for softening the jute fibres. It smells awful.'

Chrissie was hurt and insulted, but couldn't think of a suitably cutting reply. Then suddenly he smiled. It was a smile that warmed and lit his merry, blue eyes, and made her feel breathless.

'But you smell sweet, wee lassie. You smell like flowers.'

And that was Chrissie's first meeting with Danny Murphy, whose tongue had a cutting edge, and whose sweet words could warm a lass's heart, so that she never, never forgot them.

Chrissie's eldest brother, George, had married his Jean in 1897, the year of Queen Victoria's diamond jubilee. The marriage had been very quiet and simple, in the midst of the lavish jubilee celebrations. Jean brought nothing to George except her own cheery, loving self, for she was just a fisher lass from Easthaven, up the coast. Without a word being said, the family knew George's choice of wife was a sore disappointment to their papa, although Chrissie wasn't clear why. She loved Jean dearly. She looked forward to the dutiful visits Jean made with little Georgina and the baby, Hugh, when William Kennedy returned from his trips to the Antarctic, more gaunt and tight-lipped as years went by. Only Chrissie could bring a smile to his lips these days.

Ernest, who worked in the office of the Kennedy Whaling Company, explained to his sister that Papa was disappointed because Jean brought no dowry, and times were hard in the whaling industry. There were no whalers being built in the Dundee Shipbuilders' yard now, only a ship called the *Discovery*, launched in 1901 for the purpose of exploring the Antarctic.

As if her own papa hadn't explored most of that fearsome place already, thought Chrissie scornfully, as she watched the new ship set off on her trials. She was a fine ship, but in Chrissie's opinion not half so fine as

11

the *Christina K*, berthed idly for the moment in King William IV dock.

William Kennedy had higher hopes of a well-endowed wife for his second son, Arthur. Arthur had his eye upon Miss Lizzie Bowers, a jute merchant's daughter, and more importantly, Lizzie Bowers had her eye set firmly upon Arthur. The Bowers family were a little less than pleased, but Miss Lizzie was a determined young woman. The wedding ceremony was arranged for June, the reception to be held afterwards with some pomp and style in the Bowers's newly built mansion in the West End.

'You are to be bridesmaid, Christina, with my sister, Harriet. You will wear pale pink,' Lizzie decided.

'I loathe pale pink!' Chrissie stuck out her lower lip mutinously.

'Why not a deep rose-pink for the attendants, my love? The colour will set off your own bonnie white gown much more emphatically,' Arthur suggested diplomatically.

Lizzie agreed graciously, while Arthur winked at Chrissie behind his beloved's ramrod-straight back. Chrissie suspected her quiet brother had the measure of Miss Lizzie, and would handle her whims and foibles with good-natured dexterity. From then on, she felt happier about the match.

Harriet Bowers, Lizzie's young sister, thought Chrissie was the most beautiful girl she'd ever seen. Harriet's admiration was completely untainted by envy, because she had no illusions about herself. Although she and Christina were both newly turned fifteen, Harriet was already a head taller, skinny and gawky, with a thin, clever face and dark, fly-away hair that was always untidy. The two girls smiled shyly when they met for fittings of the rose-pink gowns. They both liked what they saw.

12

'Which school do you go to?' Harriet asked Chrissie, when she got the chance.

'Mrs Brough the minister's wife teaches reading, writing and arithmetic to the girls in our district, but my papa says I'm to go to Miss Black's school next term. Your papa recommends it for finishing off young ladies,' Chrissie answered without enthusiasm.

Harriet was excited. 'Why, that's where I go, Chrissie! We can be friends if you like. I don't have a best friend,' she offered hopefully.

'Oh, I'd like that, Harriet.' Chrissie smiled.

Harriet was dazzled by the smile, but thoughts of Miss Black's Establishment for Young Ladies brought her down to earth. She sighed. 'I want to go to the Public Seminary, but my parents won't hear of it. I want to study science and algebra and geometry, like the boys do,' she confided. Frustration gripped Harriet. Her woman's role felt tight and restricting, like the whalebone corset the dressmaker had just laced her into.

Chrissie's eyes were wide. 'Ooh! You must be very clever.'

'How can I be, if I don't get the chance?' said Harriet, sadly.

The dressmaker turned her attention to Chrissie, leaving Harriet to her thoughts and plans.

If I marry Charles Rankine, as Papa hopes I will, then I shall study anything I please, Harriet thought hopefully. Charles is a darling, and will let me do it, I know. Her heart beat faster when she thought about Charles, whom she'd worshipped in silence for years. She closed her eyes tight, and prayed fervently. Please, God. Let me marry Charles Rankine one day, because I do love him so. Ah, please, make him love me, too. For ever and ever, Amen.

* * *

13

The weather was kind, when Arthur Kennedy married Lizzie Bowers, and it was a stylish assembly that congregated afterwards in the sunshine, on the closecut lawn of the Bowers's stately mansion.

The two attendants of the radiant bride stuck closely together. Harriet's stays confined her so tightly she wanted to fling them off, publicly, if need be, but Chrissie endured the restriction patiently. Her waist was a handspan anyway, and she'd grown womanly and shapely recently. The deep, rose-pink colour of the gown suited her well, and the golden-haired girl drew many speculative glances, particularly from the elegant, young gentlemen gathered to wish the young couple well. On the bodice of her dress, much to the bride's chagrin, Chrissie defiantly wore the emblem of her father's trade, the silver replica of the *Christina K*.

Chrissie, while well aware of interested eyes on her, felt strangely detached, as if she were a spectator watching a play. It was an odd sensation, but her emotions were so deep and muddled these days, she wasn't unduly surprised. As she grew up, she became more aware that her settled life was changing, and she didn't know why.

Only the other day, Biddy Murphy, whose crowded tenement had become Chrissie's second home over the years, had cradled the young girl's face in her rough, red hands, and stared long and hard with an oddly sorrowful and wistful expression.

'Ah, lassie! Such a sweet and bonnie face to break a poor laddie's heart!' Biddy had remarked, sighing.

A remark which had shaken Chrissie badly, and had not been explained to her, despite all Chrissie's pleading and blandishments.

So she stood with Harriet beside the laburnum tree, sipping iced lemonade, and hoped anxiously that she wouldn't break any hearts that perfect afternoon.

Charles Rankine was also standing a little apart, quietly observing the guests. At twenty-five, he looked a solemn young man, not very robust after a childhood rheumatic fever that had caused him to grow taller than most. He seemed a dull stick. Those who didn't know him would have been astonished by the quiet humour of his thoughts as he observed the dressy gathering.

He viewed the blushing bride with unfeigned relief. Lizzie Bowers had been put forward by his parents as a suitably well-endowed wife for himself at one time. Fortunately, Lizzie had had other ideas, and being a strong-willed and formidable young woman, had cowed her parents into submission. A lucky escape!

'The bride and bridegroom!' the toast rang out.

Charles lifted his champagne glass towards Arthur Kennedy with goodwill. He looked a strong, capable chap with good shoulders, well fitted to cope with Mistress Lizzie. The best of luck to you, old chap! thought Charles.

Charles's parents were not to be deterred, though, where a suitable match for their highly eligible only son was concerned. Their interest was now concentrated upon the younger sister, Harriet, still available, young, and infinitely more amenable. Union with the Bowers was certainly desirable from a business point of view, Charles was forced to agree, and the jute trade had its problems at the moment.

He turned his attention idly to young Harriet. His lips twitched in amusement as he watched her wriggle in the grip of rigid stays which made nothing of her thin, angular frame. Rose-pink did little for Harriet, he decided. The colour did not emphasise her remarkable eyes, which he liked for their clear, frank intelligence. A nice lass, caring and thoughtful. He could do worse, Charles thought. He could afford to wait. He'd enjoyed studying at St Andrews University, and was now ready to learn all he could about the running of the Rankine Mills. There was plenty time for Harriet, and matrimony.

The other bridesmaid came suddenly into his view, stepping from the shadow of the tree into full sunlight. She stood for a moment with her face turned up to the sun, as fresh and lovely as a dewy rosebud. Charles caught his breath, his heart giving a sudden, uncomfortable lurch. He had noticed the lass, walking down the church aisle. What man wouldn't pay attention to such a bonnie face and figure? But now, as she lifted her head on her graceful neck and smiled with such youthful abandonment at the blue sky, he felt the sight tug at his heartstrings. It started a quickened beat, and almost without realising it, he was drawn towards her. Charles stopped in front of the two young girls.

'Harriet, you – you performed your duties well,' he said, ponderously. It sounded pompous, but he could think of nothing else.

Harriet had watched Charles walk purposefully towards them, and her heart had begun to sing. She was almost afraid to look at him, because her eyes might reveal too much, and tell him indecorously of her fierce and painful love. In confusion, she turned to Chrissie.

'Charles, have you met Arthur's sister, Christina Kennedy?'

'Not yet,' he said quietly. Chrissie held out a hand shyly, and he took it and held it in both of his, looked deep into her eyes, and was smitten forever.

'Christina, I am pleased to meet you,' he said formally.

Harriet watched their meeting with dismay and a sick foreboding. There was a light in his eyes, as he looked down at Chrissie, that seemed to illuminate his grave, serious features, making Harriet love him more, long for him more desperately, and despair of ever having him. She was weeping inside, her chest ached with weeping, but nobody could have told. Harriet had a fierce, stubborn pride to save her face.

Chrissie was not impressed by Charles Rankine.

A long dreep o' misery, Bessie would have called him. Still, Chrissie was prepared to be friendly, because Harriet had confided to her that she cared for him. When she felt him press her hand and looked up with a start into his eyes, she was astonished and horrorstruck to see the dawning light of love and admiration there.

She wanted nothing to do with him. He belonged to Harriet, who was her dear friend, and she wouldn't hurt Harriet for anything. Chrissie pulled her hand away hastily and stepped back.

'If you will excuse me, Mr Rankine, I must go to my papa now.'

She turned and ran, but not towards the mansion house, where her father was deep in conversation. Chrissie hurried blindly down a path through wooded shrubbery, where dark laurels hid her confusion.

She let out a little scream of alarm, when a man stepped out of the bushes in front of her. Then she recognised him.

'Och, Danny! It's only you!'

'Aye, it's only me,' Danny Murphy said grimly.

Chrissie smiled at him. She felt better, safer, with Danny around. Since that first meeting when they were children, they'd played together, talked together when Danny wasn't in the mill, had heated arguments and rows, laughed and joked together. He'd been like a brother to her.

No, thought Chrissie suddenly, that wasn't quite right. More special even than a brother. Different altogether.

'What're you doing here, you gowk? If they catch you, you'll be out on your ear,' she warned.

'I was outside the kirk. I wanted to see how the gentry got wed. I've been watching the carry-on in the garden. It makes me sick,' he growled, his black brows frowning.

Chrissie giggled. 'Och, you're jealous, man!'

'Maybe I am, Chris.'

He stared at her so intently it frightened her, and yet in a strange way she rejoiced, as if she'd been hoping long for this look. His eyes travelled slowly over her from top to toe, and she stood quiet, waiting. For what, she didn't know.

He must have moved closer, perhaps she had moved forward too, drawn irresistibly close. She could smell the oily jute on his clothes, pleasantly familiar to her senses. Danny, at eighteen, was well built and powerful, his black hair thick and curling. Chrissie caught her breath. She hadn't noticed how fine and handsome he'd grown. It was as if she'd slept for years and just wakened, and met a handsome stranger.

A stranger but for the merry, blue eyes. So blue. She'd always loved his eyes.

Loved? Chrissie's thoughts paused, startled, then leaped forward. Aye, loved!

'Chrissie—' His hands rested on her shoulders, his face close to hers. 'I'll make something o' myself, one of these days. I'll work and read and learn, and be somebody. As good as any of these folk.' He jerked his head angrily towards the garden.

She touched his face gently. 'I know you will, Danny-boy.'

His arms went round her, and he kissed her lips gently for the first, sweet time. 'Chrissie, will you wait? Will you promise?' he whispered anxiously.

Nestled in his arms, she nodded. 'I promise.'

He drew back for a moment, frowning. 'Who was the tall man, holding your hand?'

Chrissie gave a gurgle of contented laughter.

'Och, just a long dreep o' misery, Dan,' she said.

With Arthur's wedding on the go, Bessie McCutcheon had taken the chance to visit her sister. It was easier these days, with a horse-drawn tram running from Broughty to Dundee. Child-bearing and millwork had taken its toll on Biddy, and with her bad legs she couldn't manage the tenement stairs now. She didn't complain. Biddy's great joy was to lean elbows on the window sill and watch all that went on below.

Bessie was looking after William Kennedy's grandchildren, Georgina and wee Hughie, and had brought them with her. George and Jean Kennedy had been invited to the wedding, and Jean had been nervous about it.

'Bessie, I'll be a fish out o' water, among all those fine folk,' she'd wailed.

Bessie had given the bonnie woman a reassuring hug. 'Jeanie, you could hold your end up wi' Queen Alexandra herself.' And she'd meant it.

Georgina was at the mouth of the close with some of Biddy's brood, playing hopscotch, and Hughie was outside in the back court with a crowd of other barefoot urchins armed with fistfuls of marbles, absorbed in a game of bools. Bessie picked up his discarded boots and socks, just as Danny came in.

'Where have you been, son? You missed your dinner,' Biddy remarked.

He gave a tight grin. 'I've been to the wedding, to see Chrissie in her finery.'

'Oh, aye?' Biddy studied him warily. Her smile had faded.

'I hid in the bushes and watched her. She was like a rose, Ma. All the young men were after her, but it was me she chose, when I let on to her I was there.'

19

His mother snorted scornfully. 'What blethers! Why should she look at the likes of you, with her pick of all the toffs?'

He lifted his chin. 'Because I'm the one for her. I'll be somebody, one day, better than them all.'

Biddy lifted her eyes to heaven. 'Will you listen to the lad havering! She's not for an orraman like you, son. She's born a lady. Besides, she's little more than a bairn yet, and bairns are fickle,' she pointed out.

'Chris knows her mind,' he argued stubbornly. 'She gave me her promise the day.'

Groaning, Biddy shook her head to and fro. 'Aw, Danny son! Dan, it can't be. It's no' possible, with you and her.'

He came close, his blue eyes blazing. 'Aye, Ma, it's possible, and it will be, one day. Chrissie Kennedy is the only wife I'll ever take!'

He turned on his heel and stormed out, slamming the door with a crash that loosened flakes of plaster on his mother's head.

Bessie McCutcheon had turned pale with distress. She stared at her sister in utter dismay.

'Oh, Biddy! What have I done? Where will it end? I should never have brought that lassie to your house!'

Chrissie enjoyed her two years at Miss Black's. Miss Black and her staff taught little else but the perfecting of an elegant copperplate hand; enough arithmetic for a lady to keep a check on the household budget; knitting and embroidery; and above all, ladylike manners and deportment. Miss Black had had grave reservations about accepting the daughter of a whaling skipper. The stench emanating from Whale Lane at times was certainly not socially acceptable. The Bowers spoke up in Chrissie's favour, however, and Miss Black was pleasantly surprised to find the girl well-disciplined and accomplished.

She wished she could say as much for Harriet Bowers.

Harriet's behaviour puzzled Chrissie. Harriet's shy, easy-going manner had changed drastically since her sister's wedding day. She and Chrissie were still the very best of friends, sharing the same desk, but there was a subdued restlessness within Harriet. It smouldered like a volcano just beneath the surface, and Chrissie feared an eruption. Harriet had no patience with writing. Her writing was like a hen scraping on a midden, as Bessie said. She flew accurately through arithmetic problems and totted up long columns of figures swiftly, while others laboured, then sat staring idly out the window. Her embroidery was an impatient disgrace.

The eruption came one day when Harriet was struggling to master crochet. She flung the grubby cotton on the classroom floor and stood up.

'Miss Black, I want to study biology.'

Miss Black turned pale. 'My dear, that's an indelicate subject for young ladies.'

'Oh no, it isn't! I want to find out how my body works, and yours too, for that matter, Miss Black. If you're not prepared to teach me, then I shall leave!' Harriet declared.

And leave she did, that very day, striding out with head held proudly high, never to return. Mr and Mrs Bowers discovered to their consternation that they had another stubbornly determined daughter on their hands. They gave in with stunned resignation, and allowed Harriet to attend the Public Seminary, where she rapidly carried all before her.

Chrissie, a few days after her seventeenth birthday, told Danny about Harriet's latest examination success. They sat in mild sunshine, at the top of the Law Hill, the river estuary and the Fife coast beyond spread out before them. They came here whenever they could, to talk and be alone. It was a wild, high place, dominating the town, with only a rough track to the top. You could see all the factory chimneys from it, belching black smoke.

'She had top marks in most subjects, Danny.'

He lay on his back, chewing a blade of grass. 'Och, I canna stand clever women.'

'Thanks very much for the compliment, you beast!' Chrissie cried indignantly.

He pulled her down into his arms. 'You're different. You're clever in other ways, and beautiful.'

She stroked his hair. She never tired looking at him. He was so handsome, so strongly built and shapely, she felt as if she melted inside, when she looked at him. She counted the days and the hours, until she could be with him.

'Chrissie, I've joined the Volunteers,' he said.

She felt a sudden chill. 'You mean, the soldiers?'

'Aye. It's one way to get ahead; be somebody. The sergeant says if I keep on, I'll get a stripe by Christmas.'

'Oh, Danny!' She felt tearful, afraid, even though they did little else in the Volunteers but drilling and marching on the Magdalen Green, with little urchins running behind, mimicking them.

'Don't cry, sweetheart.' Danny begged. He couldn't bear to see her cry. He kissed her. His kisses were expert now, and searching. His love for Chrissie Kennedy was like a fire, consuming him. Sometimes the longing for her was almost unbearable, and then Danny studied his books on engineering, fiercely studying them at night by candlelight until his eyes ached and he was ready to drop into an exhausted sleep.

With a supreme effort of will, Danny pushed her away.

22

'Chrissie, Chrissie, we must get married soon, lass, or . . . or else—'

Chrissie was flushed, breathing fast, her eyes shining.

'Yes, Danny, yes. We will be married, now that I am seventeen. You must bide in patience for a little while though, dear. My papa believes I'm still a bairn, and I must persuade him otherwise!' she laughed confidently, as happy as a lintie.

Contrary to Chrissie's belief, William Kennedy was very much aware that his little girl had grown into a marriageable young woman. His dear Chrissie might yet save them all, he thought, now that she had turned seventeen.

Pulling gently at his moustaches, he watched his daughter alight from the electric tram and hurry along the garden path. Oh, but she was bonnie! It was almost as if there was a halo of happiness around her today, he thought. And he could make her happier still, with the news he had for her. Happy, aye, and secure for life. That's what he wanted for his dear lass.

When he heard her in the hallway, he opened the study door.

'Chrissie dear, will you come in?'

'What is it, Papa?' Chrissie looked up into his face, her joyful happiness fading a little. It was something serious, she knew. His face, scarred by frostbite, was set in solemn lines. He sat down, and she sat opposite, wondering.

'Chrissie, you must know how bad trade is. Ernest has told you our stocks of oil are dwindling. We lost a good order last month, because folk complain the smell of whale oil taints the bacon wrapped in sackcloth. If I had more capital to spend, to refit the ships, I could mechanise. That's the way ahead, Christina, to make use of the engines being made,' William said enthusiastically. He paused, smiling at her puzzled

23

face. He'd been carried away. He couldn't expect a young lass to understand his worries.

'Aye well, that's by the way. I've worked the *Christina K* hard, Chrissie, and she'd badly needing an overhaul. We must have an infusion of capital very soon if we're to keep our heads above water, and today I was given a chance to have all the capital we need.'

She touched the brooch at her neck, and her eyes shone. 'Oh, Papa, that's good news.'

He shifted uncomfortably in his chair. 'Aye. The fact of the matter is, Chrissie, that young Charles Rankine has formally asked my permission to come courting you. He hinted that if the outcome is – er – favourable, his firm will put up the money we need. What d'you say to that?' He leaned forward eagerly.

Chrissie couldn't hide her shock and dismay. She'd met Charles Rankine from time to time since Arthur's wedding, but he'd always been formally correct, much to Chrissie's relief. There had been no hint of this lightning bolt. She didn't know what to say.

'But . . . but he's such a long dreep o' misery, Papa.' she wailed.

William Kennedy laughed indulgently. 'Och, don't judge the man too harshly, lass. I'll grant you he's no oil painting, but they say he's a couthy man and kindly. He's had the running of the mill since his father's illness, and the workers like him well, and trust him, which is more than you can say for most.'

He looked at his beloved daughter thoughtfully. 'I think Charles Rankine has long had his eye on you, Chrissie, waiting with patience till you were a grown woman. That says something for the man. You know I'll not force you, dear, if you're dead set against the match, but think on it, lassie. You could be the saving of us all, aye, and the saviour, too, of your bonnie ship, the *Christina K*. Oh, Chrissie. What d'you say?'

She turned her head away. Her thoughts seemed wee and frightened, scudding round and round in terror in her head.

Danny. Oh, Danny. My dear Danny-boy! Chrissie thought.

Chapter 2

William Kennedy studied his daughter. She was obviously dismayed, but dismay was quite natural when a young and innocent lass was suddenly faced with the prospect of a suitor. Perhaps he had broached the subject of Charles Rankine's courtship rather clumsily. Chrissie isn't bold and forward, running brazenly after the boys like some other lasses he knew, thought William. She had turned pale, and the joyful light in her bonnie, blue eyes had been snuffed out like a candle.

He leaned forward and took her hands.

'My dear, you're a grown woman now, and I'll be very frank with you. The whaling grounds have been cruelly exploited, Chrissie, and stocks of black whales have dwindled almost to nothing. I'm at my wits' end, to tell the truth, but even your brothers don't know just how desperate our state is.' He gave a twisted smile. 'Mind you, Chris, I suspect our Ernest has an inkling of this perilous state, because he has a good head on him, and he's studied the ledgers. I've never owed anyone a penny, but if this season's no better than last, we'll slip into debt and I'll be forced to sell the *Christina K* to pay the creditors.'

'Oh, Papa, not my own bonnie ship,' Chrissie cried.

He nodded heavily. 'It could come to that, without Charles Rankine's capital to tide us over, dear.'

She struggled to hide her anguish. She could see

Danny so clearly it was almost as if he were by her side. She was promised to Danny. How could she break a solemn promise which she longed with heart and soul to keep?

'Oh, what shall I do?' she murmured, distraught.

His daughter's unhappiness upset William Kennedy, but he imagined he knew the reason for it. He could understand his daughter's feelings for her ship, because they mirrored his own. To lose the *Christina K* would be like losing one of the family. He had every sympathy with Chrissie in her dilemma, but oh, if only she would take a fancy to Charles Rankine.

William had satisfied himself that Rankine was a good man, a gentleman, or he would never have considered him as a husband for his beloved Chrissie. A long dreep o' misery, she'd called him! William's moustache twitched in amusement. Aye, it was but a sign of immaturity to set too much store on good looks. Chrissie would find that you can't judge a book by its binding.

'Chrissie,' he continued gently, 'I'm not forcing you to take Charles Rankine if you're dead set against it. Your happiness is much too important to me. Just get to know him, Chris. You may find you have a liking for the man, which will grow to a stronger attachment, given time.'

She said nothing, her eyes cast down. He still held her hands, and could feel the tension in her. He was sympathetic to her plight, but he must fight to save his failing business, and this was the only way.

'Oh, Chrissie, please let the man come courting,' William begged softly.

Chrissie couldn't bear to listen to her father's abject pleading. He was a proud man, fiercely independent. Why, he'd never even borrowed a halfpenny in his life, and here he was begging humbly for her help.

She looked at him sorrowfully. Rough though a whaler skipper's life was, it hadn't coarsened William Kennedy. He was still a kindly gentleman, and she'd never heard an uncouth word pass his lips. The hands she held in hers lacked four fingertips, mutilated by frostbite in harsh Arctic conditions. Her father had worked uncomplainingly for many hard, cold years for his children's sake, to keep Chrissie herself warm, well fed and in luxury. His sacrifice shamed her. For her dear father's sake, she must let Charles Rankine come courting, and risk breaking Danny Murphy's heart.

Oh, Danny, my only love, forgive me!

Tears glistened on her lashes, but she spoke up bravely. 'Very well, Papa, you may tell Charles I agree, but . . . but I don't promise to care for him.'

William Kennedy was jubilant. He kissed his daughter's brow. 'I swear you won't regret it, my love!'

She bowed her head to hide her anguish. Danny would never understand the pressures that had forced her to accept Charles Rankine as a suitor. But what else could she do?

As ever, Chrissie flew for comfort to the woman who'd been like a mother to her. Bessie McCutcheon was in the kitchen making rabbit stew. Rabbits were plentiful in the fields around the city, and she had an understanding with her many nephews to keep the Kennedy household supplied.

Martha, the cook, had been paid off long ago. There was only Bessie now to do everything. Chrissie paused suddenly at the kitchen door, surveying the scene. For the first time the shabbiness of it dawned upon her, scrubbed scrupulously clean though it was. The kitchen walls hadn't seen a lick of paint for years, and neither had the rest of the old house. It was rabbit stew again, and yesterday it had been broth and bannocks.

Chrissie felt chilled with forebodings of disaster. She'd been so happy and so much in love she hadn't noticed how poor they were becoming. She'd blithely eaten Bessie's bannocks and supped Bessie's wholesome broth, and never missed the roast beef and lamb that was seldom seen on the table now. How blindly selfish she had been.

And Bessie, herself, had grown thinner. She was still a bonnie woman, and an old maid, at thirty-seven.

Chrissie put her hands to her cheeks. 'Oh, Bessie! Bessie!'

Bessie stopped stirring the stew. She gaped at Chrissie's tears, then opened her arms. Chrissie flew, weeping, into them.

Bessie stroked the golden hair of the lassie she loved like a daughter. She felt Chrissie's tears against her cheek, and her heart was heavy. Aye, she'd been watching and waiting for this. Such unhappiness was inevitable one day, with her and Danny keeping such close company.

'What is it, my bonnie doo?' Bessie asked gently.

The whole story came pouring out in gasps and sobs. Bessie listened gravely. Chrissie raised a tear-stained face and looked at her. 'Bessie, you know how it is with me and Danny. We love each other. We want to get married soon. But how could I tell my father?'

Bessie's heart grew heavier still at mention of marriage. She hadn't known the affair with her nephew had gone so far. She bitterly regretted taking the Kennedy lass to the Murphys' tenement and letting her consort with handsome Danny and his winsome ways. Biddy had been uneasy about the relationship for many a year. And now this had happened.

Bessie knew her nephew's mettle. When Danny hears that Charles Rankine is courting Chrissie, there'll be fur flying, thought Bessie with dread. Chrissie's future

30

happiness was her main concern though. She must try to undo the harm she'd done unwittingly to the dear lass.

She stroked the tears off Chrissie's cheeks. 'Chrissie, listen. I loved a lad when I was seventeen. I loved him sore, but if I'd married him, it would have been the mill for me for the rest o' my days.' Bessie closed her eyes, shaking her head. 'The mill sickened me, Chris. The noise made my head spin like a peerie, the smell and dust made me choke, cough and wheeze until I thought I'd die. When your folks' soft job came up, I tried for it in desperation. Your ma liked me, and I was taken on, but I lost my bonnie lad, Chrissie. He was proud, and I lost him forever.'

Chrissie hugged her sympathetically. 'Bess, I guessed there was something.'

Bessie sighed. 'Aye well, there were compensations, and that's what I'm trying to get over to you, Chrissie. There are always compensations. Losing Danny wouldn't be the end of your world, my lass, but marrying him would be.'

Chrissie's eyes flashed. 'I love him, Bessie!'

'Aye, but do you love hard work an' scrubbing, living in the shadow o' the mills? It's hard enough for them that's born to it, and you're not, my hennie!'

Chrissie's mouth set obstinately. 'I love Danny, and he loves me. That's all that matters.'

'And I'm telling you love's not enough for the likes o' you,' Bessie cried.

Presently, her expression softened and she put an arm gently round the girl's slim shoulders, pleading with her. 'Chrissie, give Charles Rankine a chance. He's your kind, not Danny. Mr Rankine's well thought of by all that know him. Oh, I'll not deny Danny's a braw lad, with many good points going for him, but you've

31

been brought up a lady, Chrissie, and Mr Rankine's a gentleman.'

Chrissie threw off Bessie's arm and stood stormy-eyed. 'Do you think that weighs with me? He's a bore, Bessie. A big dreep!' Turning on her heel, she stormed out of the kitchen. Bessie stood motionless until the thud of the front door released her from the spell. Then she sagged wearily against the dresser.

'Eh, eh, where will it end?' Bessie groaned.

Chrissie ran out into the street. The driver of the electric tram clanged his bell and slowed down invitingly, for all the drivers and conductors knew the whaler's bonnie lass. She shook her head, and kept walking. She walked fast along the Ferry Road, and entering the town, climbed the steep brae that brought her by Dudhope Castle to the slopes of the Law. Mounting the track she'd walked with Danny only that morning, she stood at last on the summit, the wind tugging her skirts and coldly drying tears on her cheeks.

How happy they'd been for a short stolen time before Danny went back on the noon shift. Now their happiness was threatened, and Chrissie didn't know what the outcome would be. She longed for Danny with all her being. Looking down on the long roof of the mill where he worked, she imagined she could see him, bonnet pulled well down over his black, curling hair, admiring the new engine that ran the main shaft. A hundred and fifty belt-driven machines in the spinning flat depended upon it.

On the breath of the wind she heard the whisper of a little mill lass, plaintively weeping. 'The mill runs so fast, I canna keep my ends up.' Chrissie found herself shivering. The mills would run faster than ever now, with the bigger, better engines they were making.

Her gaze wandered to the east, to another spread of blue slate roof, another tall, red-brick chimney.

Rankine's mill!

She felt the beat of panic in her throat. Surely, she wouldn't have to marry the man? How could she, when Danny was her dream, her loved one, and she was promised to him?

Her vision blurred with tears, she looked beyond the old steeple to the harbour where the *Christina K* lay idle. Chrissie's fingers closed protectively over the silver replica of the ship pinned to her bodice. She knew she would fight, make great sacrifices if need be, to save her ship.

She turned away from the panorama below and scrambled recklessly down the path. This time she headed west towards the huddled tenements of Lochee, and walking fast she struck over the lip of the Balgay Hill, through silent tombstones and downwards towards the road to Perth, bordered by newly built mansions of the well-to-do.

Harriet Bowers was surprised and delighted when the housemaid showed Chrissie into her study. She jumped up from the desk, and the two friends hugged one another. Their friendship had never wavered, and was strong as ever. Harriet knew all about Chrissie's love affair with Danny, and if she had reservations about the wisdom of it, she tactfully kept her doubts to herself.

'Chrissie, how grand! We haven't had a good blether for ages,' Harriet exclaimed. All the time she was studying her friend alertly, and what she saw troubled her. Chris was pale, her hands cold as ice, her eyes dark with unhappiness. Harriet led her to the warmth of the fire, blethering away.

'Of course, I've had my nose in my books all winter, Chrissie, and have been most unsociable, I'm afraid.

I shall take the exams for the Higher Grade Leaving Certificate quite soon, and if I pass in all subjects I hope to train as a doctor.'

This incredible ambition drove Chris's sorrows out of her head for the moment. She gaped at her friend.

'A doctor? Harriet, you couldn't be!'

'I don't see why not!' Harriet retorted blithely.

'But . . . but the men wouldn't like it.'

Harriet gave a wicked chuckle. 'They'll just have to put up with it, Chrissie. There are more and more women qualifying as doctors, and I'm going to be one of them.'

She poked the coal into a cheerier glow. It flared up, and she was glad to see the warmth bring colour to Chrissie's cheeks. Harriet went on blethering, confident her friend would tell her what was troubling her, in her own good time.

'Chris, I've joined the suffragette movement.'

'You haven't!' Chris's eyes grew round. Word of the militant women campaigning for the vote had reached Dundee recently, and her father's remarks on the subject had been scathing. The women had been making themselves a right nuisance, even defying the police. Chrissie hoped anxiously that Harriet would behave herself.

'We're organising a grand march through Dundee on October the first, Chris. I'm to carry a banner with "Votes for Women" on it, and Daisy Marchmont will walk in front, banging the big drum. You will march with us, won't you?' Harriet asked eagerly.

'Oh, Harriet, I don't know what my situation will be by then,' Chrissie cried miserably. Bit by bit, the whole story came tumbling out.

Harriet listened quietly, a bright hope fading. Charles Rankine loved Chrissie, and wanted her as his wife. He had no intention of marrying Harriet.

34

He had continued to visit the Bowers's house since Lizzie's marriage to Arthur Kennedy, and Harriet's passion for him had grown and matured. Her hopeful parents confidently believed he came on purpose to see Harriet, and she had come to believe it too.

Sometimes Chrissie had been there when he called, but Charles had shown no more than polite interest in her. Harriet had dared to hope that his love for Christina Kennedy had cooled. She had begun to dream of being his wife one day.

Harriet could make him laugh, shaken out of his natural reserve by Harriet's frank observations, which made poor Mrs Bowers reach for the smelling salts. Others thought him a dry stick and a sobersides, but Harriet knew better. He was her dear, her darling, the only man she could ever love.

And he wanted Chrissie.

Harriet bent to poke the fire. 'Will you marry Charles?'

Chrissie wrung her hands, for she knew how Harriet felt about Charles Rankine. Chrissie was sure Harriet would make him a perfect wife. They were two of a kind, with interests in common, yet he was dazzled by golden hair and a bonnie face and form. Oh, why must the daft man be so blind to Harriet's excellent qualities? she thought despairingly.

'I may *have* to marry him. I love Danny so much, but—but I may have to marry Charles to save Papa from ruin. But oh, Harriet, dear Harriet, I don't want to break your heart!' she cried in anguish.

Harriet lifted her chin. 'Don't you worry, my dear. You won't. I have the perfect antidote for heartbreak, Chrissie. Hard work!'

She stood up abruptly, tall and slender, fly-away hair as impatiently dressed as ever; her only pretension to beauty the large, remarkable eyes lit by a determined light. 'I shall be a doctor. It will take years of hard work, and after that, years of fighting stupid prejudice. I shall have no time for heartbreak, I assure you, Chris,' Harriet declared.

Charles Rankine didn't let the grass to grow under his feet once he'd gained William Kennedy's permission to court his daughter. He sought and was granted an invitation to afternoon tea, throwing poor Bessie into a frantic tizzy of preparation.

He arrived by hansom cab, and was greeted most warmly by William. The house gleamed with polish, the air was succulent with baking, but Charles scarcely noticed. He was eager as a schoolboy to meet the woman he worshipped.

He had watched Chrissie mature and become even more beautiful as the months passed. It had been a torment, waiting until she had turned seventeen when he deemed she was old enough to take a husband.

William Kennedy opened the parlour door with a flourish. 'Chrissie, here's Mr Charles Rankine to see you, my dear.'

Their eyes met across the room, and Charles felt breathless. Bessie had brushed Chrissie's hair until it shone like smooth gold when pinned high on her head. After much deliberation, Bessie had laundered and ironed a blue gown that was most becoming. She had even daringly brushed her lass's pale cheeks with a hare's foot dipped in a little rouge, and applied the same to enhance her rosy lips.

'Not a word of this to your pa, mind, Chrissie, or I'll get my head in my hands and my lugs to play wi'!' Bessie had warned.

Chrissie was glad of the rouge, because she was sure she'd gone white as milk. He seemed taller than ever, standing in the parlour doorway. Och, and so solemn, not a smile on his lips. What a dreep.

Hastily recalling the good manners drummed into her at Miss Black's establishment, Chrissie smiled and shyly held out a hand.

'How do you do, Mr Rankine?'

'I'm very well, thank you, Christina.' He took her hand, just the tips of her fingers. The touch thrilled him, though it was quickly withdrawn.

'Sit yourself down, man,' invited William heartily. He plumped himself into the only armchair, leaving Charles the option of a seat upon the sofa beside Chrissie. He sat down gingerly.

William had scarcely embarked upon an outline of the whaling industry, when Bessie trundled in a trolley loaded with dainty sandwiches, scones, pancakes and a sponge cake oozing with fresh cream and strawberry jam. The best delicate china was out, and the silver tea service gleamed in the firelight. Bessie was dressed like a parlourmaid for the occasion; a wee bit of swank. She gave Chrissie a broad wink as she deposited the trolley and withdrew.

Chrissie giggled, but hastily smothered her mirth with her hand. She stole a quick glance at Charles, and found he was watching, amused. She quickly poured out the tea and handed him a cup.

'One lump, or two, Mr Rankine?'

'Three, please, Christina.'

Och, he was teasing her, or had an awfully sweet tooth. He accepted a genteel sandwich which vanished in one bite. Silently, Chrissie pushed the plate towards him. He looked as if he needed a good feed.

'Aye, September and October is the best time for the big whales out by Greenland, if they're to be had,' William was saying, having started upon the subject he knew best. 'I sailed with the Antarctic expedition in

1893, when Chrissie was only a baby, but Dundee ships are underpowered for the Antarctic, Charles. There's where the future lies, in bigger, faster ships.'

He paused, sighing. 'I doubt I'll not see it. Aye well, I'll take the *Christina K* to the Baffin Sea with Arthur, and George will sail on the *Windward*, and we'll see what the future holds for us by October—'

Charles met William's eye, which held a significant look. He guessed accurately he was given a free hand to woo and win Chrissie between now and October.

'Harriet's going to be a doctor,' Chrissie announced suddenly. Charles turned sharply. This was news to him.

'Is she really?'

'Yes. She's joined the suffragettes too. She wants me to march in procession through the centre of Dundee,' Chrissie went on recklessly.

Her father fixed her with a warning glance. 'Aye, but no daughter of mine would be seen dead with thon rowdy besoms! If you want my opinion, Mr and Mrs Bowers don't have their sorrows to seek, wi' Miss Harriet and her daft notions.' He delicately wiped cream off his moustache and folded the lace-trimmed napkin with an air of finality.

'Chrissie, when you've finished your tea, take Mr Rankine into the garden and show him the daffodils. There's a grand show this Lent, I've never seen a better, even after such a chill winter,' he said artlessly.

Oh, Papa, you naughty schemer, thought Chrissie.

She rose dutifully enough and led the way outside, glad to feel the cool spring air on her cheeks. Charles followed, his heart singing. The garden ran wild and untended down the slope towards the railway line, with the wide river and the hills of Fife beyond. It was ablaze with golden daffodils, but he had eyes only for Chrissie.

She had paused on the path, lifting her head and looking far out towards the estuary with the rapt look he had first loved in her, and would love all his life. She spoke dreamily, forgetting for the moment that he was there.

'This is where I stand when my ship goes to sea. I watch her until she's but a wee speck on the horizon. Then I feel as if part of me has gone with her and left a hollow space that is only filled when she comes home again—'

With a start, Chrissie remembered the tall man by her side. Danny hated her to mention the ship. It was too pointed a reminder of her station in life; so far above him. Glancing up, she found Charles Rankine regarding her gravely. She met his eyes frankly for the first time, and found herself suddenly liking him. It was a strange, inexplicable feeling.

'You understand, don't you, Charles?' she said softly.

It was a statement of her wonder, not really a question.

'Yes, Chrissie, my dear. I understand,' he answered, and dared to take her hand and hold it, as they watched the ships go to and fro upon the river, and the swaying of the yellow daffodils in the breeze.

There was a new baby in the bottom drawer of Biddy Murphy's dresser, but it wasn't hers. Biddy's older daughters were in the mill, and she had become their bairn-minder. Biddy's working days were over, and the pennies earned from minding other women's babies were welcome. She was sitting by the grate, knitting, when Danny stormed in.

'Wheest, you'll wake the wean.'

'I don't give a damn!'

Biddy rested the knitting on her lap. 'What's up with ye, Danny? Your face is as long as a wet week.'

'It's her, Chrissie,' he said through his teeth. 'She's taken a fancy man, a big, long dreep. I saw them together in Kennedy's garden in the Stannergate, holding hands.'

Biddy's heart missed a beat. 'It's Saturday, son. What took you to the Stannergate on a working day?' she demanded sternly.

Danny wrenched off his cap and flung it at the hook behind the door. 'The axle broke on the docker's cart and the bales spilled off, giving the horse an awful fright. The carter stayed to calm the poor beastie, and I was sent to Stannergate on the tram to fetch the blacksmith.' He ran his fingers distractedly through his hair. 'I jumped at the chance, thinking I might see Chrissie, and I saw her. Och, I wish I hadn't.'

So, he'd found out about Chrissie and Mr Rankine sooner than expected, thought Biddy. Bessie McCutcheon had been round in a right state to tell her sister all about Charles Rankine courting Chrissie, but Biddy had decided to keep her own counsel until she saw the way clear. She studied her son's thunderous countenance.

'It's young Mr Rankine, from Rankine's Mill. A fine man. One of her own kind, Danny. I warned ye, mind.'

He pushed his face close, so close she could feel the heat of him, and was afraid.

'And I warned you, Ma. I'll be better than him one day.'

She flapped a hand impatiently. 'Och, Dan, have sense. You and your books. Buying books is like throwing money down the Scouring burn!'

'It's the way to get on and make money. Chrissie's mine, Ma, and no other man will have her!' Danny declared fiercely.

* * *

40

The sermon that Sunday morning seemed endless, and William Kennedy frowned at Chrissie's fidgeting. She picked like a bird at Sunday lunch, and was off as soon as her father settled for his afternoon nap. Her heart singing, she set out to keep her Sunday tryst with Danny on the Law. They had to watch they weren't seen by members of the Kennedy family. Ernest was walking out with a grocer's daughter from Hilltown, and George and Jeannie and their family lived not far from the Infirmary on the slopes of the conical hill. The real danger though, was Chrissie's brother Arthur, or rather his wife Lizzie, Harriet's sister.

Lizzie had had several miscarriages, and was expecting again. Bessie shook her head gravely over Lizzie. 'I doubt that one'll ever carry a bairn,' she predicted. But Lizzie was determined to succeed. This time she was taking great care, and hardly ever walked anywhere. Arthur drove his wife gently around in a sprung carriage behind a placid pony, and there was no knowing where they'd turn up when Lizzie was out taking the air. Chrissie didn't feel safe until she reached the rough track, and then her feet flew.

He was standing staring broodingly at the factory roofs, his back to her and the wind singing in his ears. She stole up behind him and put her hands over his eyes, kissing the back of his neck beneath the strong, curling hair.

'Guess who, Dan, and it's no' your ma!' Chrissie laughed.

He reached up and gripped her wrists, then turned. She flinched from the look on his face.

'Chrissie, how long have you been daffing wi' that dreep Rankine?' Danny glared at her, and had no words to express his misery. If men could cry, he would be weeping now. His tears were pent up in his chest, aching.

Chrissie looked at him, colour draining from her

41

cheeks. 'Oh, Danny, Danny, it's a new thing. I was going to tell you, but oh, my darling, I didn't know how.' Hesitantly, she began to tell him of her terrible dilemma. She made a poor job of it, stammering and pausing often to wipe away her tears. He heard her to the end, grim-faced.

His blue eyes flashed. 'And you're to be sacrificed to save your pa! You're to be forced to take up with Rankine, because he's rich and has a fancy for a bonnie face, and I'm of no account because I'm just an orraworker making my way. I'll no' stand for it, Chrissie.'

He looked so bold and brave, her heart melted for him. She laid her head on his breast and they clung together. 'Danny, what can we do? How can I fight when it's my father and brothers that'll suffer?'

He kissed her tenderly. 'It's a cruel decision, and one you shouldna have to make, sweetheart. You must mind only that you love me as I love you, Chris, when Rankine comes to call. We're promised to one another honourably and truly. There's your ammunition for the fight.'

Chrissie was silent. It was a simple matter of choice to Danny, who was honest and forthright in his thinking, but to Chrissie the repercussions were complex and frightening. It was no simple matter to bring ruin to her family.

Danny pulled her into the lee of their favourite rock, a secluded, sheltered spot they'd made their own, and they sat down on the grass, the panorama of the river estuary spread out before them. Chrissie put her head on his shoulder, and for a little while was happy and contented in her love for him, his arm warm around her.

'I'll be a better man than Rankine one day, Chris. Folk will look up to me for what I've done. Man, maybe they'll raise a statue to me on the top of the Law, where I kissed and cuddled with my Chrissie!' Danny grinned.

And so they laughed and dallied as long as they dared in the shelter of the rock, parting company reluctantly at the gates of Dudhope Park before the leerie came with his pole to light the gaslamps.

William Kennedy and his sons sailed from the Tay at the beginning of June, in search of the black whale. Arthur was despondent and reluctant to leave, for Lizzie had lost the bairn she was expecting. George sailed with the *Windward* this time, his bonnie Jeannie waving him goodbye upon the quay with the brave smile she'd learned as a child in the trawler-owner's house. Georgina and wee Hughie fluttered white handkerchiefs, waving forlornly to their father, long after the depleted whaling fleet had passed Broughty Castle and skirted the Gaa Sands, heading northwards for Greenland and the Davis Straits.

Chrissie was once more left in Bessie's care. Bessie had been given strict instructions by her master concerning Charles Rankine's courtship.

'I want no breath o' scandal to touch those two, mind now, Bessie,' William had warned her. 'Mr Rankine's a grand catch, and there's plenty mothers in Dundee green-eyed because he's settled on Chrissie. They'll be on the lookout for scandalous titbits, and cats have sharp claws. I trust you to guard my lass, Bessie. I know you'll do your best.'

'Aye, Mr Kennedy—' Bessie had replied awkwardly. Knowing what she did about Chris and Danny Murphy, she couldn't look the poor man square in the face.

On 20th August, a hurried memo came to Charles Rankine in his mahogany-panelled office that sent him post haste in his carriage to Chrissie. She received him in the parlour with the door left wide, so that Bessie could be a chaperone. His eyes shone with suppressed excitement.

'Christina, how would you like to meet the Queen?'

Chrissie clasped her hands, eyes shining. 'Queen Alexandra? I'd love it. But she never comes to Dundee, Charles.'

'Well, she's coming now. The Royal yacht will berth in Dundee harbour, and the Queen will travel from Aberdeen by train on the twenty-third, to board the *Victoria and Albert* before sailing for Denmark to visit relatives. I have been asked to join the list of persons being presented to Her Majesty on the platform, and I'm permitted to bring a partner, Christina,' Charles explained triumphantly.

His courtship had been progressing slowly, and he was impatient to be seen publicly with Chrissie on his arm. The royal visit presented a perfect opportunity to reveal his intentions to the matriarchs of Dundee who still kept pestering him with their marriageable daughters. The tongues would wag mercilessly. Well, let 'em, Charles thought.

Chrissie hesitated. She was also aware that her presence by his side would cause a furore of speculation, which she'd been trying hard to avoid. Oh, she longed to meet the Queen, but the price was so high.

'I don't know, Charles—' she demurred.

He reached for her hands. He couldn't bear it if she refused. He was as lovesick as a lovelorn school laddie.

'Oh, Chrissie dear, please say yes! It . . . it would honour me to have you with me,' he said sincerely.

The plea went straight to Chrissie's heart. She could never love him as she loved Danny, but she liked him.

44

He had never been anything but courteous and kind. How could she refuse his request?

Och, let the tongues wag, I'm going to meet the Queen, thought Chrissie recklessly. She smiled at Charles.

'I'll trim my best hat and practise my curtsey, Charles, and we'll meet Queen Alexandra.'

'Oh, Chrissie, my darling!'

He was exultant, catching her in his arms. For a breathless moment something flared between them, a warmth that startled Chrissie. She was not the innocent girl he believed her to be, and she recognised at once the glowing light of passion, the longing to be kissed. She held her breath, then he released her quickly and stepped back. Danny would never have hesitated to kiss her as this man had done, but then Danny was not a gentleman, thought Chrissie, and she was immediately shamed by the thought.

The Royal Yacht, *Victoria and Albert*, had a stormy passage as she steamed into the Tay, escorted by the Royal Navy cruiser, *Argyll*. However, the rain ceased and the wind moderated next day, fortunately for an array of pretty hats assembled around Tay Bridge Station when the royal train pulled into the platform at three o'clock precisely.

The Lord Provost welcomed Queen Alexandra and her daughter, Princess Victoria, when they stepped from the train. There were gifts of fruit, and bouquets of roses, then Chrissie was dazzled to find herself curtseying to the Queen and Princess and exchanging a few words with the regal and gracious Queen Alexandra. Her moment of glory lasted but a few seconds before the royal party swept on and out of the station to face cheering crowds, but Chrissie knew she'd never forget the meeting. Deeply moved, she held fast to Charles Rankine's arm, not caring what interpretation the dowagers of Dundee put upon their closeness. They lingered behind the others in their party, knowing it would be impossible to reach their carriage in the crush around the station.

'Oh, Charles, thank you for giving me such a wonderful experience!' she sighed.

He smiled down at her fondly. 'This is but the first of many, Chrissie, my dearest.'

'No, sir, it's no'! It's the last, the ending for you and my lass!'

Danny's shout stopped them. He had stepped out of the doorway where he'd been hiding, and stood with legs braced, eyes glaring. Chrissie gave a frightened cry: Dan in a rage was a force to be reckoned with, as she knew only too well.

'Danny! Aw, Dan, please!' Her eyes begged him not to make a scene.

Charles was startled by the appearance of the hot-eyed young man. He looked down at Chrissie.

'You know this man?'

'Aye, she does,' broke in Danny. 'I'm Daniel Murphy, and Chris is promised to me, Mr Rankine. We were to wed, until her father sold her to you to save himself.'

These were shocking, emotive words. Charles stared hard at Danny. He looked beyond the orraworker's clothing and saw a handsome young man with angry, honest eyes set in an intelligent countenance, and his heart missed a beat.

'There was no question of selling Christina's favours when I asked her father's permission to court her,' Charles countered. 'I mentioned to him that our union might be mutually profitable, that's all. The decision to marry me or not is Chrissie's, of her own free will.'

Danny snorted. 'What free will does the poor lass have, when her father is ready to lay the ruin of his

46

whaling business at her door? If Chrissie married you, your patronage would tide the man over for a spell. Aye, maybe so, but you and I know the tide's ebbing for whaling in Dundee, Mr Rankine.'

There was an aching sorrow in Charles's breast as he considered Danny's words, which had a hard edge of truth to them. He was silent for a moment, before turning to Chrissie.

'Is it true, Chrissie? Are you promised to this man, do you love him and want to wed him? If so, Chrissie, have you considered well? Do you know what your life will be with him?' he demanded sternly, his eyes boring into hers. They were harsh words, but they must be said.

Danny took an indignant step forward. 'Aye, she knows, Mr Rankine, and she's willing to take the rough wi' the smooth. I'll not be an orraworker all my days. I may be a poor man the now, but I'm a better man than you will ever be!'

Looking down, Charles envied his rival's vitality, his looks, the broadshouldered frame that spoke of powerful strength. It was no boastful claim that Daniel Murphy was making. He was the better man of the two.

Charles bowed his head. 'It's your decision, Chrissie, and I'll abide by it. I refuse to take you on your father's terms. I'll not take you unwillingly, my dearest. You must give me your decision now.'

Oompah-oompah! The brass band at Craig Pier seemed loud in the silence of that deserted part of the station. Chrissie could hear loud bursts of enthusiastic cheering as Queen Alexandra and the Princess were driven off to the reception the Town Council had prepared for them. Dundee hadn't seen such a sight for many a year, with flags and bunting fluttering loyally in the windy spatters of rain.

She heard it as if in a dream. She looked from Danny's handsome, beloved countenance, to the grave, kindly

47

man she had grown to like and respect, and there was a heaviness in her breast because she knew what her decision was.

'I'm sorry, Charles. I have given Danny my willing promise to marry him, because I love him, and want to be his wife. I shall tell my father so, when he returns,' Chrissie said quietly.

23rd August 1907: an historic day for Dundee, a day Chrissie would never forget. A day when she'd had a taste of the gilded life she could have led with Charles Rankine, and had turned her back on it to settle for the hardships of a juteworker's wife.

But when Danny smiled at her, with the glorious lovelight in his blue, blue eyes, Chrissie's heart lifted, and sang with the patriotic chorus outside.

Chapter 3

The news that the whaler's daughter had turned down the most eligible bachelor in Dundee went round the drawing rooms of Broughty Ferry and the West End with the speed of an outbreak of influenza. The story was given an added twist by the rumour that Chrissie Kennedy had rejected Charles Rankine in favour of a juteworker. Every ambitious mama with a marriageable daughter shuddered with horror at the very thought, and hopes were revived.

Those Dundee folk who took an interest in such things settled down to wait with heightened anticipation for the return of the whaling fleet, and William Kennedy's reaction when he heard what his rebellious daughter had been up to in his absence.

'Och, lassies, nowadays!' the old men shook their heads despairingly, in the shelter of the Town House Pillars, where they met most days to enjoy a peaceful pipe, and there was much genuine sympathy for the poor man. News was seeping through of another disastrous trip for the whalers, and there were alarming rumours of foul weather and a ship lost in the Baffin Sea.

'Aye, the whaling's done for,' grumbled the old lads. Everyone knew demand for whale oil had dwindled away now streets and houses were lit by gaslight instead of smoky whale-oil lamps. Why, even the Overgate, a cheery, narrow artery leading into the very heart of town, was soon to be lit by the marvel of electricity, and there was a grand new electricity power station being built not far from William Kennedy's own house.

'Och, Captain Kennedy has enough on his plate the now, without the added sorrow of a wilful daughter,' the old ones agreed, puffing away gravely before the polis appeared, after a tactful interval, to move them on.

Chrissie, herself, shed bitter tears in private at the talk, but she walked out in the lovely September weather with her head held high. Most of the mamas and dutiful daughters shunned her, but not everyone condemned her. The bleachers, who were embarked on a bitter strike against their employers, cheered as she passed the empty bleach-fields.

'Good for you, lass! You show 'em!' someone shouted.

But that was small comfort to a lass who loved her father dearly, and for the first time in her life dreaded his homecoming.

The jingle of harnesses brought Chrissie to her feet one warm day in mid-September. She'd turned her attention lately to the unkempt garden, and had been on her knees, wrestling with weeds. She guessed correctly who the visitor was, and looked round wildly for means of escape. There was none, unless she risked a dash across the busy railway line. Sighing, Chrissie went resignedly to meet Arthur's wife, the former Lizzie Bowers.

'How nice to see you, Lizzie.' Chrissie greeted her sister-in-law warmly with a peck on the cheek.

Lizzie tethered the pony and cart to the porch rail and slipped a nosebag over the placid, little animal's head. She looked grim.

'Could we go inside please, Christina?'

Chrissie's heart sank, but she smiled brightly. 'Yes, of course.'

She led the way in, pausing by the kitchen door.

'Here's Lizzie come to visit, Bessie. May we have tea and a piece of your shortbread, perhaps?'

Bessie and Chrissie exchanged a significant glance, and Bessie nodded and tightened her lips.

The two young women were no sooner in the parlour with the door closed than Lizzie rounded on Chrissie.

'What's this I hear about you turning down Charles for a juteworker?'

Chrissie lifted her chin mutinously. 'It's true, Lizzie. I don't love Charles Rankine, and I'll not marry him. I'm pledged to marry someone else.'

Two angry spots of colour appeared on Lizzie's cheeks. 'You're daft, Christina. Quite mad. Charles will be one of the richest men in Dundee one day, and you've dared to insult and humiliate him. Taking up with a juteworker, indeed. Who is this man?'

'His name's Daniel Murphy and he works in the High mill. His father's a road-sweeper, and his mother's one of the kindest women I know. They live in a tenement in Lochee,' Chrissie answered defiantly.

'His father's a . . . a scavenger?' Lizzie's voice rose to an outraged squeak.

Chrissie was angry. Tutored by Danny, she was fluent in Dundee's distinctive dialect, and she slipped into it now. 'Aye, Lizzie. Mr Patrick Murphy's a scaffie, and he's kept busy. There's plenty work for scaffies in this town.'

Lizzie all but wrung her hands. 'The Kennedys will never live this down. I can only imagine you've been led astray by an unscrupulous rogue, Christina, and haven't the good sense to see through the man.'

Chrissie stepped closer. 'Lizzie, Danny is hardworking and honest, like his father before him. I love and respect him. I'll thank you not to insult him. If you make any more hurtful remarks, I shall ask you to leave,' she warned coldly.

51

Lizzie plumped herself on the couch, glowering.

'I'll not leave until I've driven some sense into your head. I feel responsible for your welfare in your father's absence, Christina. I'm afraid that woman, Bessie, has been lax in her duty; letting you run wild on the riverbank as a child and consort with rude, common folk.'

There was a muffled snort of indignation from the region of the keyhole, and Lizzie was on her feet in an instant and had the door wrenched open. Bessie was caught in the act, her ear at the keyhole. Lizzie drew herself up to her full five foot two inches.

'So! I'm glad you heard that, Bessie McCutcheon, because in my opinion you're to blame for this disastrous alliance which will ruin Christina's life. I shall tell Captain Kennedy so when he returns, and insist that you be dismissed.'

'Lizzie, no!' Chrissie cried in horror.

Bessie rose with as much dignity as she could muster. 'That's for the master to decide, Mistress Lizzie. I did what I believed right for the lassie in my charge. I wanted her to see how other folk live. I'd no idea she'd fall for my nephew Danny, and to tell the truth I'm as heartsick as you are. I wish with all my heart it hadna happened.'

'Aah-hah! The man's your nephew. Now I understand. You hope to advance yourself at Christina's expense,' exclaimed Lizzie grimly.

'Stop it! That's not true, Lizzie. You're twisting everything,' Chrissie cried in dismay.

Bessie's dander was up. She glared at Lizzie. 'I'll tell you one thing for sure, Mistress Lizzie—'

'And what's that?'

'You're no' getting a single bite of my good shortbread!' Bessie sniffed. She headed for the kitchen and slammed the door.

Lizzie stared after her angrily. 'Well really, what cheek! Your father will be told about this, Christina. That woman must go!'

Chrissie had never been so angry. To hear Lizzie threatening dear, loyal Bessie was more than she could bear. She rushed to the door and held it wide open.

'Get out of here, Lizzie! It's none of your business how I live my life, so will you please go?'

Lizzie gathered up her gloves with dignity. 'There's gratitude for you. I only wanted to help. I needn't have bothered.'

She swept outside with Chrissie following. Chrissie's anger had quickly fizzled out, and now she was sorry she'd been so unkind to Arthur's wife. Lizzie was busy with the pony, stowing the nosebag behind the ponycart. Stony-faced, she untethered the wee beastie and climbed aboard the trap. Chrissie touched her arm hesitantly.

'Lizzie . . . I'm so sorry you lost another baby. It . . . it's so sad.'

For an illuminating moment Lizzie Kennedy was caught unawares, and Chrissie glimpsed a startling depth of sorrow and suffering. Then the little woman gathered the reins and nodded coldly. She urged on the little pony and manoeuvred the ponytrap skilfully through the gate onto the Dundee Road without another word.

Harriet Bowers didn't know what to think when she heard Chrissie had turned Charles down. She admired Chrissie's steadfast devotion to Danny, but her own emotions were left in a chaotic state. Harriet pitied Charles because he'd been rejected by her friend, and she couldn't stop hoping he might turn to her for comfort. Hope was tempered by other considerations, however, namely Harriet's fierce ambition to be a doctor. She loved Charles, but she didn't want to be married yet. Oh, it is a muddle, she thought as she strolled pensively in the rose-garden.

'Penny for them, Harriet?'

Charles was leaning against the summerhouse in the sunshine. Smiling, he held out a penny, which she took gravely and slipped into her pocket.

'I was thinking about you and Chrissie,' she admitted.

His expression grew pained. 'To tell the truth, I try not to think about Chrissie. I work harder than usual, smoke and drink more than I ought, but still the thoughts will persist.'

She remained silent, studying him. She loved everything about him: his tall, spare frame, the quirky curve to his lips, the kindness of his steady, intelligent eyes. He studied her thoughtfully.

'Chrissie tells me you want to be a doctor?'

'Yes, I've applied to the medical faculty, and have been accepted on the strength of my exam results. Are you shocked, Charles? Mama had to be revived with smelling salts when I told her.'

He grinned. 'No, I'm not shocked. A liberal dose of Harriet Bowers' common sense is just what the medical profession needs to blow away the dusty cobwebs of centuries.'

'You're teasing me!'

He put his hands on her shoulders. 'My dear girl, I'm not.'

Charles looked down into Harriet's wide eyes. He was very fond of her and they got on well. Charles knew he must marry one day, it was expected of him, and Harriet was his favoured choice now that he had lost the woman he loved so dearly.

'Harriet, when you complete your studies and become a fully fledged doctor, will you be content to give up your profession one day, to marry and have children?' he asked curiously.

Her heart gave a wild leap, but she paused gravely to consider the question and tried to answer him honestly. 'I think it would be a great wrench, Charles, but if I truly loved the man that asked it of me, I would do it for him.'

'Yes, I believe you would,' he said softly, then bent down and kissed her chastely on the brow.

The mild, misty spell of September weather broke at last, and the suffragettes marched through the High Street on 1st October in chilly rain. Chrissie marched with them, persuaded against her better judgement by Harriet's infectious enthusiasm.

'Don't you want the vote, Chrissie?' Harriet had challenged her.

'Well, yes, I suppose so, but—' Secretly, Chrissie wasn't sure what she'd do with a vote if she had it. Surely, her small mark upon a ballot paper wouldn't change anything? She said as much to Harriet.

'Of course it would. Imagine a whole army of women with the power to vote. We could change the world, Chrissie. There could be women in Parliament, keeping an eye on the men. A woman Prime Minister, even!' Harriet's eyes glowed with fervour.

'The Prime Minister a woman? Och, Harriet, what nonsense!' Chrissie giggled.

'Well, maybe that's going a wee bit far,' her friend agreed with a grin. 'But you must march, Chrissie. You must help hold my banner. It's huge, and I can't manage the wretched thing by myself.'

So Chrissie marched, holding one end of a rain-soaked banner which proclaimed in red paint VOTES FOR WOMEN . . . NOW! They marched to the vigorous beat of Daisy Marchmont's big drum, shepherded dourly by most of Dundee's impressively tall policemen, and Chrissie felt horribly conspicuous and embarrassed.

She spotted a disapproving group of matrons waiting for the tram outside the Town House Pillars, and recognised some of the ladies who'd been her sternest critics. Her feet dragged reluctantly towards them, then she realised the interested crowd had suddenly swelled in number. The shifts had changed at the mills, and there was Danny with a group of millworkers, all cheering loudly. He caught her eye and waved furiously, blowing a kiss.

'Look, lads, there's Chrissie, my own bonnie lass. Votes for women, say I!' Danny flourished his cap, and all the millworkers cheered themselves hoarse.

Chrissie felt a lump in her throat. Danny wouldn't treat her like some of the frustrated ladies she knew, who sat aimlessly at home and filled in time at the embroidery frame. She would be his companion and helpmate, working shoulder to shoulder with her man to make ends meet. It would be hard, she knew, but the effort would strengthen her and make her the equal of any man. She would earn her right to vote.

Chrissie hoisted the banner higher, giving it a defiant shake as the procession wound past the scandalised group by the Pillars.

'Votes for women, now!' Chrissie and Harriet shouted gleefully in unison.

This time, when the whaling fleet was spotted far out beyond the white water of Abertay Sands, Danny stood at Chrissie's shoulder on the quay, waiting for the *Christina K* to dock.

They stood hand in hand, not speaking much, a good bit apart from the others waiting in an anxious group for their loved ones to return. Chrissie was as sorrowful and anxious as any, for word had gone round that the *Windward* had been lost at sea.

George had sailed on that ill-fated ship, and there was no word of him so far. She could see his wife, Jeannie, standing motionless, facing into the keen wind from the east, her hands clutching her two bairns to her as if she would never let them go.

Seven-year-old Hughie wriggled and broke away. He raced over to Chrissie, his favourite aunt. 'Auntie Chris, my ma's greeting! Is my daddy dead?' he whispered, wide-eyed.

She hugged him. 'We hope not, lovie. Some of the *Windward*'s crew were saved, maybe your daddy's among them.' It was all the comfort she could give the wee lad. Nobody knew for sure.

Danny gave the small boy a gentle push. 'Away back to your ma, Hughie. Hug her and care for her. She needs all your love the now.'

'Aye, Danny,' Hughie nodded solemnly. He had great respect for Danny, who was a dab hand at bools and had taught Hughie a trick or two when he visited the tenement with Bessie.

Lizzie Kennedy sat in the pony trap, straight-backed, not looking at anyone, least of all the young man standing by Chrissie's side. She would not allow her eyes to rest on him, yet she could have given an accurate description of his looks. Very handsome, in a bold sort of way.

The little pony stirred restlessly in the cold wind, and she quietened it with a word. From the corner of her eye she could see George's wife, their two lovely children hanging onto their mother. A familiar stab of jealousy and longing went aching through Lizzie's veins.

When would she have a bairn of her own to hold? Ah, when?

The *Scotia*, captained by Captain Roberts, berthed

first. There was the nervous laughter of relief from some of the group gathered on the quay. The *Scotia* had done well, taking two black whales. Most of the other whalers in the fleet were 'clean', they said. It had, indeed, been a disastrous trip.

Chrissie felt her heart swell with pride when the *Christina K* sailed in. This was a memorable moment, for Danny was watching the arrival of her ship for the first time. She clutched his arm.

'Oh Dan, isn't she beautiful?' Chrissie breathed.

He frowned. He had no love of the sea. Apart from a trip by pleasure steamer up the Tay to Newburgh once in a while, Danny preferred to keep his feet on dry land. He could see little to commend the weatherbeaten hulk.

'It could do wi' a lick o' paint,' he observed truthfully.

Fortunately the remark was drowned by the bustle of the ship's arrival. Chrissie's fingers tightened anxiously on Danny's sleeve as William Kennedy appeared on deck to supervise the ropes. When all was secure and the gangplank lowered, he was first down, making for Jeannie, who stood white-faced and motionless on the quay. He took her cold hands.

'Your man's safe, my dear. There was many a brave deed done when the *Windward* went aground, and George was saved.'

She seemed to come back to life, leaning against her father-in-law. 'Oh, thank God!' Jeannie cried.

'Aye, well—' William Kennedy cleared his throat. 'George was in the icy water, dear. Not too long, but it weakened him. It's my opinion George will never go to sea again.'

She looked up quickly and met his grave eyes, her joy fading.

'Where is he?' she asked quietly.

'In the sick bay. You'd best go to him, Jeannie.'

He watched her climb the gangplank with the two children, then heaved a sigh and turned away. William Kennedy caught sight of Chrissie and his face lit up. He held out his arms.

'Chrissie, my lass!'

She hugged him. He smelled of tarry rope and the sea, and pipesmoke; a comfortable, remembered blend that held no comfort for her now, because she knew she must disappoint him. He held her at arms' length.

'Let's look at you. Man, you're a sight for sore eyes, Chrissie. Lovelier than ever. You *must* be in love!' he laughed.

Tears stood bright in her eyes. 'Oh, Papa, dear—'

He frowned, then glanced around sharply. 'Where's Charles? I thought . . . I expected to find him by your side.'

Danny stepped forward. 'I escorted Chrissie to the dock, Captain Kennedy. The foreman gave me leave to take time off.'

'Who the devil are you?' William Kennedy demanded in bewilderment.

'I'm Daniel Murphy, and Chrissie and I . . . well, we've been courting for years. I've come to ask your permission to marry your daughter, sir,' Danny announced, coming straight to the point as usual.

William Kennedy stared at Chrissie. 'Chrissie, surely this lad must be blethering. I expected you and Charles Rankine to have reached an understanding by now.'

This was even worse than Chrissie had expected. She wished Danny had broken the subject of their marriage more gently, but that was not Danny's way.

'Papa, Charles and I did reach an understanding. I told him I couldn't marry him, because I love another. I love Danny, Papa, and we hope to be married with your blessing,' she explained nervously.

59

William Kennedy's disappointment knew no bounds. He'd been sustained during the gruelling trip by the thought that his bonnie daughter's future was secure, and now she was telling him she intended marrying this – he took in Danny's working clothes in a quick, outraged glance – this labourer! William Kennedy turned beetroot-red.

'Chrissie, how long has this folly been going on?'

Her hand dropped from her father's arm and she moved closer to Danny. 'It's not folly, Papa. I've known Dan since I was a child. I love him very much.'

'Love!' Her father snorted. 'You're only seventeen, Chrissie. What d'you know about love?'

That roused Danny's indignation. 'She kens more about true love than you do, Captain Kennedy. You were willing to sell her to Charles Rankine to save your trade. You took no heed o' Chrissie's feelings in the matter.'

'Why, that . . . that's impudence!' William blustered. He was all the more angry because he knew there was truth in what Danny had said.

Chrissie was dismayed as the two men she loved most looked daggers at one another. She stepped between them.

'Papa, you must not fight with Danny, because I intend to marry him and I will not change my mind.'

'I'll not allow it, Chrissie. I'll not give you my permission to marry.' William Kennedy growled furiously.

She looked suddenly older than her seventeen years. 'Then I will leave your house, Papa, and go to Danny, married or not.'

'Chrissie!' her father gasped, severely shocked. The determined woman before him seemed like a stranger, not his sweet, biddable Chrissie. There was a long silence, broken only by the screech of gulls and the welcoming cries of women on the quay, then he bowed his head and spoke in a different tone. 'If you're intent on ruining your life I can't stop you, my dear lass, but when you go to this man, you'll go as a married woman. At least I'll see to that.'

'Oh, Papa!' Tears sprang to Chrissie's eyes and she would have hugged him, but he pushed her aside.

William Kennedy slowly climbed the gangplank of his ship. He went to the stern and stood gripping the rail, staring blindly across the estuary like a man surveying the wreckage of his fondest hopes and dreams.

'I just hope you ken what you're doing, Danny Murphy,' his mother said wearily. Biddy Murphy was sorely troubled by the recent turn of events. Her son had won the whaler's lass, but at what cost? Captain Kennedy was a broken man they said, close to ruin, with his precious daughter promised to a juteworker and his son, George, sick with a congestion of the lungs.

To crown it all, Bessie McCutcheon would lose her job if Mistress Lizzie Kennedy had her way, and what of Chrissie herself? thought Biddy worriedly. The poor lass wasn't fit for life in the one-roomed tenement flat Danny had rented. He couldn't see it, of course. Danny was an optimist, like his father before him.

'Och, dinnae fash yoursel', Ma,' smiled Danny.

He was always grinning these days. As well he might, Biddy thought grimly. He'd fought hard for his lass, and won her by sheer brass neck.

'I'm thinking of Chrissie in thon wee mousehole, and her used to luxury in the big house,' she grumbled.

'It's a start,' he retorted calmly. 'We'll no' bide there long, don't you worry. I'm on the climb, Ma. The foreman's got his eye on me for promotion at the mill, because I've been learning mathematics and I'm quick at figuring. And I've been given my stripe in the Volunteers. I'm lance-corporal now.'

'Marching and drilling and capers on the Magdalen Green. Much good that'll do ye,' his mother snorted.

'It's a way to get on. If I stick at it, I could be sergeant one day.'

Biddy laughed. 'What, you, a sergeant?'

'Aye, me! Why not, Ma?'

But she shook her head and wouldn't answer, gripped by a sudden queasy fear she couldn't explain.

Chrissie should have been blissfully happy as she prepared for her wedding day, but a cloud lay over her happiness. Her father had become resigned to the marriage, for he loved his daughter too much to disown her. However, William Kennedy and Danny couldn't get on. They were too much alike: both down-to-earth characters. William generously offered to give Chrissie a handsome dowry he could ill afford, an offer which Danny proudly refused.

'Thank you, Captain Kennedy, but I'll support my wife without any help from you.'

The refusal enraged and offended poor William so deeply he turned on his heel without a word and stalked from the room, much to Chrissie's distress.

'Och, Danny, my father meant it kindly,' she protested.

Danny looked contrite. 'Aye, I know he did and I'm sorry, but he made it sound like charity, and that put my back up, Chris. I'm damned if I'll accept charity!'

She had no answer to that, for she remembered a poor, little mill-lass on the beach, and two precious farthings lost amongst the shingle.

The health of George had improved, but his cough remained troublesome. Chrissie visited George and Jeannie often, because she felt relaxed and easy with them, and she needed friends. Those two kindly souls had quietly accepted her decision to marry Danny, but Chrissie rarely visited Arthur and Lizzie. Lizzie had not mellowed.

Of course, Chrissie was on very good terms with her bachelor brother, Ernest, who had rooms in the Seagate, close to the office. Ernest was very sympathetic to his young sister's plight, but the grocer's daughter had broken off their engagement, and in consequence, poor Ernest was broken-hearted and not very cheerful company at present.

Chrissie was visiting George not long before her wedding when Jeannie announced startling news. It was cold and foggy, a bad day for George's chest, and he'd been forced to go to bed. The two women could hear his painful coughing as they talked together quietly in the kitchen.

'We're leaving Dundee, Chrissie,' Jeannie told her.

'Oh, no! Where are you going?'

'To a hill farm in Isla. The doctor says mountain air might help George's cough, and George has heard of an old farmer in the glen who'd be glad of help to run the farm.'

'But you know nothing about farming,' Chrissie objected.

'We'll learn,' answered Jeannie. She stood up abruptly and went to the window, looking out at the silver ribbon of the river below. 'I'm a trawler-man's daughter, Chrissie, and I hate the sea with all my heart. Look what it's done to my man. I don't care if I never see the river again,' she said bitterly.

'Nor do I, Auntie Chris,' added ten-year-old Georgina staunchly. 'My daddy says we'll have dogs and kittens at the farm. I'm to have a dog of my own to help Daddy herd the sheep.' The little girl's eyes shone like stars at the prospect, and her mother smiled, laying a gentle hand on the girl's dark head.

'Ina's daft about animals, Chrissie. She's been prigging at me for years to let her have a dog. Well, she shall have one now.'

There was a whimper of protest from wee Hughie, at Chrissie's side. 'Mam, I don't want to go to the farm. I want to stay in Dundee with my school chums. I like it here, and I'm to be in the football team. Why can't I stay?'

Jeannie sighed patiently. 'I'm tired of telling you, son. It's for your daddy's health. You're going whether you like it or not, Hughie, so you must make the best of it.'

The boy said no more, but Chrissie looked down apprehensively into the tearful, mutinous little face. Oh, dear, there's trouble in store here, she thought to herself.

The wedding was arranged for 22nd November 1907. It was to be a quiet, simple affair, because Danny refused point blank to allow Chrissie's father to pay for anything ostentatious. It was only a short step from the kirk to the Captain's house, and Bessie, who had so far weathered the storm of Lizzie Kennedy's disapproval, had agreed to provide a wedding breakfast for the bride and groom and their guests.

The day before the wedding, Chrissie was too restless and excited to settle to anything, and Bessie shooed her out for a walk in the cold, frosty air.

'Enjoy your leisure, lass. There'll be little enough of it where you're going,' Bessie said darkly.

Nothing could dampen Chrissie's spirits today, however. The sharp air brought colour to her cheeks as she walked briskly towards Broughty Ferry. The outskirts of the little fishing village had been transformed by the houses of jute barons, vying with one another to build larger and more ostentatious mansions, but

Chrissie paid little attention to these. She watched the busy commerce of the river at high tide, trawlers and sprat boats, and another jute steamer heading for the docks where the *Christina K* lay idle. Chrissie sighed, her gloved hand going to the brooch pinned to her lapel. The ship needed refitting, but there was no money to do it now she had turned down Charles Rankine's offer. How sad to be filled with remorse, the day before she became Danny's wife.

Walking on, Chrissie became aware of a mechanical sound behind her, and a new-fangled motor car drew alongside and stopped. Colour flooded her cheeks as she recognised the man who'd been in her thoughts, the very last person she wanted to see, today of all days.

'Charles! How . . . how are you?' she asked.

He climbed out of the car. He was beautifully dressed for motoring in a long leather coat, with a smart cap which he doffed politely.

'I'm well, thank you, Chrissie,' he answered, although his heart was pounding painfully. How beautiful she looked, lovelier than ever. He smiled at her. 'This is fortunate, meeting you by chance. I had so hoped to see you before your wedding, Chrissie, to wish you well,' he said sincerely.

'Thank you for your good wishes, Charles.'

She spoke formally, but she wanted to hug and comfort him in his disappointment. Her thoughts of him would always be tinged with warmth. He was so kind, a true gentleman.

'I have a wedding gift for you, Chrissie,' he said.

She put up a hand in protest, distressed. 'Oh, no. You mustn't.'

It would be too painful to look at his gift and remember him. Besides, Danny wouldn't have it in the house. He'd fling it out.

Reading her thoughts accurately, Charles smiled.

'Don't worry, Chrissie, it's not a tangible gift, yet I believe it will please you greatly. I've persuaded my board of directors to agree a formal contract with your father for batching oil. It means I can offer him an advance to refit his whaling fleet.'

Her heart leaped, and tears shone in her eyes. Impulsively, she reached for his hand and held it for a moment in hers.

'Charles, I don't know what to say,' she whispered brokenly.

'Don't say anything, Chrissie. Just be happy, my dear. That's all I ask.'

Charles lifted his cap, then good-naturedly shooed away the crowd of little boys that had gathered round this rare sight on Dundee streets, and clambered into the car. He was glad the complexities of driving the vehicle occupied his mind as he drove off, because he discovered his vision was misted with tears.

Bessie had organised everything perfectly, down to the spray of small white chrysanthemums pinned to Chrissie's blue suit. It had to be blue, Bessie insisted.

'"Married in blue, Your love will be true!"' Bessie had quoted firmly, and that was that.

Bessie stood back and surveyed her lassie critically, once she'd helped Chrissie dress for her wedding. She clasped her hands and her eyes shone with proud tears. 'Oh, my lassie, you're so bonnie!'

Chrissie hugged her. 'Thank you, Bessie dear. Thanks for everything you've done for me. But most of all, thank you for giving me Danny,' she whispered.

Aye, well, that remains to be seen, my dear lassie, Bessie thought, as she tearfully wiped her eyes.

Chrissie walked to the kirk on her father's arm, with Bessie following. It felt strange, like a Sunday, yet it was a working day, and Danny had been given the whole day off for his wedding. Entering the kirk, Chrissie saw that Danny's side was packed with well-wishers, but her own turn-out was sparse, only her brothers and their wives, and wee Hughie and Georgina.

And Harriet, of course. Harriet turned and smiled her wide, friendly, joyful smile as Chrissie and her father came down the aisle, and Chrissie's heart soared with gratitude. Then she saw Danny waiting for her before the altar, looking strange and solemn in his best clothes. Their eyes met, and his expression lit up with such joy and love it took her breath away. She went forward, serene and confident, and the minister quietly began the simple service that made Daniel Murphy and Christina Kennedy man and wife, for richer or poorer, for better, or for worse.

'Man, but it was a lovely service. Did ye no' think so, Mistress Kennedy?' beamed Patrick Murphy, whom Bessie had mischievously positioned at the big table right next to Lizzie.

Lizzie eyed Patrick warily. 'Yes, indeed. Very moving.'

'Aye. Minds me o' the day me an' Biddy got spliced. The lads from the Cleansing Department made an arch o' brushes for us to walk under. That was a very moving moment, dearie, I'm tellin' ye,' Patrick said mistily.

'Most . . . most unusual, Mr Murphy,' Lizzie agreed.

Danny whispered to Chrissie with a wicked grin. 'My pa and your snobby sister-in-law are getting along like a house on fire!'

Chrissie covered her mouth and giggled. Patrick had launched into the finer points of keeping Dundee's hilly streets clean with so much horse traffic going up and down to the mills, and poor, fastidious Lizzie seemed for the moment to have lost her appetite.

The wedding breakfast over, there was no excuse to

linger. The contingent of Danny's relatives prepared to leave with the bride and bridegroom, on the tram.

Now that the moment of parting had arrived, William Kennedy was overcome. He hugged his daughter with an emotion too deep for words, then turned to Danny.

'You take care of her, now.'

'I will. Dinna fash yoursel', Captain Kennedy.'

The two men shook hands solemnly on the promise, in total agreement for once. Bessie was sobbing openly and quietly. What was left for her to do, now her dear lassie was going? she wondered. There was a dark fear for the future in her, even on her lass's happiest of days.

Harriet planted herself in front of Chrissie, and the two friends hugged fondly. Chrissie had never seen Harriet in tears, because Harriet was not the weepy kind, but there were tears on her cheeks today.

'You be happy, Chris. And if ever you need me, I'll come no matter what. Remember that,' Harriet whispered fiercely.

'I'll remember.' Chris held her dear friend close for a moment, then she was swept away, hanging onto Danny's arm, urged out of the house by the boisterous crowd of Murphys. Looking over her shoulder, Chrissie saw her father standing alone, outlined against a calm sea. The others stood apart in a group, waving, and she waved back, touched by the support they'd given her, aye, even Lizzie. But it was the image of her father that stayed with her, that lonely man.

The tram arrived, clanking along, and the conductor's jaw dropped.

'Help my boab, what's this? The Band o' Hope?'

'Hold your wheest, man! It's ten pennies an' six ha'pennies for the Tramway Company.' Patrick Murphy counted the lordly sum into the man's hand as his brood scrambled aboard.

Chrissie's spirits lifted, and she laughed happily and

enjoyed the riotous journey with the rest. They all descended when they reached Lochee, the little village, in the eye of the Balgay Loch, that had become a sprawl of close-packed tenements and dwellings around the mills and great towering chimney stack of Cox's lum.

Biddy hugged her new daughter-in-law, her heart sore for the lass.

'Mind now, hen, I'm just a few closes down the street. You come to me, if you need anythin'.' She turned to Danny, and gently ruffled the curly, black hair of this, her dearest lad. 'Be good to her, Dan. Be happy, and mind an' carry her over the threshold for luck!'

He grinned and kissed his mother, but his eyes were moist. 'I will, Ma.'

And he did. After unlocking the door with a flourish, Danny swept Chrissie up in his strong arms, and made a play of staggering over the threshold with her slight weight, while Chrissie laid her head on his shoulder and laughed merrily. He set her on her feet and they stood hand in hand, looking round the single room that was to be their home.

Danny's spirits dropped to his boots. 'Ach, Chrissie, it's no' near good enough for ye, my dearest,' he said miserably.

Chrissie took him into her arms and kissed him.

'You're good enough for me, my darling lad, and that is all that matters.'

Chapter 4

Chrissie wakened with a start on Monday morning, roused by an unaccustomed din. She propped herself sleepily on one elbow and found Danny was already up, washed and shaved, dressed in his working clothes.

'Dan, what's that racket?'

'It's the factory, it's time for the first shift.' He came and sat on the edge of the bed. It was built into the wall of the wee room like a cupboard, and had a curtain that pulled across for privacy. She stretched out her arms and pulled her husband down to her.

'You should've wakened me, Dan.'

'Och, you were sleeping like a bairn. Snoring, too!' he grinned.

She giggled, kissing his clean, shaven cheek. Reluctantly, Danny eased her warm arms gently from his neck. It was a wrench to leave her, so bonnie and loving. He stood up resolutely.

'I'm away now, Chrissie. The fire's lit and the kettle's singing on the hob. There's fifteen bob saved in the tea caddy. We'll need something for our tea. I'll be in for my dinner before the one o'clock gun goes off at Dudhope, but a sup o' soup and a bite o' bread'll be enough for me, lass.'

He stooped to kiss her. Could he ever get enough of her kisses? He had to tear himself away, reaching for his working-bonnet hanging on the hook, looking over his shoulder so that he could keep the image of her lovely face before him all morning.

Chrissie lay back languorously. She could hear his boots clatter along the stone platform outside and down the stairs to join his workmates thronging the street. A man's lusty voice floated up to her, joking. 'You're awfy late the day, Dan. I wonder why you dallied?'

'Ach, the lad's taken a bonnie, gentry wife, lucky devil!' laughed another.

She heard Danny reply jauntily, the words drowned by the steady tramp of feet heading downhill to the mill. They'd never get the better of her Danny: he had an answer for everything.

A gentry wife, though, Chrissie frowned.

Well, she'd show 'em! She threw back the covers and climbed out of bed, glad to put her feet on the raggy rug her father-in-law had made. Patrick had fashioned the rug from an old jute sack and rags gleaned from his job as scaffie, and it had been his wedding gift to them. Privately, Chrissie had thought it an odd jumble of colours at the time, but now she appreciated its cosiness on the bare wooden floor.

She washed and dressed quickly, for even with the fire, the room felt chilly. Danny, bless him, had made enough porridge for two and left a pot of tea stewing on the trivet. There was just enough milk left in the churn to make the strong tea drinkable and wash down the porridge, and Chrissie sat at the table and let out a happy sigh of pure content. She'd keep an ear open for the milk-cart, then go out shopping armed with Danny's fifteen shillings, a really princely sum. This was the life!

But first, this place needed a good clean. Chrissie rolled up her sleeves.

She was tired, wet and dishevelled by the time she'd scrubbed the floor and washed the window, humping buckets of water from the tap in the back yard, and to tell the truth she couldn't see much improvement. There were generations of grime ground into the floorboards. If only they could afford a bright, pretty linoleum, she thought wistfully.

Chrissie replenished the churn at the milk-cart, braving the stares of her curious neighbours. She surrendered the last few pennies of her own in payment and returned to the room a little unnerved. She'd brought only a few serviceable skirts and dresses with her, but even those seemed out of place. The other women had eyed her attire and muttered to one another, and one had laughed outright. That wasn't very kind, thought Chrissie.

As a gesture of defiance, she wore the blue suit she'd been married in, to go shopping, and topped it with the flowery hat Bessie had created for that happy occasion. Lochee folk stopped and stared, and the butcher's jaw dropped when this elegant vision of loveliness walked into his shop. He hastily stubbed out a Woodbine and stuck the fag-end behind his ear.

'What can I do for ye, missis . . . er . . . madam?'

'A pound-and-a-half of mince and a marrow bone, if you please.'

Mince was easy, Chrissie had decided: Bessie made mouth-watering mince, served with fluffy mashed potatoes. It looked a simple, nourishing dish, well within her capabilities, and Bessie made beautiful broth with a marrow bone.

Bowed out of the butcher's, she headed for the grocer's. There was so much her small store-cupboard lacked, Chrissie went quite recklessly wild in the grocer's, selecting items at random from the well-stocked shelves. Beaming, the proprietor stood with pencil poised, ready to tot up her purchases.

'Anything else today, madam?'

'Oh, yes. And a stone of potatoes,' she finished triumphantly, with the mince and tatties in mind.

There wasn't much change from the fifteen shillings when it was all added up, and Chrissie eyed the large heap of groceries with dismay. She'd never carry that!

'I'll send the laddie round with it, madam,' the grocer offered. He coughed delicately. 'I'm afraid there's a thruppenny delivery charge.'

Chrissie accepted with relief and handed over a silver threepenny bit. The grocer blinked when she told him the address, but she walked out with her head held high, leaving him staring after her, open-mouthed.

Back home, there was still plenty of time to make soup, and she'd used some of the remaining pennies to buy a large loaf at the baker's. The fire had burned low in her absence, so she cheerfully banked it up with drossy coal from the bunker. It took exception to this treatment and began smouldering sulkily, giving off yellow, sulphureous smoke that made her cough.

Chrissie sang gaily as she sliced onions and other vegetables. She emptied the whole lot into the iron pot with the marrow bone and a few handfuls of barley, filled it up with water from the jug, then swung the soup pot over the flames.

Only there weren't any flames.

She hovered anxiously over the fire, poking it now and then, but it refused to respond. The little grocer's laddie came puffing up the stairs, staggering under the weight of the basket, and she was so worried and abstracted and sorry for him, she sent him away beaming with another threepenny piece from Danny's sadly diminished store.

When Danny took the steps two at a time and charged in at dinnertime, he found his wife smeared black with coal dust and reduced to tears.

'Oh, Dan. The broth!'

He lifted the lid of the broth pot, surveyed the watery, greasy, uncooked contents and hastily clamped the lid on again. He turned and took poor, woebegone Chrissie in his arms.

'Never mind, my dearie, we'll have bread and butter.'

'And cheese,' Chrissie remembered, brightening up. 'I went shopping this morning, Dan. I bought ever such a lot with the fifteen bob. There's the change,' she told him proudly, pointing to a few remaining pennies.

Danny turned pale. 'Chris, we were meant to pay the rent and buy coal out of that, and the factor'll be here the morn, seeking his siller.'

She burst into tears. 'Oh, Danny, I didn't know. I'm sorry.'

He kissed and comforted her, and to her amazement, began to chuckle. 'Oh, Chrissie, you're a card! Two days married, and you'd have me bankrupt. Lucky I've got savings. There's another ten bob hidden beneath the mattress.'

Danny worked his magic on the fire before he left, and it blazed up. Wickedly, the contrary beast scorched Chrissie's attempt at mince and tatties, but Dan, who could have eaten a horse when he returned ravenous from the mill, declared it was the best meal he'd ever tasted, and his Chrissie the finest cook in Lochee.

After that humbling experience, Chrissie laid the wedding suit and hat in the bottom drawer of the dresser and gratefully accepted the shawl Biddy had knitted for her. It was skilfully knitted, with the expertise of years, and lined with cloth from an old overcoat Patrick had picked up on his rounds. Pulled over head and shoulders and reaching down to Chrissie's knees, it kept her snug and cosy even in the fiercest winter gale.

At first, the strangeness and hardships of her new life occupied most of Chrissie's time. Gradually she adapted, her muscles aching with humping unaccustomed loads of water and washing. She mourned silently for her smooth, white hands. Now the skin was roughened by washing soda and bars of strong yellow soap, her fingers so chapped and painful with hacks and chilblains she was ashamed of them, and hid her hands beneath the shawl.

But she made friends at the wash-house, or the steamie, as everyone affectionately called the steaming, perspiring building where clothes could be washed with the benefit of piping hot water on payment of a few pennies. Scrubbing away on the washing-board at Danny's oil-stained shirts, Chrissie joined in many a joke and cheery laugh with the other loud-voiced, raucous women. It seemed to Chrissie all Lochee women spoke at full pitch of their lungs. They were used to shouting above the din of the looms, of course, and had a well-developed sign language also, which was expressive, and not always polite.

The women were curious about Chrissie's background, and intrigued when she gave details of Bessie McCutcheon's menu in more affluent days.

'Roast beef an' Yorkshire pudden on the Sabbath? What swank!' roared Nellie Cafferty as she mangled sheets. 'My man doesna look for more than a pie an' a pint.'

The shirts and sheets washed and mangled, it was home again carrying the laden basket, for Chrissie grudged pennies to the little lads who hung hopefully round the wash-house door with the constant piping cry,

'Humph your washin' for ye, wifie?'

By such small economies, she tried hard to spin out Danny's wages, but sometimes her back ached sorely as she pegged out the clean washing on her return home. The washing line ran through a pulley from her window to the tall and massive wooden pole rising from the Green behind the tenements. The greenie pole, bedecked with its lines of fluttering washing, reminded her of the masts of her own bonnie ship, the *Christina K*. She would look at the pole, and touch the brooch she always wore, and sometimes the secret tears would fall.

'I'll have to get a job, Danny,' Chrissie announced at last in desperation. She was tired of struggling to make ends meet on one wage, and more tired still, of looking at the bare walls of their one small room. Most of her neighbours worked all day in the mill, their young bairns lodged with obliging grannies, and it was lonely.

'No, Chrissie,' Danny's square chin set stubbornly. He was being unreasonable, and it infuriated her. She'd marched with the suffragettes fighting for votes for women. Why shouldn't she work if she wanted to?

'You can't stop me, Danny Murphy,' she flashed at him.

'Oh, can't I? I'm your husband, my lass!'

'You're not my master, Dan. I've a will of my own, and I'll do what I think fit for us.'

'I'll not have you working in the mill. Never that, understand?' he shouted angrily.

'Who said anything about the mill? I wouldn't work in thon place, even if you paid me pounds!'

'Too posh, are ye?' Danny growled contrarily. 'I suppose you'd rather slave in a shop, or behind the bar counter, Heaven forbid!'

'Aye, Danny, I would.'

Danny suddenly dissolved into disarming chuckles. 'Och, Chrissie love, see you behind a bar! You'd be preaching temperance in no time. You'd have all the seasoned drunks signing the pledge an' wearing the blue ribbon, 'cause they'd fallen in love with that bonnie face of yours. You'd be a more disruptive influence on hardened drinkers than the Salvation Army, and the proprietor would kick you out.'

And, of course, Chrissie laughed, and fell into his arms, and lost interest in the quarrel for quite some time. But she got her way in the end, and by the beginning of February 1908, she'd been taken on as a shop assistant by the grocer.

The hours were long and she was on her feet all day, but Chrissie enjoyed the work. She was nimble-fingered, and was soon weighing sugar and other dried stuffs, packaging them in blue paper as neatly as the grocer.

Her wages were small, but enough to buy a few comforts. Danny had slippers on his feet instead of jute rovies, as they sat cosily by the fire of an evening. He would be poring over his books, as usual, in the light of the hissing gas mantle, while Chrissie wrote letters to her family.

The writing desk had been Harriet's inspired wedding gift. It contained everything a dedicated correspondent might need, and Chrissie made full use of it. She loved writing in the beautiful copperplate, taught at Miss Black's establishment, and her letters were a joy to read.

One freezing night in March, the wind whistling and howling along the plettie outside, Chrissie settled down with a sigh of pleasure, to write.

My dearest Ina and Hughie,
Little of note has happened since last I wrote you, my dears, except that I believe I have mastered the art of cheese-cutting. You use this contraption which has two handles and a wire to embrace the mother cheese, then 'wheek!' a sharp pull, and there you have a baby cheese to present to

78

your customer weighing more or less the desired
amount . . .

Wee Hughie splashed through mud and slush on the
farm road, clutching Chrissie's letter. He couldn't wait
to read it to Georgina, who was out at the sheep pens.
Och, this awful road, Hughie thought with disgust.
In Dundee you could run like the wind on stone
pavements; you could take off your boots in summer and
run barefoot on warm stone. But in this God-forsaken
glen – words failed him.

The snow had been grand to start with, white and
sparkling, but there was nobody to throw snowballs
or toboggan with except Ina, and she was a girl. If
only his friends from Dundee had been here, they'd
have had fun. And the snowfall went on getting deeper
and deeper until he couldn't get out. Hours of boredom
followed, until he'd been glad to go back to school,
where the talk was boring: all about sheep, cattle and
grain. He missed the sea; Hughie's heart felt sore when
he thought about the sea. His dad wanted him to learn
farming, but Hughie vowed silently he never would.
The moment he was old enough, he was going to sea.

Hughie splashed on dourly through brown slush.

Georgina was leaning on the dyke by the sheep pens,
trying to whistle. Girls never could, somehow. Tam, the
shepherd, was with her, and four sheepdogs lay around
their feet. One of the dogs growled at Hughie and Tam
shushed it. Hughie kept his distance.

'A letter from Auntie Chrissie, Ina. It's a funny one. I
haven't seen Mum and Dad laugh so much for a while.'

Ina smothered her annoyance at her young brother's
appearance. She spent long hours with Tam; a quiet,
restful, young man with endless patience. She'd just
tried to pen some sheep with her boisterous pup. The
results had been disastrous, making Tam laugh.

'You've a lot to learn about running dogs, Miss Ina. You've to learn to whistle first, like this—' and he'd put fingers to his lips and let out a shrill, echoing whistle that made the dogs' ears perk alertly.

'Oh, Tam.' Ina's eyes shone with hero-worship.

She'd been trying to imitate Tam's whistle when Hughie arrived and spoiled her concentration. Still, a letter from Auntie Chrissie was something to be savoured. Ina forgot about the shepherd for the moment.

'Race you back to the house, Hughie. We'll read the letter in front of the fire and make cinnamon toast at the same time, shall we?' Ina cried gaily.

The two children ran off, splashing recklessly through the slush; Ina's sheepdog pup racing madly after. The shepherd leaned on his crook and shook his head in amusement. What a lassie, always up to some ploy. She was winsome though. Aye, she'd be a right winsome lass one day, Tam thought.

Lizzie Kennedy was expecting again. Lizzie's sister Harriet came specially to tell Chrissie the news. Danny was at home, too, that spring holiday, but he made himself scarce when Harriet arrived. Brainy women made Danny uneasy.

Chrissie seated her friend by the fire, proud to play hostess in her own home. 'It's a pity it's not a better day for the Fast,' she said.

Harriet agreed, trying hard not to show how shocked she was by the pokey, little room and lack of all amenities.

She gave her friend a keen look. 'Are you happy, Chris?'

'Yes, I'm happy.' Chrissie bent to poke the fire into a brisker flame. 'I believe I'm a stronger person now, Harriet, because of what I've seen and the folk I've met, good and bad. Life's hard, you know, without the velvet cushions.'

Harriet put a hand on her arm. 'Chrissie, it needn't be so. Your father's business is doing well because of the contract with Rankine's to supply batching oil. Your father would be only too glad to help.'

Chrissie averted her eyes, for Harriet had unwittingly touched on a point of conflict between Chrissie and her husband. 'Papa rarely visits us when he comes home from sea, Harriet. He and Danny will never get on and Dan refuses to accept Papa's charity.'

'Good Heavens, it's not charity.'

'It is, to Danny.'

Harriet gripped her friend's hands. 'But if there were children?'

Chrissie looked at her. 'There *will* be a bairn come October or November, God willing.'

Harriet hugged her delightedly. 'Oh, Chris, a baby. Danny must accept your father's help now, for the baby's sake.'

'Don't tell Lizzie just yet, will you, Harriet?' Chrissie begged anxiously. They looked at one another, and Harriet nodded. She was a medical student, and knew better than most how precarious her sister's condition was.

Lizzie carried her baby for seven months, then lost him. She nearly lost her life as well, and the surgeon attending the new maternity wards of the Eastern Hospital decided enough was enough. Lizzie Kennedy would never have another pregnancy.

Harriet tiptoed in to see her sister who lay very straight and still, staring at the ceiling. Harriet took her hand and kissed her cheek.

'How are you, love?'

She didn't answer right away, and then replied harshly

with another question. 'Christina's expecting a baby, isn't she?'

Harriet was flustered. 'Why, yes, dear, but how did you . . . ?'

'I saw her walking in Lochee. She didn't see me, but I knew right away what her condition was.' Lizzie turned to face her sister. 'That self-willed woman humiliated Charles Rankine and went off and married a juteworker, yet she's to be blessed with a child. Arthur and I will never have the baby we long for now. It isn't fair, Harriet.' Tears stood bright in the poor woman's eyes. Harriet felt like weeping for her sister, but she did not. An emotional outburst would do little good. It was more important for Lizzie to have a positive outlook.

'Lizzie dear, there are many little children in need of a loving home. You could adopt a child.'

Lizzie's eyes blazed. 'A child with unknown vices, a stranger's baby? Never!'

Harriet lifted her shoulders helplessly. 'Then I don't know how you are to be helped, Lizzie.'

Lizzie turned her face away. 'I am strong, Harriet. I will survive. But I will not visit Christina, if her bairn is born alive and healthy.'

Charles Rankine came upon Chrissie by chance. He had deliberately avoided the precincts of Lochee for fear of a meeting, only to bump into her in Dundee's Nethergate. The shock took his breath away. Carefully controlled emotions surfaced and he could hardly speak. He discovered he still loved and wanted her as fiercely as ever.

She stepped back, smiling with surprise and genuine pleasure, and he noted for the first time the thickening of her waistline beneath the concealing shawl. The knowledge she was going to have a baby struck him like a blow. This might have been his child, his own little one. He smothered his aching sorrow and doffed his hat.

'I hope you are well, Chrissie?'

She laughed softly. 'Very well, Charles. Blooming, as they say!'

He dropped all pretence at formality. 'Chrissie, any help I can give, anything I can do for you and the baby, I'll do it,' he offered earnestly.

She studied him gravely, and it came to him suddenly that this was a very different Chrissie from the young, uncertain girl he'd courted.

'Thank you, Charles, but I have a husband. A hard-working lad. I have work, myself, and an errand to see to in the Overgate for my employer,' she answered with dignity.

He was taken aback. 'But you shouldn't be working in your condition, so far on.'

She was obviously amused, her eyes twinkling. 'Charles, it's not an illness, having a bairn. I shall work until I'm brought to bed with my wean. We need the wage more than ever now.'

He blinked. She was as forthright in her speech as Harriet, but she had a new pride and independence he respected. He smiled gently.

'You've changed, Chrissie. Do you still march with the suffragettes?'

She laughed. 'Och, no. I'm too busy earning my right to vote. I leave the campaigning to Harriet and the other ladies.'

'Ladies? They're a militant bunch,' Charles said. 'Poor Winston Churchill had a hard time of it as Liberal candidate in the Dundee by-election. Did you know one harridan rang a muffin bell repeatedly when he tried to speak? Mr Churchill was not amused!'

Chrissie nodded. 'It wasn't polite. Still, he was elected.'

'Yes, he seems quite an able man, and the female campaigners had the worst of it when opposing him at the hustings—' He paused, for she was fidgeting to be on her way. '—I won't detain you, Chrissie. It has given me great pleasure to see you again,' he said sincerely.

'Goodbye, Charles.' Her cheeks were soft rose-pink, her blue eyes warm and friendly. She touched his arm lightly, then hurried off.

He watched until she turned the corner into Thorter's Row and he could see her no more. She had scorned his help, but there were other ways of helping her, Charles thought. Devious ways, perhaps, but just as effective.

Bessie McCutcheon arrived when summoned, to offici- ate at the birth of her dear lass's bairn. She looked at Danny and jerked a thumb towards the door.

'Away to your ma, Danny.'

'Na, I'll bide.' He folded his arms across his chest.

Bessie turned beetroot. 'Danny, I'll no' have ye in here getting under my feet. Away to your ma, I said.'

'It's my bairn as much as Chrissie's. I want to be with her, Bessie,' he insisted stubbornly.

Bessie gave him a long, aggravated look, then sighed irritably.

'Well, keep out the way, mind.' She thrust an empty bucket at him. 'Here, make yourself useful. Away to the tap and fill this. We'll need plenty hot water.'

Danny worked obediently all that long, fraught Sunday afternoon, and Bessie had no complaint of him. He held Chrissie's hand when the pains were bad, and kept his suffering to himself. It was evening, the gaslamp hissing in the small, cramped room, when Bessie cleaned Chrissie's baby and wrapped the tiny mite in flannel and handed it to Danny.

'Here, Dan. Hold your little lass, while the doctor sees to Chrissie.'

He looked down at a tiny face surmounted by a thatch of black hair like his own. The baby opened blue eyes, and he swore she recognised him and smiled. Danny Murphy felt a tender new love enter his breast, strange and compelling. He bent his head and kissed his daughter, and a tear dropped upon her perfect, little cheek.

'Alexandra. That's what we'll call her, Chrissie,' Danny declared later, when all the excitement was over, and Bessie dozed exhausted in the armchair. They were examining their new daughter with breathless wonder, as she lay sound asleep in the crook of her mother's arm.

Chrissie laughed. 'It's an awful big name for a wee scrap, Danny.'

He stroked the baby's soft, black hair with a fingertip. 'D'you mind the day Queen Alexandra came to Dundee, Chris? The day I won you fair and square from Rankine? I stood hidden in the doorway, watching Queen Alexandra step from the train. She was so stately. I've never forgotten that sight of Her Majesty. I never will. I want my daughter named for the Queen.'

She lay and looked at him, seeing the emotion he couldn't hide, the tears she'd never seen near him all the years she'd known him. She had always loved him for his joyful strength, but she loved him then as never before, for his weakness.

Alexandra was barely a month old when Danny came racing home one freezing November night, the sulphureous fog, bred from every smoky Dundee lum, lying thick over the town. He burst into the room and grabbed Chrissie by the waist, whirling her round.

'Dan, Dan,' she protested, laughing. 'What's up with you? You've brought in a draught fit to blow the fire up the lum.'

'Promotion!' he cried. 'We're really on the climb now, my dearie. All the bookwork and hard graft has got me noticed at last, my lass. The mill manager called me into his buckie the day, and told me there's a vacancy for a foreman in the weaving shed. I'm to be on probation for a spell, but if I come up to scratch, it's permanent. What d'you say to that, Mrs Murphy?' He was bursting with pride.

She put her arms round his neck and kissed him. 'I say it's well deserved, Dan, for the work you've put in. They must've had an eye on you all this time.'

'And I was thinking studying had been a waste of time,' Danny beamed. He couldn't keep still, striding about the room. 'I'm to get a grand wage, Chris, enough to make you blink. First thing, we'll get out o' here.' He looked around, curling his nose distastefully. 'We can afford better than this, a place with two rooms and our own tap, even. I'll be chapping on the factor's door, first thing the morn,' Danny vowed.

Chrissie viewed the little room with mixed feelings. She had hated it at first, but now it was home. They'd had ups and downs, but they were happy here. She shivered, suddenly afraid. Would they be so happy in the braw, new house, even with two rooms and a tap of their very own?

They moved a month later to a tenement flat in Liff Road, approved by Danny because there was a school handy. It had two rooms and a boxroom with a skylight, which served as Alexandra's nursery. It also had a tiny scullery containing a sink and tap, and Chrissie no longer had the chore of humping water up the stairs. There was no prouder man in Dundee than Danny Murphy, as he filled the kettle at his own tap and set it on the hob to boil.

William Kennedy paid a visit to view his new grand-daughter shortly after the move, accompanied by his two sons, Arthur and Ernest.

'By Jove, she's a wee charmer, Chrissie.' Arthur was boisterously jovial, trying to make up for the pointed absence of his wife. Lizzie had refused to come, despite all Arthur's coaxing.

'She's her father's double,' remarked Ernest, then wished he hadn't, noting William Kennedy's stony stare.

William had become taciturn and gruff since Chrissie's departure. The decline of the whaling industry continued, and although William still sailed with the diminished fleet, it was Arthur, the businessman, who had secured alternative supplies of batching oil to honour the contract with Rankine's, and had branched out into handling more lucrative shipments of Baltic timber. The Kennedys were doing well enough.

William stumped over to the crib and peered in. The beautiful baby stared up at him curiously, then smiled and gurgled and waved her tiny hands. Some of the lonely longing for his bonnie Chrissie eased, and a little spark of joy lit in William's heart.

He fished in his pocket and brought out a gold sovereign. He placed it in the baby's palm, and watched the little fist close tightly over it. William looked up and met Danny's eye.

'That's no' charity, Danny Murphy. It's the bairn's gift, man. You can't refuse that,' he grunted triumphantly.

Danny laughed. 'It'll go into the bank for her, Mr Kennedy, and thank ye kindly. I've been thinking of opening a bank account for the wee lass, and that's a braw start to it.'

Danny settled down well to the foreman's job. He stood no nonsense from his weavers, yet they liked and respected him for his good humour and sense of fair play. Despite the ups and downs notorious in the jute trade, Danny's weavers were kept content. His appointment was made official in due course, and there were strong hints of further promotion.

It seemed, to Chrissie, anything Danny Murphy turned his hand to must succeed. A near riot outside the Kinnaird Hall, to further the suffragette cause, resulted in a strengthening of fibre amongst the Dundee Volunteers, and Danny was made sergeant. He swelled with pride and happiness, coming home of an evening to his little, toddling daughter, whirling her round and round in his arms while the bairn screamed for joy.

Sometimes Chrissie experienced a secret pang of jealousy when she watched the two of them together. Black curly hair, blue-eyed, father and daughter were so alike in every way, she felt excluded. Much as Chrissie loved Alexandra, the child worshipped Danny, pushing her mother aside to run to him. Chrissie was delighted to find she was expecting another baby. This bairn would redress the balance of their little family, she hoped.

Chrissie and Danny's second daughter was born on the day of King George V and Queen Mary's coronation in 1911, when Dundee streets were a sight to be seen with fluttering loyal flags and bunting.

Danny laughed joyfully when he held his second wee lass.

'Chrissie my darling, this one has to be a Mary.'

He placed the small bundle in Chrissie's arms and she lovingly examined her baby. Unlike Alexandra, this wee mite had a fuzz of fair hair, a pink, crumpled face just like a little rosebud.

'Let's call her Mary Rose, Danny. She's so beautiful, my wee Mary Rose,' Chrissie said softly.

They were busy, happy years for Chrissie and Danny as their two little lasses grew. Alexandra and Mary Rose were much admired as they played together in the back court, the one so dark-haired, blue eyes sparkling with mischief, the other fair and quiet, with shy, thoughtful, smokey-grey eyes.

Chrissie, at twenty-four, had little time to spare to glance in the mirror, but she still caused heads to turn when she had occasion to board the tram for Dundee. The town itself had changed to accommodate an increase in traffic, with the old Cowgate widened recently for the trams that vied with a steady stream of horses and carts plying to and fro between the mills and the harbour. One thing Chrissie noted with pleasure: the tramlines aided the horses labouring up Dundee hills, for the cart wheels fitted exactly.

There was little time for Chrissie and Danny to be bothered about unrest in the outside world. The warring Balkans seemed very far away, and the assassination of the heir to the Austrian throne and his poor wife, while shocking, seemed far distant from the busy jute mills of Dundee. Then suddenly the name of Kaiser Wilhelm of Germany was on everybody's lips and the dark menace of war was looming closer.

Mr Asquith, the Liberal Prime Minister who'd had the foresight five years ago to introduce a five shilling old-age pension, had the heartrending task of announcing to the nation on 4th August 1914, that they were at war with Germany.

Chrissie's first thought was for her husband. She hugged Danny, frightened and worried. There were posters springing up everywhere with Lord Kitchener's commanding countenance, his finger pointing, ordering young men to join his army. Many Dundee lads had gone already, most of them just for a lark.

'Oh, Danny, you won't have to go, will you?' she asked anxiously.

He laughed and kissed her. 'No, my dearie, I'm

needed in the mill, the manager says I'll be in a reserved occupation, especially as he's retiring. Jute cloth'll be needed as never before, and we'll be working full out. Wars are aye profitable for the jute trade, Chris.' He looked regretful. 'Mind you, lass, I'd have liked a crack at Kaiser Bill. The cheek of the man, thinking he can walk into Paris. Our lads will stop him, though, and I wish I could join them.'

Alexandra wormed her way between her parents, to show her father the satchel Chrissie had bought in preparation for the wee lass's first day at school. She was to attend Liff Road School, and could hardly wait to get started.

'My wee lass is to be a big schoolgirl. You'll no' need your daddy now, Sandra.' Danny ruffled his daughter's hair fondly.

'I will-so need my daddy, even though I'm big! You're not to go fighting Kaiser Bill, Da!' She flung her arms passionately round his knees to keep him trapped. Mary Rose came through from the scullery to see what all the stushie was about. She watched solemnly, thumb in mouth. Danny picked her up and kissed her rosy cheek.

'Och, it would take a team o' horses to drag me away from my three bonnie lassies!'

So, Chrissie was reassured. She could watch recruiting sergeants visit the town, and admire their smartness and swinging kilts with an easy mind, because they posed no threat to her own dear lad. A patriotic fervour followed the soldiers, and more Dundee men volunteered. Dundee folk were singing war songs in the music halls and in the streets now. Cheery, marching tunes that lingered in your head.

Chrissie was preparing to write to Harriet that September, just after the Kaiser's soldiers had been repulsed at the battle of the Marne, and folk said it would be all over by Christmas. Harriet was a fully fledged doctor, but her last letter had been rueful, addressed to Chrissie from a far-off hamlet in Caithness.

> I am an embarrassment to the established medical profession because I am a woman, Chris, and have declared an intention to do research into many ailments. They have tried to sweep me under the rug, sending me here, I will prevail, however. Do not fear!

Chrissie smiled. She knew Harriet's mettle, and had no doubt she would win through. She had just put pen to paper when she heard Danny's step on the stair outside, and he burst in so wildly she started to her feet.

'Dan, wheest, the bairns are sleeping!'

Then she saw his face, and her heart almost stopped beating. She went to him. 'Oh, Danny dear, what is it?'

'It's Rankine. Charles Rankine. That's what it is.' He gave her a look containing such a black depth of bitterness she turned icy cold.

'I don't understand, Dan. What has Charles done?'

'Only made me accept nothing but his charity, all these years.' He thrust Chrissie aside and began pacing the room.

'I told you the mill manager was retiring. Well, I had a wee dram with him in his buckie the night, aye, more than one, enough to loosen the man's tongue. He told me I'd been singled out in the first place because Charles Rankine wanted it, and he was such a good customer they dare not refuse him.'

Chrissie put her hands to her cheeks. She knew what a blow this must be to her husband, what a let-down to his fierce pride.

'Oh, Dan. Danny!' she whispered in horror.

He couldn't keep still, pacing to and fro, clenching a fist as if to strike out at someone.

'So it wasn't studying and skill wi' the engines that earned me promotion, nor yet my quickness at figuring. They never had their eye on me, Chris, until Mr Rankine pointed me out. Aye, and only to keep *you* in comfort. He aye had a strong fancy for you, and I could forgive him that, but what galls me is, the man didn't believe I had it in me to support my wife in the way she'd been accustomed. He wouldn't even give me credit for hard work, Chrissie, but must interfere in my life with his damned charity.'

Danny crashed his fist angrily on the table, and one of the little lasses roused and wailed sleepily. He paid no attention, his voice raised.

'I'll not stand for it, Chris, I'll not take the man's patronage a day longer. It's the army for me.'

He strode to the door, and Chrissie came suddenly to life, racing after him, hanging on to his arm, terrified.

'Danny, no! Oh, Danny, let's talk.'

'The time for talking's past, Chris.' His face was like stone. He pulled his arm away and gave her a push that sent her staggering, then he was out of the door and away. She ran after him, screaming, not caring who heard.

'Danny, come back! Please Danny, listen to me. Come back!'

But all she heard were his firm footsteps, hurrying off. Both bairns were awake now and wailing with fright, but Chrissie sank down on the stairs and covered her face with her hands, weeping for her man.

Chapter 5

Chrissie dried her eyes and went to the frightened children. It took time to settle them, for though she tried to hide her distress they sensed it immediately. Alexandra kept crying over and over: 'Where's my da? I want my daddy!' until Chrissie lost patience.

'Wheest! Your daddy's gone out.'

'When's he coming back?'

'Soon. Go to sleep, Sandra. You'll not be fit for school tomorrow,' Chrissie warned.

Sandra turned her head away. Despite the comforting glow of the nightlight candle standing in a saucer of water, the little room she shared with Mary Rose seemed dark with menace. She'd never heard her father raise his voice so angrily before. Even when she'd been naughty and he was stern, she wasn't usually afraid, but tonight he'd shouted so loudly she'd been terrified. She was still cold and shaking with fear.

Sandra put her arms round her sister, hugging the warm, little body close to her. It was strange, Mary Rose was just three years old, yet she had a calming influence. Mary Rose planted a sympathetic kiss on Sandra's cheek, and the icy coldness of Sandra's fear began gradually to melt. Clasped in one another's arms, the two little sisters drifted off to sleep.

Danny didn't come home that night, although Chrissie sat up waiting until dawn. He returned wearily at dinnertime just before the one o'clock gun, and slumped in a chair.

'Well, Chris, it's done. The army took me like a shot. They said I'm just the man they need, a sergeant in the Territorials, but I noticed they sniggered behind my back. The Town Clerk's army, the real soldiers call the Territorials. Being a sergeant in the Terriers counts for nothing in this war, Chrissie,' he said dully.

'Aw, Danny.' Chrissie hugged him. The spark of pride had gone out of her man, his shoulders sagging; and it was Charles Rankine who'd done this terrible thing to her proud Danny, with his meddling in their lives, she thought with a bitter surge of anger.

'I've been to the mill and handed in my notice,' Danny went on. 'They begged me to change my mind, but it's too late for that. I've to report for a medical, then I'll go to Perth barracks to be kitted out and trained for soldiering with the Black Watch, the recruiting sergeant said.'

She couldn't speak, she could only hold him close to her breast and comfort him as their happy little world fell apart.

More and more men were rushing off to join Kitchener's Army. A trainload of Dundee lads left with Danny for the Black Watch barracks in Perth. The station had an air of unreality about it that cold day, and Chrissie stood on the platform holding her little girls by the hand, wishing she could waken from this bad dream.

The frosty air reeked of coal-smoke from the waiting engine, its steam shrouding everything. Her eyes were bright with unshed tears, but she smiled bravely at her man. The men were cheerful and excited. It was easier for them in a way, she thought. They had one another's rough companionship to bolster them, but what cheer would there be for the women, with their husbands and sons gone to fight in a foreign land?

'Don't worry, wifies, the war'll soon be over now. The Dundee lads are off to give Kaiser Bill a black eye,' shouted one of Danny's companions, raising a wan cheer from those standing on the platform. Chrissie glanced anxiously at Sandra. The child had been unusually quiet and withdrawn lately. Sandra's eyes were fixed longingly on Danny, and the little girl looked so lost and bewildered Chrissie forgot her own misery. It was almost time for departure.

'Here, my pet,' she lifted Sandra and held her so that Danny could hug his daughter.

'Bye bye, my wee hen. I'll be home soon, Sandy. You take care o' your mummy for me, mind,' he told her gruffly.

Chrissie then lifted Mary Rose for her father's kiss. The guard was unfurling the little green flag, and Danny and Chrissie looked at one another speechlessly. The flag waved, the crowd gave a ragged cheer as the train moved off, slowly gathering speed. Danny waved and waved until he could see his wife and bairns no more, then turned away resolutely to face the trials of a new life.

Chrissie tried to be cheerful for the children's sake. They came out of the station and walked across the road, their feet dragging miserably. She smiled at them. 'Do you remember when the King and Queen and Princess Mary came to Dundee, not long ago?'

Sandra nodded, remembering that warm, lovely summer day. 'Daddy had a holiday. We stood in the street and waved flags, and the girls from Keiller's sweetie factory gave Princess Mary caramels.'

'Yes. We saw King George and Queen Mary drive past in their carriage, and your daddy swore Queen

Mary waved specially to Mary Rose.' Chrissie glanced down at her small daughter, toddling along by her side.

'You're named for Queen Mary, you know, Mary Rose.'

Sandra gave a skip. 'And I'm named for Queen Alexandra.'

They had reached the corner of the Greenmarket where the old Crown Hotel used to stand. The ancient part of the city they called the Vaults was being hauled down to make way for a fine new City Hall. Such changes in the town since I was a girl, Chrissie thought. She pointed to a corner of the wall where the stonemasons were working.

'Look, that's the stone the King and Queen set in place when they visited Dundee.'

Sandra's jaw dropped, and Mary Rose goggled solemnly. 'They must be awful big an' strong to lift that,' Sandra said.

Chrissie laughed. 'No, dear, they pressed a wee button in a jute mill a mile away, and the stone moved into place as if by magic. That is called electricity, and it is a very wonderful thing.'

With an anxious eye on her pennies, Chrissie recklessly treated them to tea and cream cakes. A justifiable expense, for when they boarded the Lochee tram, the children were smiling and cheerful.

Bairns soon forget, Chrissie thought sadly, as she watched her two little ones laugh and giggle together. But, in fact, Chrissie was mistaken: Sandra Murphy never forgot the day her father went to war. The memory of that event stayed with her all her life, bright and clear in every detail.

Chrissie was forced to go back to work at the grocer's, to make ends meet. Biddy Murphy willingly took charge of

Mary Rose and Sandra while their mother worked, and did not refuse the few pennies Chrissie offered her.

'Although my Patrick's doing fine, Chris, and we're not short of a bob or two,' Biddy told her daughter-in-law proudly, 'he's been put in charge o' the other scaffies in the Dock Street depot. My, but he looks real braw these days, Chrissie, in a not-bad bowler hat he found on the tip, an' a tuppenny Norfolk jacket out o' Raggie Mary's.'

'I'm sure he does.' Chrissie tried to keep a straight face. 'It's very good of you to look after my weans, Biddy. I don't know what I'd do without you,' she said gratefully, and Biddy squeezed her arm.

'Ach, you'd manage fine, Chris. You're a hardy one, for all your fine, gentry looks. Besides, it's nice to have wee bairns to care for even though I'm nearly off the legs. My youngest lassie's gone off to be a tram conductress in Glasgow. A man's job for women. Did you ever hear the like? It's a good while since I'd a wee baby in the dresser drawer or a little one under my feet,' Biddy added, smoothing Mary Rose's shining, golden hair with a loving hand.

Even so, Chrissie wasn't happy leaving her children in another woman's care. She was forced to allow Sandra, in particular, more freedom than she considered good for a six year old. The child made her own way home to Biddy's close after school, and Chrissie suspected she did not always go straight to her grandmother's, but ranged around Lochee exploring its wynds and alley-ways. Sandra, when questioned about her activities, buttoned her lip and would tell her mother nothing. Chrissie secretly despaired. She felt she was losing her daughter's trust, and didn't know how to retrieve the situation.

Oh, if only Danny were here, she often thought, studying her mutinous little daughter anxiously.

The harassed grocer was glad of Chrissie's services, all the young men in his employ having volunteered for the army. In recognition of the fact she was doing four times the work, he paid her another two shillings a week on top of her small wage, and on that, they managed.

The letter arrived on Charles Rankine's desk by the afternoon post. He slit open the envelope, then sat staring at its contents.

One white feather, the symbol of cowardice.

He'd heard they were sending white feathers to some of the men that were left behind. Nobody ever discovered who the culprits were, though the suffragettes were suspected. The sight sickened and angered him. There was no way of fighting back, no way of defending himself against the smear. How could he tell the cruel person who'd sent this that the army had already rejected him on medical grounds?

Charles stood up restlessly. If only he'd had Chrissie by his side. If only he'd had the support of the woman he loved, this wouldn't hurt so much. He watched the feather flutter from his fingers into the office fire, its pure whiteness shrivelling and turning black, then he strode out of the building, the office staff staring after him in surprise.

He had to see her. He needed to see Chrissie.

Dundee was used to motor cars now. There were more cars and lorries appearing on the streets, and Charles Rankine's motor caused little interest in Lochee. He parked discreetly in Liff Road, close to the tenement where Chrissie and her man lived, and settled down to wait.

Charles had no clear idea what he would do if he saw her. Just to look at her would be enough to soothe his agitated mind. He sighed and rubbed his eyes. At least he'd done all he could to ensure she'd be comfortable, with her husband safe in a reserved occupation. Danny would be permitted to stay at home, doing valuable work essential to the war effort. Chrissie and her family would be secure.

It was almost dark when he saw her trailing wearily up the street towards the close-mouth, holding two bonnie little girls by the hand. His heart lurched. The scene wasn't as he'd anticipated, but he gave no thought to that. He was out of the car and walking towards her before he realised what he was doing.

Charles stopped in front of Chrissie, blocking her path.

'How are you, Chrissie?'

Eagerly, he took in every detail of her appearance. The girlish roundness of her figure and features had fined down, but she was no less desirable for that. She had an ageless beauty; but she was so thin, he thought with a rush of anxiety. Didn't she have enough to eat?

She was staring at him as if confronted by a ghost, the colour leaving her cheeks, then her eyes suddenly flashed fire and he backed away, startled.

'How dare you come here, Charles. How dare you!' she cried.

He was staggered by this reception. What had he done? He gripped her arm. 'Chrissie, Chrissie dear, I'm sorry, I didn't mean to—'

Indignantly, she shook off his hand and pushed past grimly without a word, dragging the children with her. The smaller child looked back over one shoulder curiously.

'Mummy, who's that man? Is he a friend?'

Chrissie's reply floated back to Charles through the chilly darkness.

'No, Mary Rose, that man is no friend of ours.'

* * *

Chrissie was still seething with outrage as she prepared to cook something for herself and the children.

The cheek of the man. What had he hoped to achieve, accosting her like that? Had he hoped she'd fall into his arms now her man was away at war? Some women would, she knew; for the old virtues of loyalty were breaking down.

Chrissie dismissed that thought. No, whatever else he might be, Charles Rankine was an honourable man. Watching bacon and eggs sizzle in the pan, her temper cooled, and she was sorry.

Perhaps she'd been hasty. Maybe the man had been trying to make amends for what he'd done. He'd been sorely troubled. She'd sensed that at once, for she could often tell the emotions of other folk. Chrissie turned the bacon unhappily. She wished she'd been kinder to the poor man, for after all, he'd meant his patronage of Danny kindly, and had kept quiet about it. If it hadn't been for the mill manager blethering, Danny would never have known. Well, it was too late now: Charles Rankine wouldn't come seeking her company again.

Danny came home on leave, having completed his training. He looked very fit and fine in uniform, with the dark Black Watch kilt swinging on his hips and the red hackle in his bonnet. Chrissie's heart was full to bursting with loving pride in her man. She organised a party for members of his family, and even Biddy puffed and struggled her way up the stairs, with Patrick heaving from behind. There were Murphys everywhere, sitting on the stairhead singing Irish songs soulfully and swigging beer, and spilling out on to the washing green to boot a ball with the excited bairns. Their neighbours in the close joined in enthusiastically, and everyone voted it one of the best homecomings in the long history of Lochee.

Lying together in bed that night when everyone had gone reeling home and their two little daughters slept the sleep of exhaustion, Chrissie snuggled close to her husband and gave a sigh of pure content.

'Oh, Dan, it's so good to have you home.'

He was very quiet for a few moments. 'They're sending us to the front after this, Chris.'

Her heart contracted with dread. 'Aw, Danny. So soon?'

He lifted a strand of her lovely golden hair, lying loosened about her shoulders, and put it to his lips. 'They tell me I'm a good soldier, my darling. Very good. I've been thinking that's maybe the way to get on, signing up with the army for good. They've hinted I could get a stripe soon. How d'you fancy being a regular soldier's wife once this war's over and done with?'

'If that's what you want, Danny.'

'Aye, it is. I won't go back to the mill, Chris. I could get on in the forces, be an officer in time, even,' he said with the familiar determined lift of the chin. He kissed her, his mouth warm on hers. 'Another thing I want, sweetheart, I want a son. A little lad to call my own. Another Danny, only brainier, and not so ready to fly off the handle when his pride's dunted.'

'Och, Dan!' she laughed, her eyes brightly shining. 'You can't order a bairn just like that, dearest. We could fill the house with lasses, looking for a lad.'

He held her close to him, smiling. 'Why not? We're young, Chris. The war'll soon be over, and I'll come through it, for it's just a stalemate: two armies sitting in the trenches, glowering at each other. The only sensible solution is to make peace soon, then there are years ahead of us,' said Danny confidently.

Sandra felt as if she was walking on air. Her daddy was home, and folk turned in the street to admire him in his kilt, with the proud red hackle in his hat. On the tram, ladies smiled at him coyly through their lashes, and old men clapped him on the shoulder, and told him he was a braw soldier-laddie, and to give Kaiser Bill a good punch on the nose, Jock, from them. Sandra walked in his shadow, adoringly.

'Come on, we'll away to Broughty Ferry and visit your Grandpa Kennedy. It's time the old man had a sight of you,' Danny announced to his two little daughters one Sunday towards the end of his leave. Sandra wasn't keen, and her mother looked even more reluctant.

'Should we, Danny? Papa hasn't been near us since the row over Sandra's schooling.'

Sandra pricked up her ears. Her father laughed. 'As if I'd send my lassies to a dame school, and let your father pay for it. No, Chrissie, I know you tend to agree with your papa, but I say our lasses will learn more about real life from Lochee lads and lasses. It's high time Captain Kennedy stopped sulking about it, and came out of the huff, though.'

A dame school. Sandra wrinkled her nose in disgust. She suspected the gang of lively little boys she tagged on to after school wouldn't be allowed over the threshold of such a posh establishment.

William Kennedy was not sulking, nor was he in a huff. It was a more delicate matter that kept him from his daughter's door, and he didn't know how to resolve it. He was dozing that Sunday afternoon, when Bessie came rushing into the parlour in a terrible flap of excitement, forgetting even to tap on the door.

'They're coming, Captain Kennedy! They're walking up the path!'

He sat bolt upright. 'Who? The Germans?'

Bessie looked disgusted. 'Och, no, not them. I'd not

get excited about that lot. It's Chrissie and Danny and the bairns, Captain.'

'No!' He felt the colour leave his cheeks and his heart thump. Smoothing his ruffled hair with a hand, he hurried into the hallway and opened the door. There she was, his bonnie lass, bonnier than ever. He held out his arms, and Chrissie ran into them.

When they were all settled in the parlour round Bessie's tea-trolley, his two grandchildren sitting on the rug at his feet, William took cautious stock of his son-in-law. He had to admit the lad looked very handsome in uniform. He wore the kilt well, and wasn't bandy-legged, like some.

'Aye well, Danny, you'll soon be off again?' he asked gruffly, then wished he'd kept silent when he noted the pain in his daughter's eyes: she was still loyal to the man although he'd brought her low. Her clothes were spotlessly clean, but well-worn, though he noted that the bairns wore new red velvet dresses, white pinnies trimmed with lace, and bonnets decked with flowers. Chrissie's self-sacrifice brought an unbidden lump to William's throat. He stood up and went to the window, filling his pipe from the tobacco pouch, keeping his back turned to them.

'I've something to tell ye, Chrissie. Something I should have discussed with you first, but couldna, for it was taken out of my hands. I'm just the figure-head o' the firm now, you see; a done old man. It's Arthur that's the boss, with Lizzie behind him.'

'How is Lizzie, Papa? I haven't seen her since Mary Rose was born. She never calls on us now,' Chrissie said.

He shrugged. 'Och, she's fine. Arthur's got a good enough head on his shoulders and Ernest keeps the books, but Lizzie wears the breeks. She's aye poking her nose into the business. She's got little else to do except

103

drive thon motor car and be a menace to decent folk on the road. It's an awful pity she couldn't—' He paused and sighed. '—Ach, well, poor Lizzie,' he said more gently. He braced himself and turned round. 'The long and short of it is, Chrissie, they've sold your ship.'

'Papa, no!' Her hand shot protectively to the brooch on her blouse, as if she'd shield her bonnie ship from harm. Poor lass, it was too late.

'I'm afraid so, Chris. The *Christina K*'s on the Newfoundland register now. It made sense, Chrissie, though it broke my heart to consent. Only two whalers sailed in 1913, and now the war has finished the Dundee whaling industry for good. It's fortunate Arthur had the sense to turn to more profitable cargoes years ago, or we'd be ruined.' William sighed and pulled at his pipe. In fact, the firm was doing quite nicely, but it wasn't like the old days.

Chrissie's eyes filled with tears. Newfoundland. So far away in a cold, strange land. She'd never again see her ship come sailing proudly up the Tay. Chrissie ducked her head in case Danny noticed her sorrow. He'd think she was daft, crying over a boat. Chrissie herself couldn't explain why the ship meant so much to her. It was complexly linked to the loss of her mother, and her own life. William, watching his daughter keenly through a cloud of pipesmoke, saw her distress and understood, and his heart bled for her.

'I can add an' take away, an' next week we're starting to multiply, Grandpa,' chimed in Sandra, who'd been silent for too long.

Her grandfather's expression softened. 'My, but wee lassies are getting brainy these days!'

'It's a grand school, Liff Road School. Sandra's very bright, the teacher says.' Danny couldn't resist the dig, and William scowled darkly.

'There's more to being a lady than book learning, Danny Murphy.'

'A lady? Huh!' grunted Danny scathingly.

'Can I pour you another cup of tea, Papa? Danny, have one of Bessie's scones, they're scrumptious,' intervened Chrissie hastily, shoving the plate at her husband with a warning glance.

It was no good, she thought. Danny and her father would never get on.

Another parting. How could she bear it? Chrissie wondered, smiling brightly. She was growing to hate the station and the huge steaming engine that waited impatiently to carry her man away.

'Have you got your sandwiches, Danny?' she asked as he leaned out of the carriage window.

'Aye, lass, they're in my kitbag for later.'

'"Pack up a sandwich in your old kitbag,
An' smile, smile, smile!"' trilled little Mary Rose suddenly.

They all laughed uproariously; a welcome relief from the almost unbearable sadness of parting.

Danny looked at Chrissie. He never tired of looking at her. He wasn't much of a hand at writing letters, nor at speaking out about his innermost feelings, but oh, how he loved her. He hadn't told her so for a good while, not since they were courting on the slopes of the Law, and he couldn't bring himself to tell her now in front of all these folk. He could only look at her, and hope that somehow she knew.

She did. Chrissie caught her breath at the love blazing in her husband's eyes. She reached up and held his hands.

She wanted to tell him how much she loved him, but there were people watching and listening, and it wasn't done to make a public show of your feelings.

105

'Mind and wear the warm socks your mother knitted, Dan, and the balaclava and scarf, when it's cold,' she said.

'Aye, Chris, I will that,' he nodded dutifully.

'Hey, wifie, stand clear,' the guard warned, raising the whistle to his lips, his flag poised. The train jolted, and Danny released her hands. She could hardly see him through a blur of tears, but she kept smiling. She wanted him to remember her smiling, not miserably weeping. She smiled and waved until the last carriage disappeared far down the track, then covered her face with her hands.

Somebody kicked her ankle. It was painful, and Chrissie cried out. She turned to find Sandra glaring.

'You didn't let me say goodbye to my daddy! You stood there blethering about silly socks, and wouldn't let me say goodbye! I hate you!'

'Sandra dear, I . . . I'm sorry,' Chrissie didn't know what to say. How could you explain the pain of loving a man, to a child? How could you make her understand the emotions hidden beneath banal words?

Mary Rose looked from one to the other in distress. There were bad feelings between the two people she loved, and she didn't know how to cope with that. Her lower lip trembled, great tears welled up and spilled down her cheeks, and she bawled loudly.

Once again, Mary Rose saved the situation. Sandra turned to her sister with a sympathetic cry and hugged her, then their mother bought them each a penny bar of chocolate out of the machine on the platform, and they went home quietly, to a sadly silent house.

'Drat!' Harriet Bowers had made a blot on her letter to Chrissie. She mopped it up with blotting paper and chewed the end of the pen as she read over what she'd written.

You'll never believe it, Chris, but I'm in Dover, waiting to embark for France with a group of stiff and starchy nursing sisters and a giggling gaggle of raw little VADs – members of the Women's Voluntary Aid Detachment; Red Cross, to you! I can't tell you where I'm going, dear, because that's hush-hush, but I'm off to do a worthwhile job at last.

The folk of Caithness, bless 'em, are extremely healthy, and I doubt if I'll be missed. Doctors are badly needed in France, even women-doctors, and when I offered my services I was snapped up right away. It's been all hustle and bustle since then, Chrissie dear, with no time to visit Dundee. I was given a short training course in London on various procedures, then received my marching orders. No time to say goodbye, I'm afraid, but we'll have a good blether when I come home.

If you see Charles—

That was where the blot formed, like a tear. No time to say goodbye to Charles. No time to tell him how much she loved him. War intensified feelings, speeded everything to a frantic haste, so that vital words were left unspoken forever. Harriet dipped the pen in the inkpot.

If you see Charles, dear Chrissie, give him my kindest regards.

Shortly after receiving Harriet's letter, Chrissie had a visitor. A stylish young lady with rosy cheeks that spoke of the sparkling health of a countrywoman. Chrissie opened her arms with a cry of recognition.

'Georgina! Oh, Ina, my dear!'

They hugged, then Chrissie held her niece away from her, smiling admiringly. 'Oh, Ina, how bonnie you've grown. So fashionable in the shorter skirt, too, and showing such neat ankles. A young lady now!'

Ina pouted. 'Not really. Fine feathers don't make good hens, Auntie Chris. I *hate* the town.'

Chrissie seated Ina by the fire and looked at her with amusement. 'Why come to Dundee, then?'

Ina grimaced. 'It wasn't my idea. Daddy wants me to learn typewriting and Sir Isaac Pitman's squiggles. He says that's the way for women to get on, thudding away on typewriters in offices, so he's arranged for me to do a course and stay with Grandpa Kennedy. He says I could earn thirty shillings a week as a secretary, when I'm trained.'

Chrissie's jaw dropped. 'That's a fortune!'

Ina looked glum. 'Maybe, but I don't want to do it, Auntie Chris. I didn't want to hurt Daddy and Mum by refusing point blank, but I wish Dad would get it into his head that I want to be a farmer. Instead, he's trying to turn poor Hughie into one, and Hughie hates it. Hughie's terrified of cows and can't herd sheep and hates getting his boots covered in mud.' Ina couldn't resist a giggle at that point.

Chrissie smiled. 'Poor wee Hughie!'

'Yes, if only we could change places,' Ina sighed. 'Hughie would be perfectly happy in Dundee. All he wants is to go to sea. Dad'll not let him, though. Since the old farmer died and left the farm to his nephew in Australia, Dad's been in sole charge. He needs somebody to help him, but there's Mum and me and old Eck, and . . . and Tam, of course.' Her colour heightened as she mentioned Tam's name.

'Who's Tam?' Chrissie asked with interest, noting the blush.

'Tam's a wonderful shepherd, Auntie Chris. You

should see him with the dogs, out on the hill. He's quiet and thoughtful, and, oh . . . so caring and nice . . .'

Ahhah! thought Chrissie. She was beginning to understand why her brother had made haste to send his daughter to Dundee. George hoped she'd meet more eligible young men there, who'd drive all thought of the gentle shepherd out of Ina's head.

Ina had been studying her aunt. Auntie Chris was still lovely, but too thin, in Ina's opinion, and there were dark smudges beneath her eyes.

'How are you, Auntie Chris? You look tired,' she ventured.

Chris laughed. 'Oh, I'm fine. I'm always a little tired at first when I'm expecting a bairn. That passes in time, love, then I'm right as rain.' She tried to make light of the dragging exhaustion and nausea that plagued her this time. The grocer had noticed, and warned her. 'You'll have to buck up, Chrissie. There's plenty would be glad of your job.'

Ina hugged her. 'Oh, I didn't know about the baby. Are you hoping for a boy this time, Auntie Chris?'

'Danny's got his heart set on a boy, Ina, but I—' she turned away, weariness overcoming her for a moment. '—I don't care one way or the other, dear, so long as the bairn's strong and healthy.'

'Thanks.' Hughie got down from the cart that had brought him from Perth, and generously handed the driver a shilling.

The driver grinned. 'You're welcome, son.' He urged the horse on, and Hughie was left standing in Dundee's Nethergate. Och, it was great to have cobbles beneath his boots again. He crossed a road that was much busier than he remembered, the tackets in his boots making a cheery clatter on the cobblestones. He'd done it, he'd got away from the farm!

It was good of the McGregor boys to enter so whole-heartedly into his plan, Hughie thought gratefully, as he made his way towards the docks. His father had been pleased when he'd begged to go to Perth market with the McGregors. Poor Dad, Hughie thought contritely. He'd believed Hughie had come round to farming at last, now he was fourteen and old enough to leave school. I never will be a farmer though, Hughie thought passionately. That's why he'd decided to run away to sea. He'd write to his parents as soon as he could and try to explain how the sea kept calling him, and wouldn't let him settle.

Hughie rounded the corner where the Greenmarket was. He had happy memories of fairs held in that open space, with roundabouts and sideshows. He stopped dead. Och, it was all changed, the old houses gone and a big wall going up, narrowing the open space. He passed the horse trough and went under the Royal Arch built for Queen Victoria years ago.

He put a hand on the stout stonework and grinned up at the towering archway, its crevices liberally streaked with bird droppings. Pigeon's Palace, they called it. At least they couldn't change this famous landmark, Hughie thought. Whistling cheerfully, he headed for the wharf where the jute ships berthed.

They said France was a bonnie enough country, but this part of it certainly wasn't bonnie, thought Danny. It was a sea of mud and broken stumps of trees. The trenches weren't one long orderly line, as he'd imagined they would be, but were like a rabbit warren, zigzagging here and there.

It was almost dawn and nobody'd had much sleep that night, because of the furious bombardment the artillery lads were putting up, to soften the German defences.

One of the old soldiers threw a Woodbine stub into the mud beside the catwalk, and grinned at Danny. 'Jerry'll be keeping his head well down. D'you think this is the Big Push at last, Corp?'

Danny was a corporal now, with two stripes on his sleeve. The army had its eye on him, and he was on the climb again. He smiled, 'Aye, it could be. We're going over the top, that's for sure.' All round them, men were mustered and ready.

He thought about Chrissie. A strange time and place to be thinking of a woman's golden hair lying loosened around her shoulders, and a tender smile on her lips.

'I hope it's the Big Show,' the old soldier was saying. 'I'm sick o' filling sandbags day after day. Man, I enlisted to save France, no' to shovel it into bloomin' sacks!'

'Never mind, they're jute sacks made in Dundee. It's an ill wind that doesna blow somebody a bit o' good, Geordie,' Danny said cheerfully. He cast a quick glance over the twelve fighting Jocks in his section. They were ready. He saw the sweat of fear on one young lad's cheek. A very young lad, barely seventeen, if that, Danny suspected. They sometimes lied about their age to be taken on, too young to realise what they were doing. The laddie caught his eye.

'Are . . . are you scared, Corporal?' the boy asked tremulously.

'I'd be daft if I wasn't, son,' Danny answered, and the boy smiled at him, comforted.

The bombardment had ceased suddenly, and the silence was uncanny. There were streaks of light in the eastern sky and a grey concealing mist lying over No Man's Land. The whistles started blowing furiously, all along the line.

Danny grinned at his men. 'This is it, lads. Good luck.' With one hand on the ladder leading out of the trench, he paused and smiled at the white-faced youth.

'Stay behind me, laddie. You'll be all right,' Danny said.

* * *

Chrissie was ill again, and unable to go to work. She'd dragged herself in yesterday, but today she was sick, her back ached, and it was beyond her strength to creep down the stairs. She wrote a note for Sandra to hand in to the grocer's on her way to school, and prayed that the man's patience wouldn't finally snap.

She was over seven months gone now. If only she could keep working till the baby was born, she thought worriedly. Food prices kept going up and up, and it was getting harder to feed herself and her little family on the wages the grocer paid. Her pay was docked for every day she missed, and was becoming less and less as her time dragged on. With the price of a small loaf risen to fourpence, Chrissie was sometimes at her wits' end.

Chrissie saw Sandra and Mary Rose off, hand in hand; Sandra to school, the little one to her granny's. She poured another cup of tea, and shivered as she listened to the utter silence in the house. It seemed quieter than usual today, the silence broken only by footsteps coming up the stairs. They stopped outside, and there was a brisk tap on the door.

Chrissie eased herself out of the chair and went to answer the summons. She stared stupidly at the laddie holding the telegram. At first she felt nothing but mild surprise. He held the envelope out to her.

'Are you Mrs Murphy?'

She nodded and took it. She even had a silly smile fixed on her lips as her slow fingers fumbled to open it. The words made no sense at first, then they seemed to bore painfully into her head.

Danny had been killed in action.

'No!' She shook her head at the boy. 'No. There must be some mistake. Not Danny. He said he would come back!' Chrissie's voice had risen and the boy stepped back nervously. He hated this task, and it fell to him all too often these days. You never knew how they'd take it, the poor souls.

Her neighbours on the stair were alerted by her cries. The kindly women came running to Chrissie and led her gently inside, the telegram still clutched in her hand.

'There, there, hen. You have a nice, hot cup o' tea,' they advised, ladling in plenty of sugar.

She stared at them, a hand held to her aching back. 'Not Danny. He said he'd come through it. He's going to be an officer one day. It can't be Danny, can it?'

The women looked at one another. 'Lassie, come and lie down. We'll send for Bessie McCutcheon to see to ye. We'll bide until she comes,' one of them said kindly.

She let them lead her to the bed she'd shared with Danny, and made no protest when they undressed her and made her comfy in her nightie. They sat with her patiently, these kind, busy women who had plenty of work of their own to see to, but Chrissie was hardly aware of their presence.

She lay numb and quiet until a sudden sharp pain roused her. Then she came alive, with a wild cry that brought the women to their feet.

'My baby!'

The baby that Danny Murphy would never see would be born that day, in sorrow, and too early. Chrissie buried her face in the pillow, and at last, began to weep piteously.

Chapter 6

Danny's son was born that cold November night, and afterwards Chrissie drifted into a stupor of grief and exhaustion. Bessie marvelled as she hastily tended to the boy. She had never seen such a tiny baby. The doctor pursed his lips doubtfully.

'He'll need special care, this little one, and I doubt his mother's in a state to give it. She's undernourished, the poor woman, and with her man gone, her life'll no' be easy. It might be better if—' He stopped and glanced uncomfortably at the tiny baby Bessie had laid in the crib.

'He's maybe wee, but he'll fight. All the Murphys are fighters,' Bessie said staunchly.

'Aye, well, this one'll need to fight harder than most,' said the doctor.

He lifted Chrissie's thin wrist and took her pulse, frowning. 'She should never have worked these past few months in her state. It'll take time to rebuild her strength.'

Bessie sighed. 'This is a good flat, Doctor, and Danny was proud of it, but it must have been a sore struggle for his wife to keep it on, with the rent rising and only her allowance as a soldier's wife. The poor lass had to work. She had no option.'

The doctor looked sceptical. 'Hadn't she? Her father's well-off, isn't he?'

Bessie sighed. 'She has her pride, Doctor, and who's

to say that's a bad thing? Asking her pa for help would have reflected badly on her man, and the Captain didn't want her to marry my nephew. Aw, poor Danny!' She dabbed her eyes with a corner of her apron, overcome by grief.

The doctor patted her shoulder. 'Anyway, I've given the lass something to make her sleep. I'll be in again in the morning. In the meantime, Bessie,' he glanced at the wee scrap in the crib, 'keep the fire stoked and keep him warm. I've a feeding bottle, glucose and powdered milk in my motor, which I'll give you. Try to get him to feed. If not, then, I'm afraid—' he broke off and shrugged eloquently.

Chrissie drifted gradually back to reality after hours of oblivion. It was a painful reality, and it finally brought acceptance of her Danny's death. The room was hushed, and she turned her head in sudden fear to find Bessie dozing by the fire.

'The baby?'

Bessie was by her side in an instant. 'He's sleeping, Chris. He's smaller than a rabbit, with a mew like a kitty, but he sucked at the bottle and he's fighting. He's a Murphy, that wee one,' Bessie said proudly.

Chrissie levered herself up. 'I want to see him.'

She was so weak, Bessie almost had to carry her to the crib. But there he was, Danny's tiny son. Her eyes filled with tears. She'd thought she had no tears left, after crying for Danny, but she cried again for his wee baby. She cried helplessly, because she feared she had neither the strength nor the means to give their son the care he needed. She reached out and touched his soft cheek, her heart filled with a deep and tender love.

'Samuel. That's a good name, isn't it, Bessie?' she said softly. The name had just come to her, unbidden, but she was certain Danny would have approved.

116

'It's a grand name, dear. Samuel Murphy has a proud sound, yet Sammy sounds couthy for a wee bairn,' Bessie beamed.

The baby's life hung in the balance. He lost precious weight, although the doctor assured Chrissie that was to be expected with premature babies. Chrissie was on her feet again, and had sent Bessie away, despite her vigorous protests. All Chrissie's resources were concentrated on fighting for her son's life.

Biddy Murphy, bless her, had put aside sorrowing for her son and was caring day and night for Danny's two bewildered lasses, leaving Chrissie free to look after the frail baby. Sammy was a week old and still clinging grimly to life when Chrissie had a visitor. She answered a tap on the door and found her father standing on the doormat.

Once she would have flung herself into his arms, but she had changed greatly from the headstrong girl who had left her father's house on Danny Murphy's arm. Sorrow and adversity had given her a dignity that William Kennedy found touching. His eyes misted.

'How are you, my dear?'

'I'm well, thank you, Papa.' Her lips lightly brushed his cheek, then she stood back, inviting him in.

He accepted awkwardly, looking about him. The tenement flat was spotlessly clean, but to his eyes lacking in all the creature comforts. William was saddened. His beloved lass had been accustomed to better than this. He stood in the middle of the room. It was warm, the fire blazing from coals heaped on it.

'I was much saddened to hear about Danny, my love. One more terrible tragedy. These are sad times, Chrissie,' William said gruffly.

'Yes. I'm not the only one mourning today, Papa.'

Chrissie realised a barrier of awkward memories was

rising between them, made more painful by Danny's death. Emotions ran so deep she didn't know what to say.

William crossed to the crib and peeped in. He was shocked to find such a frail, tiny mite. He turned urgently to his daughter.

'Chrissie, my grandson needs special care. This draughty hovel is no place for an ailing bairn. Come home where you belong, dear, and bring your weans with you. I'd welcome you gladly.'

She stiffened. 'You forget this is my home, Papa, the home my husband made for us. I prefer to stay in it.'

William frowned. She was putting her children at risk because of stubborn pride. He couldn't understand her attitude.

'Don't I have any say in the welfare o' my grandchildren, Chrissie? Och, this is no time for pride, lass.'

Her blue eyes blazed fiercely. 'Oh, yes, it is, Papa! My man gave his life for King and country, yet you *still* believe he wasn't good enough for me. You never got on with Danny, for in your heart you despised him and his background. It would have suited you fine if I'd married Charles Rankine and his money. You could have boasted about your fine son-in-law then!'

William quailed before the onslaught. 'Chrissie, please—'

She spread her arms to encompass the room. 'This is my home, Papa. Don't you dare belittle it!'

He had his pride too. He glared at his daughter angrily. 'Very well, you've made your choice and I'll abide by it. I'll not come here again, Chrissie, seeking to change your mind,' he warned darkly.

Chrissie wasn't angry any more. She leaned weakly on the table, filled with remorse yet unable to take back a single word. The accusations she'd heaped on her father were only too true, and he knew it.

William went quickly to the doorway, but hesitated on the threshold. Turning his head, he took one last, worried look at the crib where his tiny grandson lay. Such a wee bairn, a bairn that already felt like part of himself, its life seriously threatened by Chrissie's pride. There were tears of anguish choking him, hard and painful after the anger. He bowed his head, afraid she might see his suffering.

'Goodbye, Christina.'

Chrissie stood motionless. Once, she would have run into his arms and he would have made everything come right for her. Not any more. She had changed too much, and so had he. She remembered how many times she'd stood waiting on the shore for the *Christina K* to come sailing up the Tay. In those innocent days the beautiful ship had carried everything her childish heart held dear. Once, her father had been the only strength and comfort she'd known, and today she had destroyed the image with a few harsh words.

Seeing him more clearly, Chrissie noticed for the first time how much her father had changed. His features were careworn, the keen light gone from his tired eyes. The broad shoulders, always held so proudly on the bridge of his ship, were hunched as if he'd spent too many long hours seated at his desk. With deepening distress, Chrissie viewed the toll that the war had taken upon her father as he struggled to maintain his trade. She couldn't let him go like this, saddened and bitter. Somehow she must make him understand what her humble home meant to her, and then perhaps he would have some comfort.

'Papa, wait!' she cried as he turned away, and he wheeled around at once, his face alight with hope.

'Chrissie, have you reconsidered? Will you come with me?'

The room blurred as she shook her head. The cheap

119

oilcloth on the table was cold to the touch despite its bright colours. Her fingers caressed it.

Danny had laughed, presenting the oilcloth to her on her birthday. 'I canna afford red roses, Chris, but these roses'll never fade.' A wave of desolation washed over her.

'No, Papa, I've not changed my mind. This is my home.' She looked round the room, tears running unashamedly down her cheeks.

'Everywhere I look, everything I touch holds a memory of Danny,' she said softly. 'Memories are all I have now. Don't ask me to leave, because I can't. Happy memories of my man lie buried here, Papa, and memories are the only comfort I have.'

Hope died in William as he listened. He knew very well how memories could bind you to an empty house. He'd loved his bonnie wife dearly, and long mourned her in the shabby old house he stubbornly refused to leave. Aye, he knew, and understood at last.

He summoned up a shaky smile for the daughter who was no longer his dear, little girl, but a determined grown-woman. 'So be it, Chrissie,' he muttered.

This time he didn't hesitate, but went out, quietly closing the door behind him. Chrissie listened to his footsteps going downstairs, faltering a little at the dark turn where the gaslight was dim, then she let out a sigh that sounded more like a groan and crossed to the window. Outside, she watched her father walk away heavily, like an old man, into the grey, smoky chill of the November twilight. Tears ran down her cheeks. Danny's death, which should have united father and daughter, had only served to drive them apart.

The baby seemed stronger, so Chrissie sent for her two little daughters. She longed to have them with her, but she'd thought it prudent to leave the girls with Biddy

120

meantime. They came into the room quietly, and stood hand-in-hand. Chrissie opened her arms. 'Oh, my poor darlings!'

They ran to her and she hugged them. Mary Rose wept loudly, but Alexandra remained silent. Looking at the child, Chrissie became worried: Sandra seemed suddenly older than her years. Bright-blue eyes that had once sparkled mischievously, were dull and lack lustre, and her springy black curls hung lank. Chrissie's heart went out to the lost and lonely little soul who'd idolised her father. She tried to draw her daughter into her embrace, but Sandra wriggled free and stood aside while her mother consoled Mary Rose.

'Come and meet your brother, Sammy,' Chrissie said presently. She held a warning finger to her lips. 'Shhh, you must tiptoe and be very quiet, because he's been fractious, and I've just rocked him to sleep.'

She led them to the crib, and the two little girls craned over their brother in breathless wonder.

'Oh, Mum, is he real? He's just like a wee dollie,' whispered Mary Rose, in awe.

Chrissie smiled. 'Yes, love, he's a real baby, only very small and delicate. We must take great care of him.'

Sandra said nothing, and Chrissie wondered what was going through her head. Was she jealous? Oh, if only Sandra would talk to her. Surely it couldn't be good for a little girl to be so withdrawn? Biddy had marvelled because Sandra hadn't shed a tear or mentioned Danny's name, but that had frightened Chrissie. It wasn't natural. She watched her little daughter anxiously as Sandra peeped into the crib.

Sandra never forgot the first sight of her brother. His perfect little face stayed pinned brightly to her memory like the ship-brooch her mother always wore. Somehow, this tiny person helped to fill the huge void left in Sandra's heart by the loss of her dear daddy.

The tiny baby's helplessness touched Sandra deeply, releasing tears dammed up inside. Her eyes filled, the stiff muscles in her face slowly relaxed, and she found she could cry at last, because of Sammy. A great, rending sob tore from deep in her chest.

Blindly, the little girl turned to her mother and clung to her until the storm of grief had passed. Chrissie held her daughter and stroked her damp hair, silently giving thanks for those painful, healing tears.

The weather turned bitterly cold, with a raw, damp chill that seemed to seep through cracks in the door. Chrissie was at her wits' end to keep an even temperature in the room, for it was becoming difficult to make ends meet. The doctor tactfully presented her with a bag of coal to top up the bunker, and when she thanked him with tears in her eyes, he waved her thanks aside.

'Och, lassie, say no more. I picked it up here and there on my rounds from folk that have less need o' it. We must keep that wee man warm and free from infection, you know.'

But it was easier said than done. Sandra came home from school coughing with a feverish cold, and Mary Rose went down with it too. Within the confines of the small flat, it wasn't long before Chrissie herself was coughing and sneezing. She lived in terror lest delicate wee Sammy caught the infection.

Biddy came to the rescue once more, taking the two little girls to her house to convalesce, leaving Chrissie free to nurse the ailing baby.

Sammy wasn't so well. He was restless and cried a lot. Chrissie feared she hadn't enough milk to satisfy him, and the thought filled her with dismay. Prices were rising steadily because of wartime shortages, and the landlord had hinted the rent would go up. She must find work, yet how could she leave her baby? Chrissie rested her head in her hands and groaned, then succumbed to a fit of coughing.

A discreet tap on the door roused her, and she opened it to find an unexpected visitor. She was surprised to see Lizzie Kennedy, her sister-in-law, for Lizzie hadn't come visiting since Mary Rose was born. Lizzie looked ill-at-ease.

'Christina, may I come in?'

Chrissie stood aside, and Lizzie swept quickly past. She stood taking off her gloves, her eyes going to the crib.

'Your father told me about the baby,' Lizzie said. She looked at Chrissie compassionately. 'My dear, I'm so sorry about Danny. It's tragic.'

'There's many in the same situation, Lizzie.'

'Yes, indeed. It's a dreadful time.'

Lizzie walked over to the crib and stood looking down searchingly at the sleeping baby. Her face was impassive. Chrissie couldn't tell what she was thinking.

'He's perfect, but *so* tiny. He needs so much care.' Lizzie said softly, as if to herself.

Chrissie was overcome by a fit of coughing, and Lizzie turned, frowning anxiously. 'Christina, you're not well.'

'It's just a cold, Lizzie.'

'Maybe, but if this little mite were to catch it—' Lizzie paused and stared at Danny's son, then faced Chrissie. 'I've come here with a proposition to put to you, Christina. Your father says you've refused help, but I don't see how you will manage with your two girls and a sickly baby to care for.' She stopped for a moment, her eyes shining with a pathetic eagerness. She took a step forward, clutching Chrissie's arm.

'Chrissie, give me the baby. Arthur and I are well-off. We could give your baby all the love and nursing care he needs just now.'

'No, Lizzie!' Chrissie cried. She wrenched her arm away, horrified. How could she give her baby into another woman's care? It was unthinkable.

And yet she must be practical. How could she keep him? How would she manage on a widow's pension with two growing girls to feed and clothe and a premature baby requiring constant attention? Desperate, anguished tears sprang to Chrissie's eyes, and she backed away.

'No, Lizzie!'

Lizzie followed, pulling at her arm. 'Oh, Chrissie dear, I know it's hard for you, but if I take Samuel you can see him whenever you wish. Your baby shall have skilled nursing care, I promise. He'll have a better chance of life, Chrissie.'

Chrissie hid her face in her hands. 'Lizzie, I can't!'

Sammy stirred and whimpered, his faint cry weak and forlorn. Lizzie went swiftly to the crib and soothed him.

'Hush, my little pet, my little darling—'

Chrissie watched in wonder. She was witnessing a transformation. Gone was the haughty, abrasive Lizzie Kennedy, replaced by a gentle, motherly woman. Chrissie's heart ached with pity. Anguished, she suddenly made up her mind.

'Take him, Lizzie!'

'What?' Lizzie stared. Chrissie turned away, unable to bear the pitiful expression on the poor woman's face.

'Take my baby, Lizzie. Take Sammy away with you this minute, before I weaken and snatch him back.'

Lizzie's eyes were bright with tears. 'Oh, Chrissie, I'm so sorry for you, but it's for the best, I'm sure of it.'

Chrissie was speechless with misery. She could only nod.

Lizzie stared unhappily at her sister-in-law, wondering what to do, then the baby began whimpering in earnest. Swiftly, Lizzie picked Samuel up and wrapped him cosily in his shawl. Holding him protectively against her shoulder, she hurried to the doorway. Lizzie hesitated for a moment, looking back. She longed to comfort Chrissie somehow, but she knew better than most that words were of little comfort when you had lost a child.

Shielding the baby tenderly from the freezing air, Lizzie ran lightly down the tenement stairs and headed towards the waiting car. Once outside, an ecstatic joy made her heart beat fast. She had vowed she'd never take a stranger's child into her home, but this wee one wasn't a stranger. She knew the virtues of Samuel's parents, aye, and the vices too.

Chrissie put as cheerful a face as she could upon the baby's absence when her daughters returned home.

'Your Auntie Lizzie is to look after Sammy, in Uncle Arthur's big house in Downfield. Isn't he a lucky, wee lad?' She smiled to hide her heartbreak. The two little girls looked uncertain, staring doubtfully at the empty crib.

'When will Sammy come home again?' Sandra asked wistfully.

'Oh, when he's big and strong,' Chrissie answered airily, folding tiny baby clothes that had been drying on the pulley. Her hand rested gently on the small garments for a few moments, before she resolutely opened the dresser drawer and put them away, out of sight.

Bessie McCutcheon was furious when she heard what Lizzie had done. She barged into William Kennedy's study with scant ceremony.

'Captain, you canna permit that woman to take Chrissie's bairn. It's heartless, prevailing upon the poor lass when she's weak and sorrowful with nowhere to turn.'

He looked at her coldly. 'Bessie, you forget I offered my daughter and her children the sanctuary of this house, and she chose wilfully to reject me. I consider Lizzie's offer a humane and generous one. In fact, it's an ideal solution for all concerned.'

Bessie tapped her chest angrily. 'Listen, Captain Kennedy, I'm the bairn's great-aunt. Am I not to have a say? I think it's criminal of you, allowing thon starchy, stuck-up, wee besom to steal my dead nephew's son.'

William Kennedy's eyes glinted dangerously, and his cheeks took on a choleric hue. 'Mind what you're saying, Bessie McCutcheon,' he warned ominously. 'I'll not have my daughter-in-law insulted and my actions criticised by you. Our association's been long, Bessie, but I'll not stand for your unkind remarks. If you don't like what's been done, you're free to go.'

'Are you giving me the sack, Captain Kennedy?' Bessie demanded with icy dignity.

William glowered. She'd driven him into a corner he couldn't wriggle out of without loss of face. 'If you put it that way, woman, I suppose I am.'

'I see. Then I'll be out of your house once I've worked my week's notice, Captain. I'll no' stay where I'm not wanted.' Bessie turned on her heel and marched out, banging the door.

She went to the kitchen, trembling and shocked by her temerity. She was acting on a matter of principle, and she vowed she would never give way. All the same, Bessie quailed at the thought of leaving this fine house that was her home. She looked round her spotless kitchen with misty eyes. Where could she go when she left this safe haven?

Not to her sister's, for poor Biddy had quite enough on her plate, what with grief over Danny and her bad legs. That left one other option. Bessie's heart was heavy as she contemplated the future.

Och well, Bessie, beggars canna be choosers, she thought bravely.

William swore inwardly when Bessie stormed out of his study in high dudgeon. Och, he'd done it now. Well, he was damned if he'd retract. She would apologise, when she had cooled down, and he'd be lenient. He couldn't imagine the house without Bessie. It was quiet enough already without his grand-daughter, Georgina, who'd been with him for the past few months until wee Hughie ran away to sea on a jute ship.

Ina had given up her typewriting course at once and gone back to the farm to help her father and mother. William sighed. She was a grand lass, and he missed her. But now Bessie was threatening to go. Where would it end?

He went to the window and absently studied angry stormclouds gathering to the west beyond the railway bridge. Last May, Mr Asquith had brought in conscription for all men between the ages of eighteen and forty-one, and Ernest had recently received his calling-up papers. William shivered; he'd be lonely when Ernest went. He'd be a worried and lonely old man, with nobody to care a jot for him. Not even Bessie.

Ina went back to the farm with mixed feelings. She was excited at the prospect of seeing Tam again, but worried about Hughie sailing on the high seas. The Germans had sunk the *Lusitania* early in the war with the loss of many lives, and Lord Kitchener himself had been drowned last June when *HMS Hampshire* struck a mine off Orkney. The seas were dangerous, with mines and submarines lurking everywhere.

Ina saw her own anxiety mirrored on her parents' faces, as she hugged them, her excited sheepdog romping round her heels. Jeannie and George Kennedy had aged appreciably. Her mother's bonnie, smiling face was thin and prematurely lined with anxiety and hard work.

'If only the laddie had told us how he felt,' Jeannie said worriedly. 'I could have arranged for Hughie to go to sea with my father on the trawler. At least his grandpa would have kept an eye on him.'

'Och, Jean, nowhere's safe,' sighed George, drawing on his pipe. 'You'll mind the Zeppelin airship dropped five bombs at the mouth o' the Tay last April, alongside the fishing fleet, and there were folk killed by bombs in Leith and Edinburgh. I don't know what the world's coming to.'

'It's getting smaller, that's for sure.' Jean smiled at Ina, for she'd a tit-bit of news for her. 'We had a letter from the owner of the farm, the old farmer's nephew in Australia. He is enlisted in the Australian forces, and has been posted to England. He hopes to come north sometime to view his inheritance.'

Ina wasn't particularly interested. She fidgeted, looking out of the window towards the snowy brow of the hill. 'Where's Tam?' she asked.

Her mother and father exchanged a quick glance. 'He'll be at the sheep-pens. The ewes are all down from the hills now,' George said.

Ina slipped away as soon as she could, on a pretext of walking the dog. Her feet flew along the track, muddied with the first snow of winter. Oh, it was good to wear boots again, and feel the clean air on her skin. And there was Tam, just as she'd dreamed of him, standing in front of his cottage, the dogs at his feet. She paused, seized by an emotion so strong it brought tears to her eyes. She put her fingers to her mouth and whistled. The dogs perked their ears, and Tam looked up.

'Tam!' Ina waved and started running, the dog tearing after her. Once started, she couldn't stop. She ran straight into his arms, and they closed tightly around her. She looked up into his face. 'Oh, Tam! How I've missed you, dearest!'

She couldn't pretend any more, she loved him too much.

Tam looked dazed, pale beneath the tan. He held her close and felt the magic that had always been there between them, even when she was a young lass, but wonderfully strong and irresistible now she'd come back a lovely, young woman.

'Ina! Oh, my dearie!' He closed his eyes in anguish.

An indignant screech cut across his thoughts. 'Tam, what d'you think you're doing?'

A young woman had appeared in the cottage doorway. She stood glowering, fists planted on her hips. Tam released Ina and stepped back hastily. His head drooped, and he couldn't meet Georgina's eyes.

'Ina, that's Margaret, my wife. We got married three weeks ago.'

'Married?' Ina repeated in a small, dazed voice. She'd gone icy cold. She stared at Tam. 'Oh, Tam. Why didn't you wait for me?' she whispered.

Tam shook his head blindly. 'I was so lonely, when you went away. I didn't know, Ina. I never guessed how it was with us, until now, when I held you in my arms . . .'

The grocer was adamant. He wouldn't give Chrissie her job back. Her ill-health had sorely tried his patience. There was nothing else for it, Chrissie thought, she'd have to try her luck at the jute mill. She was hopeful, for the mills were on overtime, keeping up with the demand for sackcloth.

The man on the gate knew her by sight, and was

sympathetic. 'It's Massie, the foreman, you want to see, missis. Through that wee door there,' he directed, pointing.

The roar of machinery made the ground tremble beneath her feet. A gust of hot, stoury air struck her when she opened the door. Massie was in a wee, glass buckie of an office. He chewed his moustache and frowned when Chrissie stated her business.

'And you've no experience?'

'I'm quick to learn,' said Chrissie eagerly.

He frowned. 'Aye well, Mrs Murphy, your man was favoured by the high heid yins, but you'll get no favours from me, mind, if you're taken on.'

Chrissie looked at him coldly. 'I'd expect none, Mr Massie.'

He scowled. 'And don't you be hoity-toity with me, my lady!'

With that, Chrissie was taken on. She was put under Bella Duncan's wing to learn the intricacies of keeping the yarn bobbins filled. Bella was a big, cheery woman with a voice like a foghorn that carried even above the deafening noise of the machinery. The factory was a bewildering scene of noise and movement, overhead shafts and pulleys all contributing to the din. Chrissie put her hands over her ears, and Big Bella chortled.

'Och, you'll soon get used to that.' She caught sight of Massie glaring, and picked up the spinner's hook. 'Look, Chrissie, the rove bobbins are atop the spinning frame. That's thick thread loosely twisted on big bobbins for the warp, see? The weft's a looser twist, to fill in a' the wee windows i' the cloth. The thread's fed through rollers and delivered wi' a twist to the yarn bobbins, spinning awa' on the frame. There's twenty ends to a frame, and your job's to keep the yarn bobbins filled from the rove, like this.'

Big Bella went into action, using the hook to join

the ends of the rove yarn to the fast-spinning bobbins. Her hands flew so fast, Chrissie couldn't follow the movements. She looked crestfallen. 'Oh, Bella. I'll never do that!' she shouted in dismay.

'Ach, there's nothin' to it. Here, you have a go. It's the only way to learn,' bellowed Big Bella, handing Chrissie a spare hook.

She managed not too badly at first, but it was hard, relentless work. It was an endless process, the full bobbins being replaced with empty ones. The machinery drove on and on tirelessly, spinning fast, requiring deep concentration to keep the ends of yarn up, until Chrissie's head began to spin dizzily. She got in a muddle, panicked, and found Massie standing over her.

'What d'you think you're doing? You're no' keeping your ends up!'

She wiped the sweat off her brow. 'I . . . I'm sorry.'

'I'll let you off this time, but you'll have to do better, or you're oot,' he growled.

Big Bella sorted out the frame for her. 'Don't you mind Massie, lass. He's no' half the man your Danny was, an' he kens it,' she roared.

Shortly before Christmas, Chrissie received a note from Lizzie, inviting her to bring the children to see Sammy. Her spirits lifted. There were changes afoot that might end the stalemate of the war, and everyone was more hopeful. Asquith, Freeman of Dundee, had resigned, and the firebrand Lloyd George had taken over. They said the Welshman got things done.

Chrissie patiently unpicked an old white shawl and knitted a delicate, tiny matinée jacket. The two little girls drew self-portraits for their brother to hang over his cot, so he wouldn't forget what they looked like.

The three of them were in a fever of excitement as the appointed Sunday afternoon approached.

They sat in the Downfield tram marvelling at the fine houses and neat gardens. Arthur Kennedy's house, when they reached it, was the grandest of the lot. The little girls were awed when a uniformed maid answered the bell, but Lizzie was right behind, arms outstretched.

'Come in, my dears!'

Chrissie could hardly believe this gracious, smiling lady was her stiff and starchy sister-in-law. Lizzie had filled out, and her eyes sparkled with happiness, only clouding when they rested on Chrissie. She squeezed Chrissie's arm.

'He was so desperately ill for a spell, Chrissie. He'd caught your cold, and we thought we would lose him.'

Arthur came up behind his wife, a portly, successful man now. He put an arm proudly round Lizzie's shoulders. 'This wonderful woman saved the wee man, Chrissie. She sat with him night and day, nursing him until the fever abated. He grows stronger every day, the wee lamb! Come and see—'

He led the way into a room that made the children's eyes goggle. There was a Christmas tree in the window, hung with tinsel and coloured baubles, and a blazing fire reflecting its cosy light on shining brass and polished wood. A cradle trimmed with white lace and blue ribbons stood beneath the tree, and Chrissie went towards it as if in a dream.

He had grown, put on weight. He was awake, as if watching the glitter of the decorated tree, but he looked up at her with a dark, unfocussed stare. She could see no resemblance to Danny or herself. His downy hair had a gingery tint, almost like Lizzie's. This finely dressed baby could have been Lizzie's child, not hers. Chrissie backed away, a chill in her heart. She handed the little matinée jacket to Lizzie.

'For the baby, Lizzie. It's not much, I'm afraid,' she murmured, her vision blurring with tears.

At least the children enjoyed the afternoon, and found nothing amiss. Lizzie was wonderful with them, down on her knees helping to open their presents. The gifts were carefully chosen to delight the girls. Mary Rose crooned happily over the baby doll with blue eyes that opened and closed in a smiling, china face, and Sandra was overcome with joy at the elaborate wooden pencil case, and the five-year diary with its own private lock and key. She snuggled close to her aunt. 'Have you really met Queen Alexandra, Auntie Lizzie? What's she like?'

Lizzie smiled. 'She's a very brave and gracious lady, pet. She's so easy to talk to, you'd never guess she is deaf, and she glides along so gracefully you don't notice her poor leg is badly afflicted with rheumatics.'

Sandra hugged her knees and dreamily studied pictures in the fire. She wished they didn't have to go home. She wanted to stay with Sammy, lapped in warmth and luxury for ever.

It was Harriet who broke the news to Chrissie that Ernest had been wounded in battle on the Somme, in a letter written in the spring of 1918.

I suppose it was no coincidence he should be brought to Etaples, where I'm based. He was remarkably cheerful once the shrapnel was removed, congratulating himself on collecting 'a Blighty one'! Indeed, Ernest should be in Blighty by now. I pulled some strings, and arranged for him to recuperate at Glamis Castle so you can visit your brother more easily, my dear.

133

He is well, but his soldiering days are over. Ernest will limp for the rest of his life, and should count himself lucky to be alive. Oh, Chrissie, how I long for this awful war to end, and a return to sanity. I dream of peace, of settling down to quiet, domestic life. Have you seen Charles? Is he well? He sends me such amusing letters, but they do not tell me what I want to know—

Chrissie let the letter lie in her lap. Poor Ernest! And yet, he had survived. How weary everyone was of the war. Even the popular songs on everyone's lips had lost their jauntiness, and had a sad, yearning note, a longing for peace. Chrissie herself was weary, although her hands flew as fast as Big Bella's now, and she could keep her end up in the mill. The noise and humid heat, the fibre dust, and most of all the small injustices of the work sickened her. Her girls were growing fast, and Mary Rose had started school. The bairns must be clothed and shod, and there was no respite from the mill for Chrissie.

She made up her mind to visit Ernest on her own, and set off for Glamis Castle one Sunday morning. This time, she left the children with an obliging neighbour, for Biddy was far from well.

As the bus left Dundee behind and climbed laboriously over the Sidlaw Hills towards the Strathmore Valley, Chrissie looked back at the grey city with a sense of freedom and a lighter heart. For the first time since Danny's death, she was almost happy. How delightful to be free to go anywhere she wished, to order her own life as Harriet did, she thought. Chrissie had never known freedom since the childhood days of Bessie's benign rule, and suddenly she longed passionately to be free of care and responsibility. She sighed. A hopeless dream, indeed!

* * *

Glamis was like a fairytale castle, Chrissie thought, as she left the bus with a few other visitors and went through gates leading to a long driveway. Sunlight lit the grey stone turrets ahead, and the green fields of the estate lay all around. A lark rose as Chrissie walked on, and she lifted her head with the quick joyous movement that had won Charles Rankine's heart, to listen to the birdsong. For a moment she felt young again, carefree and lightsome.

Wounded soldiers were congregated in the gardens, the men in light blue suits making a welcome show of colour against the grey walls. They were very cheerful, hailing the visitors with a hearty rendition of 'Hullo, hullo, who's your lady friend—?'

Chrissie found she was laughing.

She located Ernest, assisted by admiring backchat from his companions that did much to boost her morale. Her cheeks were rosy and her blue eyes sparkling with laughter when she reached her brother's side. She kissed his cheek, to a chorus of whistles and shouts of 'Ernest, you lucky devil!' and 'Hey, Miss, what about me?'

'Chrissie, what a surprise! You look great!' Ernest smiled at his young sister fondly. She was very dear to him, and the poor lass hadn't had her sorrows to seek.

Chrissie sat down, examining her brother anxiously. To her relief, Ernest looked remarkably fit. It was hard to tell he'd been wounded, apart from the telltale crutches resting by the seat. A dark-haired, pretty young lady appeared beside them. She smiled at Ernest.

'How's the leg today, Ernest?'

'Not so bad. I'll be doing the eightsome reel any day now.'

She laughed merrily. 'We'll see about that!' She turned to Chrissie. 'Have they given you tea yet? No? I'll make sure you get a cup.'

Smiling, she hurried away. Chrissie stared after her, warmed by her concern. 'Who's that, Ernest?' she asked.

'That's the Earl of Strathmore's daughter, Lady Elizabeth Bowes-Lyon. She's an angel, that girl. She's comforted many a homesick Tommy with her lovely smile, going round the wards day after day.'

Ernest paused for a few moments, then glanced sideways at Chrissie.

'Chris, I'm awfully glad to have this opportunity to talk to you. I've got something important to tell you – at least it is, to me – I've fallen in love.'

'Oh, Ernest, I'm so happy for you,' Chrissie squeezed his arm. It had taken her brother many years to recover from his unhappy experience with the grocer's daughter.

'Her name's Geraldine Mason and she's American,' Ernest went on eagerly. 'She came over to England with her father after America entered the war, and we fell in love when I met her on leave in London. Her father's been doing research into motorised vehicles, armoured tanks mostly, and he's offered me a job when I'm fit. I'd work with him in England at first, and then America, in the engineering works in Detroit.'

Ernest's eyes glowed with enthusiasm. 'I thought I'd be a clerk in Papa's office for the rest of my days, Chris, but to be offered a chance like that, near the woman I love, is miraculous.' He stopped abruptly, and the glad light in his eyes faded as he sighed. 'But it's no use, Chris. How can I leave Father?'

She put a hand urgently on his arm. 'You must accept, Ernest. Arthur can look after the business, and Bessie will care for Papa, surely?'

He looked at her strangely. 'You don't know, do you?'

Chrissie felt a chill of foreboding. 'What is it?'

'Papa has no head for business, you know. He bungled the batching oil contract and Rankine cancelled it. Arthur's affairs are separate and well managed, fortunately, but the old man's ill and broken-hearted, and living all alone.'

Chrissie clutched her brother's arm. 'But Bessie's there!'

He shook his head. 'No, Chris. The old man and Bessie had a row and parted company when Lizzie took your son. Nobody knows where Bessie is.'

Chrissie stared at him in horror. 'Oh, Ernest! What are we going to do?'

Chapter 7

'There's only one solution, Chris,' Ernest said gloomily. 'When my gammy leg heals and I'm discharged from the army, I'll go back home and care for Papa. I must refuse Mr Mason's offer, and tell Geraldine to forget about me. I love her dearly, but you couldn't expect a rich, young American lady to marry a penniless cripple and settle in Dundee. The city is facing hard times even if we do win this dreadful war.'

'If Geraldine loves you, that won't put her off,' Chrissie said.

Her brother sighed. 'Maybe not, but I love her too much to let her make sacrifices. Besides, I have some pride!'

Chrissie was silent. The other wounded soldiers had drifted towards a trestle table set up in the garden. The pretty, young Lady Elizabeth Bowes-Lyon was helping to dispense tea to the convalescents, and Chrissie could hear laughter and the homely chink of teacups. It was a scene to lift anyone's spirits, but Chrissie felt thoroughly depressed. Some of these brave young men had three or more wound stripes on their sleeves, and had been sent back to the Front again and again. They'd all suffered so much pain and anguish, and now Ernest must give up his chance of happiness. It was so unfair!

A thought suddenly struck her. Why shouldn't she step into the breach to save her brother? For a moment the possibility chilled her. She'd be loath to give up her independence, and the home where memories of Danny still lingered so vividly that she sometimes thought he would come whistling up the close.

But what independence had she? Only the hard discipline of the mill six days a week. Aye, and the tenement flat was no home with Danny gone, for she was hardly ever in it, and her wee lasses must fend for themselves while their mother slaved. Memories? Those were locked away in her heart forever with her love for Danny.

Besides, Ernest said Papa was sick and needed care, and she loved her father dearly and had a duty to care for him in old age. Oh, and what about Bessie, her nurse and dearest friend? Bessie had championed the cause of Danny's tiny son and been dismissed for her pains. Bessie *must* be found, Chrissie thought worriedly.

The crutches leaning near her brother's chair caught her eye, and that settled it. Harriet had written that Ernest would limp for the rest of his life. He had suffered enough.

'There's no problem, Ernest. I'll give up the flat and look after Papa,' Chrissie offered.

Ernest's eyes lit with hope. 'Oh, Chris, would you? The decline of the whaling industry and the loss of so many shipmates and fine ships has hit the old man hard. Papa's sick and difficult to handle, I'm told, but you were always the apple of his eye!'

Tears rushed to her eyes at that, and he squeezed her hand sympathetically. 'Mind now, Chrissie, it won't be easy. Arthur tells me the batching oil side of the business is in a bad way since I was called up, because poor Papa couldn't cope. I don't know if enough can be salvaged to give the old man a comfortable old age. Och, how can I leave you with such a worry, lass?'

Chrissie brushed the tears away and laughed. 'If I can

140

keep my end up in the mill, I can cope with anything, Ernest!'

He smiled and nodded admiringly. 'Aye, you've had more than your share of trouble, yet won through. Arthur and Lizzie will be a help, Chris. Arthur has a good head on his shoulders, and everything Mistress Lizzie touches seems to prosper.'

'Yes, I know.'

Her brother didn't know how much his innocent remark hurt her. Lizzie was fostering Chrissie's premature baby, and the little chap was thriving under Lizzie's care, although he still had a long way to go. To give Lizzie her due, she was generous with invitations, and Chrissie had made frequent visits on a Sunday afternoon to see her son, with his little sisters in tow.

She had held Sammy in her arms many times and kissed the fluff of gingery down on his tiny head. Perhaps some hint of his mother's longing and frustration disturbed the baby, because the wee mite would begin wailing fretfully and wouldn't be comforted until Lizzie took him and cuddled him. Sammy didn't even act like Chrissie's child any more.

A nurse was approaching, balancing cups of tea: Lady Elizabeth hadn't forgotten her promise. Ernest squeezed Chrissie's hand. 'I'll never forget this, Chris. You can't imagine how it feels to be free at last to live my own life.'

'Oh, yes, I can, Ernest dear,' she replied, remembering a young girl who had willingly left comfort and ease, to go her own way.

Chrissie continued to work at the mill during the summer of 1918, anxiously awaiting word from Ernest, who had urged caution in dealing with their father. William Kennedy was quite likely to refuse Chrissie's offer point blank, Ernest said. The old man was stubbornly set against involving his daughter and her children in the disaster he'd created. It was a delicate situation to be handled with diplomacy.

She asked around, to discover if anyone knew what had happened to Bessie McCutcheon, but nobody could tell her anything. Biddy said her sister had turned up with all her belongings in a carpet bag one morning towards the end of last year. 'She made me swear I'd not tell ye she'd got the sack, Chris, because you'd enough to worry about at the time. I tried to get her to bide wi' me, but she said she'd manage fine on her own, an' stumped out the door. I havena seen hair nor hide o' her since.'

At least they needn't look for Bessie in the jute mills, Chrissie thought, because the damp, stoury conditions made Bessie ill. She must be in domestic service somewhere, but how could Chrissie track her down?

The humid heat of that warm summer drained the mill-workers. The long lines of spinning frames beneath the cast iron beams were manned by tight-lipped women with sweat running down their faces. There was talk of wages being cut and women laid off because of bad trade, and everyone was on edge. Even Big Bella grumbled.

'I'm sick o' this, Chris, for the heat's fair murdering my corns. The weavers have the best job, ye ken. The roof's higher in the factory than in the mill, and you can open a' they big windaes too,' she bellowed above the thunder of the machines.

Chrissie was quite familiar with the various departments of the works. She knew that yarn was prepared and spun in the mill, and woven into cloth in the factory. There was rivalry between spinners and weavers, who were inclined to think themselves the bees' knees, and could be toffee-nosed in consequence. The foreman came stalking along the frames, scowling.

'No talking, you!'

Bella glared at him. 'Can we no' have a breath o'fresh air in this place?'

'Fire risk. One spark wi' a wee puff o' wind behind it could start a mighty conflagration in the oily yarn. You ken the rules, Bella,' growled Massie smugly.

Bella's hands were a blur of movement at the frame. 'Och, there's mair danger from the fags you puff on the sly behind the partition, you daft ass!' she muttered.

He advanced threateningly. 'What's that you said the now?'

'I wis thinkin' aboot the fluff ahent the partition, Mr Massie. A fag-end dropped carelessly could set it aff. Somebody ought to tell the manager,' roared Bella sweetly.

The foreman turned purple and Chrissie started to laugh. The merriment welled up and refreshed her like cool water. It was a while since she'd laughed.

When she went home after work that Saturday afternoon, Chrissie was still light-hearted. She smiled at her two little daughters.

'How'd you like to go to the pictures? Charlie Chaplin's on at The Rialto.'

Sandra's eyes lit up. 'Oh, Mum, can't we go to the La Scala?'

'Well—' Chrissie swithered. The new cinema had opened in the Murraygate in 1913, but she'd never been. It was in the centre of town and sure to be more expensive than the local flea-pit, as Danny had called it. She studied her little daughter's eager face. 'Oh, all right, love,' Chrissie agreed recklessly.

The bairns cheered. Sandra insisted on wearing her best clothes and straw hat wreathed in roses, despite thundery showers. Of course, Mary Rose must follow suit. While the little girls were getting ready, Chrissie surreptitiously raided the tea-caddy. One pound twelve and sixpence. She smiled as she recalled the foolish young bride who'd squandered Danny's cash. She'd learned good sense since then, but this was a special occasion. She slipped the precious savings into her handbag.

Sandra walked with her nose held so high she was in danger of tripping over her feet. She held Mary Rose's hand in a restraining grip and wouldn't let her skip. In her imagination, they were princesses, and their mother was Queen Mary. Princesses wouldn't play at stottin' the ball – One two three, a leerie, Four five six, a leerie, Seven eight nine, a leerie, Ten, a leerie, post man – then you kicked one leg up high to let the ball stot under, and sometimes folk could see your knickers. Och, no, princesses would never do that. Princesses wouldn't chalk on the pavement at the head o' the close for a game of hopscotch, nor be seen dead skipping down the street on a Saturday on the way to a matinée, thought Sandra. She pointed her toes daintily, trying to avoid treading on the cracks in the pavement, in case she fell through.

But oh, the sight of the La Scala when they reached it. The gilded luxury of the cinema made Sandra's jaw drop as they joined the queue and began to shuffle across the marble floor. Her eyes goggled when they reached the glass boley and the scarlet-lipped woman behind it, and her mother asked boldly for 'A shilling and two halves, if you please.'

Oh, my, the balcony. Wait till she told them at school she'd been in the balcony. Sandra mounted the wide staircase as if in a dream. She really was a princess at that moment, walking on thick red carpets past white and gold plaster pillars, with an awed Mary Rose gripping her hand like grim death. There were stylish ladies bearing torches waiting to take your ticket and show you to your seat, and one of them winked at Sandra.

'Better tak' aff your bonnet, hen. Folk behind'll no' see the picters for yon rose-gairden,' the stylish lady joked.

A man in a black suit came out and stood in front of the velvet curtains on the stage, and the spotlights fixed admiringly on him. He flexed his muscles and bowed, then sat down in front of the piano, flicking out the tails of his jacket with a flourish to trail down the back of the seat. He began pounding away on the keys ten to the dozen as the lights died.

The film was about daft policemen chasing robbers acting so silly the Murphys almost choked themselves laughing, while the man's music trilled with mirth or thundered like a train, where appropriate. Sandra stole a glance at her mother. There were tears of laughter pouring down her mother's cheeks, and her mouth was wide open, laughing like the old days when Daddy said something funny.

Oh, Daddy, my dear Daddy, I miss you sore! Not a bad place to cry for a lost daddy, amidst gales of laughter, with nobody to see.

Afterwards, they came out into a throng crowding the Murraygate so thickly the trams couldn't get moving and kept grumpily clanging their bells. The Murphys were carried along with the crush of folk right through swing doors into Woolworth's. You could hardly squeeze a postcard between the people crowded in there, because the rain was pouring down outside. Everyone steamed in the heat. That was the big joke at school, of course. 'It's warm in Woollies!'

Gosh, it certainly was no joke, Sandra thought, submerged in a sea of warm bodies, her hat knocked squint.

Chrissie bought them both a threepenny bangle. Sandra fitted hers on her wrist and her nose went higher in the air. They jouked out of the packed store through the back pend and made their way hand in hand to the Mid Kirk Style. In the narrow wynd behind the Steeple Kirk, it seemed the crowds swarming round the wee Overgate shops had grown hungry at the same moment and made for the Buster stalls. The air was rich with the smell of frying onions and sizzling chips, and the shouts of the folk selling things from the stalls rang like cheering in Sandra's ears.

Chrissie used her elbows well and came out with her hat askew, clutching three pokes of chips and peas. They found a quiet corner beside the City Churches and ate hungrily with their fingers, then washed their hands genteel-like and drank from the drinking fountain which spilled clear water from a little lion's mouth.

Going home in the tram, nursing Wallace's meat pies for their tea in a paper bag transparent with hot fat, Sandra had her future mapped out crystal clear in her mind.

She was determined to marry a very rich man, and live in luxury for the rest of her life.

Shortly after that happy outing, Chrissie received a disturbing letter. It was from wee Hughie, written in a shaky hand and post-marked Bombay, India. It had taken weeks to come.

Dearest Auntie Chris,
I've written to Mum and Dad, saying I'm sorry for running away to sea, but I can't be a farmer. I'm no good at it, and anyway I'm scared of cows. I hope they will forgive me someday. I've told them everything's fine and I'm doing well, because I don't want them to worry, but I'm not fine, and I've hardly any money left, Auntie Chris. It was awful hard work on the ship. I was seasick and

scared most of the time in case a German submarine torpedoed us. When we reached Bombay I
went down with a very bad fever. It was so bad
the Captain wouldn't have me aboard in case he
and the rest of the crew got it, and I was put in
hospital ashore.

I'm better now, but the ship sailed without me
days ago and nobody else will take me on because
I look so weak and weedy. A friend has advised
me to go to the Samnuggur Jute Works in Calcutta,
which has links with Dundee. I might get work
there and save money for my passage home. So
that is what I will do, Auntie Chris. Please don't
tell Mum and Dad. You may tell Ina if you wish,
though, about the misfortunes of . . .

Your loving nephew, Hughie

Chrissie didn't know what to think. She fetched a map
contained in one of Danny's books, and was aghast
to find the vast distance her nephew must travel from
Bombay to Calcutta. He was obviously weak and nearly
penniless. Oh, whatever had happened to the lad? she
worried.

After some anxious deliberation, Chrissie wrote a
cautious note to Georgina, outlining briefly Hughie's
plight. Someone in the boy's family ought to be kept
informed, though there was little anyone could do.

Georgina Kennedy read Chrissie's letter seated on
a rock on Craig Dubh, her sheepdog flopped at her
feet while the sheep grazed peacefully on the hill. She
looked more like a slender, long-legged youth than a
young woman, for she'd taken to wearing a shirt and
trousers, her hair tucked under a bonnet, much to her
mother's disgust.

'You'll never get yoursel' a man dressed in that rig,
Ina,' Jeannie had wailed on more than one occasion.

Ina didn't care. Tam was married to another. What did it matter what she looked like? Trousers were grand for scrambling up the hillside after the dog. She kept her distance from Tam, never looked his way, never spoke to him. It was safer.

Margaret, Tam's wife, was expecting a bairn quite soon. She flouted her condition triumphantly when Ina was around, and Ina spent more and more time alone on the hill, the wind blowing in her face, the sun tanning her skin a golden brown.

She frowned anxiously over the letter. Oh, poor wee Hughie. And nothing could be done while the miserable war dragged on.

'Hey, you there!'

Ina hadn't heard a sound, but she looked up to find a soldier standing on the track, his uniform strangely out of place in this peaceful spot. She stood up, shading her eyes to see him better.

'Yes? Are you lost?'

He came closer. For a big man, he walked softly. 'Well, I'll be . . . You're a sheila!' he exclaimed.

'A sheila?' Ina stared at him, taking in the bush-hat turned up at one side, the sunburst badge on it, and light suddenly dawned. She smiled.

'Oh, you must be Bruce, Mr Cameron's Australian nephew. We've been expecting you. Have you come to view your inheritance?'

He nodded. 'If I can find it.'

Ina laughed and waved an arm towards Craig Dubh.

'This is it. Nearly two hundred acres of hill and forest, fifty acres of arable, a farmhouse where my father and mother live, and three cottages.'

He had a trick of narrowing his eyes thoughtfully so that only a glint of grey showed. 'Hmmm. That all? Hardly worth bothering about.'

She stared. 'How much land do you have in Australia?'

'Oh, around a hundred an' fifty thousand acres of grazing in the outback,' he shrugged. 'Australia's a big country. Not many men though, nor women neither. Women are scarce in the outback. Leastways, the right sort of women.'

At that, he looked at her appraisingly with his keen, narrowed eyes, and she felt herself go beetroot-red beneath the golden tan.

'If you will follow me, Mr Cameron, I will take you to my father,' Ina said coolly, turning her back on the intense scrutiny and leading the way down the track.

The Germans had launched another attack and driven the British and French back ten miles. It seemed to the sorrowing and weary folk at home that the war would never be won. But General Haig kept his nerve. This time he deployed armoured tanks, which Mr Churchill and Lloyd George favoured, and the fearsome things lumbered across the scarred and pitted battlefields in sufficient numbers to turn the tide of battle and save many infantry lives. The enemy fled, screaming that the Devil was after them, and Ludendorff's offensive ran out of steam, and crumbled. The end was in sight at last.

In September 1918, Chrissie received a postcard from Ernest.

Dear Chrissie
Papa has agreed at last, and will welcome you and your bairns when you arrive. I have been discharged, and leave for London tomorrow (10th inst) to join Mr Mason and Geraldine. I get around pretty well on one stick. I will write you at greater length soon.
God bless you, my dear! Ernest.

149

Chrissie drew in a breath and straightened her shoulders. There was much to be done. First she must give her notice at the mill.

The workers were sad to see her go. They'd grown attached to the bonnie woman who never flaunted her gentle birth, and worked as hard as anyone to feed her bairns. Even Massie, the foreman, was put out.

'Just when you'd got the hang o' it and were some use tae me in the spinning flat, woman,' he growled in disgust, which was high praise, coming from him.

They made her a wee presentation on the last day, gathering in the courtyard when the bells rang for the end of the shift. She was surrounded by beaming, kindly faces, with Bella at the forefront, who draped a pretty, blue shawl around Chrissie's shoulders. It was so light and finely knitted it would have passed through a wedding ring. The others cheered, and tears ran unashamedly down Chris's cheeks.

'Oh, thank you all! How can I ever thank you?' she sobbed.

Bella wiped her nose emotionally on her cuff. 'Och, Chris, it's nothing, just a wee bit shawl knitted frae bits an' pieces. Here, lass, fix it at your neck wi' your bonnie ship brooch.' She pinned the shawl and arranged it becomingly. It matched Chrissie's blue eyes. Bella stepped back and clasped her hands together admiringly.

'Oh, it's exquisite, isn't it?' she said in hushed tones, and everyone agreed.

Meanwhile, Sandra was saying her own farewells. She headed for the backcourts of the tenements, after school.

The courts were a bustling scene of activity, with hordes of bairns playing and yelling around the greenie poles, under lines of washing fluttering overhead like signal flags strung from the windows. There had once been grass on the greens, but it had long ago succumbed to the pounding of tackety boots during the 'seven-weekies', the long summer holidays.

Sandra picked her way past a line of little girls waiting their turn at the skipping rope tied to a greenie pole. One of their number was cawing away energetically at the rope's end, while a little lass skipped, pig-tails flying.

'C'mon, Sandra, jump in an' keep the pot bilin',' one of her pals yelled.

But Sandra moved on, her eyes searching the various groups. There was a screaming bunch playing high tig on the walls, and driving a wifie daft by jumping on newly scrubbed steps. A more sedate group were bowling hoops down the close and catching them with cleeks just before they rolled into the street and took the feet from unwary passers-by.

Stepping fastidiously around a tangle of laddies wrestling happily over a football in the mud, Sandra at last found what she was looking for, an intent little circle of boys in a quiet corner, playing bools.

'Hey, you, Norrie Gallacher!' Sandra cried.

Nobody moved, but a red-headed boy deftly knuckled a marble into the centre of the ring and grunted, 'Uh-huh?'

'I'm leaving tomorrow wi' my mum an' my wee sister. We're going to live with my grandpa in a great big hoose in Broughty,' Sandra continued, not without a hint of pride.

'Oh aye?' The boy swooped on three bools he'd knocked out of the ring. The others groaned.

'I'm to go to the Grove Academy, Mum ses. I'll not let on if I meet you when I'm oot wi' my new posh friends, Norrie Gallacher, but I'll give a wee wink, so's you'll ken it's still me,' Sandra offered generously.

'Aye.' He squinted and knuckled another bool.

'I'm to marry a very rich man an' live in luxury noo, so I'm breakin' aff our engagement,' she announced.

'Oh aye?' His favourite glassie with yellow and white swirls in it had scattered all the other marbles centred in the ring.

'I just called to say bye bye,' said Sandra.

Norrie Gallacher collected his winnings and stuffed the bools into bulging pockets.

'Ta ta,' he said.

A corner on Jimsie the carter's cart was all Chrissie needed to shift her belongings. Harriet's little writing desk and one or two precious bits and pieces were all she took. The rest went to Maggie Glancey's for a few welcome bob.

Jimsie generously offered transport on the cart, which Chrissie accepted. She'd no intention of letting their possessions out of her sight. When the carter had carried everything down and stowed it on the flat cart, Chrissie stood for a moment in the empty flat, looking round. Danny's presence wasn't there any more. The place felt dead and cold in the fitful sunlight. She went out, closed the door behind her and descended the echoing stone stairs for the last time, fighting back the tears that threatened to overcome her.

The two little girls were thrilled with this form of transport, perched up with Jimsie behind the big brown horse.

'Has this horse been to the war?' Mary Rose asked in all seriousness.

'Naw, he wisnae called up. Mind you, he'd've gone if he'd got his papers. He's that willin', the big saftie,' Jimsie answered, geeing-up his old friend. They moved off at an easy pace, heading down Lochee Road.

'I gave my Saturday penny to the teacher to help the wounded horses,' Mary Rose said proudly.

'You're a kind wee lassie to spare a thought for the poor suffering beasties. There's no' mony folk does, hen,' said Jimsie with a sigh.

It seemed to take ages to reach William Kennedy's house, for Jimsie went by devious routes and stopped at least once to water his horse at a trough. At last they came to a halt outside the gate, and Chrissie clambered down stiffly. Jimsie lifted the little girls after her, then brought a nosebag from the back of the cart and draped it round the horse's neck before spitting on his palms and beginning the removal.

The door opened, and William Kennedy came out. Chrissie and her father looked at one another. Her heart missed a beat when she saw how he'd aged, and how gaunt and stooped he'd become. He had a sad, uncared-for look which she found unbearably pitiful.

He frowned at her. 'Must you come on a cart? Why didn't you get the removal van, and come in a cab like decent folk?'

'That costs shillings, Papa,' she smiled. She went to him, feeling his proud aloofness as they embraced.

Mary Rose was staring, mouth open. 'Why are you greetin', Grandpa?' she asked curiously.

'I'm no' greetin'! I've got the cold.' He hastily took out a hanky and blew his nose.

Sandra gave him a knowing look. 'It'll be the Spanish flu, Grandpa. It's terrible bad in Lochee. You'll need to get away to your bed wi' a hot toddy.'

He looked down at the two concerned wee faces, and his poor tired, worried features relaxed into the glimmer of a smile. 'I see I'm to be well looked after. A toddy, you say?'

Mary Rose took his hand for comfort, and Sandra nodded wisely. 'Aye, Grandpa. A hot toddy wi' cinnamon, and go easy on the hot water. That's what

153

Norrie Gallacher's granny takes when she's oot wi' the rag-and-bone cartie in a' weathers.'

Chrissie hid a smile as she turned away to pay Jimsie his due. Somehow she had a feeling her two daughters had broken the ice.

The house had been sadly neglected with Bessie gone, although Chrissie was touched to find her father had done his best to make them comfortable. There was clean linen on the beds and fires burning in her bedroom and the girls' room next door.

'There's stone piggies been in the bairns' beds all day, in case o' damp,' William grunted.

'Oh, thank you, Papa.'

Chrissie turned to him with misty eyes. She hugged him. Although he made no move to reciprocate and showed no emotion, she guessed he needed to be hugged, and frequently. He turned his head away.

'I dinna ken where Bessie is,' he said gruffly.

'Would you take her back?'

'Maybe.' He looked sideways at Chrissie. 'Will you take the baby away from Lizzie, now you're home?'

Chrissie had been thinking about that. It had filled her thoughts for days. She could care for Sammy herself now she'd stopped working at the mill. She lifted her chin.

'Yes, Papa. He's my son. I want him back.'

Why did she feel so badly about the decision? Chrissie wondered. Surely she'd a right to care for her own baby.

The old man hesitated as if he might say something, then changed his mind and shuffled from the room.

Chrissie was kept so busy cleaning, cooking and seeing her little girls settled into their new schools, the ending of the war caught her quite by surprise. Perhaps it caught everyone by surprise. There was little joy in Dundee at the news, only a great upsurge of relief and mounting

154

sorrow. There were so many empty places, scarcely a family that hadn't lost a father, son or brother. A generation of young Dundee lads, all gone.

Kaiser Bill, the cause of the trouble, jouked out of Germany and hid himself away, well aware that legions of sorrowing women were crying aloud for vengeance. The bitterness felt in the city was as raw and biting as the November wind.

Chrissie's brother Arthur arrived the Sunday after the armistice was signed, ostensibly to rejoice with them over the good news. Arthur had a more personal matter on his mind though, as Chrissie found out when their father went off to take a nap.

'Chrissie, do you intend taking Sammy away from us?' Arthur demanded bluntly when they were left alone.

'I—' She faltered and stopped at the look on her brother's face. He leaned towards her urgently.

'Chrissie, I know you've every right to take him, but *please* don't.'

'Arthur, he's my baby – and Danny's,' Chrissie protested.

'It will be the death of Lizzie,' said Arthur quietly. 'She says nothing, but I know she could not live without the baby. You have your two little girls, but Lizzie has nothing, no hope. There's no future for her if you take Sammy away.'

Greatly agitated, Chrissie rose and went to the window. She couldn't sit still, for she trembled in every limb.

'But he's my baby, Arthur,' she said brokenly. Her vision blurred with tears as a picture of Lizzie tenderly cuddling the baby took shape before her.

Arthur had risen. He put a gentle hand on his sister's shoulder. 'We love him so much, Chris. We love him like our own son. Perhaps the loss would be easier to bear when Sammy is older and less dependent. I can't say, Chrissie. It must be your decision.' He picked up hat and gloves and prepared to leave.

'Please consider it well, Chrissie. I'm off to London tomorrow to a meeting to discuss trade with India now the war's over. When I return, I'll accept whatever decision you've reached,' Arthur said.

Left alone, she rested her forehead against the cool pane and closed her eyes in anguish. So many complications in her life, such sorrow to bear. Always, such sorrow.

Dr Harriet Bowers had returned to Dundee shortly before the armistice. Harriet was exhausted by the horrors she'd faced, and her superiors had persuaded her to leave the hospital at Etaples for a rest. Mr and Mrs Bowers, justly proud of their daughter's achievements, would have immediately thrown a dinner party for thirty guests, if Harriet had allowed it, but she wouldn't hear of it, so Mrs Bowers settled instead for a small, intimate dinner, with Charles Rankine as the sole guest.

Charles was still unmarried, though his reputation was somewhat besmirched because he hadn't gone off and got himself killed in the war. Even so, thought Mrs Bowers optimistically, he was still an excellent catch.

Left alone together diplomatically after an excellent dinner, Harriet studied Charles with loving eyes. He had changed. There were deep furrows in his brow and the gently humorous eyes looked tired and saddened. In his own way, Charles Rankine had had a cruel and punishing war.

He lit a cheroot, watching her through the blue, scented smoke.

'Was it very bad, the war?' he asked quietly.

A spasm of pain crossed her face. 'Yes. Very bad.'

Harriet stood up restlessly. She placed another log on the glowing fire and stared into the flames she'd created.

She'd been called to a Casualty Clearing Station just behind the Front Line once, and been shocked by the primitive conditions in the war-torn marquee. No running water, sugarboxes as medicine chests, sterilisers heated by meth burners in biscuit tins, wire cages baited to catch the rats. And the wounded boys lying everywhere, covered in blood-soaked blankets. Harriet shivered.

'Harriet—' Charles broke gently into her thoughts, and she turned to face him. She met his eyes honestly. Perhaps he could see the love shining there. If so, she was too tired to dissemble.

'I asked you once if you'd ever be willing to give up your career, settle down and have a family. Has the time come, my dear?' Charles asked.

Harriet considered his words gravely. Were they tantamount to a proposal? She felt none of the joy she'd expected, her mind was abstracted, the thoughts shooting off at tangents.

'Charles, did you know that when Kitchener's volunteers were medically examined, a great many were undernourished and unfit? They were stunted; bodies deformed by rickets and disease caused by poor diet, appalling slums and evil working conditions. The men were skilful and intelligent, but sadly ill-educated. So much remains to be done. *Someone must do something.*'

He rose and framed her vehement face with his hands.

'Does it have to be you, Harriet?'

'Perhaps.' She looked up at him steadily. 'Charles, what about Chrissie?'

She felt the shock of her words quivering through his fingers, but his voice was calm.

'Chrissie will never forgive me because I meddled in her life. Her man was safe in a reserved occupation until he discovered I'd put him there. The sad thing is, the lad had great ability. He didn't need me to speak for him. I was no friend to Chrissie, Harriet. She told me so herself.'

'Ah, poor Chrissie,' Harriet sighed.

'Yes, poor Chrissie,' Charles said. He bent his head and gently kissed Harriet on the lips.

William Kennedy wakened on Monday morning in no fit state to attend the office.

'Maybe I have caught this damned Spanish flu,' he groaned.

Chrissie ushered him back to bed and tucked him in. 'You've been overdoing it, Papa, that's all. You need a break from the office.'

'Och, how can I? There's only me to manage the place. The clerks were called up, and now Ernest's deserted the sinking ship.' He sneezed pathetically.

She looked at him thoughtfully. 'You've forgotten one thing, Papa. You have me now. Why shouldn't I look after the office until you're well again?'

'What?' His eyes opened wide. 'That's out of the question, Chrissie. You're a woman. An office is no place for women.'

Chrissie laughed. 'The world's changing, Papa. Women over thirty are getting the vote. I've worked long hours in a grocer's shop and in the mill. Why not work in an office?'

He spluttered weakly. 'It's no' seemly. I dinna ken what the world's coming to!'

She bent and kissed his cheek. 'You lie still and keep warm. I'll man the ship!'

'The customers'll no' like it. The jute merchants'll be fair scandalised at having to deal with a woman, Chrissie,' her father warned her anxiously.

She was almost out of the door by then. She turned and blew a kiss.

'Then they'll have to get used to it, Papa. Do them good!'

Chrissie was glad to get out of the house for a spell. She'd grown used to going out to work, and sometimes found her father's house lonely and stifling. She ran joyfully to catch the tram, enjoying the freedom of shorter skirts.

Reaching the Seagate, Chrissie unlocked the office door and walked boldly in. She stopped in the doorway and took stock. There were papers lying here, there and everywhere, some of them thick with dust. The office was dingy, dirty and smelled of stale whale oil. She wrinkled her nose in disgust, hung her coat on the coat-rack and wondered where to start. There was a massive ledger lying open on the desk, and that seemed as good a place as any.

Chrissie's sojourn in the grocer's shop had taught her some elementary book-keeping, and she pored over the figures entered in the ledger. They were depressing, indeed. She turned her attention to the chaos all around, and her spirits sank. Everything must be read and documented and filed away in its proper place. It was a monumental task.

'Well, sooner begun, sooner mended, my girl,' she said stoutly. She pulled a pile of invoices towards her and began going through them. With increasing indignation, she discovered that some of her father's debtors had taken advantage of the old man's good nature and given themselves a handsome credit. That would end forthwith, Chrissie determined.

By mid-day, she was dust-covered and her head ached, and she had only done a fraction of the work needed. Much of it was a mystery to her. Chrissie sat down before the ledger and sank her head in her hands.

The office door opened, and she looked up in

surprise. She hadn't expected any customers on a Monday morning. She was even more surprised to find that the caller was Charles Rankine. She had long ago shed most of her bitterness for his part in Danny's death. Too much had happened since then for rancour to flourish, and Chrissie's first sensation on seeing Charles was one of relief. Perhaps he could explain mysteries of the batching oil trade which baffled her.

She gave a friendly smile, and held out a hand.

'Oh, Charles, I need help!'

Charles Rankine hadn't moved from the doorway. The shock of finding Chrissie had overwhelmed him and left him speechless. She was as lovely as he remembered, and he wanted her as much as ever, but his inclination was to turn and run. She had hurt him very badly long ago, and Charles had no intention of being hurt again.

Chapter 8

Chrissie guessed accurately that Charles Rankine was reluctant to become involved with the Kennedys. She could hardly blame him. Her family had brought the man little joy. She had rejected his offer of marriage, her father had let him down badly over the oil contract, and such treatment was bound to rankle.

But why stare at her in tongue-tied silence, as if he'd seen a ghost? It upset her: she was accustomed to down-to-earth folk who spoke their minds and left you in no doubt as to their feelings.

She sighed. Charles was a gentleman born and bred, and that's where the difference lay, no doubt. He was still an eligible bachelor, and scheming Dundee mamas were forever trying to coax him into matrimony. No wonder he was wary of her advances. At least she could reassure Charles her interest in him was strictly businesslike.

She gave him a friendly smile. 'Charles, I'm trying to bring a semblance of order to Papa's affairs, but it's all so new to me, and there are some terms I don't understand yet. I'd be grateful for your help. I promise I won't detain you, and I shan't trouble you again. I'm not a helpless female, you know.'

Charles relaxed a little. 'Very well, Chrissie. What d'you want to know?'

'To start with, why did you cancel your contract?'

He was shaken. This wasn't the sweet Chrissie of his

dreams, but a young woman with shrewd blue eyes, challenging him as an equal. It was disconcerting.

'I was forced into it because your father couldn't deliver on time, Chrissie. I know whale oil is scarce these days, but he was unwilling to experiment with other sources. That's no use. The batching department must have suitable oil to soften the jute fibres, otherwise the fibres break on the carding machines and the whole procedure is held up, with workers standing idle. They don't like it any more than I do.' He gave her an apologetic glance. 'Forgive me, Chrissie, I forget you don't understand the manufacturing process.'

'Oh, yes, I do.' Her smile was grim. 'I've cursed my father's trade often! You can smell the fishy smell of whale oil off the rove bobbins as they feed on to the spinning frames. The smell gets on to your clothes in spite of a thick linen apron wrapped around you. I've boiled my linen in the steamie, and still the smell of stale fish clung until I thought I'd be sick. I've watched the manufacture of jute sacking from start to finish when I worked in the mill, Charles. I understand perfectly!'

He was staggered. 'You worked in the mill? Oh, Chrissie, I didn't know.'

She shrugged. 'I had to exist somehow after Danny died. It's difficult for a soldier's widow to live on the pittance they give you, with two young bairns to feed and clothe.'

Charles stared, seeing Chrissie in a new light. She had never been far from his thoughts since the day they met at Lizzie's wedding, but he had never dreamed this lovely woman possessed such resourceful courage.

'Oh, Chrissie, I could have helped.'

Her lip curled contemptuously. 'How could you? Could you persuade the jute barons to pay another two bob a week instead of cutting wages? That's the only help I'd take from you and your kind, Charles.

162

Why can't they pay decent wages to poor hardworking folk?'

He shook his head to clear it, for he felt dazed.

'Chrissie, you're so bitter!'

Charles looked dejected and she felt sorry. Maybe she'd been harsh. How could you expect a rich man to know what it was like to be poor? Studying him more closely, she saw he had not escaped unscathed from the war, although he hadn't fought in it. She'd even heard it whispered he'd been a conscientious objector, though he hadn't gone to jail.

Brash folk had shouted after him in the street, jeering, 'Conshie! Conshie!' The man had obviously suffered great stress and driven himself hard to keep his factory going. Scars of his suffering were etched on his tired features in deep lines and furrows, and his eyes looked haunted and melancholy. Chrissie had a sudden desire to make him smile, but didn't know how.

'I'm sorry, I don't mean to be bitter, Charles. The past is over and done with, so let's forget it. Now, how can I restore your faith in the Kennedys? Tell me what I must do to regain the Rankine contract, and I'll do it.' She smiled and laid a hand persuasively on his sleeve.

'Well, Chrissie, you must be dependable and keep your price keenly competitive. You must have the hide of a rhinoceros, yet be the soul of tact. That takes some doing in a man, but if you want my opinion, I think a woman would find it well nigh impossible,' he replied bluntly.

Looking down at the small hand resting on his arm, Charles wondered if she guessed how devastating her touch was. It took only the slight pressure of her fingers to reawaken his love. His vulnerable state dismayed him, because he'd believed himself free from her spell at last. He'd even been on the point of asking Harriet to marry him.

163

Yet he knew this futile infatuation for Christina Murphy had no future, for she'd made her aversion to employers like himself quite clear. She wanted security for her children, not an unwelcome love affair with a man she despised. He couldn't blame her, after all she'd been through.

Chrissie narrowed her eyes thoughtfully. 'Hmm. I see I've a lot to learn, and male prejudice to overcome as well. But if I offer high-quality oil at a fair price and organise reliable delivery, you might reconsider?'

'Certainly.'

'Then I can't wait to get started, Charles,' she laughed gaily.

He was amused and touched by her high hopes. Didn't she realise the capital expenditure involved? He'd heard disturbing rumours in the city about old William Kennedy's difficulties. It was said he was nearly bankrupt. Charles had visited the office that morning to offer the old man some practical help, and instead he'd found Chrissie. What an ironic twist of fate.

Chrissie turned to the ledger. On it lay a pile of invoices she'd sorted out from the muddle.

'Look at these, Charles. I've checked the ledger, and these men haven't paid Papa a penny.'

He peered over her shoulder as she flicked through the invoices one by one. He whistled in amazement. 'But this money should have been paid into your father's account months ago!'

'Exactly. Some of his customers have been taking a loan of him, trading on Papa's good nature and ill health. That's awfully mean! There's three or four hundred pounds due, possibly more, and I'm getting it out of the scoundrels, Charles, even if I have to twist their arms!' she declared, lifting her chin.

Charles gave a secret smile of delight, though there was a lump in his throat. He'd recognised that glorious tilt of the head, that joyous eagerness of eye. It was the look that had made him fall head over heels in love with the young lassie, years ago.

'You'll be mighty unpopular with the high heid yins, Chrissie,' he warned.

She laughed. 'Frankly, I don't give a hoot!'

Charles eyed her with growing respect. 'Can I help in any way?'

She looked at him thoughtfully. 'Well, yes, Charles, there is something. I want a typewriter but I don't know where to buy one. Can you advise me?'

'I can do better than that. We have a spare machine in the office that's seldom used. I could lend it to you if you want.' He glanced at her speculatively. 'Can you type, Chrissie?'

'Not yet, but I'll learn. It's faster, more efficient, and bound to impress these fly lads.' She tapped the invoices with a fingertip, grinning.

His heart was beating uncomfortably fast. He longed to sweep her into his arms and kiss her soundly, to show how deeply he appreciated her brave spirit, but wiser counsel prevailed. If he wanted Chrissie, he must tread warily.

He stopped himself abruptly. His thoughts were following a risky path, and he couldn't risk being hurt again. It would finish him this time. Harriet could make him content, even happy, but Harriet could not bring love vividly alive with just a touch. Ah well, Charles sighed. Perhaps marrying Harriet would be the saving of him. Who could tell?

He pressed a fist just underneath his quickened heart, and presently the ache eased and allowed him to concentrate on other matters. Putting their heads together, Charles and Chrissie went methodically through William Kennedy's papers to see exactly what was to be done to make the Kennedys solvent.

* * *

In the next few days Chrissie struggled with the intricacies of the typewriter Charles had loaned her and thought longingly of her niece Georgina, who was an accomplished typist. She was tempted to write and ask for Ina's help.

Ina, however, was otherwise engaged at the moment. The sudden appearance of Bruce Cameron, the Australian owner of the farm, had brought about a crisis in her life.

'He wants to sell the farm, Ina,' her mother whispered tragically, when the Australian had been closeted all morning with George Kennedy.

'Oh, no!' Ina was aghast. The mountain air suited her father's weak chest and he was much better in health. He loved the farm, and rarely left it except to visit Forfar market. Where would he go if the farm was sold, and who would employ a man in his forties with a weak chest?

Her mother was sobbing quietly. 'It'll be the death of your father if he has to leave the farm, Ina. He's had enough worry as it is, with Hughie running off to India,' Jeannie wept.

There was a scheme forming in Ina's head. It seemed shocking when it first occurred to her, but as she examined the idea more cautiously, she saw it had merits. She went in search of the tall Australian.

She found him leaning on a dry-stone dyke, reflectively chewing a stem of grass and studying his hilly inheritance.

'I want to talk to you,' she said.

He turned lazily and leaned back on his elbows against the wall. He looked amused. 'Fire ahead, I'm listening.'

'Are you married?'

His eyes narrowed. 'No. The right sort of woman's not easy to find in the outback. It's a man's life, hard and lonely. Women can't stick it, unless they're the right sort.'

She stood very straight and slim in her mannish clothes. 'Am I the right sort?'

He fingered his chin doubtfully. 'We-ell . . . I dunno. You might be.'

'Then I'll strike a bargain with you, Mr Cameron. If you want a wife, I'll marry you. On one condition, though.'

'Oh, yeah?'

Ina came closer. She wanted to pierce the cover of those narrowed grey eyes. She wanted to know his emotions, find out what he was thinking. She thought she detected something akin to a gleam of amusement beneath the lowered lids. It encouraged her.

'Please don't sell the farm. Leave my mum and dad in peace to manage it for you. If you do, I'll marry you whenever you like. If . . . if you want to marry me, that is—' she ended bleakly.

Ina thought about Tam, and the blissful life they might have shared in the little sheiling on the breast of the brae, if only he'd waited for her. But that was just a wistful dream now, and Tam's wife was proudly carrying Tam's unborn baby. How different Ina's life would be in a huge, parched country at the other end of the world, living with a stranger she hardly knew. Suddenly tears stood bright in her eyes.

Bruce Cameron alertly noted the tears and wondered at them. This unusual girl didn't seem the weepy type. He couldn't make her out, but he admired her style. Perhaps he had found the woman he'd been looking for to share his tough and lonely life. This tiny farm wasn't important. He'd more than enough land already, back home. If her folk wanted it that bad, it was all right by him.

167

He studied Ina reflectively. She was a no-nonsense sheila with no frills about her, and he liked that. There'd been no mention of love, but he guessed that would grow, given time. Bruce felt suddenly light-hearted, as if a weight had been lifted from his shoulders. This proposal must be unique in outback history. Wait till the boys lounging outside the Billabong store learned he'd gotten himself a little Scotch wife while fighting in the war! They'd be green with envy. Envy was just about the only thing that was green, in sun-parched Billabong, he thought, and grinned widely.

'Yes, Georgie. Your pa and ma can keep the farm. I'll settle for marrying you, girl!'

Ina felt weak with relief. There would be time for regrets later. She held out a hand, and they shook hands on the deal.

It was a milder variety of Spanish flu that had struck down William Kennedy, not the virulent virus that had claimed the lives of old and young that year. It was bad enough, however, to keep the old man indoors for weeks, giving Chrissie free rein in the office. Everything was tidy and orderly now, and she was negotiating with a local seed-crusher for linseed oil. When her father's debtors settled their bills, she would go ahead and order a batch. The overdue statements had been sent out, being greeted with ominous silence. Chrissie decided to send terse reminders to the worst offenders, and fitted paper into the machine. Nimble-fingered, she could type quite well now.

The door crashed open, bringing with it a flurry of December sleet borne on the freezing wind blowing up the Seagate. A red-faced man strode in, icy droplets melting on his macintosh. He flung an envelope on the desk.

'What's the meaning o' this?'

She picked it up. It was one of the invoices she'd sent out.

'Your firm owes my father one hundred and twenty-five pounds, sir. Payment is well overdue. It's all set out quite clearly,' she answered pleasantly.

'Oh, I can read, lassie,' he scowled. 'Mr Kennedy and I had an agreement. I wasnae to pay until the beginning o' March.'

Chrissie raised her brows. 'Oh? You'll have that in writing from my father, I expect, along with a calculation of the interest involved?'

He spluttered and turned beetroot-red. 'Och, no, of course not, I just had a friendly word or two wi' your pa, as usual.'

'I'm sorry, but if you demand such long credit I will add interest. Ten per cent is normal,' she pointed out sweetly.

'What?' his voice rose to a roar. 'You've already plumped a hefty credit charge on my bill, woman! This is extortion.'

'No, sir,' smiled Chrissie. 'It's good business.'

She giggled to herself after he'd gone, still blustering. He'd settled the account with a bad grace and sworn he'd never darken her doorstep again. Well, she didn't need his sort. She could expect more abuse though, because she was a woman in a man's world. Chrissie sighed. Surely there must be honest men in Dundee who'd deal with a woman, without prejudice?

Lloyd George, the Prime Minister, called for a general election within a month of the armistice. He assured the electorate his aim was to make Britain a country fit for heroes to live in, and he wanted to get started right away on the task.

'Well, I'm havin' nothin' to do wi' warmongers like thon,' stated Biddy Murphy, who had the vote for the first time in her life, and was proudly aware of a heavy responsibility.

'Who'll you vote for, Granny?' asked Mary Rose curiously.

'Ah, that would be tellin', pet,' replied Biddy coyly. 'Winston Churchill's a wise-looking cheil, but I'll maybe plump for Neddie Scrymgeour, seeing he's for Prohibition an' the banning o' strong drink.'

She gave her husband a meaningful look. Patrick had been out with several of his merry cronies the night before, and looked sadly the worse for wear.

Sandra and Mary Rose visited their gran once a week to help put the washing through the mangle. That done, they pegged the clothes to the washing line that ran via a pulley from the kitchen window to the greenie pole. The little girls managed this quite well, standing on the coal bunker in the kitchen.

Chrissie insisted on this regular visit, and although Sandra grumbled as a matter of principle, secretly she enjoyed visiting her gran and granda. She could relax and be herself in the tenement flat, and needn't watch her p's and q's all the time. She'd let slip casually to her posh new Academy-friends that her granny lived in the West End. That was near enough the truth, and sounded swanky.

Sandra found life an awful strain these days, keeping up appearances. She was terrified her friends would find out about her lowly tenement upbringing and mock her. They hadn't suspected anything amiss so far, but danger lurked round every corner. Take yesterday, for instance, Sandra had been walking arm in arm with her new bestfriend, Caroline. Caroline's father had a big house in Broughty Ferry with a paddock attached. Caroline owned a shiny, black pony and the riding togs to go with it. Sandra was walking proudly along Brook Street with Caroline, when who should come whistling round the corner but Norrie Gallacher, Sandra's ex-fiancé. She turned icy cold and tried to make herself small so he wouldn't notice. A vain hope, for Norrie had eyes like gimlets.

'Oh, hullo there, Sandra. How're you doin'?' he beamed.

Sandra hauled frantically at Caroline's arm, but her friend had stopped dead, gaping curiously. No wonder, for Norrie had flipped over into a handstand, and was teetering around on his hands, waving his legs in the air.

'Hey you, Sandra! Notice onything? I've left the school and I'm into my first pair o' long breeks. One an' six oot o' Maggie Glancey's, wi' a kirkcaldy strippet shirt thrown in for luck!'

He fell over into the gutter and picked himself up, much muddier but still cheerful.

'Me an' my gran have two rag-an'-bone carties now, Sandra, and we're thinkin' o' buyin' a cuddy an' a flat cart come the spring. Has your ma ony rags or jeely jars the day? I'm payin' a guid price, mind. You could hae a balloon an' a paper dolly free, if I get a wee kiss.'

Sandra turned hot and cold with embarrassment, but maintained her dignity.

'I will inform Ma . . . er . . . Mother. Kindly step aside, boy!'

Dragging Caroline, Sandra pushed past and raced to safety round the corner. Caroline kept looking back curiously.

'Sandra, who was that?'

'Och, just a poor boy my mother gives her cast-offs to,' answered Sandra loftily.

'He's good-looking, isn't he?' remarked her friend.

'Is he? I hadnae noticed,' sniffed Sandra.

* * *

171

In the December election, Mr Churchill won a Dundee seat for the Liberals, in spite of Biddy's vote for Edwin Scrymgeour.

There was peace in the land at last, but the standard of living of Dundee folk didn't improve. Civil war in Russia did away with a lucrative market, and the Indian mills which had prospered during the war took vital work from the city. Men came home from the army full of hope, to find themselves standing aimlessly on street corners while their womenfolk worked. It was demoralising. It took the heart out of a man.

The Spanish flu, mild though it was, had weakened William Kennedy. He was quite content to stay at home and potter in the garden when spring came, and let Chrissie take over the business. She gritted her teeth and worked hard, and managed to scrape a fair living for her father and her children, with her brother Arthur's help. Charles Rankine's advice was invaluable, too. He was one of the few men who didn't condescend when speaking to her, and they'd had some interesting discussions about the jute trade, and the way it was going. Chrissie had gained respect for his views. He was usually right.

She was writing up the ledger and attempting to ignore warm summer sunshine beckoning outside, when Lizzie entered the office. Lizzie held little Sammy by the hand, an unusual occurrence. Lizzie usually came alone, or with Arthur.

Chrissie's son was toddling now. He was pink-cheeked and sturdy, though still rather small for his age. He looked delightful in a white sailor-suit with navy-blue collar. Chrissie's heart gave a lurch, and she held out her arms. The little boy immediately retreated behind Lizzie's skirts, peeping out at his mother with suspicious blue eyes.

The awful truth was that Sammy was afraid of the smiling woman. She seemed friendly and smelled nice, but she held him so close and looked so sad, strange emotions disturbed him and made him wriggle and cry. He wanted to cling fast to Lizzie. He sensed that pretty, smiling Chrissie threatened his security somehow.

Ever since he was a tiny baby, Sammy's sensitive antennae had picked up disquieting signals when Chrissie was near. Undercurrents of emotion emanating from Lizzie and Arthur rocked his happy existence; frowns and whispers behind his back disturbed him. Sometimes he would wake crying in the night, dreaming Chrissie had arrived, and was carrying him away from those he loved.

She was reaching for him now, and he was scared. He buried his small face in Lizzie's comforting skirts and clung on with all his might. Lizzie patted Sammy's curly head.

'I'm sorry, Chrissie, he's shy. He won't let me out of his sight. It's just a phase he's going through, poor lamb.'

She picked up the little boy and held him in her arms. Sammy felt secure there. He sucked his thumb, watching Chrissie warily.

'Chrissie, Arthur's been offered a position in India, at the Titaghur mill. It is a wonderful opportunity for him,' Lizzie announced.

'Oh, Lizzie, I *am* pleased!' cried Chrissie warmly.

Lizzie rocked the child, looking away. 'Yes, we are both delighted. I will go to Calcutta with my husband, Chrissie.'

There was a long silence. A bluebottle buzzed frantically, trapped on the window pane, but that was the only sound.

'And Sammy?' asked Chrissie carefully. Her heart was pounding with such hope she could hardly speak.

Lizzie looked up. 'Chrissie, we've been assured the standard of life in India will be excellent. Arthur has made stringent inquiries, and has talked to others with children who have lived there. They are all agreed the risks involved in taking a young child to India are no greater than those to be faced in this chill climate.'

There was a coldness in Chrissie's heart. A hopelessness.

'You hope to take Sammy to India with you, don't you?'

Lizzie looked miserably uncertain, almost scared. 'Chrissie, he clings to me. He . . . he's devoted to Arthur. What would it do to the child to take him from us now? He would be a sadly distressed little boy who might be emotionally scarred for life. How could you care for him and give him the attention he'd need, while attending to your father's business? It . . . it's impossible, Chrissie. It would be disastrous for you, and the child!'

Chrissie stood up. She slammed the ledger shut with a bang and flung down the pen with such force the nib spattered ink on the blotter.

'Am I never to get my son back? Am I fated never to have him, Lizzie?'

Lizzie was on the verge of tears, hugging the boy. 'Chrissie . . . Chrissie, he loves us,' she pleaded frantically.

Chrissie held out her arms. 'Sammy, I love you so much. Come to me, my darling. Oh, Sammy, why won't you love me?'

He cringed away from his mother and flung his arms round Lizzie's neck, screaming a frantic, high-pitched scream that went on and on. His nightmare was coming true, right here in bright sunshine, and this woman wanted to take him away. Sammy screamed in terror, hardly pausing to draw breath; beside himself with fear.

Chrissie covered her face with her hands. 'Lizzie!

Lizzie, stop him! I can't bear it. I can't! Oh, please, Lizzie, stop him!' she moaned.

Lizzie kissed the hysterical child and rocked him against her breast, whispering to him, soothing him, and gradually the dreadful crying stopped. Sammy lay spent against Lizzie's shoulder, with only an occasional sobbing hiccup to show how great his distress had been.

Chrissie slowly uncovered her face, and the two women looked at one another over the boy's curly head.

'You see, Chrissie? You do see?' whispered Lizzie.

Chrissie nodded. The heart had gone out of her. She wanted to touch her son's soft, curling hair, but she didn't dare in case he started screaming again. She turned away and watched the poor trapped bluebottle beating itself against the window pane.

'You'll write to me, won't you? You'll keep me informed?' she said huskily.

There was a feverish light of gratitude in Lizzie's eyes, and tears on her cheeks.

'Yes. Yes, of course I will, my dear Chrissie.'

The woman and child must have stolen quietly away, because Chrissie roused herself with a start some time later to find she was alone. She sank down on the chair, giving way at last to sorrow and despair.

Bessie had foreseen this, she thought. Oh, if only Papa had heeded Bessie's warning and taken Sammy away from Lizzie, this would never have happened. Bessie would have fought for the little one, helped Chrissie to care for him right from the start. Even now, Bessie would have fought like a tigress to keep Sammy with his mother.

But Bessie had gone. Chrissie had searched diligently, but her dear friend, her nurse, had completely disappeared. She wept anew, for Bessie.

175

A hand touched her shoulder, and she started up, ashamed to be caught red-eyed and weeping. Especially by this visitor: Charles Rankine. Charles was studying her with such a strange expression, as if her sorrow affected him very deeply. She pushed wildly at her disordered hair. She must look such a sight.

'What's wrong, Chrissie? What's happened?' he asked quietly.

The whole story came tumbling out. She hadn't meant to tell him, but she couldn't help herself. It was so long since she'd had a sympathetic ear, so many weary years since she'd had a shoulder to cry on.

'What else could I do, Charles? I love my boy, I want him, but if I take him it will cause so much unhappiness to the child, and to Lizzie and Arthur—'

Her lips trembled and she would have wept again, but he took her hands and held them tight. 'Chrissie, your boy will come back to you one day. He'll come of his own free will, whatever Lizzie says. Until then, you will have to let him go, I'm afraid. The damage was done when you entrusted him to Lizzie as a baby.'

'I blame myself, Charles,' she cried.

He smiled. 'Don't. It's not your fault, or Lizzie's; it's a twist of fate, difficult to understand until time passes, and you see there was a purpose behind it after all.'

He pulled her to her feet. He smiled, and looked suddenly younger, more carefree. 'You need the afternoon off, Mrs Murphy! A breath of fresh air, the sun on your face, and never mind about freckles. I know just the place for a gentle promenade in the sunshine.'

Chrissie hung back. She felt a little breathless at this turn of events. 'But . . . but the ledger, Charles.'

'Blast the ledger!' he said cheerfully. He flipped over the printed card hanging on the glass door so that it read 'Closed' to the outside world.

'Come along, Mrs Murphy, put on your bonnet!'

Charles was in a reckless mood. He set his bowler at a rakish angle and twirled his walking cane.

'Just a moment, Charles—' Chrissie went to the window and opened it. The bluebottle escaped. She turned, smiling. 'I'm ready now.'

What instinct drew him to the harbour? Charles wondered afterwards. They walked along Seagate, which had once formed the heart of old Dundee and now held a different spirit, in the bonded whisky warehouse rebuilt after a disastrous fire. They turned instinctively south, down an old, narrow street realigned by the building of the new Caird Hall, towards Queen Victoria's Royal Arch that led to the bustling commerce of the riverfront.

Harriet Bowers, buying a newspaper in the shadow of the Pillars, looked up just in time to see them disappear. It was like receiving a blow to the heart. She actually put a hand on a stone pillar for support, she felt so shaky.

Charles had been very attentive to Harriet recently, so kind and companionable that her hope and confidence in a future together had grown. He had kissed her. Oh, not passionately or anything like that, but he had kissed her, a gentle, fleeting token. A love token? She had persuaded herself it was. He never mentioned Chrissie. Harriet had discounted Chrissie as a rival, until this awful moment.

He was laughing, looking down at the lovely woman by his side. His bowler hat was tilted, and he looked as young and eager as a schoolboy with his first, calf love. Tears stung Harriet's eyes. She would have given all her medical skill, all the honours won in war, of which her parents were so proud, to have Charles Rankine look at her like that.

He hadn't told her he was seeing Chrissie. That's what hurt most. She could have borne the shock bravely, if only he'd told her he was seeing Chrissie. It was like a betrayal. Harriet walked away blindly. She bumped into others in the pleasant shade of the Pillars, and hardly heard their indignant protests as she walked out into a blaze of sunlight.

'Hey, wifie, you forgot your change!' shouted the newsvendor.

Harriet walked on unheeding. The man shrugged and grinned and cheerfully pocketed the unexpected bonanza.

Chrissie hadn't visited the harbour since they sold her ship. She'd been reluctant to go there in case it reopened old wounds, but now as she strolled along the wharves with Charles, she responded to the familiar atmosphere with nostalgic delight. The smell of sea and tar and fishing nets was just as she remembered, as the little sprat boats went out on the ebb tide to come back with the flow.

There was a neglected old hulk in the berth where the *Christina K* used to lie. Steamers loaded with wood from the Baltic occupied the quays where the whaling ships had once anchored. Chrissie turned away abruptly. Was her ship lying deserted in a Newfoundland harbour, rotting and forlorn?

Further along, men were unloading a jute ship newly arrived from India, dockers swarming round the bales. Chrissie paused to watch, thinking anxiously of her nephew Hughie. There had been no word of him for months.

'My niece, Georgina, has married an Australian, did you know? It surprised us all, it was so sudden. George and Jeannie must be lonely, with Ina so far away and Hughie seeking his fortune in India,' Chrissie remarked lightly, trying to hide her misgivings from her companion.

'There are great opportunities for young people in both those countries, Chrissie, one so old and the other so new.' Charles smiled down at her kindly, and somehow she felt comforted, less anxious about her niece and nephew. They would survive. They were Kennedys!

It was pleasant, walking in the sun. They left the docks, laughingly dodging a pug engine chuffing along the rails, and strolled along by the riverside. The marine parade stretching before them to the railway bridge was one of the finest in the country, a popular walk. Charles stopped and leaned his elbows on the sea wall, watching the *Fifie*, the ferry linking Dundee with Fife, forge its busy path across the river. He was completely happy, acutely aware of Chrissie beside him. This afternoon had sealed his fate for good or ill. Charles had made up his mind.

He watched a small fishing boat battle against the strong tidal rip, flowing down through the bridge towards the open sea. He knew he had a battle of his own to fight.

'Chrissie, I want to kiss you. I want most desperately to kiss you. I want to take you in my arms and never let you go. I want to marry you, Chrissie,' Charles told her quietly, his heart beating crazily, an uneven, palpitating beat.

Chrissie had been happy and content until that moment. The pleasure of warm sunshine on her face and the soothing lap of water against the sea wall had been enough. Now Charles had spoiled the perfect afternoon, forcing her to face a momentous decision that would alter her life.

Oh, she liked him. More than that, she felt warmth in her heart for him, tenderness and pity. But these emotions were pale shadows of the love she'd had for

Danny. How could she marry Charles, when she felt only fondness for him?

And then there was Harriet. Harriet loved Charles staunchly, and would be the perfect wife for him. Chrissie turned to face him, and they looked at one another.

'Charles, I don't love you, not . . . not in that way,' she told him frankly.

He had expected it to be difficult, painful. 'I can accept that, Chrissie. To have you as my wife would be enough for me.'

'Would it? I don't believe it would be fair to marry you, without love.' She turned away. 'Charles, Harriet loves you. What about Harriet?'

He smiled, grim and sad. 'I don't love Harriet, not in that way. I can't marry Harriet, without love.' He cast her own words back at her, then touched her bare arm, caressing it.

'It's an impasse, Chrissie, but it doesn't change the facts. I love you, I want to marry you. On your own terms, if I have to.'

She drew her arm away, shivering, although the blood coursing through her veins felt hot. She didn't know what to do.

'Charles, I have to think. You must give me time to think.'

'Of course.' He nodded gravely.

She turned to go, and he would have followed, but she stopped him.

'No, Charles. Please, leave me. I must be alone for a while.'

He looked at her, and the yearning in his eyes made her heart beat faster. 'Just remember I love you, Chrissie. Enough for both of us, my darling.'

Chrissie hurried away, almost running. She couldn't feel any more the pleasant warmth of the lovely afternoon, because she was cold and dark inside. One part of her wanted to marry Charles for the comfort and security of her father and children. Aye, and perhaps for herself, too. How wonderful to have his strength behind her to face the worries she must face day after day. But it wasn't a fair bargain for Charles, without love. He deserved better.

She was in terror in case she hurt him again. And yet, whatever she decided, she feared she must hurt him. Yes, and Harriet too. How could Chrissie marry Charles, without wounding her dear friend Harriet?

Chrissie let herself into the office. Automatically, she took off her hat and opened the ledger and sat staring unseeingly at the columns of neat figures. Presently, a shadow darkened the glass door, and she looked up.

Harriet came in quickly. Quite composed, she looked at Chrissie. 'I've been waiting for you to come back. I must talk to you, Chrissie.'

Chapter 9

Harriet sat in the chair reserved for visitors to the office.

'I saw you out walking with Charles just now, Chrissie.'

'Yes, it was such a beautiful day. Charles took me to the harbour. I hadn't been there since Papa sold the *Christina K*, you see, and . . . and, oh, Harriet, I'm . . . I'm sorry!'

Chrissie felt so guilty, and yet her behaviour had been beyond reproach. She'd done nothing to encourage Charles Rankine. His proposal had taken her completely by surprise.

Harriet smiled. That took considerable effort, but nobody would have guessed. 'Chrissie dear, don't apologise. You've helped me out of a very awkward situation, you know.'

'Have I really?' Chrissie looked mystified, and Harriet laughed.

'Yes, dear! I'm very fond of Charles, and I've flirted with him shamefully since I came home. Mama and Papa haven't helped, sending frequent invitations to dine, as if Charles and I were already engaged. I'm sure the poor darling feels almost duty bound to marry me now, although he doesn't really want to. If he did propose to me, I couldn't think how I was going to refuse without hurting his feelings badly. When I saw you two together this afternoon I realised I'd found a perfect solution to my problem, Chris. You can take Charles off my hands!'

Chrissie stared at her friend in bewilderment. 'But you're in love with him. You mean you'd refuse to marry him?'

'Yes, of course! For a woman, marriage means total commitment to husband and home, but that's not possible for me. How could I abandon my medical career when so much remains to be done?'

'But, Harriet—'

Chrissie would have argued, but Harriet pressed on hurriedly. 'You see, Chris, I looked after women workers in a munitions factory for a short time before I went to France, and was shocked to find many were suffering from chronic complaints which could have been cured easily if caught early enough. Call it false modesty and ignorance if you like, but they wouldn't dream of consulting a male doctor and would rather suffer in silence. I want to change all that.'

There was a zealous glow in Harriet's eyes which Chrissie found convincing. Chrissie herself had seen millworkers shrug off 'women's troubles' lightly and go on working until they dropped, rather than visit a doctor or pay precious sixpences for a consultation.

She eyed her friend thoughtfully. 'Well, there's certainly a great need for doctors who understand the trials and tribulations of womenfolk.'

'I knew you'd understand, Chris,' Harriet said, smiling her relief. She'd succeeded in her objective, which was to convince Chrissie she was a dedicated career woman. Now she must remove herself from the scene and leave Charles free to marry the woman he loved. Harriet was reasonably confident Chrissie would accept Charles, if he proposed. The lot of a penniless widow was hard, and Chrissie had her children and an ageing father to consider. Harriet leaned forward, eager to press home the advantage.

184

'Charles has always been fond of you, Chris. I know you rejected him once and resented his interference in your married life, but you've made friends with him again. Please, look after Charles for me. I wouldn't want him to be lonely when I leave.'

'Don't worry, Harriet dear. Charles won't be lonely, I'll see to that,' Chrissie promised recklessly.

Harriet stood up. If she didn't get out of the cramped little office soon she feared she would break down. The role she had played for Chrissie's benefit had proved very demanding. She smiled brightly.

'Well, that's a weight off my mind! Now I can go ahead with an easy conscience and accept the job I've been offered. A doctor in Glasgow contacted me recently, looking for a lady practitioner to care for women patients on his panel. Apparently my name had been suggested by one of my former colleagues who knew of my interest in the effects of malnutrition. There should be plenty scope for research in the Glasgow slums!'

Chrissie shuddered. She was sad because Harriet must leave Dundee, and distressed at the thought of her dearest friend working in Glasgow's dreadful slums. Harriet would work her fingers to the bone trying to solve insoluble problems bred by deplorable living conditions. Chrissie wished Charles had fallen madly in love with Harriet; it might have been the saving of her.

'Oh, Harriet. Please take care,' she begged tearfully.

'I will, don't worry. Just make Charles happy, Chris. That's all I ask.'

Harriet hugged Chrissie and walked out of the office.

Outside, the rumble of wheels heralded the arrival of a string of horses and carts laden with jute bales. She

185

stood patiently to let them pass, her eyes misted with bitter tears. A tramcar clanged and clattered fretfully as it ground along the rails, hindered by the carts. Harriet paid no heed to the impatient sounds and earned a glare from the driver, as she crossed the road in a daze.

She walked past shops whose windows usually delighted her with a display of the latest fashions, but she didn't pause. The streets were thronged with shoppers enjoying the sunshine, but Harriet scarcely noticed. Charles had never loved her. Their love affair had been just a figment of her imagination, her hopes of married life with husband and children only a wistful dream. Harriet faced up to the reality, then turned away resolutely to begin quite a different future.

Christina Kennedy married Charles Rankine in the autumn of 1919, when the leaves had turned rich gold and fallen in rustling carpets on the pavements. It was a quiet wedding in an empty, echoing Broughty church, but Chrissie's two daughters were proud little bridesmaids and her brother George served as Charles's best man.

Chrissie's other two brothers were not present. Ernest had married his Geraldine in the States, and was living in Detroit. Arthur had sailed for India a month ago, accompanied by his wife and foster son.

William Kennedy, wiping his eyes with emotion throughout the simple ceremony, was delighted by the match, but there was a marked snubbing of the happy occasion by Charles's relatives and friends. Chrissie had heard it whispered she was marrying Charles for his money. Broughty folk recalled she'd always been a wilful lass who'd broken her father's heart by marrying a common juteworker. A taste of the hard life in the slums had turned her into a wee gold-digger out to catch a rich husband, they said.

As for Charles Rankine, he wanted his heid examined, marrying a poverty-stricken widow with three bairns, when there were plenty of rich young Dundee spinsters eminently more suitable.

Chrissie paid no attention to the blethers, although they were near enough the truth. She didn't love Charles with the single-minded passion reserved for Danny, but she liked and respected him, and above all she needed a man beside her to help with her father's struggling oil business. She'd been completely honest about her feelings and Charles had been willing to settle for what she could give. On that understanding, Chrissie had agreed to marry him.

Chrissie had dreaded telling Sandra and Mary Rose that they would have a step-father, but the two girls had taken the news well. A week or so before the wedding, they'd had a frank discussion with Charles, from which Chrissie had been excluded.

'What shall we call you?' Sandra asked Charles seriously. 'We can't call you Daddy, because we already have a daddy in heaven. Papa is out of fashion, Father sounds a bit too swanky, and Mr Rankine sounds awful – like a school teacher.'

Charles considered this very important question with due care. 'Don't you think Charles sounds nice and friendly?' he suggested.

'Charlie is my darlin', my darlin', my darlin'—' warbled Mary Rose cheerfully.

'Yes, indeed, Mary Rose. Charlie would also be acceptable between good friends such as ourselves,' agreed Charles, endeavouring to keep a straight face.

Sandra studied the new man in her life critically. He was tall and thin and so unlike her beloved daddy in heaven, it was impossible to make comparisons. Maybe that was a jolly good thing, thought Sandra wisely.

'How big is your house?' asked Mary Rose.

'Quite big. It has four public rooms, eight bedrooms and two bathrooms. Oh, and a large conservatory tacked on to the drawing room.'

Mary Rose's face fell. 'Och, isn't there a kitchen for Mummy to work in? Where's she to do the cooking if you haven't got a range, and how's she to do the washing if there isn't a tub? Is there a steamie nearby?' she demanded.

Charles smothered a grin. 'Your mummy won't work in the kitchen any more, dear. Cook and the maids will see to the meals and housework, and the washerwoman will do the washing and ironing for us all.'

Sandra's eyes grew round as she viewed dazzling possibilities.

'Charles, is there a paddock?'

'Yes, there's a field behind the house. Would you like a pony, my dear?'

'No, thank you, Charles, not a pony, just riding togs. But only if you can afford it, mind. I'm afraid they're awful expensive. Caroline's cost a whole pound,' Sandra replied. She was scared stiff of horses, but she dreamed of cutting a dash in Broughty Ferry, walking out in riding togs.

Mary Rose climbed hopefully on to his knee. 'I'd love a pony, if you wouldn't mind, Charles, but I'm no' fussy about the togs. You could pawn something out of your big hoose to buy Sandra's togs an' my pony. If there's two bob to spare you could maybe buy a pussycat to catch mice an' rats in your hoose, an' a wee canary in a cage to whistle an' keep you cheery, like my granny's.'

'I'll consider the good advice concerning my finances and general well being, and let you know my conclusions in due course, my dear girls,' said Charles gravely, a twinkle in his eye.

* * *

Her daughters scattered rice with joyful abandon as Chrissie and Charles came out of church. It felt strange to be another man's wife.

Thinking of that other wedding years ago, overwhelmed Chrissie with sadness. Although she laughed merrily and shook showers of rice from her hat, her eyes glistened with tears. Charles's hand tightened on hers, and Chrissie smiled at him gratefully. He was attuned to her every mood, and guessed she was thinking of Danny at this poignant moment. The knowledge hurt him, yet his eyes were clear and kind and brimming over with love for her.

They were to spend the honeymoon at Beechyhill, Charles's family home near Broughty Ferry. His father and mother had died some years previously, and Charles had been living there on his own. He looked forward to the house coming alive again, reawakened from its gloomy silence by children's voices and happy laughter.

William Kennedy had offered to look after his two granddaughters for a week, to give Chrissie and her husband a little time to themselves. Chrissie had found a housekeeper for her father, who had refused point blank to leave his home and move in with his daughter and son-in-law. The housekeeper was a pleasant and kindly woman, though not a patch on Bessie, Chrissie thought privately.

Chrissie watched her father and the children set off for home in a cab, the two girls waving frantically. She was suddenly terrified by what she'd done. It seemed a great risk: could she be happy marrying without love, and more important, could she make Charles happy? She thought for a few panicky moments that she could revoke the solemn vows she'd just made and resume her former life, then she turned towards Charles. It was too late now for regrets.

Charles helped Chrissie into the motor car and climbed into the driver's seat. Tooting the horn joyfully, he set off. Chrissie waved to George and Jeannie and a few curious onlookers, then set her face resolutely towards her husband's house.

The servants were waiting by the front door, drawn up in a line according to rank. Chrissie counted a cook, parlourmaid, housemaid, a nervous, wee tweeny who looked frightened out of her wits, and a string of elderly gardeners, all eager to cast a critical eye over their new mistress.

Charles looked apologetic. 'I'm sorry, dearest, but most of the female domestic staff left during the war to work in munitions.'

'You mean there were more?'

He laughed as the car drew to a halt. "Fraid so! Come and charm your household, Mrs Rankine!'

Chrissie did her best, exchanging a word with everyone and being careful to note the wee tweeny's name. She was encouraged to overhear a whispered exchange between cook and head gardener as she and Charles passed into the hallway. 'Well, the new mistress seems a decent-like woman, Archie. No' the stuck-up, bossy kind, and that's a God's blessing!'

'Aye, Cookie, she'll no' wear the breeks in this hoose. Maister Charles has a mind o' his ain.'

Having passed muster with the staff, Chrissie paused and looked in wonder at the carved staircase and ornate ceilings.

'Come, I'll show you round your home, Chrissie,' Charles offered, watching with a smile.

Holding her hand, he led her from room to room. Chrissie was staggered by the beautiful furnishings and the size of the apartments, but the ultimate luxury to her mind was the downstairs cloakroom and two sumptuous bathrooms upstairs. She couldn't help comparing these with her tenement flat in Lochee, and the single tap of which Danny had been so proud. They'd shared an outside toilet with five other families. With an effort, she stifled a feeling of outrage.

'And this is your bedroom, Chrissie. I've had it redecorated for you. Mine is at the end of the passageway,' Charles was saying, opening a door at the head of the stairs.

She went slowly and thoughtfully into the rose-pink room with its delicate, feminine draperies and mirrored dressing-table, and stood looking round in silence. Then she wheeled to face her husband, colour in her cheeks.

'Charles, I appreciate what you've done for me, I thank you for it with all my heart, but you're making a grave mistake. I won't be a wife in name only.'

He put his hands on her shoulders and looked down at her, and his face became sad, the happiness wiped from it.

'But you don't love me. You told me so. I can accept it, Chrissie. I'll make no demands on you, I promise. It's enough to have you near.'

There was warmth in Chrissie's heart for this husband who would place his wife on a pedestal, untouched, if that's what she wanted. But that was no marriage. It was a mockery of marriage, and she'd have nothing to do with anything so false and hollow. She put her arms round her husband's waist and looked into his eyes.

'There are many different ways of loving, Charles. I want to be your wife and your companion. I want to be beside you always, good times and bad, not kept apart like a golden goddess in a rose-pink shrine.'

His arms tightened round her. She reached up and kissed him gently on the lips. His shoulders began to shake, and it took Chrissie a minute or two to realise he was laughing.

191

'Oh, Chrissie! Chrissie, you're wonderful! I spent hours agonising over this blasted pink bedroom, and I needn't have bothered! Och, I could've saved the money and bought myself a new car!'

Still laughing, Charles grabbed his wife by the hand and led her merrily along the passageway to his room.

What a holiday the honeymoon was for Chrissie, who was waited on hand and foot by the staff. Charles drove her around the countryside, for the weather was clear and fine. They visited Forfar, and the hilly, little burgh of Kirriemuir. From the Northmuir, Chrissie viewed the foothills of the Grampians with pleasure, lifting her head to let the keen wind blow through her golden hair. Charles watched, enchanted. He was happy, even though he knew Chrissie had only married him for the security he could give. That thought lay always at the back of his mind. He wouldn't let himself forget, even when she kissed him with an appearance of warmth.

He was too happy. It couldn't last, he thought suddenly with a cold shiver that had nothing to do with the chilly wind.

'Come, Chrissie. Let's go home, my darling,' he said, putting an arm protectively around her shoulders.

Chrissie went willingly. Tomorrow the holiday would end. Her two little daughters would arrive and Charles must return to work at the factory. Their married life would begin in earnest.

Sitting together after dinner that night by a roaring fire, Chrissie began making plans. Her hands were busy, embroidering roses on a dress for Mary Rose.

'The children can go to school with us in the mornings, Charles. We'll all travel together in the car, but I shall come home from the office by tram, as usual, in the evening.'

He glanced up from the paper he'd been studying.

'But, Chrissie, you don't have to work in the office any more. I'm putting a clerk in your father's office to handle day to day transactions, and keeping an eye on everything myself. There's no need for you to work, my darling.'

She stopped sewing, the needle poised in mid air. 'But I must work, Charles. I've always worked.'

He smiled. 'Not any more. Your place is here, Chrissie, running our home.'

She stood up in dismay, the sewing falling off her lap. 'But the house runs like clockwork without me. I'll check household accounts and order stores and see the linen's mended, of course, but there's nothing else for me to do. I'm waited on hand and foot. I can't lead an idle existence, Charles, it would drive me daft!'

'I gather married ladies meet regularly for tea parties. Some of them play bridge in the afternoons, go shopping, or do a little voluntary charity work. I'm sure you'll find some way of filling in your time, darling,' Charles said.

His fiery wife frowned furiously. She stamped her foot with frustration. 'I won't waste my time with gossip and cards! I've no intention of buying clothes I don't need and giving condescending help to poor folk! Put a clerk in Papa's office by all means, Charles, I could do with a help, but I shall work in the business as usual, and you won't stop me!'

Charles looked aghast. 'Chrissie, it isn't done for the wife of a man in my position to work. What will people say?'

'I don't care what they say. I've never paid the slightest attention to malicious blethers, and neither should you!'

He sat in silence for a moment. 'I'll tell you what they'll say. The men will blame me for not keeping my wife in order, and the women will condemn me for sending you to earn a living for yourself in the wicked world. Either way, I can't win. You and Harriet will start a Dundee revolution between the pair of you!'

'Good! It's not before time!'

She plumped down angrily into the chair and picked up her sewing, stabbing the needle into the delicate fabric.

Presently, she peeked across at her husband cautiously and met a humorous eye and raised eyebrows. Chrissie's lips began to twitch. She couldn't stop herself, his expression was so comical. She was only just beginning to plumb the depths of her husband's sense of humour, so different from Danny's boisterous wit. She burst out laughing.

'Oh, Charles! You've been teasing me all the time!'

'Just a wee bit. You're so beautiful when you're angry,' Charles admitted.

Chrissie returned to her father's office, and found her task lightened by the clerk Charles had employed. Joseph was a pleasant man in his late fifties. He worked quietly and efficiently and didn't mind taking orders from a woman. Joseph and Chrissie got along famously.

Dundee had been badly hit by the post-war recession in trade. The crowds of grey men standing aimlessly at street corners grew steadily larger, and now more women were out of work too. There were many families cold, hungry and poverty stricken that winter. Charles Rankine struggled to keep his workers in full employment, but he worked long hours himself and called upon all his resources to do it.

A slump in jute orders hit Chrissie's firm too. She was at her wits' end casting around for new outlets for oil, when Charles inadvertently gave her an idea. He usually arrived at the office to drive her home. Chrissie had become used to motor travel and was determined to learn how to drive when Charles had the time and energy to teach her.

He'd been having problems with the old car, and that day was no exception. He cranked the starting handle, cursing beneath his breath. When he got the engine to turn over and splutter to life, he climbed in beside Chrissie.

'Charles, cars need oil, don't they?'

'Yes, to lubricate the engine. That's what's wrong with this one, it's burning too much oil. The engine needs to be re-bored.' Charles glanced at Chrissie curiously. 'Why d'you ask?'

'Couldn't Kennedy's supply lubricating oil for engines as well as whale and linseed oil? Trams and buses must use a lot. Why can't we tender for that market, Charles? It must be growing daily with so many vehicles on the road.'

He changed gear thoughtfully. 'I'll look into that, Chrissie. We can cost it out and try our luck, if it's feasible.'

Harriet's little writing desk had gone with Chrissie to Beechyhill. Chrissie wouldn't be parted from it. She wrote regularly to Ernest in America, George on the farm and Arthur in India. She also wrote to her niece, Georgina, far away in Australia. Chrissie's letters were a godsend to Ina, a precious link with home as she struggled to adapt to life in the outback with her taciturn husband.

One day, Chrissie sat down and wrote a simple letter to Sammy, her little son, telling him how much she loved him and thought about him every day. Sammy was still too young to read, of course, but Chrissie hoped Lizzie would read the letter to him. She illustrated the pages liberally with drawings. She drew Mary Rose riding her pony and Sandra decked in riding togs that had never seen a horse's back. She sketched the tabby cat purring by the fireside, and the canary trilling in its cage. Chrissie discovered she had an aptitude for sketching, and smiled to herself as she read over what she'd written. It read like a storybook. She hoped the little boy would enjoy stories about his big sisters and their pets, and think more kindly of his mother in consequence.

Lizzie Kennedy frowned when a bearer brought a letter addressed to Sammy in Chrissie's handwriting. Lizzie had just finished tiffin and was dining alone that afternoon, a punkah fanning the air gently above her head, keeping the room pleasantly cool. The ayah had removed Sammy for his nap, which was a blessing, because the little boy would have been interested in the letter from Scotland, and Lizzie might have been forced to read it to him. She stared at Chrissie's letter thoughtfully. Who was to know it had ever arrived? The bearer couldn't read.

Sammy had forgotten all about his mother, and seemed much more settled. He'd grown into a sturdy little boy who seldom cried, and played happily all day long. His ayah adored him and Sammy was devoted to the kindly Indian woman. Was it fair to remind the little boy of this threat to his security? Should she read Chrissie's letter to him, and risk upsetting the child?

Surely not, thought Lizzie. Time enough for the problem to be faced when the boy was older and more able to cope with the complex situation.

The decision made, Lizzie couldn't bring herself to destroy the letter. She crossed to the bureau she'd had shipped out to India, and unlocked it. One of the ornamental brackets inside was not what it seemed; it could be pulled out like a drawer to reveal a roomy secret compartment behind. Lizzie slipped the letter inside, and quickly closed the opening.

Just in time. She heard Arthur exchange a word or two in Urdu with the stoic punkah-wallah who operated the fan hour after hour, then her husband came into the room. He had brought with him two strangers who hovered shyly in the background.

'Lizzie dear, a most remarkable thing has happened!' exclaimed Arthur excitedly. 'You know I've been on the lookout for my nephew, Hughie, and had no idea where to start? Well, my dear, Hughie walked into my office this morning right out of the blue, and here he is, Lizzie!'

Lizzie studied the young man Arthur presented to her. Hughie was very brown, dressed more like an Indian than a European. Only the clear, blue eyes reminded her strongly of Chrissie, as Hughie came forward and dutifully pecked Lizzie's cheek.

'Hullo, Auntie Lizzie! I'm jolly glad to arrive at Titaghur at last! I've had loads of hair-raising adventures on the road from Bombay. Remind me to tell you all about it sometime,' Hughie grinned.

Lizzie thought him a little too forward for a youth of eighteen. There was no deference in his manner, and in her position as one of the leading mem-sahibs of the community, that rankled. Hughie put his arm round the other visitor Arthur had brought to Lizzie's elegant bungalow.

'Auntie Lizzie, this is my wife Jani. I met her at the mission in Tundragore, and we fell in love at first sight. The missionary performed the marriage ceremony just two months ago,' Hughie announced happily.

Lizzie gazed at the beautiful, dark-eyed Indian girl in Hughie's arms and tightened her lips ominously. Lizzie Kennedy could foresee many problems lurking ahead.

Charles continued his desperate battle to keep Rankine's factory going. Indian mills had captured the market for cheaper jute cloth, but Charles was one of the first in Dundee to adapt his looms to cater for a higher quality product. The factory began producing carpet yarn and jute backing for linoleum, and Rankine's workforce was kept employed during hard times. Chrissie's firm was doing modestly well, supplying an increasing demand for engine oil.

The country had grown disenchanted. Lloyd George's promise of a better life for heroes had not materialised. The cost of food rose, and wages fell. Men who'd fought bravely for their country couldn't find work.

There were riots in Dundee when the Jute Trade Board announced another cut in basic wages. Men and women were bitterly angry, and the whole country was in a ferment of discontent. In October 1922, Lloyd George resigned as Prime Minister.

The prospect of a General Election on 15th November 1922 excited Chrissie. She remembered she'd carried a suffragette banner with Harriet before the war. Now she was over thirty and had the vote for the first time. It seemed a great triumph for women.

Dundee was in the grip of election fever. There were crowds of men at every street corner and outside every pub, arguing loudly. There were six candidates standing for two Dundee seats, but one candidate was seriously ill. Winston Churchill had just had his appendix removed in London and was in no state to electioneer in the seat he'd held for the past twelve years. His loyal wife, Clementine, took over. She arrived in Dundee with her infant daughter Mary, and set to work.

Clemmie was appalled by the misery she saw as she campaigned in the city. She wrote and told her husband so. She wrote of the unrest abroad in the town, and how she couldn't blame the poor folk. She experienced that bitter unrest at first hand: in the newly opened

Caird Hall, her large audience barracked her speech repeatedly, and in Larch Street Hall the meeting she bravely attended ended in uproar.

Enough was enough. Winston got out of his sick bed and travelled north. An LNER engine in gleaming green and black livery brought him to Taybridge Station, but he fared no better than his Clemmie, in the noisy hustings.

Sandra found the election procedure wildly exciting. All the schools closed on polling day, and gangs of children roved the streets, shouting slogans. Mary Rose was out riding on her pony, but Sandra put on her best coat and hat and walked into town to join in the fun. The scenes in front of the Pillars were enthralling. Crowds of people watched Mr and Mrs Churchill drive up Reform Street in a bright-red car, smiling and waving. Everyone was in high spirits on this fine November day. William Gallacher, one of the other candidates, was doing a tour of the polling booths in a gaily decorated horse-drawn landau. It was like Band Day at Magdalene Green, only better and noisier, Sandra thought happily.

There were crowds of rival supporters in the streets, waving banners and shouting slogans, and as she'd expected, Norrie Gallacher was among them. He spotted her and came over waving a placard. He'd grown tall.

'Mind now, Sandra. Vote for my namesake, Willie Gallacher!' he urged.

'Och, save your blethers. I'm only fourteen,' said Sandra cuttingly.

He scrutinised her from head to toe. 'Oh aye. I can see you're just a wee lassie yet. Never mind, I can wait!'

'You neednae bother, Norrie Gallacher. I've tellt ye till I'm tired, I'm to marry a rich toff!'

Sandra put her nose in the air and marched off, leaving him grinning after her.

* * *

Chrissie and Biddy Murphy were excited, and a little stunned, when the man they'd voted for polled many more votes than Mr Churchill.

The millgirls went shouting through the streets, wildly excited because their vote for a man of peace had changed the course of history.

'Neddie Scrymgeour's in!' was the shout all round the town.

Chrissie soon had another reason for rejoicing. She found she was expecting a baby, after a long, fruitless wait. In fact, she had quite given up hope of having the child she and Charles wanted. Now the doctor had confirmed recent suspicions, and Chrissie could at last tell her husband the joyful news.

'Oh, Chrissie, my dear!' Charles pressed his fist to his chest to stop the painful hammering of his heart. He was overjoyed, of course, but suddenly very frightened for the safety of his wife and child. Women died in childbirth, and babies were always at risk.

A little of Chrissie's joy faded at his expression. He had turned pale with shock and didn't look well. He'd been working too hard as usual. She knelt beside his chair and took his hand.

'What is it, dear? Aren't you pleased?'

'I'm delighted, Chris, but absolutely terrified at the same time! Oh, darling, will you be all right?'

Holding his cold hand, she felt a protective warmth flow from her hand to his. It was a warmth that came straight from a heart deeply touched by his concern. She laughed at him gently, with emotional tears in her eyes.

'Oh, Charles, I'm as strong as a horse! Promise me you won't worry any more.'

And so he promised faithfully and tried to hide his fears from his wife, but he worried in secret. Another worry, another weight of heavy responsibility on his shoulders, another ache in his brave heart.

Biddy Murphy died as she had lived, quietly, and with no fuss. Patrick found her sitting in her chair as if she slept, a gentle smile on her lips, her old hands folded across a framed photograph of the soldier laddie she'd loved so dearly.

Chrissie wept many sorrowful tears for her dear friend and mother-in-law, and insisted on attending the funeral although she was heavy and awkward, with the baby on the way. Charles would have gone with her, but Chrissie asked to be alone, and he respected that. The girls were at school, and she let them bide there. They were sad enough as it was, to lose their beloved granny.

And what a turn-out there was, at the cemetery on the high hill! Patrick wiped his nose emotionally as he surveyed the crowds of folk who'd been blessed by Biddy's kindliness at one time or another, and had come to bid her a last farewell.

'Oh, she'd have been fair dumbfoundered to see a' the folk, Chrissie. She'd have been proud. Mind you, she'd have been worried sick in case she hadnae bought enough biled ham to go the rounds afterwards!' Patrick sniffed.

At the end of the moving service, Chrissie lifted her head and dabbed tears from her eyes. The crowds were dispersing quietly, while Patrick was led away, comforted and supported by a phalanx of Murphys. A shadowy face turned towards Chrissie for a fleeting instant, staring at her from a group of dark-clad, shawled women on the path.

Chrissie felt the blood drain from her cheeks. Bessie! Was that Bessie? She started forward, pushing her way through the mourners.

'Oh, please . . . let me pass! Bessie! Bessie, where are you?' she called frantically.

She broke through, pushing the startled millworkers aside, but there was no sign of anyone resembling her old nurse. Chrissie looked round wildly. A movement caught her eye on the side of the hill behind a tombstone, it was the shawled figure of a woman, hurrying away.

Chrissie stared. But it couldn't be Bessie. Why would Bessie run away from her without a word? It made no sense, and yet she'd glimpsed Bessie's face in the crowd.

'Bessie, wait!' Chrissie called again, then set off in pursuit.

She was soon forced to rest, despairing of ever catching up with the figure hurrying ahead, but despite the slowness of the pursuit, she was always quick enough to catch sight of the woman in front, hobbling along.

Once, the woman paused and glanced over her shoulder, then broke into a shuffling run as if terror-struck.

It couldn't be Bessie. This was a scraggy, old, ragged woman. Chrissie hesitated. What was the point of going on, alarming the poor old soul?

Maybe she knew where Bessie could be found. Chrissie hurried on. If only she could run, but she dared not, she was so heavy with this bairn, heavier than she'd been with any of the others. The doctor had warned her it might be twins.

'Wait! Please stop!' she called out desperately, but the old soul had reached the Hawkhill and was gaining confidence amongst a maze of wynds and pends. Chrissie thought she'd lost her, then suddenly she jouked out of a close-mouth, with a woman shaking a fist after her, and shuffled away down the street towards the slums they called the Blue Mountains. Chrissie hurried on.

She caught sight of the tail of a skirt disappearing into the darkness of a filthy close strewn with rubbish. Taking a deep breath, Chrissie plunged after her. Ahead, a broken door creaked gently on its hinges, and beyond she could hear someone panting, gasping and coughing. Chrissie pushed open the door cautiously and stepped into a miserable room. The woman she'd been chasing was crouched upon the bed, huddled into the shawl, coughing.

Chrissie went over to the crouching figure and put a hand gently on her boney shoulder.

'Oh, I'm so sorry, chasing after you like this, but I'm looking for a woman called Bessie McCutcheon. I'm sure I saw her at the funeral. Please, do you know where Bessie is?' she asked.

The woman didn't answer. Clutching the shawl close to her chin, she turned slowly and stared up at Chrissie in dumb silence.

Chapter 10

Chrissie gave a heart-broken cry.

How could this poor old soul be bonnie, buxom Bessie? Yet it was. The eyes were the same, and in the gaunt features a recognisable ghost of bonnie Bessie McCutcheon still lingered. Chrissie flung her arms thankfully round her old nurse. 'Oh, Bessie dear, I've found you at last!'

Bessie sobbed. 'I didna want you to! Oh, Chrissie, I didna want you to see me brought so low! That's why I ran.'

Chrissie glanced round the rat-infested cellar with a shudder. She could smell the damp decay of the awful place. She knew Bessie to be a proud woman, but the old Bessie would have abandoned pride long ago rather than live in such conditions. Chrissie simply couldn't imagine why Bessie hadn't asked for help. William Kennedy would have welcomed her back gladly.

A fit of coughing overcame poor Bessie. Chrissie held her close as a hacking cough tore at Bessie's chest. When the paroxysm of coughing eased, Chrissie laid Bessie on the bed. She took off her own warm coat and covered the sick woman in its thick folds. Bessie mumbled a weak protest.

Chrissie smiled. 'You bide here and keep warm, Bessie. I'm away to get a cab. I'll not be long. I'm taking you home with me.'

Bessie shook her head frantically. 'Aw, Chris, no,

dinna! Away home and forget you saw me. It's too late, lass, I'm done for, and glad to join poor Biddy on the hill. Ah, Chrissie, dinna bother wi' me, I'm feenished.'

'Never give up, Bessie McCutcheon! Heavens, Bessie, you lectured me often enough when I was a wee lass, so just heed your ain good advice for once. The boot's on the other foot now, Bessie!'

Chrissie paused in the doorway.

'Don't run away, mind. I'll be back in a tick!'

For the first time came a glimmer of Bessie's smile. 'Bless ye, Chrissie, I'll no' run. I couldna take another step if Auld Nick himsel' was after me.'

Chrissie walked as fast as she could to the cab rank in the Nethergate. There had been cabs for hire in front of the Steeple for as long as she could remember, horse-drawn hansoms in her girlhood, but today she approached a gleaming black motor car. Its proud driver had just put an extra shine on the bonnet with a duster.

Chrissie asked him to drive to the dilapidated area of Hawkhill where she'd just left Bessie, and the driver looked uneasy.

'If those Hawkhill bairns scratch my paintwork, Missis, it'll be you that pays,' he warned.

He drove the short distance, and Chrissie left him waiting apprehensively at the close-mouth, eyeing a crowd of barefoot youngsters who'd appeared as if by magic. Bessie had sunk into a dull stupor, and stared at Chrissie vacantly. Chrissie had to support her to the waiting cab. The driver shot out of his seat when they appeared, his face a picture of horror. The bairns cheered.

'You're not taking that dirty auld wifie in my cab!'

'Oh, yes, I am!' Chrissie jumped on the running board and managed to load Bessie into the back seat. The driver was hopping with anxiety.

'I'll have to fumigate my motor after her! This cab is used by clean, decent folk!'

Chrissie calmly ordered him to drive to Beechyhill, and slammed the door in his face.

The good address effectively silenced the driver, and there wasn't a chirp out of him until they pulled up outside the house. He sheepishly helped Chrissie to lift Bessie out of the car, and beamed when she paid the fare and added a generous bonus for his trouble.

Agnes, the parlourmaid, appeared in the hallway to see what all the stir was about. She shrieked when she saw Bessie.

'Oh, Mrs Rankine! What are ye doing wi' that auld tinker?'

Chrissie gave her a stern glance. 'Don't judge folk too hastily, Agnes, my dear. This was a fine woman once, and will be again, if I have my way of it. Please help me take her upstairs.'

Between them, they carried Bessie up. Chrissie ordered the maid to run a hot bath while she undressed Bessie, then dismissed the girl with orders to burn the wretched rags. Agnes left with alacrity, the clothes well distanced between finger and thumb, rushing downstairs to tell Cook and the others the news.

Tenderly, Chrissie bathed Bessie and wrapped her in a warm bathrobe. Gently, she shampooed the matted hair and carefully teased out the tangles, combing Bessie's hair in front of the bedroom fire until it dried and shone silver in the fireglow. All the while, Bessie remained in a bewildered state, only reviving enough to groan, 'Ah, Chrissie, I'm so ashamed!'

Chrissie put Bessie to bed in the rose-pink guest room with a hot-water bottle at her feet. She sat by the bed holding her hand and gazing anxiously into Bessie's face. Bessie lay moaning and coughing, and it was clear she was very ill. Presently, there was a tap at the door and Charles came in.

'What's going on, darling? Agnes is having hysterics about tinkers in the guest room—'

Chrissie explained quickly what had happened. Charles looked grim as he studied the sick woman, for he remembered Bessie in her heyday, presiding over Captain Kennedy's household. She was in a piteous state today.

'I think we should call the doctor without delay, Chris,' he said gravely.

The doctor looked gloomy after he'd examined Bessie.

'Asthma and chronic bronchitis, aggravated by near starvation.' He sighed heavily. 'Aye, Mrs Rankine, I've seen many poor souls like her recently. Her symptoms are similar to the bronchial fever that millworkers call "mill-hoast". Has she worked in the mills, d'you know?'

'I shouldn't think so. She told me once, mill dust made her ill.'

The doctor patted Chrissie's shoulder. 'Well, she's in the best place now, thanks to you. It's not so much the illness that worries me, more her lack of spirit. The poor woman seems to have no will to live. I'm afraid she could just fade away.'

All night Chrissie kept watch by Bessie's side, soothing her when she tossed restlessly; rejoicing when at last she drifted into a more natural sleep. When dawn's grey light filtered into the bedroom, Chrissie studied Bessie hopefully. There was no change. Sadly, Chrissie went to the fireplace and added another lump of coal to the glowing embers. She put her hands to the small of her back, wearily easing her heavy body.

'Why, Chrissie, you're having a bairn!' Bessie cried

out suddenly. Startled, Chrissie looked up. Bessie was lucid again, at last.

'Of course I'm having a bairn! Why else would I come seeking you, Bessie McCutcheon? You know fine I can't have a baby without you!'

A gleam appeared in Bessie's eye and grew brighter as she studied Chrissie's shape.

'My, I'll need to get my strength back quick by the look of ye!'

Chrissie laughed joyfully. 'The sooner the better. You'll take some broth today for a start. Cook's broth is nearly as good as yours, Bessie!'

Bessie grinned weakly, then coughed.

Chrissie waited until the spasm passed, then sat facing her on the bed. 'Bessie, I'll never understand why you didn't ask us for help months ago.'

Bessie was silent a long time. 'Your pa never wrote me a reference, Chrissie. I thought at the time maybe he didn't want to 'cause I was impudent about Mistress Lizzie. Nobody'll take on a servant without references, ye ken, so there was nothing for it but the mills. I trekked eighteen miles to a jute factory in Kirriemuir, for I thought country air would suit my chest, but it made no difference. It's the dusty air in the factory makes me wheezy, you see. I got very sick, then I got the sack an' trailed back to Dundee completely skint, and lived like a beggar. Oh, I was ashamed to be seen!'

Chrissie hugged her. 'Bessie dear, Papa would have given you an excellent reference if only you'd asked. He didn't want you to leave, but you know how proud and stubborn he is. I suppose he was so upset, he forgot all about a reference. I'm so sorry, my dear!'

Bessie closed her eyes wearily. 'Och, begging for crusts taught me which side my bread's buttered.' Presently she stirred again. 'Chrissie, did you get your wee laddie back?'

'No, I didn't. Lizzie and Arthur took him to India.'

Bessie tut-tutted. 'I knew fine, Mistress Lizzie wouldn't let Sammy go once she'd got her hooks into him.' She lay thoughtfully silent for a bit. 'I was glad when I heard you'd married Charles Rankine at last, Chrissie. He's a fine gentleman. When's the bairnie due?'

'The middle of May. The doctor's sure it's twins.'

'Twins!' Bessie's eyes opened wide. 'Heavens, Chris, I'll need to get oot o' this bed!' She lay staring at the ceiling, grinning delightedly. 'Twins, eh? Weel, Chrissie, fancy you wi' two wee twins!'

The twins were born a fortnight early, on 28th April 1923, two days after Lady Elizabeth Bowes-Lyon married her Prince Bertie and became the Duchess of York. News of the royal wedding had delighted Chrissie, who had fond memories of Lady Elizabeth as a young woman at Glamis. It seemed a good omen when Chrissie's babies chose that week to arrive.

Charlotte was first to put in an appearance, followed by Ewan. Presently, Bessie placed the two wee bundles in Charles Rankine's arms.

'There, Mister Charles, a fine lad an' a bonnie lass. A gentleman's family, all in one go!'

He hugged his children. 'Oh, Bessie, this'll be enough for me. I couldn't go through all that again!'

He carried the babies tenderly to his wife, looking so proud and awkward, Chrissie almost laughed outright. Watching Charles with his children flooded Chrissie with such a surge of love for her husband, the laughter died in her throat.

Danny had captured her youthful heart, but the mature emotion she felt for Charles at this magical moment was quite different, and no betrayal of her dear, dead Danny.

She longed to tell Charles of her discovery, but

Bessie hovered nearby and the doctor was buttoning his shirt-sleeves, and so the moment passed. Charles placed the babies safely in Chrissie's arms, then kissed her.

'Thank you, my dearest darling, for our two lovely bairns.'

She looked at her man with tears in her eyes, and couldn't manage a word.

1923 was an eventful year for Dundee. The new city hall, donated by one of the city's benefactors, was officially opened by the Prince of Wales. Sandra went with Mary Rose to view the festivities on a damp, showery day, and promptly fell in love with the handsome young Prince. She hung over the barrier hopefully, trying to catch his eye.

Mary Rose knew all the signs by now. She giggled. 'You haven't a chance, Sandra. He's to be King one day, so he has to marry a princess or a titled lady. Queen Mary wouldn't let you in the door of Buckingham Palace. You're not pan-loafie enough.'

Sandra tossed her head. 'I could be, if I set my mind to it.'

At that moment she caught sight of Norrie Gallacher. He was half-way up a lamp-post to get a better view, and was yelling cheek down at her as usual. Sandra stuck out her tongue defiantly at her tormentor, just as the Prince of Wales happened to glance in her direction.

Amid all the fuss surrounding the new Caird Hall, there were rumours the old Town House, designed by William Adam, was to be demolished. Nobody believed such blethers. Why would the high heid yins knock down the dear old Pillars? They'd stood at the very heart of the city for years, sheltering its citizens and housing the Tramway offices and some good, wee shops.

There were plans to raise a war memorial on top of the Law, the ancient volcanic pinnacle dominating the city. Charles told Chrissie squads of navvies had already started laboriously digging a road through Dudhope Estate, winding up the steep slopes to the top of the hill.

Chrissie was nursing the babies at the time, for Charles always headed straight for the nursery when he came home. Bessie was installed in the nursery to help his wife care for the twins, and this had proved a very happy arrangement. Bessie grew stronger and more energetic day by day, and the twins were her pride and joy. Today, while their parents chatted, she lifted the babies one by one from Chrissie's lap and tucked them cosily in their cots.

'The memorial's to be built to the winning design in the competition thcy held recently, Chrissie.' Charles knew the news must waken sad memories for his wife, so he hurried on. 'They say it's an impressive design, and the monument's to be built of Cornish granite, a stone that's particularly white and enduring. There's to be a beacon on the top, and it'll be seen for miles when it's finished, as a constant reminder of the men Dundee lost in the war.'

She was quiet a while. 'How strange, Charles. Danny and I used to go courting on the Law when we were youngsters, and he claimed he'd be famous one day and they'd raise a statue for him on top of the Law. And now they'll do it. Danny was joking, of course, but it's strange all the same.'

Charles turned away, struggling with a wretched sense of inferiority. He hadn't been deemed fit to be a soldier, because of the fever that had damaged his heart in childhood. That cruel white feather, sent during the war to a sensitive man, had left wounds that would never heal.

He sighed. 'Danny was always the better man, Chrissie.'

She put her arms round him and kissed him. 'Not better, my dearest. Never better. You kept the factory going for men to come home to. That took great courage, too.'

Some weeks after the birth of Charlotte and Ewan, Chrissie received two letters from India by the same post. The first was from her sister-in-law. The tone of Lizzie Kennedy's letter was effusively joyful.

> So you have a dear baby boy to call your own at last, my dearest Chrissie – and a lovely little girl as well. I cannot find words to tell how delighted we were to have your letter with news of the twins' birth. Arthur asks me to send his fondest love to you all.
>
> You must be so busy and happy, my dear. I quite envy you the hard work of caring for your two little ones. Sam is such an independent six-year-old, Ayah is not permitted to tie so much as a shoelace!
>
> Sam attends an excellent European school, and can already read and write. The head of the school is a man after my own heart, Chrissie, and the standard of education is so good we have decided not to send Sam to school in Britain. I have campaigned long and hard for good teachers to be sent out to teach expatriate children, and it seems I have succeeded.
>
> We will keep Sammy in India to complete his education, knowing you have your own dear youngsters to care for now . . .

Chrissie crushed the letter angrily.

We will keep Sammy; calm as you please! The cool cheek of the woman! Chrissie shook with futile anger.

And another thing: Sammy could read and write, but had made no attempt to answer Chrissie's loving letters. That's what hurt her most.

Recovering somewhat, Chrissie ripped open the second letter with trembling fingers, and found it was from her nephew, Hughie. The whole family had been vastly relieved to hear of Hughie's reappearance in India. George and Jeannie had been so overjoyed to find their son was safe and well, they'd taken the news of Hughie's marriage to an Indian girl quite calmly.

Hughie's letter was short, and Chrissie detected bitter undertones.

Jani and I have decided to leave India for good. We have suffered many hurtful slights and insults from Jani's people, and mine, and don't feel welcome in this country. Uncle Arthur kindly gave me employment in the mill, but I'm no land-lubber, Auntie Chrissie. My heart's not in the job and I long to be at sea again. I have made friends with the captain of a jute ship, who suggests I should join his ship and take a mate's ticket eventually. Who knows, I may be ship's captain myself one day! I shall work my passage on my friend's ship, and bring Jani to Dundee with me.

Please, dear Aunt Chrissie, could you find a place for Jani to stay? I must sail with the ship when it leaves Dundee, and will have little time for house-hunting . . .

Chrissie took the problem of Hughie's wife to Charles. Lizzie's letter she kept prudently to herself, for she knew it would infuriate her husband.

Charles frowned thoughtfully. 'There's the lodge,

Chrissie. It's stood empty since old Henderson died last autumn. Jani could stay there.'

Chrissie hugged him delightedly. 'Darling, that's perfect! I can make sure Jani's not lonely while Hughie's at sea. What a kind man you are, Charles. What would I do without you?'

'Oh, you'd manage, dear,' he answered lightly. He knew she was a resilient and capable woman, who ran her own successful family business with very little help from him. Chrissie didn't really need him, Charles thought sadly.

Ewan Rankine was just a little lad when he learned he had an older brother. Chrissie told the twins about Samuel, their half-brother, as soon as they were old enough to understand. The news made no impression on Charlotte, who was perfectly content to be petted and admired by her half-sisters, and had no need of further attention, but Ewan was thrilled.

Chrissie had tried hard, but couldn't hide her feelings as she told the two little ones about Sammy. Ewan was an unusually bright and perceptive child, and his mother's sad expression worried him. Her sadness cast a shadow over Ewan's happy existence so he pretended to play with the tin motor-car Hughie had brought him from Hamburg.

He pushed the car along the patterned carpet. 'Brrm, Brrm, Brrm!' he went, so his mother would think he didn't care two hoots about Sammy being far away. Anything to stop her looking so sad.

Chrissie watched the little ones play. Sammy was lost to them, too, but they didn't care. She sighed. Well, who could blame them?

But Ewan did care. His heart sang. He had a big brother called Sammy, who for reasons Ewan couldn't grasp, lived in India. Oh, if only Sammy lived in

Dundee, Ewan thought. They would have such fun. They could climb together into the high branches of the monkey-puzzle tree. Ewan had tried yesterday, but Bessie'd had hysterics and he'd fallen off and skinned his knees.

That night when Bessie was hearing the twins' prayers, Ewan slipped in a special one which he kept to himself. Please God, bless my brother, Sammy, and bring him home soon, Amen.

Then he lay contentedly while dear old Bessie tucked him in and kissed him. Ewan didn't feel lonely any more in this family of girls.

He had a brother!

The years seemed to fly. The twenties was a frantic decade, in which life speeded up, whirling some into a heedless round of pleasure, others into the very depths of despair. Grimly, Charles kept Rankine's going through strikes and depression, patiently fostering links forged long ago between Dundee and America. His brother-in-law, Ernest, was a great help to him. He was a successful man in the States now, with a happy, growing family, and a stake in the carpeting and upholstery of automobiles manufactured in Detroit.

Harriet's writing desk was in constant use, for Chrissie was a loyal correspondent. From Harriet's hurried scrawls in response to Chrissie's beautifully penned efforts, Chrissie gathered her friend was running a clinic in one of the most deprived areas of Glasgow. She was fighting against poverty, disease and prejudice with all her considerable skill and dogged determination.

'Sometimes I'm even daft enough to believe I'm winning,' wrote Harriet ruefully.

Chrissie had news to pass on to Georgina in Australia, concerning Jani. Hughie and Jani had a little boy called Jamal, now aged three, but looking after her son was not enough to keep Jani occupied. She'd sought out Chrissie diffidently, holding the dark-eyed boy by the hand.

'Aunt Chrissie, there is a small shop to let opposite the school. I am thinking it could be a good business, with newspapers and sweets and groceries. I have little to do now Jamal is not a baby and Hughie is at sea for many long months. Would it offend Uncle Charles if I leased the shop and worked in it? Would it be seemly for the wife of a First Mate, do you think?'

'Jani, I worked for many months in a grocer's shop myself. I think it's a wonderful idea!' Chrissie had answered, smiling.

'And you can guess what the Broughty Ferry folk call Jani's little well-stocked shop, can't you?' Chrissie wrote to Georgina. 'Yes, that's right, my dear – Jani a'thing!'

William Kennedy was a very old man, but still spry and lively. Secretly, he thought his granddaughter, Sandra Murphy, the loveliest lass in the whole of Dundee, though he'd never tell her so.

Sandra loved visiting her old grandda. William had taken Biddy's place in her affections, poor Patrick having drunk himself to death years ago.

'Sandra, that skirt's scandalous short,' complained William, when his stylish granddaughter appeared one day, showing her shapely knees.

Sandra laughed merrily and admired her dashing silhouette in the mirror above the mantelpiece.

'It's the latest fashion, Grandda. Skirts are worn short, if you have the legs for it.'

'Lassies didna have legs in my day,' he grumbled. 'And look at your hair, cropped short like a wee laddie's. Young ladies used to put their hair up when I was young, nowadays they let their hair doon once they leave the school!'

She kissed him fondly on his bald patch. 'Poor Grandda! I'm afraid you'll never get used to the idea that I'm a flapper, and proud of it!'

'Sounds mair like a daft wee fish.' He heaved a sigh. 'Aye, the Kennedys are long-lived, but that's a mixed blessing, my lassie. Times change, your friends slip awa'. All the whaling skippers are gone, bar me. What I'd give to see the whaling fleet go sailing up-river just once more. The bonnie *Balaena*, the *Eclipse*, the *Active*, my ain lovely *Christina K*!'

'That's the brooch Mum always wears, isn't it?' asked Sandra curiously.

He wiped his eyes with his hanky. 'Aye, your mother knows how it feels to love a ship, because the *Christina K* was hers, too. A ship's only baulks o' timber, sheets o' metal, an engine and the pull o' wind in the canvases, Sandra, but somehow love grows in ye for it. When you love your ship and lose her, it's like a part of you goes with her for ever.'

The visit to her grandda sobered Sandra, and she walked home instead of taking the tram, to the detriment of her high-heeled shoes. When she reached Beechyhill she had cheered up, and was in plenty of time to prepare for the tennis dance that evening. Life was a whirl of parties, sport and pleasure; and pretty, popular Sandra was in the thick of it. Ostensibly, Sandra helped run the household for her mother, having completed a year's course at domestic college followed by six months typing and book-keeping. In reality, the household ran itself perfectly smoothly, leaving twenty-year-old Sandra plenty of scope to enjoy herself.

She ran lightly upstairs to her room. Bessie had laid out Sandra's new dance-dress on the bed. It was a short-skirted, daring gown of midnight-blue satin encrusted with dark-blue beads and finished with a deep, swinging

218

fringe round the hemline. The whole creation was supported by thin shoulder-straps. Sandra could well imagine the startling effect against bare, creamy-white shoulders, and long, silk-stocking-clad legs.

Belle o' the tennis ball, that's me! she giggled.

The thunder of hooves broke into Sandra's thoughts. She glanced out of the window and smiled tolerantly. Mary Rose was returning from her daily gallop along the sands, fair hair tousled, pink cheeks glowing.

Affectionately, Sandra watched her young sister guide the horse expertly into the stable-yard and slide from its back. Mary Rose patted the beast's neck and kissed it. Sandra turned away, shuddering.

'Wow!' exclaimed Charles, when a vision of loveliness descended the stairs later that evening in a waft of 'Evening in Paris'. 'Er . . . a bit daring, isn't it, my love?'

'Oh, Charles, you sound just like Grandda!' Sandra wrinkled her nose in disgust and wrapped herself in a dramatic black-velvet evening cloak lined with white silk. 'Ready, Charles?'

He crooked an arm. 'Your carriage awaits, princess!'

Laughing, they swept out together to the waiting car.

After Charles had deposited Sandra at the dance hall, she cast an expert glance around and sighed. The same old crowd of boring youths gaping goggle-eyed at her, and a gaggle of her green-eyed girlfriends eyeing the dress. Och, sometimes she wondered why she bothered!

And then she saw him.

Even without the tuxedo and fashionably baggy Oxford bags he was wearing, he would have stood out from the common herd. He was tall, with an aristocratic air of boredom that made Sandra catch her breath. As if he'd sensed her interest the young man looked up and their eyes met. His eyes widened and the bored look disappeared. Sandra hardly dared to breathe, but he came across as she'd known he would, and was even more breath-taking at close quarters. He smiled, his eyes still studying her, admiringly.

'Excuse me, but do you do the Charleston? The band is just striking up, and it's my favourite dance.'

It so happened the Charleston was one of Sandra's accomplishments. She'd practised the steps night after night to the sound of the gramophone, much to the amusement of Chrissie and Charles, who'd laughed at her antics until the tears ran down their cheeks. She'd mastered the dance at last, though, and could Charleston with the best of them.

With a smile, she took his hand, and they were off, dancing so energetically that the other dancers cleared a space and clapped and cheered them on. When the dance ended, they collapsed into one another's arms, laughing.

The young man looked down at her. 'You're jolly good. I didn't expect to find such a good dancer in a place like Dundee.'

She could tell by his accent he was English, and looked at him archly. 'We are very civilised in Scotland, you know!'

He laughed, taking her arm and guiding her towards the buffet table. 'Let's sit this one out, and you can tell me all about yourself.'

They ended up sitting cosily on a turn of the main staircase, eating sausage rolls and drinking the innocuous fruit punch served up traditionally at the tennis dance. Sandra introduced herself, but they talked mostly about him.

'I'm named after my father, Sir Roderick Stirton. The eldest son is always called Roderick. It's a sort of family

tradition, like inheriting the title and the family estate,'
he told her.

'You mean you'll be Sir Roderick, one day?'

'Well, Sir Roddy, probably. I'm an informal sort of
chap,' he smiled.

Sandra played with the stem of her glass, her eyes
cast down thoughtfully. 'You must be rich.'

'I've never thought about it, to be honest. My
allowance never seems to go far enough.'

He went on to tell her he'd taken a degree in
economics at Oxford, and was now preparing to enter
the family textile business. 'Cotton spinning mostly, but
I'm in Dundee to get an insight into the linen trade. My
uncle, William Weatherall, is a shareholder in one of the
mills here, and I'm staying with his family.'

Sandra was excited. 'I know the Weatheralls. They
live quite near Beechyhill, our house!'

He took her hands and gazed into her eyes. 'Then
I hope we shall see a great deal of one another,
Sandra.'

'Oh, yes, Roddy, I hope so!' Sandra answered breathlessly. Her heart was singing like a lintie. She had met
the rich, young gentleman of her dreams, and fallen
head over heels in love with him.

They arranged to meet next day in Smith Brothers'
Tearoom, and after that they met nearly every day,
playing tennis at the tennis club, or walking dreamily
by the riverside. For Sandra, it was an enchanted time
during which the sun always seemed to shine. It must
have rained in the weeks they spent together, but she
didn't notice. She was in love for the first time, and she
wanted to keep her loved one all to herself.

Chrissie could hardly fail to notice what was going
on. She came across the young couple now and again,
but Sandra was so absorbed in her young man she didn't

even notice her mother. It worried Chrissie, and she determined to broach the subject tactfully.

'I saw you yesterday in Reform Street with your friend, my dear. He looks a nice young man. Why don't you ask him to tea, so that we can all meet him?' she suggested.

Sandra's heart sank. She'd been trying to protect her tender love from the ridicule of her boisterous family. They could so easily spoil everything by teasing her, and thus break the enchantment. The twins were a lively pair of scamps who led Bessie a merry dance. Charlotte was always up on her tippy-toes, dancing around, and was quite liable to break into a Highland Fling for the benefit of an English visitor. Ewan spent most of his time climbing into the tree house the gardener had built for him in the monkey-puzzle tree, and usually emerged filthy, with skinned knees.

Mary Rose was less of a risk, being completely absorbed in her horses, but even *she* was liable to turn up at table cheerfully muddy and unkempt, and humiliate poor Sandra horribly. Sandra met her mother's eye, which had a certain determined glint she recognised. She sighed and gave in.

'Oh, very well, Mum. I'll bring Roddy to tea tomorrow.'

Roderick Stirton's visit to Beechyhill was strewn with pitfalls where Sandra was concerned. He'd no sooner arrived and been introduced to Chrissie in the drawing room than Charlotte appeared, dressed in a kilt outfit. She laid down two crossed walking sticks and proceeded to do a wildly energetic sword-dance for the Englishman's benefit. Her twin brother watched, grimacing horribly.

Roddy raised his brows and whispered to Sandra. 'I thought you said Scots were civilised!'

'That's enough, Charlotte!' Chrissie said firmly. She frowned at her son. 'If the wind changes, your face will stay that way, Ewan.' She turned to their guest, smiling. 'Don't pay any attention to these scamps. You'll stay for high tea, won't you, Roddy?'

Sandra looked agonised. 'You mean dinner, of course, Mother!'

Her family were letting her down, and she was mortified. She stood up and smiled at Roddy. 'My step-father keeps a small stable of horses, Roddy. I know you're interested in horses. Would you like to see them?'

Roddy agreed with alacrity. Her mother had a way of looking at him as if she could see right inside his head, and it made him nervous. He excused himself and went thankfully outside with Sandra. They linked arms. She was a dear girl, and he was madly in love with her. He pulled her into the shelter of the rhododendrons and kissed her soundly.

'I love you. You know that, don't you?'

Sandra nodded happily. 'You keep telling me so, darling. But it makes it very special, telling me in my own home.'

He let her go abruptly, suddenly remembering her mother's clear, blue eyes. Sandra took his arm, and they walked on towards the stables.

Mary Rose had set up several obstacles in the field, and was going round the course on Thrawn Janet, her favourite mare. Sandra and Roddy leaned on the wall to watch, and Sandra swelled with pride as her young sister soared over the jumps on the big, black horse. Mary Rose on horseback was something wonderful to see. She had never carried a whip or riding crop in her life, never jagged a tender mouth with her light hands. Whatever Mary Rose asked of the big animals, they did for trust of their young mistress.

Roddy leaned his elbows on the wall and watched the slight figure with an expert eye. 'Your sister rides well.'

Sandra beamed with pleasure. 'Yes, doesn't she?' She could have hugged Mary Rose. Roddy must have a better impression of their family now.

Chrissie was annoyed. She'd specifically asked her husband to come home promptly at six to meet Sandra's young man, but it was nearly seven-thirty and there was no sign of Charles. It was typical of him. When some problem arose at the works, he forgot about everything else.

Chrissie fumed. If he really loved her he would be home right now, helping to make conversation with Roderick Stirton. It was hard going as time dragged by. Chrissie had developed a pounding headache, and Cook would be grumbling furiously as the meal slowly spoiled.

Sandra kept giving her mother thunderous glances. What had gone wrong? The conversation had become stilted, and even Roddy was running out of topics.

Mary Rose had changed into a blue dress that merely skimmed her slight figure. It was modest, yet somehow disturbing, and Roddy found his eyes being drawn to her unwillingly. She hardly said a word, yet he grew hot under the collar every time their eyes met. His tummy was empty, and loudly growled its discomfort. He shifted uncomfortably in his seat. He'd accepted the dinner invitation, otherwise he would have politely taken his leave. When were they going to dine? he wondered.

Chrissie heard the car arrive at last and gave a sigh of relief.

'Ah, here's Charles!'

She rose and went into the hallway. She was still

annoyed and ready to give her husband a piece of her mind. Sandra was in love with this lad, and the least Charles could do was show an interest in him. Chrissie opened the front door, then stood frozen. It wasn't Charles. It was the family doctor who'd become their firm friend over the years. He closed the car door and came towards her.

'Chrissie, my dear—'

She saw his expression, the compassion mirrored in his eyes, and felt her heart lurch. She'd had this experience before, years ago, this terrible, icy feeling. Her hand went to her heart.

'Is it . . . Charles?'

The doctor reached for her hand and held it in his warm, comforting grip. 'Yes, I'm afraid so.'

'An . . . an accident?'

'No. He collapsed in the mill. I warned him some months ago he was working too hard. Fortunately, they contacted me quickly and I got him to the infirmary right away. He's very ill, Chrissie. I must warn you I don't hold out much hope, my dear,' he said.

She felt her heart start to beat fiercely. Where there was life, there was hope. She felt strong again, ready to fight for her man's life if need be.

Chrissie looked at the doctor. 'Would you take me to the infirmary, Doctor? I want to be with him.'

Chapter 11

Chrissie ran to the drawing room and broke the news of their step-father's illness to her daughters. They were very upset, but fortunately Roddy Stirton's presence helped. Chrissie left Sandra in floods of tears in his arms, while Mary Rose sat numb and pale.

Rushing upstairs, Chrissie hurriedly told Bessie what had happened and left her in charge before dashing outside to join the doctor. He drove down the driveway in a spray of gravel and sped towards the infirmary. The doctor's reckless haste told Chrissie the seriousness of Charles's condition. She hung on apprehensively as the car negotiated the final curve of the steep brae leading to the red-brick building perched high on the slopes of the Law.

But Charles was still alive and fighting. The doctor had a hurried consultation with the ward sister, while the night nurses studied Chrissie curiously. Chrissie turned away, embarrassed by the inquisitive stares. She was dressed in her most expensive dress and wore the beautiful Rankine rubies Charles had given her when they married. She knew she must look opulently wealthy to these hard-working lasses. How could they know that for once she'd abandoned the modest dress she usually wore, in favour of clothes more suited to entertaining Sandra's young man?

The doctor appeared at her elbow. 'There's no change, Sister says. I think I ought to stay, Chrissie.'

She smiled at him. 'It's good of you, Doctor, but you're a busy man. I'll be all right. I'd like to sit with Charles awhile, if I'm not in the way.'

'Chrissie, are you sure? How will you get home?'

'I've a guid Scots tongue in my head. I'll call a cab.'

When the doctor had gone, Chrissie sat outside the ward feeling lost and scared. How could she live without Charles? He was the head of the household in so many ways, and her dearly loved man besides. She'd never found words to convince him she loved him, and now it was almost too late. Angrily, she brushed away tears. While there's life, there's hope.

Sister appeared, very stiff and starchy, but her eyes were kind.

'We gave Mr Rankine medication to ease the pain and make him sleep, Mrs Rankine, and he's not wakened yet. I'd be negligent in my duty if I didn't warn you there's little we can do for victims of heart trouble, but your husband's still fighting, and that's a good sign.'

She led Chrissie to Charles's bed, which was screened off from the rest of the ward. Behind the screens he lay so pale and still Chrissie's heart missed a beat. Sister pulled forward a chair.

'You sit with your man as long as you wish, my dear. I believe it helps patients to have their dear ones near, but be ready to nip out the side door if I tell you Matron's coming. She's a stickler for discipline! Give us a call if you need us, mind.'

Chrissie thanked her gratefully and sat down beside her husband. The screens were pulled round and she was left alone. She took Charles's limp hand and raised it to her lips. There was no response, so she bent and kissed him on the mouth and whispered in his ear. 'Charles, please come back to me. How can I go on without you? I love you very much.'

Still no response. She covered her face and wept

silently. Presently Chrissie heard a whisper of her name, and lifted a tear-stained face to find Charles, conscious, watching her.

'Why are ye greetin', wifie? I'm no deid yet!' he murmured in a broad Dundee accent and a brave ghost of his usual smile.

'Oh, Charles, thank God you've wakened, my darling. I wanted to tell you how much I love you!' she cried.

The smile faded. 'No, you loved Danny. You were honest with me when we married, Chrissie, and I respect you for it. Don't spoil everything with comforting lies, now I'm dying.'

Chrissie's sorrow exploded in wild anger. 'You're not dying, Charles Rankine, and I don't tell lies! Heavens, man, we've been married for years, surely you know by now if I say I love you, then I do! So stop feeling sorry for yourself, Charles. I love you and need you. I'd be lost without you—'

Chrissie stopped suddenly, horrified. What a tirade, and her poor man so ill! Charles seemed to be having difficulty breathing, and she was seriously alarmed.

'Oh, Charles, I'm sorry!' She felt utterly helpless. Should she scream for a nurse? Chrissie saw to her dismay her husband's eyes were wet with tears.

'Charles, you're crying!'

'I am not! I'm trying not to laugh in my fragile state. Folk can die laughing, and I don't intend to.' He became serious again, staring at her in wonder. 'Chris, I believe you really *do* love me! But it took one of your famous displays of spunk to convince me.' He clasped her hand with surprising strength and gave her a long, pleading look. 'You'd never lie to me, would you, my love?'

Chrissie blinked back tears, smiling. 'I swear I've lied to you only once in all the years we've been married, my darling. About the price of this posh dress, Charles. The

229

lady in Smith Brothers assured me it's the latest mode for tea-dancing, and it cost a good deal more than I dared admit to you!'

'I'll sit it out during the tea-dancing, Chrissie, but I don't give a damn about the price. It's so beautiful—' The effort of talking had exhausted Charles, but Chrissie imagined he looked better as he drifted off to sleep.

Throughout the night, Chrissie sat by her husband's side, watching and praying. He slept deeply, hardly moving. Surely that was a good sign?

At last the ward began to waken. Lights were switched on, nurses helped patients to wash, and straightened beds. Night-nurses left, day-nurses came streaming cheerily into the ward like a breath of fresh morning air. Behind the screens, Chrissie listened tiredly to all the bustle. Thankfully, Charles slept on undisturbed.

'Wha's ahent the screens?' a nurse's voice asked curiously.

'It's Charles Rankine, heid bummer o' Rankine's Works. He was brought in last night half-deid. It's his heart, Sister ses. Wheest, though. His wife's wi' him!'

The other voice dropped low. 'Is that right? You mean her that used to work i' the mills and married him for his money?'

'Keep your voice doon! Aye, that's her. Looks like she'll get his siller soon. He gied us an awfy fleg when he was brought in!'

The voices faded as the nurses continued down the ward.

I love him! Chrissie longed to scream after the gossiping girls, but what was the use? Tearfully, she kissed Charles and vowed she'd do everything in her power to care for him and make him happy. She vowed it, not because a trivial remark had touched a tender spot, but because she loved her man dearly.

* * *

The shock of their step-father's sudden illness brought Sandra and Mary Rose much closer. They'd always been affectionate sisters, but their love and concern for Charles created a special bond.

They wept when their step-father was taken ill. Roddy was rather out of his depth, faced with two tearful young women, but rose gallantly to the occasion. He comforted the sisters and persuaded them to eat the excellent meal Cook served up after Chrissie left. He tucked in heartily, and thereby gained the approval of Bessie McCutcheon, who'd appointed herself chaperone in Chrissie's absence.

'Aye, Sandra, that's a weel-brocht-up young gent you've got,' whispered Bessie behind her hand. 'He doesna pick at his meat like some posh folk. Just look at his plate, as clean's a whustle!'

Much later, Mary Rose stood in darkness beside the front porch, watching Roddy kiss Sandra goodnight. The sight made her feel very odd.

She wished she could steal away to the stables to be with her horses. There she would be comforted by the warmth of the uncomplicated animals and the familiar smell of harness and hay.

As Mary Rose watched Roddy embrace her sister, her whole body ached with a new, powerful emotion. At last she could stand it no longer and moved out of the shadows into the light of the porch lantern. Roddy looked up with a start and met a challenging gaze. Something wordless and fleeting passed between them, and he abruptly released his hold on Sandra. Mary Rose came forward and took her sister's hand.

'It's well past midnight, Sandra. I think Mum will stay at the hospital with Charles, and send word to us tomorrow. You can sleep with me tonight if you want.'

Sandra didn't look any too pleased. She'd been

revelling in Roddy's sympathetic kisses, and resented her sister butting in. 'Och, don't fuss, Mary Rose. I'm accustomed to keeping late hours, even if you're not.' She stifled a yawn just in time.

Roddy gave Mary Rose a conspiratorial wink over the top of Sandra's head, for poor Sandra sounded very weary and irritable.

'I'm just leaving anyway, Sandra. I think your mother would have got word to you somehow by now, if the news was bad.'

Sandra sighed soulfully. 'Oh, Roddy dear, you're such a comfort!'

Love for him shone unashamedly in Sandra's beautiful, brilliantly blue eyes. She obviously believed every word he said, and Roddy looked away uncomfortably. Secretly he didn't feel so confident about Charles Rankine's chances. He looked up and met Mary Rose's eyes, and again something leaped between them with the swiftness of light, as if she'd read his thoughts accurately.

'Goodnight, Roddy. Thanks ever so much for being with us tonight,' she said formally.

He nodded and walked away, wondering why his emotions were in such a whirl.

Charles maintained good progress after the heart attack, and three weeks later was allowed home. Then Chrissie became fully aware of her husband's weakened condition. As the days passed, it was borne home forcibly to her that Charles's active life would be greatly curtailed. His weakness made him despondent.

'How could I manage a full day's work in this state, Chrissie? Perhaps the time's come to sell Rankine's.'

She handed him a cup of tea. 'Do you want to?'

'No, but what option do I have? The other directors are past retirement age and would be fine pleased if the works closed, but it's my workers I'm thinking of. They're grand men and women who've been outstandingly loyal to me in difficult times. It goes against the grain to see them on the dole, and Rankine's reduced to a pile of rubble like the dear old Pillars.'

Chrissie sipped the tea thoughtfully for a moment. 'There is a simple solution, dear. You tell me what to do, and I go to the factory and do it.'

He frowned. 'That's putting a great strain on you, my darling.'

'Nonsense! It's a challenge, and I love challenges. Cook, Agnes and Sandra run the household very efficiently between them, Kennedy's needs little attention from me and dear old Bessie dotes upon our twins. I'm beginning to feel redundant. Helping you to keep Rankine's going would give me a new purpose in life, Charles.'

'More likely give you grey hairs, my love!' He stretched his long legs comfortably in front of the fire. It was a chilly day, a cold haar lying grey on the river, and he was glad he didn't have to go out. He considered Chrissie's suggestion thoughtfully. It had its merits.

'Well, it's worth trying, Chris,' Charles decided. 'There's quite a hefty price rise due, and someone has to break the news to our American customers in Detroit. I'll draft a tactful letter, and you can ask my secretary to attend to it. I'm afraid Benjamin Franklin Chester will not be overjoyed!'

'Who's he?'

'Head of Autofibres, Detroit. His firm has dealt with Rankine's for years, but he's a very shrewd chap, firmly believes that if you keep a sharp eye on the cents, the dollars will take care of themselves. He hates price rises.'

Chrissie was filled with energetic vigour, eager to

embark on this new interest. There were also new skills she wanted to master. 'Charles, I want to learn to drive. If I could drive it would be a great help to you. McIntosh could teach me.'

Charles looked apprehensive. 'McIntosh is an excellent coachman, Chris, but I'm not convinced he's mastered the complexities of the combustion engine yet. He shouts "whoa!" when he applies the brakes, and it always makes me nervous.'

Sandra was delighted to have her step-father home, and very relieved when life returned to normal. Her mother's brave efforts to keep Rankine's going and the speed with which Chrissie learned to drive impressed Sandra greatly. She decided she and Mary Rose must learn too.

Sandra drew the line at receiving instruction from old McIntosh, though. Roddy Stirton would instruct them in his own little black Morris.

He agreed equably enough, and lessons began in the environs of Beechyhill to begin with, but as his pupils gained confidence, they ventured further afield. Sandra was especially proud the first time she drove through the city centre with Roddy by her side. The scene looked unfamiliar, a gaping empty space where the old Town House had stood, the ancient buildings and narrow wynds that had formed the Vault, all gone. It was an area of wanton destruction, enough to make a staunch Dundonian weep, but Sandra paid little attention. Concentration was required to dodge buses, tramcars, horse-drawn carts, and an impatient jam of motor vehicles. Roddy was impressed by his pupil's driving. At the first opportunity he instructed her to pull into the side, and hugged and kissed her more thoroughly than he'd intended, a measure of his relief that they'd negotiated all the hazards safely.

'Jolly good show, Sandra!'

Sandra was pleased, but embarrassed. What would folk think if they saw them canoodling? He was English, of course, and couldn't be expected to know well-brought-up Scots lasses didn't hug and kiss in public. Roddy didn't notice anything amiss, but Sandra was relieved when he told her to drive on.

The day after the successful driving lesson, Sandra took advantage of a beautiful morning to walk to Broughty Ferry with a shopping basket over one arm. She had just reached Jani's thriving little shop when her path was suddenly blocked.

'Norrie! What are you doing here?' Sandra demanded of the tall, goodlooking young man.

She hadn't seen Norrie Gallacher for months, had hardly given him a thought since Roddy had appeared on the scene. There was a change in Norrie's demeanour, she noticed at once. He looked grim and serious. She'd never seen him without a cheeky grin.

'What luck! I've been hanging around waiting for you, Sandra.'

'For me?'

'Aye. They tell me you've met your rich man at last. An English toff wi' bools in his mooth.'

'What's it to you if I have, Norrie Gallacher?' She tilted her chin and walked on. He fell into step beside her.

'I saw you yesterday canoodling in the Perth Road. Are you going to marry him?'

Sandra considered the question breathlessly. All of a sudden it seemed vastly important, and her reply a really momentous decision.

'Yes, Norrie. When Roddy asks me, I'll marry him.' She glanced up apologetically. 'I'm awful sorry, Norrie.' Why she must apologise to Norrie Gallacher wasn't quite clear, but it was necessary.

'Don't be sorry. It's me that's daft, hoping and waiting. You never gave me no cuttin's,' he said bitterly.

Sandra felt like crying. 'I telt ye till I was tired, Norrie.
I was sick o' tellin' ye not to . . . to—'

'Love ye?' He wheeled round angrily, stopping her in
her tracks. 'Well, I do love ye, but I'll no' hang around
to watch you marry your rich toff. I'm away to Canada.
I've had it in mind for a while to go there an' try my
luck now my granny's weel provided for. I've bought
her a nice hoose in Broughty, big enough to take a' her
antiques an' bits an' bobs.'

Sandra gasped. 'You never!'

He gave a ghost of a grin. 'There's brass in muck, as
they say. I've got six carts and a scrapyaird, and a tidy
wee removal business forbye. My gran'll never have to
work her fingers to the bone again. There's servants
looking after her now.'

Sandra was stunned. There was nothing left to say.
Norrie held out a hand.

'You be happy wi' your rich toff now, Sandra,' he
growled fiercely.

She took his hand, on the verge of tears. 'Norrie,
could ye no' write to me from Canada to tell how you're
gettin' on?'

He shook his head. 'Better no'. Your man wouldna
like it.'

He held her hand tightly, looking deep into her eyes,
then let go abruptly and went striding off. Norrie didn't
look back, although Sandra watched hopefully until he
was out of sight. Tears blurred her last sight of him.
She had a strange notion she'd lost something rare and
precious. She walked on slowly, chilled in spite of the
warm sunshine.

Mary Rose took to driving less readily than her sister,
because Roddy's presence at her side played havoc

236

with her powers of concentration. At first Sandra sat patiently in the back seat while Roddy instructed Mary Rose. Her sister crashed the gears so excruciatingly, however, Sandra rebelled.

'Poor wee car, that's torture! I'm away in to read my library book in peace.'

After that, Mary Rose and Roddy were always confined alone together to master gear change and double-declutch.

At last Roddy decided his pupil was fit for the open road, and persuaded Mary Rose to head the Morris's bull-nose cautiously towards quiet country roads behind Beechyhill. She began to enjoy herself, birling along empty roads, passing fields of ripening grain waving in the breeze on either side, herds of glossy black cattle grazing peacefully on higher ground. And Roddy by her side.

She wove a daring fantasy that he was madly in love with her, and they were driving off to – she didn't know where. She would go with him any-where. He had just to say the word and off she'd go, trustingly—

'Hey, there's a bend coming up, better change down to third gear,' Roddy warned.

Mary Rose came back to earth with a bump. Flustered, she tried to remember what pedals she should press and which way she should move the gear lever. It was all too much. She tried to brake, but the car went faster. Roddy bellowed with alarm and grabbed for the wheel.

'Watch out!'

The little car failed to negotiate the bend, but fortunately there was an open gate ahead leading on to moorland and they trundled safely through the opening. The vehicle bumped and jolted over uneven ground and came to rest in a clump of whins.

Mary Rose was thrown forward, the breath knocked out of her.

She revived outside the car with Roddy bending over her anxiously. He breathed a sigh of relief when her eyes fluttered open.

'Thank heavens! I thought I'd killed you.'

'It's my fault. Oh, Roddy, is your car damaged?' she sobbed.

'The car's all right. Oh, please don't cry!'

Roddy sat down beside her and put an arm round her, supporting her so that her head rested against his shoulder. She felt warm and trusting as a little animal nestling against him. Her fine, golden hair was delicately scented, tickling his cheek. He looked down at her. What on earth was happening to him? He'd flirted lightly with many girls, he'd imagined himself madly in love with Sandra, but he'd never felt like this before, filled with such a conflict of wild and tender emotion it scared him.

'Mary Rose,' he murmured dazedly. He'd never noticed before, but her name sounded like music.

Mary Rose felt light-headed, yet her mind was crystal clear. She guessed Roddy wanted to kiss her, and if she allowed him to, life would become complicated and difficult. She had only to struggle free and make light of the incident and it wouldn't happen. The choice was hers. But oh, how she longed for his kiss! She didn't move, couldn't move. She lay in his arms, staring at him breathlessly.

'Oh, my darling,' he whispered.

He kissed her. Her first kiss, and yet she responded naturally and without awkwardness, her arms going round his neck with an eagerness he shared, as if she'd waited all her life for their lips to meet. They drew apart at last, laughing with a release of spontaneous joy neither had experienced before.

Roddy hugged her. 'Mary Rose, the first time I met you I was attracted to you. I thought I liked you just because you're Sandra's sister, but there's more to it than that. There's a sort of magnetic attraction between us, pulling us together. Oh, darling, I felt it from the very first moment!'

'Yes, I know what you mean. I can tell what you're thinking, though you haven't said a word. I think I've become part of you now I've met you, and I'll never be completely Mary Rose Murphy again.' She shivered with a sudden premonition of disaster. 'Oh, Roddy, it frightens me terribly. I wish it hadn't happened. I wish we'd never met!'

'Don't say that! I love you.' Roddy silenced her fiercely with a kiss.

There were tears in her eyes. 'Roddy, what about Sandra?'

His expression changed. 'She'll have to be told about us.'

Mary Rose broke down and wept in his arms.

'Please don't tell her, Roddy. Maybe she'll meet someone else soon. We have all the time in the world and I can't hurt Sandra. I mustn't hurt her!'

He held her close, stroking her hair. 'Darling, don't cry. I'll be very nice to Sandra, and won't say a word about us, so long as we can be alone together like this. Oh, Mary Rose, please take ages to learn to drive!'

She laughed shakily. 'Don't worry, I will. I'd rather have horses any day.'

Sandra was quietly preparing for matrimony. She was living in a dream world and didn't notice what was going on in front of her eyes. She was secretly gathering articles for her bottom drawer, delighting in beautiful bed linen and other bits and pieces. Sandra drew the line at studying wedding dresses though. Time enough for that when Roddy popped the question. She was confident he would very soon, because he treated her so gently these days, restraining his feelings admirably.

She could drive perfectly well, and had asked Roddy to concentrate on Mary Rose. Whenever Roddy had time off from the textile course he was attending, he and Mary Rose set off in the Morris. Sandra didn't mind. She smiled affectionately as she watched them go.

Poor Roddy! He was willing to suffer her young sister's awful driving because Sandra had begged him to. How devoted the dear man was, Sandra thought happily.

Charles was afraid he'd flung poor Chrissie right in at the deep end, because the jute trade was in a very bad state and becoming worse. Some jute works had been forced to close temporarily and other were on short time. Rankine's had kept going mainly because of American contracts. Charles was quite pleased to take a back seat in his weakened state. With his staunch assistance, Chrissie appeared to be coping. She had learned to drive remarkably quickly and Charles had bought her an Austin 7, which she'd taken to, like a duck to water. He had to smile, watching Chrissie speed off every morning in the little black car, the twins hanging out of the car window waving to him as they set off with their mother to school.

The twins gave Charles his greatest pleasure, apart from pottering around with wireless sets. He enjoyed helping with home lessons and always read books to them at every opportunity. Bessie didn't approve, and said so.

'Filling the bairns' heids wi' nonsense, Mister Charles!'

'It's not nonsense, Bessie, it's fairy tales!' protested Charlotte indignantly.

Bessie snorted. 'Och, that's one an' the same thing, lovie.'

'Did Sinbad the Sailor go to Calcutta, Dad?' asked Ewan.

'He went pretty nearly everywhere, did old Sinbad.'

Sitting on the rug, Ewan hugged his knees. 'I want to go to India, Dad. I want to see Sammy.'

Bessie wiped her eyes. 'Bless the innocent wee laddie. Mistress Lizzie'll soon put a stop to that,' she muttered.

Charles smiled and ruffled Ewan's hair fondly. 'Maybe you will go to India, Ewan. Charles Lindbergh has flown the Atlantic, the Germans have built airships and there are seaplanes riding out there on the Tay. The world is getting smaller and smaller. I'm sure you'll meet Sammy one day.'

Ewan beamed delightedly, but Charles was left curiously saddened. He couldn't think why.

Chrissie was busy and happy. Her husband had accepted his limitations cheerfully, and her involvement with Rankine's had brought them very close. They were more than husband and wife, they were partners in every sense, she thought as she drove her dear, little Austin 7 through the city towards the office.

There were great changes afoot in Dundee. The city centre was a depressing scene of mud and chaos, but there was a grand new square promised. The gaping hole left by the demolition of the old Town House would be bridged by massive steel beams to support a real piazza comparable to those in Italy. Labourers were working to east and west of the Caird Hall, new buildings were rising, stone wings which would shelter the square and transform this dismal scene.

Chrissie sighed nostalgically for the old days and the historic city she'd grown up with, then scolded herself. Just look at the employment it offered to poor souls who'd been out of work for months! She drove on, heading for Rankine's Works.

'You're in Benjamin Franklin Chester's bad books, Mrs Rankine!' smiled Maisie, Charles's secretary, when Chrissie reached the office. Maisie handed her a letter. It was from Autofibres, Detroit, deploring in strong terms the recent price rise in jute weft yarn. It ended on a sour note.

Who is this Chris Rankine anyway? The price has gone sky high since that guy took over. Send Charles back, will you? He's my buddy!

Yours etc
Benjamin F Chester

Chrissie laughed. 'Maisie, reply to Mr Chester's letter. Inform him the price of jute weft yarn has been somewhat reduced because of judicious buying. Send it with Mrs Christina Rankine's compliments, will you?'

Maisie grinned. 'That'll gie the guy a red face!'

Chrissie donned the white linen coat she wore on her daily inspection of the works. The workforce had stared the first time she made the tour, but now they welcomed it. She collected the mill manager, and they set off. She was nothing if not thorough, starting with the stowers in the warehouse where jute bales rose in tiers, then moving on through batching and carding to what she knew best, the spinning frames in the mill. Chrissie often lingered here, watching the women at work and remembering how she'd toiled on the fast frames, keeping her ends up.

Old habits die hard, and on leaving the mill and entering the factory Chrissie treated the weavers with due deference. The weavers heartily approved of Chrissie in consequence, smiling and nodding regally as she passed by the looms.

'She's no' a real toff, ken, only a half-toff wha used tae work i' the mull hersel'. She kens fine what it's like to ·feed bairns on little mair than ten bob a week. Guid luck tae her an' her puir, sick man,' was the shout.

Returning to her office, Chrissie remembered two letters she'd collected hastily from the postman before leaving home. She settled down to read her mail, noting with surprise that the letter from India was written in Arthur's hand.

Lizzie has been ill, and has asked me to reply to your recent letter. Illness struck her very suddenly, and has left her so weak and helpless the doctors are puzzled as to the cause and treatment of her ailments. I hope and pray it will pass.

We are troubled by strikes and unrest because of the demand for Home Rule led by Mr Gandhi, who was once a perfectly respectable lawyer with a thriving legal practice in Bombay. Goodness knows where it will all end, Chrissie!

Sammy continues to be a comfort and blessing to us both. The headmaster tells us he shows great promise as a budding engineer. Sammy's father was also gifted in that direction, I believe . . .

There was more, but Chrissie skimmed over it. As always, mention of her son upset her. She was sorry to hear about Lizzie's illness, but it didn't bring the day of Sammy's return any nearer. The boy never wrote, and sent no message to his mother. It was as if she didn't exist for him. Her letters to Sammy had gone unanswered, and she never wrote to him now. His stubborn neglect had finally defeated her.

With a sigh, she turned to her niece Georgina's letter, from Australia. It contained happier news.

We have a baby girl! A bouncing 7lbs 6ozs little beaut. We have named her Jean Christine, after my mum and my favourite auntie. I hope you feel honoured! I admit I never wanted children, but Jean Christine is adorable, the only beautiful thing in this hot, barren desert . . .

Chrissie studied the letter thoughtfully. Reading between the lines, she suspected Ina's marriage was not a happy one.

Mary Rose could no longer ignore the situation she was in. It went against the grain for her to deceive anyone, and now something really dreadful had happened which forced a decision one way or the other.

'I'm going to have a baby, Roddy!'

She'd waited until they'd reached their own special place on the moorland, a secluded grassy hollow surrounded by whin bushes, before she told him.

He felt as if his heart had stopped. 'But . . . but I've been so careful after that first time – Mary Rose, are you sure?'

She blinked hard, trying to be brave. 'I've suspected for some time, and I was sick this morning again. Mum was sick in the mornings when she was expecting the twins. It . . . it's a sure sign, Roddy.'

'Oh, my darling!' He held her close. He was petrified, scared. He was twenty-two, not contemplating marriage and fathering babies, yet this awesome responsibility was being thrust upon him. It turned him to jelly.

Mary Rose was sobbing quietly and forlornly. 'I don't mind about the baby. I want your baby. But they'll say I'm a bad girl, a disgrace to the family. I feel so ashamed, so wicked.'

'You're not!' Suddenly he was angry. He wanted to bash the people who would sneer at his lovely, generous

Mary Rose. He wanted to protect her and his baby from the censure of the cruel world.

His baby! his thoughts reeled. A little living creature. His son, his daughter. Roddy's thoughts steadied. He began to plan.

'Listen, love, this is what we'll do. We'll say nothing about the baby to anyone. When I've made the necessary arrangements we'll elope – to Gretna Green, if you like. That's where couples go to get married, isn't it? We'll be married there, then head for my father's estate. Mother will look after you.'

Mary Rose wiped her eyes. The speed of events left her breathless.

'But . . . but that'll cause a sensation!'

He laughed recklessly. 'Of course it will, but that's just the point! They'll think we've run off together because of Sandra. By the time the baby arrives you'll be a respectable married lady living in England and nobody can point a finger at you!'

She was quiet. It was a good idea, a wonderful idea, but—

'Poor Sandra,' Mary Rose said softly.

'Sandra doesn't really love me, I'm sure. She'll get over it,' Roddy said cheerfully.

He felt uplifted, sure of himself. He hugged his woeful little darling. 'Leave everything to me, my sweetheart. I'll see to all the details, you pack your case and be ready to leave the moment I say the word.'

The days sped by once the decision was made. Mary Rose felt strangely helpless, borne along on a tide of events whose course she couldn't change. She obediently packed a small case with a few of her belongings and hid it in a cupboard. The day Roddy told her they must leave was the strangest Mary Rose had ever spent.

Her mother and step-father, her sister, dear old Bessie and the twins, went about the daily round, unaware that this was the last day they would spend together as a happy family. When Mary Rose stole away with Roddy in the wee small hours that night, the family ties would snap, her dear sister's dream of happiness would shatter and Sandra would be shamed and pitied and mocked by cruel folk.

Mary Rose had shed many bitter tears over her horses. She had been forced to take her friend, Caroline, partially into her confidence, and Caroline had promised to exercise Thrawn Janet and Billy until they could be found good homes with kind people. Mary Rose knew in her heart she would never see her beloved horses again. That was another heavy price she had to pay.

The sun was sinking, night drawing closer, the time of parting coming nearer. Tears running down her cheeks, Mary Rose sat at her dressing-table and wrote a letter. A last, simple letter to all her dear ones, asking their forgiveness.

Chrissie found Mary Rose's letter on her plate when she came down to breakfast with Charles next morning. He smiled as he reached for the toast and marmalade.

'A billet doux, love? I haven't missed our anniversary or anything, have I?'

She smiled, but the white envelope addressed in her daughter's hand was vaguely unsettling. Her fingers trembled as she slit it open and read the few short sentences through to the end, her heart turning to ice.

'Oh, Charles!'

'What is it?'

Chrissie had turned pale, and he was on his feet in an instant. Silently she handed him the letter. He read it through swiftly and sank down in the chair. They looked at one another, the full horror of the situation slowly sinking in.

'Oh, my God, Chrissie. What about Sandra?' breathed Charles.

'Who's taking my name in vain?' Sandra laughed. She'd wakened in a marvellous mood. Yesterday she'd bought white satin pyjamas, very chic, very seductive, and laid them in the bottom drawer. It was nearly filled to the top with lovely things carefully folded and scented with lavender sachets. Whenever Roddy asked her to marry him she would say yes. She was ready, impatient.

She paused in the doorway of the breakfast room, wondering why her mother and step-father looked so serious, and why they stared at her so hard. Sandra became alarmed.

'What is it? What's wrong?'

Chrissie's heart ached for her daughter, aye, for both her dear daughters. 'My darling, you must be brave,' she said gently. She held out the letter in silence. It seemed the only thing to do.

Sandra took it as if in a dream. It registered slowly that it was in Mary Rose's careful script. She read it through, then read it through again, although every word was etched firmly in her mind.

She would never forget what it said, never forget the humiliation and shock of that awful moment, the crushing sorrow as all her beautiful plans and dreams crashed around her ears. Most of all, she would never forget it was the sister she'd loved and trusted who'd betrayed her trust and stolen her man.

Sandra's anguish tore from her in a scream.

'Forgive her! She asks me to forgive her! Well, I won't. I will never forgive Mary Rose for doing this to me. I will never speak to her again as long as I live!'

Sandra flung the letter furiously into the heart of the fire and ran from the room.

Chapter 12

Sandra did not cry when she reached the sanctuary of her bedroom. She ached with the hurt her sister and Roderick Stirton had inflicted on her, but she stubbornly refused to cry.

She sat on the window seat and stared out. The first leaves of autumn had fallen, and lay stirring and rustling in the breeze that swept the garden. Winter was coming, and she was glad. It seemed appropriate, the scene should turn bleak and cold to match the ice in her heart.

There was a tap on the door and her mother came in.

Chrissie approached diffidently. She didn't know what to do for the best. Perhaps she'd no right to intrude, but this was her dear daughter and she couldn't keep away. She sat beside Sandra, who didn't even turn her head.

'Sandra darling, I'm so sorry.'

Chrissie's sorrow was sincere. She blamed herself for not noticing what was going on. If she hadn't been so preoccupied recently she might have stopped the elopement in time and saved Sandra this humiliation. The break-up of their happy family might have been avoided. Now it was too late, and Chrissie feared the damage was done.

Sandra stirred. 'It's strange, Mum. When poor, deaf, old Queen Alexandra died I wept buckets, but I've been betrayed by the man I love and my own sister and can't raise a single tear. I'll never speak to Mary Rose or Roderick Stirton again.'

'Don't say that, love. You'll forgive them in time.'

'No, I won't, Mum!' She stood up abruptly and began pacing the floor. 'Oh, I could forgive them for falling in love, but I can't forgive them for keeping it from me. Why didn't they tell me? I could have come to terms with it.'

Sandra stopped abruptly, struggling not to weep. When she spoke it was in quiet, controlled tones. 'I'm going out. I must walk for a bit while I decide what to do. I can't stay in Dundee after this. I'm sorry, Mum.'

Sandra's unnatural calm unnerved Chrissie. She knew how stubborn her daughter could be when her mind was made up.

Sandra walked outside into the chilly autumn morning. Mary Rose and Roddy would be far away, perhaps already man and wife. The thought made her walk faster. She had no idea where she was going, but from habit she turned downhill towards the river. A car tooted behind her, startling her, and Sandra hastily jumped on to the pavement as a Ford saloon drew up beside her.

At first sight, she didn't recognise the woman driver, then recognition dawned. It was some time since they'd had a visit from Harriet Bowers, her mother's best friend, but Sandra had always been fond of her. Mary Rose and Sandra had no aunts on their mother's side of the family, so they'd adopted Harriet.

Sandra forced a smile. 'Hullo, Auntie Harriet!'

Harriet leaned over and opened the passenger door. 'Can I give you a lift into Broughty, Sandra? Hop in, love.'

As her passenger climbed reluctantly on to the running board, Harriet alertly noted signs of unhappiness on the open young face. Harriet was adept at diagnosing misery, because she'd had plenty of practice in the art. Her clinic lay in the Clydebank area of Glasgow, where unemployment was rife and the massive bulk of the largest liner ever built at John Brown's yard lay unnamed and unfinished in silent stocks, casting a black depression over all who saw her.

She smiled at Chrissie's bonnie daughter. 'My, what a lovely young lady you are, Sandra. It's a good job your mother sent me a recent photo or I would have driven straight past.'

'Were you on your way to see Mum and Charles?'

Harriet hesitated. 'No, I'm off to buy fish at Broughty harbour. My mother swears it's fresher.'

She let in the clutch and the car moved off smoothly. Since the twins were born, Chrissie's letters had been few and far between and had given nothing away. Harriet had heard about the severity of Charles's illness from another source, and she was puzzled and a little hurt by her friend's reticence.

'How is everyone?' she asked carefully.

'Fine. At least . . . that is—' Sandra hadn't meant to tell a soul what had happened that morning, but she found herself telling Harriet everything. She poured out all the pain and disillusionment, and even told her sympathetic listener about the articles collected secretly in the bottom drawer.

'So you see, I can't go on living in Dundee with folk pointing me out as the girl who was jilted because the man she loved fell for her young sister. I don't know what I shall do!' Sandra stared through the windscreen, her eyes hot with unshed tears. She wouldn't cry though. It was a matter of pride not to cry.

Harriet pitied Sandra. She could well imagine what the poor lass was going through. Hard work had dulled the ache of losing Charles, but the humiliation of that awful time still lingered. She drove to the harbour and parked on the front. There were fishing cobles drawn up on the shingle beach opposite the fishermen's cottages. It was top of high water, and a jute ship took advantage of high tide to reach its berth. Harriet watched the vessel's progress abstractedly.

'Can you type, Sandra?'

Sandra was surprised. 'Type? Yes, I took a course in typing and book-keeping. I'm not particularly fast, though.'

'That doesn't matter.' Harriet turned in the driving seat and looked at her. 'I need a receptionist at the clinic. Somebody I can trust to handle appointments and file patients' records. Would you like the job? I warn you, it's hard work. You'll see poverty that'll anger you and sights that'll turn your stomach. That's the minus side. On the plus side, you'll meet folk with a couthy humour that'll tug your heartstrings while you split your sides laughing. You'll watch quiet courage that'll humble you for the rest of your days.'

Thoughtfully, Sandra watched the busy commerce of the river, the varnished fishing boats and painted ships, the *Fifie* on its monotonous course in the distance. It would be a wrench to leave the ancient city she loved, but the blood of two brave men flowed in Sandra's veins, as she was well aware. Her grandfather had gone out many times from Dundee into a cruel and hostile environment and returned safely. Her father had left home to sell his life dearly for the peace of the world. Sandra made up her mind.

'All right, Auntie Harriet. I'll take the job. I just hope I'm up to it.'

Harriet grinned. 'You'll do fine, my dear, but please, let's drop the "Auntie". It makes me feel old!'

* * *

252

The Rankine twins were sheltered from the disaster that had split their family, but the sudden departure of Mary Rose followed very soon after by Sandra's trip to Glasgow, didn't escape their notice. Charlotte questioned Bessie, but all she got was a grim tightening of the lips.

'Mind an' pick a guid, honest Dundee laddie when your turn comes, my wee hen,' said Bessie. A warning which made no sense whatsoever to the bewildered little girl.

Ewan had more success. He was a bookworm like his dad, and could be found most winter evenings lying on his stomach in front of the fire, his nose buried in a book. He gleaned a lot of useful information by keeping quiet as a mouse, because grown-ups forgot he was there.

Chrissie was guilty of that omission when she received a startling letter from Mary Rose six months after the elopement. She hurried into the study where Charles was twiddling the knobs of the wireless set. She was considerably agitated, and didn't stop to check whether her young son was present or not.

Ewan was there, but well hidden. Curled up in a corner of the sofa, he was deeply engrossed in a book.

'Oh, Charles! Mary Rose had a baby a fortnight ago. A girl called Elizabeth, weighing eight pounds and four ounces.'

Charles looked up. 'Hardly a six-month premature baby at that weight. This explains everything, Chrissie.'

'Yes, I must admit the possibility did cross my mind.' She sat down wearily. 'Charles, should we tell Sandra? Will it open old wounds that are maybe healing, d'you think?'

He switched off the set, and the room fell silent. 'You must tell Sandra right away, Chris. It was the secrecy of the whole affair that hurt her most. We can understand that the baby drove Mary Rose and Roddy to elope, of course, but if Sandra knows, it might help her to forgive.'

Chrissie sighed. 'I do hope you're right. Oh, Charles! This is our first little grandchild, and we have no joy in Elizabeth's arrival and little hope of seeing her. What a tragedy that is for all of us!'

A slight movement from the sofa alerted Charles, and he raised a finger to his lips. Chrissie caught a glimpse of her son's fair head and covered her mouth in dismay.

Ewan read on. He'd heard all he wanted, and presently his mother and father were convinced he'd heard nothing. Charles switched on the radio and twiddled the knobs, and the happy strains of 'Alexander's Ragtime Band' floated jazzily through the air.

'Bessie, can wee babies drive cars?' Ewan asked. The conversation he'd overheard had puzzled him and he couldn't understand what it meant.

Bessie was darning socks. She frowned at Ewan. 'What are you bletherin' aboot noo?'

'Mum says Mary Rose has had a baby. She said the baby drove Mary Rose and Roddy to get married, but how can babies drive cars, Bessie?'

Bessie didn't answer. She dropped the darning and began muttering.

'Oh, michty me! The disgrace o' it, the shame. Poor Chrissie. Her heart must be sair!'

She fixed Ewan with a fierce glare that made him shake in his shoes.

'Now listen, my lad, you've no' to let on to onybody aboot babies driving folk to get married till I give you the word in three months, when it's all above board an' respectable. That goes for you too, mind, Charlotte.'

The twins nodded hastily. When Bessie was in this

mood nobody argued. Later on, Ewan cleared up the mystery surrounding the timing of Mary Rose's baby by referring in secret to a large medical dictionary Charles kept on the library shelves.

Old William Kennedy slipped peacefully away in his sleep that summer to join the brave band of whaler skippers who'd gone before. He was hale and hearty to the last, enjoying a good blether and a wee tot of whisky with friends in the tavern right to the end of his long, hard-working life.

Chrissie missed her father sorely, but she was glad for him. It was the way he would have wanted it, she knew. His housekeeper, Mrs Pearson, who'd looked after the old man devotedly for years, asked Chrissie diffidently if she might be allowed to pay rent for the old house and keep a few respectable boarders.

'Just to keep the wolf frae the door now the dear Captain's awa', ken, Mrs Rankine?' she explained hopefully.

It was an excellent idea which neatly solved the problem of what to do with the house, for Chrissie was loath to sell the family home. Maybe in time the bonds would loosen and she could let it go, but the old house still harboured too many memories. As a little girl she'd stood at this very window and watched her ship go sailing out to sea. The beautiful *Christina K*.

Chrissie sighed and turned her back upon the river scene. The ship was gone for ever, her useful life ended. All that remained of Chrissie's bonnie ship was the brooch she always wore pinned to her dress.

Sandra returned home for a short time when she heard the news, for she'd been very fond of her grandfather. Chrissie saw a great change in her daughter, though it was hard to put a finger on it. Sandra was as pretty as ever. She'd always dressed stylishly, but now her clothes, although well cut, were on simple lines and in muted colours. They were go-anywhere clothes that wouldn't stand out in a crowd.

'Do you enjoy your job, Sandra?' asked Charles as they sat in the garden, having afternoon tea in the warm sunshine.

Sandra sipped her tea, then replaced the cup carefully. 'No, I don't enjoy it, to be honest, Charles. I hate the ugliness, the poverty, and most of all the smell.' She lifted her head and looked at him defiantly. 'And because I hate it so much, I can't give it up. Does that make any sense to you?'

He looked at her hard. 'Yes, my dear. I think it does.'

She stood up with an embarrassed little laugh. 'Oh dear, I'm beginning to sound like Harriet, and I'm not a patch on her! Did you know she hit a six foot docker with the appointments ledger and knocked him cold, because he'd blacked his wife's eye? He's a reformed character after that.'

'I can imagine!'

Chrissie thought she knew what the difference was in her daughter. Sandra had abandoned the imaginary world and come to grips with the stern realities of life, at last.

The day before she returned to Glasgow, Sandra came face to face with Norrie Gallacher's granny, in Draffen's store, of all places. Draffen's held an unrivalled reputation as a 'posh' shop, and one startled glance at Aggie Gallacher told Sandra the old lady was as posh as any well-bred lady. Aggie's furs and elegant gown wouldn't have disgraced the Duchess of York.

Sandra was delighted to meet the old soul, because she had pleasant memories of Norrie's granny in the days when Sandra was six years old and engaged to him. She recalled Aggie had been of regal demeanour even when pushing a cartie loaded with rags and old junk. Despite a sharp tongue her heart was pure gold, and she'd given it wholeheartedly to Norrie, the orphan laddie she'd brought up from babyhood.

Sandra held out a hand, smiling. 'I'm so pleased to meet you, Mrs Gallacher.'

Aggie ignored the hand and the friendly smile. 'Weel, I'm no' awfy pleased to see you, Sandra Murphy, after what you did to my Norrie, sendin' him awa' frae Dundee!'

'But I didn't do anything.'

'Aye, I ken. That's what I meant.'

The conversation was taking a baffling turn. Sandra changed direction. 'How's Norrie doing in Canada?'

'Fine.'

'Is he married yet?'

Aggie snorted. 'Naw, the daft gowk. I keep tellin' him to get himsel' a guid wife, but he'll no' do it.'

Something stirred in Sandra, a nostalgic longing for the innocence of childhood, a memory of a wide, cheeky grin and carrot coloured hair, a persistent irritation she'd somehow sadly missed as the long months slipped by.

'Mrs Gallacher, could you give me Norrie's address?' she asked tentatively.

The old lady stiffened. 'Naw, I couldna. You had your chance an' muffed it, Sandra, so bye bye.'

With a glare, Aggie swept out of the store, leaving Sandra staring after her.

Although Dundee had felt the full force of the depression, life for a ten-year-old boy was packed with interest. Coming home from school in the centre of town, there were plenty of muddy dubs for Ewan and his pals to splash through as the extension from Dock Street to Ferry Road neared completion.

The boys took full advantage of all possibilities. They mourned the passing of the little sweetie shop in the demolished Pillars, where they'd bought pokes of sweeties on their way home from school. Soon, however, the setting in place of huge steel girders to bridge the cavern beneath the new city square was a stupendous sight which attracted large, aimless crowds, Ewan and friends included.

There was a silent battle going on in Dundee between buses and trams. The much-loved tramcars still numbered 79, as opposed to a fleet of 64 buses, but traffic congestion in the city centre worsened daily. The visit of the Prince of Wales in April 1933 caused traffic chaos. Ewan was in the thick of it, of course, and in danger of being squashed against the wall of the Centre for The Unemployed which the Prince of Wales was visiting. An excited crowd of cheering men and women descended upon the popular young Prince, and Ewan felt small and frightened. Prince David didn't seem to mind the crush. Smiling and joking, he disappeared inside the building to inspect what was being done in Dundee for the vast army of unemployed men and women.

'That laddie trails a' ower the place! Just look at the glaur on his guid school shoes,' complained Bessie in despair. 'I'm no' so fleet as I was, or I'd meet him from the school mysel' to keep him oot o' mischief.'

A potent threat which turned Ewan pale with apprehension.

Chrissie was also concerned by Ewan's wanderings, and told him so frankly. As usual, her son retaliated with a reasonable compromise.

'If I'd a wee dog, Mum, I'd come straight home from school and take it for walks.'

'Yes, and I'd have to feed and look after it most of the time!'

Cunningly, Ewan played his trump card. 'The Duke and Duchess of York's wee girls have a dog, Mum, and they look after him themselves. I read all about it in a magazine. It's a corgi, an' it's called Dookie, which is short for the Duke of York's puppy. So why can't I have a dog?'

Ewan knew his mother admired the Duchess of York. In September Chrissie had made a special trip into the country to see the Duchess open Belmont Castle, a home for old folk.

Chrissie eyed her son with fond exasperation. He could twist her round his little finger, the scamp. 'I'll have a word with Dad, Ewan,' she promised weakly.

Ewan smiled to himself. He knew the battle was won. Angus, a big, soft-hearted black labrador pup, joined the family soon after, and quickly wagged his way happily into everyone's affections.

Although the twins shared the closeness twins have, their interests differed. While Ewan roved the countryside with Angus, Chrissie took Charlotte to dancing class on Saturday mornings, and usually stayed to watch from the gallery. Charlotte was the star of the class. Tap-dancing, ballroom, hornpipe, Charlotte's flying feet mastered them all. Her delighted teacher said she was a natural dancer.

Charlotte's preference was for Highland dancing, and she was one of those chosen to dance a foursome reel before the Duke and Duchess of York when they visited the Royal Highland Show. It was being held in Dundee that year for the first time since 1890, and the crowds were enormous. Chrissie and Charles stood hand in hand in the throng watching their talented daughter, positively bursting with pride at her accomplishment.

Their visit to the show was a welcome break for Chrissie and Charles. Charles had never recovered his full strength, but visited the factory twice a week, despite Chrissie's protests. He was cautiously optimistic about the up-turn in trade, hoping it was a sign lean times were passing. Sandra wrote cheerfully from Glasgow to say work had started upon the huge liner in John Brown's yard, and things were looking up again in Clydebank.

By now, Chrissie was on good terms with Rankine's American customer, Ben Chester. They conversed in short postscripts, and Chrissie and her secretary shared many a giggle over his humorous comments. His latest postscript had made Chrissie uneasy, though.

Who is this guy, Hitler? They tell me he's put Germany on her feet again, building roads like you never saw. Their factories are working full time making heaven knows what. And what about the Duce Mussolini? Sure, he drained the Pontine Marshes and made the desert bloom, but I think these guys are getting too big for their boots. They want watching, Chrissie!

Chrissie took the worry home to Charles. 'Do you think there'll be another war, darling?'

'They wouldn't be so daft, Chris. Europe's just recovering from the last fiasco,' Charles answered reassuringly, for he knew his wife had good reason to fear an outbreak of hostilities.

Chrissie was reassured by Charles's comforting reply, but Charles spent more time listening to the wireless and reading newspapers, and all he heard and read was disquieting. He watched his young son grow taller as the months went by, and a terrible fear took root.

Worries about the future didn't trouble Ewan. When the weather wasn't suitable for walking the dog, there was always the pictures.

Bessie and Charlotte were also avid fans, and their

favourite pastime on a wet Saturday was to take a tram into town and visit the Majestic or the Kinnaird, or any one of the thriving cinemas showing musicals, comedies, or, preferably, weepies. After the show, their routine rarely varied. They went to Wallace's restaurant and sat in the cosy, onion-scented interior. Bessie did the ordering in a pan-loafie voice, conscious she wore her best costume and the fur Chrissie had given her.

'Twa pies, a pot o' tea an' twa sair heids.'

'Oh, Bessie!' Charlotte had been mystified by this order the first time, but now she collapsed in giggles. The waitress returned with two steaming, hot pies and two little iced cakes each wrapped around with a strip of white paper, looking for all the world like a bandage on a sore head.

Ewan didn't accompany Bessie and Charlotte, because his taste in films differed. Besides, he was horribly embarrassed by Bessie's loudly enthusiastic involvement in community singing, led by a little ball that bounced gaily along the words of the song on the screen, and accompanied by a man on the cinema organ.

Ewan preferred Laurel and Hardy, Mickey Mouse, and above all, Westerns. Tom Mix was Ewan's hero. He wished his father hadn't sold Mary Rose's horses and disposed of the field at the rear of Beechyhill to a property developer, when money was tight. Ewan would have dearly loved to try cowboy exploits on horseback. He made do with a long-legged, easy gait, hitching up his brccks frequently, eyes narrowed keenly as he smiled dangerously, hands hovering over imaginary six-guns slung low on the hips.

Being a regular patron of the cinema. Ewan was made aware of events elsewhere in the world. The Pathé Movietone news kept him up to date. He watched King George and Queen Mary's Silver Jubilee procession take place in London in 1935. More ominously as time passed, newsreels began showing flag-waving soldiers, rank upon rank goose-stepping in Germany. The sight gave Ewan a curious, squeamish feeling inside, and although he didn't want to very much, he joined the school cadet force.

Chrissie always relaxed on Saturday afternoons after a busy week. She enjoyed catching up with her correspondence, seated at Harriet's little writing desk. She wrote to a widening circle of friends and relatives around the world. She didn't write very often, though, to Harriet.

She couldn't shake off a foolish fear that Harriet would return and take Charles from her now that he was ailing and needed care. She had deliberately made light of her husband's illness in her letters to Harriet, and it had been a severe shock to Chrissie when Sandra announced she was going to work for her in Glasgow. So far, thankfully, they'd only received one brief, friendly visit from Harriet.

Chrissie wrote Sandra a chatty letter, then, more carefully, wrote to Mary Rose. She didn't know what to make of Mary Rose's short, non-committal communications, nor of the information that she and little Elizabeth were moving to a small house in London. Chrissie gathered that living with Mary Rose's in-laws had not been successful.

She picked up a pen to write the usual difficult letter to her sister-in-law, Lizzie, in India. Lizzie's illness was a progressive one, and Arthur had written that she couldn't walk or use her hands very well now. Sammy's old ayah tended to her mistress devotedly, Arthur wrote, and Sammy himself, nearly nineteen, had left school and was working as an apprentice engineer in the Titaghur mill.

Chrissie stared at the blank page and sighed. Nearly nineteen! And if she met Danny's son in the street, she would not know him.

By the end of 1936, everyone realised they were witnessing historic events. The popular prince upon whom the country had pinned such bright hopes, abdicated rather than give up the woman he loved. Mrs Simpson had been recently divorced, and a consort for the new king with such a background was unthinkable. The romantic story brought tears to dear old Bessie's eyes, but it was a shattering blow to everyone concerned.

Chrissie and Charles were glued to the wireless set. It was astounding news, and it soon became plain that the Duke of York, an unassuming, home-loving man who'd never sought the limelight, would be their next king. The lovely, dark-haired girl Chrissie had met one spring day at Glamis Castle would be queen, and Chrissie was absolutely delighted. The Coronation would go ahead as planned, on 12th May 1937.

Dundee was hit by Coronation fever. The city took a personal pride in the new King and Queen and their two little daughters. The youngest, Margaret Rose, had been born nearby, at Glamis Castle, and the family had been frequent visitors to the city over the years. The City Square, declared open three years ago by the King's younger brother, the Duke of Kent, lent itself to artistic decoration with bunting and flags, but Chrissie took the twins, who were newly turned fourteen, to a much more famous and traditional location.

Bernard Street, a narrow street of old stone tenements just off Hawkhill, was famed for its ingenuity on such occasions. Chrissie and the twins left Hawkhill and rounded the corner, then stopped in their tracks to stare. A blaze of patriotic bunting and strings of small flags criss-crossed the street. Union Jacks fluttered from most windows, alongside red, white and blue balloons and banners.

'Wow, that's jolly good, Mum! Even better than the City Square.'

Ewan was clearly impressed, and Chrissie was glad. She wanted her children to remember this old street with brave flags flying. Looking up at the brilliant colours transforming smoke-grimed stone, Chrissie felt a fierce love for her city and its folk. She had lived up a closie in her time and suffered the hardships that the proud, beaming folk standing in the doorways had suffered. She wanted to urge her children to remember this sight all their lives, but she was too choked with emotion to utter a word.

'I don't feel well, Mum,' announced Charlotte suddenly.

Chrissie studied her daughter anxiously. Charlotte had been tired and heavy-eyed at breakfast that morning, but Chrissie had thought nothing of it. The girl looked really ill now, hot, feverish, and shivering.

'My head hurts,' she complained.

Charlotte was bewildered. She didn't know what was happening to her, but she suspected it was something bad. She was never ill usually, apart from a snuffly cold or two. Her legs had begun aching so much they felt weak. She clung dizzily to her mother.

Chrissie was really concerned by now, and with Ewan's help, they got Charlotte back to the car. Chrissie drove as fast as she dared to Beechyhill, and asked Charles to phone for the doctor.

The doctor washed his hands carefully after examining Charlotte.

'Chrissie, I'm arranging for Charlotte to be taken to hospital immediately. She should be kept in isolation,' he said gravely.

'Isolation?' The word struck terror into her heart. 'What is it? What's wrong with her?'

'I believe. . .poliomyelitis, my dear. Infantile paralysis. There have been a few cases in the town.'

'Oh, no!' Chrissie felt the room sway. Charles was beside her at once. Poor dear Charles! was Chrissie's first thought. He should be protected from such worry and stress, and yet he seemed stronger than she was at that awful moment. His arm was around her, strong and comforting. He looked grey and drawn with worry, but he smiled.

'She'll pull through, my darling, I'm sure she will.'

The doctor was speaking, telling them all the things they must do. Ewan must be kept off school and in quarantine, in case he was infected by the disease too.

It was a nightmare from which they couldn't waken, as long days and longer nights dragged slowly by. They weren't allowed to visit Charlotte in hospital, only permitted a glimpse of her from steps outside the window. But Charlotte had been very fortunate, the doctors told Charles and Chrissie at last. She would recover and lead quite a normal life. Only her left leg was paralysed, and that could be strengthened by wearing a strong metal caliper. She would get around reasonably well once she got used to it. Charlotte had indeed been very lucky, considering the initial severity of her illness.

Lucky! Chrissie rested her head against Charles's shoulder momentarily and closed her eyes in anguish. The doctors hadn't watched Charlotte dancing, light as thistledown, before the lady who was now the Queen. They didn't know how graceful and talented Charlotte had been, how spirited when she danced.

Chrissie allowed herself one last moment of weakness then wiped her eyes and fiercely counted her blessings. Ewan had escaped the disease, and Charlotte was recovering. Charles had coped remarkably well with the stress of his daughter's illness. Her family had much to be thankful for.

Charlotte couldn't get used to the disaster that had befallen her. She couldn't adjust to a limb that refused to do her bidding unless encased in heavy metal that dragged awkwardly when she tried to walk. She didn't try very hard with the exercises she'd been given, and she wouldn't go out much. Anyway, she hated the pitying stares she got when her mother persuaded her to go shopping in the car. She knew she was making her mother and father distracted with worry, and she was sorry, but she hadn't the willpower to do anything about it. It hurt even to listen to music, because it made her want to dance, and she would never dance again.

Ewan was sympathetic, but he had his own ploys and amusements to occupy him. That summer he went off with the school cadets to camp at Cortachy for a fortnight. He was a lance-corporal, and extremely proud of the single white stripe on his uniform jacket.

Worn out with worry, Chrissie went down with a severe chill, which Bessie struggled to cure with all sorts of remedies, ranging from beef tea to Bile Beans. Nobody had much time to spend on Charlotte any more, for Charles was forced to go to the office every day.

Charlotte was lying moping in bed, wondering if it was worth the effort of getting up, when the bed-clothes were tugged sideways and a cold draught hit the back of her neck. She sat up indignantly, then laughed.

'Och, Angus, it's you!'

The dog wagged his tail, then sat looking at her with mournful, pleading eyes. His ears drooped, and he looked forlorn and pathetic. Nobody had any time to spare for poor Angus either these days.

'Poor old boy. We're outcasts, Angus, you and me,' Charlotte told him sadly.

He agreed, wagging his tail and whining. He then

leaped on to Charlotte's bed, nudging and prodding her energetically with his cold, wet nose.

She giggled and tried to fight him off. 'Hey, stop it, you daft dog! I can't take you for walkies!'

That was the wrong word to use. The dog's eyes brightened, and he uttered short, sharp barks of excitement. He shoved and pushed at Charlotte and created such a rumpus she was forced to get up. How could you argue with a determined black labrador who had his mind set on 'walkies'?

Reluctantly, Charlotte dressed, buckling on the hated caliper. She sat and looked at the dog with tears in her eyes. 'Angus, dear Angus, I'd love to take you for walkies, but I can't! I'm sorry, oh, so sorry!'

But, of course, Angus couldn't understand. He nudged Charlotte to her feet, then gently escorted her along the passageway. He bounded off and came back proudly, a happy gleam in his brown eyes, carrying the lead in his mouth.

She laughed. 'I hope you know what you're doing, Angus. I walk as slow as a snail!' She bent down and clipped the lead on his collar.

To her surprise, once outside, Angus padded slowly by her side. She could rest a hand on his head, and it steadied her, and when they came to a slight rise, he pulled her up it. Charlotte began to gain confidence.

'Just to the park, mind, Angus. That's all I can manage.'

Seated thankfully on a bench, Charlotte let Angus off the lead and allowed him to rove around busily on his own. She lifted her face to the sunshine. It felt good, and a little of its warmth and brightness entered into her. Life wasn't so bad. Her legs were awfully tired and weak, but that was because she hadn't been using them much. If she walked more, they'd grow stronger.

A little group of youths came noisily along the path,

enjoying the freedom of a public holiday. They whistled appreciatively and winked at her as they passed.

'What a smasher!' she heard one of them remark to his mates.

Charlotte smiled, colour in her cheeks. They hadn't even noticed her leg and she was filled with a delightful hope for the future. She called Angus to her, and hugged the big dog gratefully before setting off for home.

Charlotte's determination to conquer her disability went a long way towards making Chrissie feel better. She watched delightedly as her young daughter grew stronger and more confident. Charlotte walked with a determined, limping gait, the devoted black dog padding along beside her, patiently matching his pace to hers. It was beautiful to watch. Laughter came back into the house, music blared out from wireless and gramophone, and for a time Chrissie was happy, ignoring the threat that hung over the country.

Talk of war was on everyone's lips, however, and soon Chrissie could hardly bear to watch her young son as he left for school on Fridays, the day the cadets mustered. On those days Ewan was kitted out smartly in uniform, a khaki jacket and Black Watch kilt which reminded her poignantly of Danny. At fifteen, Ewan was almost as tall as Charles, with his father's clean-cut, sensitive features and Chrissie's wavy fair hair, which he subdued sternly with hair oil. He was a full corporal in the cadet force, and confident he would gain sergeant's stripes before leaving school.

Ewan had no idea what he would do when he left school. Go into the family business, he supposed, though the prospect didn't thrill him. He felt restless, infected by the uncertainty and the scary rumours flying around. Only Bessie, placidly knitting socks, appeared unaffected by the jitters.

'Bessie, do you think there'll be war?' Ewan asked.

She looked at him over the top of her specs. 'Wi' the Empire Exhibition on in Glasgow? Nae chance!'

It was daft, but he was reassured. 'Dad says the factory's working flat out making sandbags, Bessie,' Ewan persisted.

'Aye. The flooding's been something awfy roond aboot the River Earn.'

'My pal's dad has joined the Civil Defence, and he says they're to dig air-raid shelters in Dudhope Park opposite the hospital.'

Bessie sniffed and rattled the knitting needles. 'Och, I'm no' surprised, wi' a' they flying boats clutterin' up the Tay. No wonder they're building shelters in case their daft inventions fa' oot the sky on to decent folks' heids.'

'They say Hitler will march into Czechoslovakia, Bessie.'

'Mr Chamberlain'll no' let him. Dinna bother your heid aboot Hitler, lovie, the man's daft,' said Bessie comfortably, and gave her full attention to turning the heel.

The glorious weather in the summer of 1939 belied the imminent threat of war. The sun shone from a blue sky hazy with heat. Chrissie lifted her face to the hot sun, pottering in the garden on one of her rare moments of leisure. She was the only energetic one that Saturday; Charles lay snoozing in a deckchair on the terrace, his panama hat tipped over his eyes; Ewan lazed in a hammock slung between two tall rowan trees, reading a book, while Charlotte sunbathed, faithful Angus not far away, lying watchfully in the shade.

The birds sang and all around lay a peace and tranquillity which Chrissie knew was false. Her nephew, Hughie, had recently been given command of a new merchant ship and his wife, Jani, had visited Chrissie only that morning, in tears.

'Oh, Auntie Chrissie, Hughie's ship is heading for America, and they are saying in my shop that merchant ships will be torpedoed and sunk by submarines if this war comes. They are saying Jamal and Ruby will be sent away from me to live with strangers in the country, and there will be no food and sweeties to sell in my shop. What should I do?'

Chrissie had smiled and hugged poor, worried Jani. 'There's little we can do, I'm afraid, love. We must just wait and see.'

Jani's tears had dried after a comforting chat and a cup of tea, but Chrissie couldn't dismiss her own anxiety so easily. She couldn't settle like the others to enjoy the perfect summer day, and she gave a small sigh of exasperation when she spotted a stranger walking up the driveway. She was in no mood for visitors.

Chrissie shaded her eyes against the sun and saw that this was a young man of medium height. He was smartly dressed, but it was impossible to make out features against the sun's glare. She saw him hesitate uncertainly, then walk towards her. He stopped, the width of the rockery between them.

'Excuse me, but are you Mrs Rankine?'

Chrissie felt suddenly apprehensive, almost panicky. She answered him sharply. 'Yes. What is it?'

He studied her for a moment in silence, as if put off by her tone, then doffed the smart hat politely and held it somewhat nervously by the brim.

'Well, you see, I'm Samuel Murphy. I'm Sammy,' the young man announced.

Chapter 13

Sammy!

Chrissie had imagined her son's return many times, but never like this. Time after time she'd rehearsed what she would do and imagined the joyful words that would welcome him into her arms, but the moment had come and she couldn't think of anything to say.

'Why have you come?' Chrissie asked eventually. Hardly a promising start!

'I wanted to visit Dundee before joining up.'

She was taken aback. 'You mean . . . join the army?'

'Of course. That's why I left India.'

She was aware of a crushing disappointment. Hesitantly she negotiated the rockery steps, coming down to his level. Chrissie shaded her eyes against the sun's glare with a hand, and discovered her son's eyes were as blue and clear as Danny's, his hair not so black, but brown with coppery lights. The discovery made her want to weep, but she hastily controlled the impulse.

'So you didn't come back just to see your mother?' She kept her tone light, impersonal.

He didn't answer right away, but studied her with guarded blue eyes.

'I was curious about you. I wanted to find out what sort of woman would give her son away and take no interest in him afterwards.'

'But I wrote, Sammy!' Chrissie protested.

He looked politely sceptical. 'Well, of course, you wrote to Mother and Dad, but that's not quite the same, is it?'

She stared at him in bewilderment. Hadn't he read the letters in which she'd poured out all her love, all her longing for him? Obviously not.

Sammy's expression had softened a little. He went on talking quietly. It seemed as if he had to talk to somebody.

'Mother died shortly before I left. It broke Dad's heart. I thought about staying in India to be with him, but I want to join a Scottish regiment if there's to be war. Dad understood my feelings, so I came back to Scotland in order to volunteer. It was the only way.'

His resemblance to Danny was remarkable. As he talked enthusiastically about his plans, a shiver ran through Chrissie despite the hot sunshine. Her son would go off to war not knowing how much she loved him. Thinking it over more rationally, Chrissie suspected Lizzie had destroyed the letters she'd written to Sammy explaining the circumstances of his birth and fostering. No doubt she'd salved her conscience by arguing they would upset the boy. That would be typical of Lizzie's reasoning. Chrissie's heart felt like lead. Lizzie was dead and it could never be proved that the letters had been written. Chrissie doubted if Sammy would believe her account of the matter anyway.

'I'm sorry. I didn't know Lizzie had died,' she said.

'She couldn't move or speak towards the end. It was very sad to watch,' Sammy said briefly.

He didn't want to talk about it, because the memories of his foster mother's last days were still so sharp in his mind. She'd stared at him with such eloquent pleading, as if begging his forgiveness for some imagined wrong she'd done him. It had unnerved Sammy. He thought he'd never forget that look. He shivered and put on his hat, pulling the brim well down to shield his eyes.

'Now I've paid my respects, I'll be going.'

'No, please don't go yet,' Chrissie pleaded.

He shrugged. 'But there's nothing more to say, is there?'

'Perhaps not. That . . . that's up to you, Sammy.' There was so much she wanted to say to him, but he didn't want to hear it. He was impatient to leave.

He hesitated for a moment, scanning the old mansion house at the top of the hilly garden. 'I would like to meet my sisters, though,' he admitted grudgingly.

'They're not here, I'm afraid. Mary Rose is in London and Sandra works in Glasgow.'

He gave a wry smile. 'So you got rid of all the Murphys when you went up in the world. You must be delighted!'

Chrissie was suddenly furious with him. Whatever her faults, she didn't deserve this. It wasn't fair. 'It was no wish of mine to lose my bairns, Sammy. Fortunately, I have my twins and my dear husband for comfort,' she said coldly.

Sammy felt bitter. She shouldn't have thrown that in his face. 'Ah yes, your husband. You did very well for yourself the second time around. Better than you fared with my poor father!'

Immediately he'd spoken, he was sorry. It was true, but he was sorry all the same. He hadn't meant to hurt her, but he could read the hurt in her expressive eyes. She was a very beautiful woman, Sammy noted for the first time with a sense of shock. He reckoned she must be around fifty, and he hadn't expected her to be beautiful, but hers was the sort of beauty that didn't fade with age. He'd spent so many years bitterly resenting her rejection of him, he found her beauty very disconcerting.

Chrissie took a threatening step towards her son.

'Nobody says that to my face, not even you, Samuel Murphy! Go away, for heaven's sake! Get out of my sight!'

She was too hurt and furious to think clearly. She just wanted him to leave so that she could give vent to her misery and weep.

And that was how Ewan found them seconds later. He didn't notice anything amiss as he bounded down the rockery steps, but as he approached the pair he could sense tension in the air. He gave the stranger a curious glance. Another vacuum cleaner salesman getting the brush-off, Ewan decided.

'Hey, Mum! Dad says there won't be any sandwiches left if you don't come now!'

She turned towards him, and Ewan got a severe shock, for his mother looked strange, sort of wild. He'd never seen her look like that before.

'Ewan, this is your half-brother, Sammy. He's just leaving,' she said in a chilly, strangled voice.

Ewan could hardly believe his ears. He forgot the odd vibrations in the air in his excitement, and almost shoved his mother aside, pumping Sammy's hand vigorously. 'Gosh! I've been wanting to meet you for ages, Sammy! Have you come home for good?'

Sammy was shaken. The youngster's friendly enthusiasm was most embarrassing under the circumstances. 'Well – er – not really. I'm joining up. I'm hoping to join my father's regiment, actually.'

'That's a jolly good show!' Ewan breathed, eyes shining. 'I'm sixteen, Sammy. D'you think the war'll last long enough for me to fight?'

'Hey, it hasn't even started yet! Maybe Hitler won't annexe Poland after all. Maybe he'll abide by Chamberlain's ultimatum and this crisis will blow over.'

Sammy smiled at Ewan, relaxing a bit. He liked this kid, his brother. He liked the thought of having

274

a brother, even a half-brother. It gave him a warm feeling of belonging somewhere to someone who cared about him. He sneaked a cautious glance at his mother. Her expression was tragic, and unwillingly he pitied her. He wished he could think of something comforting to say, but nothing came to mind. He made a show of consulting his wristwatch.

'I'd better go. My train leaves soon.'

Ewan felt quite emotional. His brother was just as broad-shouldered and gallant as Ewan had imagined, and he was going away bravely to join up. Ewan could hardly wait to follow suit. If only he were older and they could go together! He caught Sammy's sleeve.

'You'll come back soon, won't you, Sammy? Please?' he begged.

'We-ell—' Sammy glanced at his mother, then met his half-brother's pleading gaze, and was forced to give in. He grinned and clapped the young lad on the shoulder. 'OK. I'll come back just to see you, wee brother.'

Sammy wondered how his mother was taking this unexpected development, but he wouldn't look at her. He turned and went briskly down the driveway and into the quiet street. Outside, he heaved a sigh of relief now the awkward interview was over. He'd been dreading it, and yet longing for it to happen.

As he'd half expected from the beginning, it had been a disaster, with his mother losing her rag and ordering him off the premises. To be fair, he couldn't blame her.

Ah, well, Samuel Murphy, your country needs you, even if your mother doesn't, he thought wryly.

Whistling cheerfully to keep his spirits up, Sammy stepped out jauntily, heading towards Broughty Station.

* * *

The fine weather continued, making preparations for war seem out of place. The river sparkled a serene silver-blue in the sunshine, and the white monument atop The Law glinted a warning nobody heeded on 2nd September 1939, the last sunny Saturday of peace.

Ewan went to the pictures that evening with a pal to see John Wayne in *Stagecoach*, while Bessie and Charlotte queued patiently for over half an hour to watch James Stewart and Carole Lombard in *Made for Each Other*.

Despite the chilling issue and fitting of gasmasks, and the air-raid shelters which were springing up all over the place, the city appeared surprisingly normal. Home football supporters were cheery and boisterous that evening in the pubs: Dundee was top of the Second Division!

'There's going to be war, Chris. Warsaw's been bombed. Poland's gone,' Charles said suddenly that evening as he anxiously monitored the wireless.

Chrissie put down the cups of Horlicks she'd brought for their supper. 'Maybe Hitler will heed the ultimatum and withdraw.'

Charles smiled wryly. 'Nae chance! Not now, dear.'

Chrissie cradled the hot drink in her cold hands. She was glad the twins and Bessie were out enjoying themselves. Tomorrow everything would be different. For a moment she weakened and became tearful.

'Oh, Charles, Sammy will be in the thick of it, and if it's a long war, Ewan will have to go, too.' She stopped, biting her lip to check the tears. Like many mothers that Saturday night, while the last precious hours of peace ticked away, Chrissie found the future too awful to contemplate.

There was almost a sense of relief in Dundee that Sunday, after the Prime Minister had spoken. The ultimatum had been ignored. We were at war.

'Aye weel, that's put the tin hat on it,' Bessie remarked grimly.

She was right. All over Dundee, members of the Civil Defence were donning tin hats and looking anxiously to the defence of the city. On the west coast the weather had broken, and thunder rumbled ominously over Greenock and Glasgow.

Chrissie welcomed the hundred-and-one tasks that landed on her shoulders, because it gave her no time to think. She'd already ordered yards of black-out material, and she, Charlotte and Bessie spent hours lining curtains and criss-crossing brown sticky tape over window panes in case they shattered. Charles had fitted out one of the underground wine cellars as an air-raid shelter. It was a large area, and he'd blithely issued invitations to most of the occupants of newly built bungalows round about to share its underground safety. The prospect of such a gang of visitors appealed to his hospitable nature.

'Looks like being the biggest party we ever hosted, next time the siren goes, darling. Lucky we still have quite a good stock of wine in the cellar,' he grinned happily.

It saddened Chrissie to watch the child evacuees leaving Dundee. She had volunteered her services to help organise the little ones on to trains at the East Station, and manfully wiped noses and dried tears – the mothers' as well as the bairns' – and located lost gasmasks and mislaid teddy bears and dollies. Jani's little girl, Ruby, went off happily with her bestfriend to a kindly farming couple in Fetter-cairn, but Jamal dug his heels in and refused to go.

'Och, no, Auntie Chrissie, that's for wee bairns!' Jamal said scornfully. 'I'll soon be fourteen anyway and leaving the school. Then I'm going into the Caledon shipyard to learn to build ships, before I go to sea like my dad.'

Jani gave a wee howl and mopped her eyes mournfully, but Chrissie smiled and gently ruffled Jamal's raven-black hair. The Kennedys' sea-faring tradition would be safe in Hughie's son's hands. Old William Kennedy would have been delighted to know it.

There were changes in the Rankine household, comings and goings. The first to go was Agnes, the housemaid. She came to Chrissie pink-cheeked and blushing.

'Mrs Rankine, ken the wee tubby air-raid warden wha comes to check on the black-out near every nicht? Well, I've clicked wi' him, and we're to get married. I'll hae to hand in my notice. I'm awfy sorry, 'cause you an' Mr Rankine have been so good tae me.' Poor Agnes dabbed her eyes with her apron, quite overcome, and Chrissie had a job calming her down and offering sincere congratulations.

Not long after Agnes left, Cook followed suit. 'My sister in Forfar's been landed wi' four evacuees, an' she's sair needin' a hand, Mrs Rankine. I dinna want to leave you in the lurch, mind. My niece, Emily McDade, is lookin' for a canny – ahem – a good job. She's only nineteen, but a rare wee cook, an' light-handed wi' the pastry,' Cook volunteered eagerly.

'I'd need to interview Emily first,' warned Chrissie cautiously.

Cook grinned confidently. 'She's down the stair. I'll send her up, shall I?'

So Emily McDade took over in the kitchen. She was an attractive girl, with large grey, lively eyes that sparkled with intelligence and fun. Chrissie couldn't understand why the girl was content in domestic service. Housemaids, parlourmaids and cooks were deserting the big houses in droves, flocking into the women's services, to munitions, or working as clippies on the buses. The war had liberated a great flood of domestics, never to return to their jobs again.

One day curiosity got the better of Chrissie, and she asked Emily outright why she'd chosen the job.

The girl turned pale. 'Oh, Mrs Rankine, you'll put me out if I tell you,' Emily said tearfully.

Chrissie smiled. 'Try me. I'm not so easily put off folk I like, Emily.'

Emily collapsed unhappily on the kitchen chair, looking tragic.

'I've had TB. I was in the sanatorium for a year, and the doctors say I'm cured, but folk are funny, Mrs Rankine. It's like a stigma on you, having TB, and your bestfriends don't want to know you. You'll maybe no' want me in your house, now you know.'

Chrissie went over and deliberately hugged the poor, unhappy girl. 'Of course I want you. More than ever now. You're cured, Emily. Put your illness behind you, love. Forget it.'

Emily wiped her eyes. 'You're good, Mrs Rankine. You mind me o' my own mum, before she died,' she sobbed emotionally.

But Emily couldn't remain depressed for long. She was up again in a trice, cheerfully making a pot of tea while she chattered away. 'Mind you, Mrs Rankine, I was fair scunnered when I found out they wouldn't have me in the Wrens because of my chest. It's an awfy smart uniform, an' you get to wear fine black lisle stockings,' said Emily, wistfully.

At the end of May 1940, the ominous calm of the first few months of war in Europe ended in disaster at Dunkirk. Charles and Chrissie listened anxiously to the radio for news of the evacuation. Ewan joined them as they tuned in. He clenched his fists uselessly.

'Sam'll be there, Dad! Oh, if only I could do something!'

'You can do something, son. You can pass your exams with flying colours and start training as an accountant as you planned. This country will need clever young men when the war's over,' Charles pointed out.

But that wasn't what his young son wanted to hear. Ewan had other ideas. He decided he could pass his Highers all right, maybe work in an office until he was eighteen, but then he would join up immediately and fight in the war. Just try to stop him.

Ewan's twin sister was also restless. Charlotte's schoolfriends talked importantly about doing 'their bit'. Some were in the junior Red Cross, prior to going on to train as nurses, others planned to join the services when they were old enough, or go into munitions. None of these avenues was open to Charlotte because of her leg. The best she could manage was a stint in the forces canteen run by the local WVS.

All the same, Charlotte thoroughly enjoyed working in the canteen. She had welcomed the new wartime fashion of smart and comfortable slacks for women, because they hid the ugly metal caliper on her leg. Standing still, nobody could tell she was different. Soldiers and sailors queuing for tea and buns and 6d packets of Kensitas cigarettes, flirted lightly with the pretty, young girl behind the counter. Charlotte laughed and joked with her many admirers and innocently enjoyed herself.

Sometimes somebody would organise a tea-dance, with one of the lads playing the out-of-tune old piano in the corner of the hall. Charlotte's feet tapped to the new, catchy tunes of 'Run, rabbit, run' and 'Roll out the barrel', but she always firmly refused offers to dance.

Until Leon arrived.

He was one of a contingent of Polish soldiers billeted in the neighbourhood. They had suffered much, these

280

young Polish men, and were popular with the ladies of the WVS, because of their exquisite manners.

The day Leon arrived a tea-dance was in full swing. He glanced around, caught sight of Charlotte standing beside the tea-urn, and came right over. His manners were beautiful, though strange and foreign. He clicked his heels and gave a polite, little bow.

'You would like to dance, please, miss?' he asked.

She blushed. 'Oh, no, thank you. I can't dance.'

He seemed surprised. He gave her a straight, considering look. 'But everyone can dance a little, and this dance is very easy, just trotting like a fox to this good music.'

She was hot with embarrassment. 'No, really, I can't dance.'

He wouldn't take no for an answer. He looked puzzled. 'Please tell me. Why not? Is it because I am not speaking Scottish so good?'

Charlotte was distressed. She hadn't meant to offend him. He looked so kind. Not handsome really, just nice. 'Oh, no, you speak very well. It . . . it's just—' Words failed her, and to her horror a lump rose in her throat and tears welled up and ran slowly down her cheeks. 'I want to dance with you very much, but I can't. You see . . . my leg is paralysed because I had polio, so I can't dance any more. I'm . . . I'm a cripple.'

She had never used the hated word before, stubbornly refusing to admit to herself it was true, but this nice Polish soldier demanded complete honesty somehow. She ought to feel embarrassed and humiliated, but curiously, she didn't. She felt soothed and oddly refreshed.

He laughed gently. 'But with me, you can dance. Come, I show you how.'

He held out a hand, and she took it trustingly. He drew her close, holding her so that they moved as one. He guided and lifted her, and set her feet down lightly with the precision of a ballet dancer. Her natural sense of rhythm helped, and soon she was dancing again, light as a feather in the support of his arm. He looked down at her, surprised, shaken by his emotion. He had pitied her at first, but now he felt differently. Her youth and loveliness moved him deeply.

'And I do not even know your name!' he said with wonder.

She told him, laughing. 'Bessie, my old nurse, would give me a telling-off if she knew. We should have been introduced first. I don't know who you are, either!'

'I am Leon,' he said. He smiled down at her with a twinkle in his eye. 'I would tell you my other name, but you will not pronounce it well. Scottish people never do.'

But she pleaded, and he told her, and as he'd predicted she stumbled over it. He laughed, and declared it didn't matter. Nothing mattered, he said, except the music and the dancing, and being together.

And Charlotte was ready to agree. After that, if Leon was there, Charlotte danced with him.

It was old Bessie who spotted the soldier coming wearily up the driveway on a damp day in early June. She put on her specs and peered out of the window, then gave a piercing skirl.

'Chrissie, it's him! I'm sure it's him.'

Chrissie had been working on Charlotte's dress, trying to make do and mend. She looked up, startled. 'Who?'

'Your laddie. He's the spittin' image of his da. Look!' She pointed with a trembling finger.

Chrissie looked, and started to tremble too. Sammy! she thought. She closed her eyes for a moment or two to compose herself, then went to the door.

'Hullo, Sammy,' she said, as her son reached the porch.

Sammy put down what was left of his pack. It flopped emptily on the ground, looking much like himself, flattened. He was unable to feel emotion any more. He'd only experienced a mild surprise when their defeated army was greeted by excited, cheering crowds on the quayside, as if he and his mates had achieved some sort of victory.

Maybe it was in a way. He was too weary to care. He studied his mother's guarded expression. She didn't know what to expect from him. Well, they were quits. Neither did he.

'They asked if I had some place to go on leave until the regiment is reorganised. I'm sorry, but yours was the only place I could think of off-hand,' he told her dully.

Chrissie's impulse was to fling her arms round him, to comfort him and wipe the terrible, hopeless, haunted look from his poor, dirty face. The moment was too fragile though. A wrong word, an impulsive touch could send him flying away like a wounded bird. She stood aside.

'Come in.'

He walked past her, trailing the half-empty pack. He stood passively studying the shabby hallway that was needing a lick of paint it wouldn't get, the high windows plastered with sticky tape. Chrissie guided him into the parlour, where Bessie was hopping from one foot to the other with excitement.

Bessie had no inhibitions. She grabbed Danny's son and planted a kiss on two days' growth of stubble. 'Sammy, my wee sojer laddie! Hame at last. I'm Bessie McCutcheon, your da's auld auntie, lovie. I was wi' your mammy when you were born.'

Sammy's head was spinning gently. More relatives he hadn't known he possessed.

Bessie gave him an expert glance. 'Och, you're

needing your tea, son. I'll away and stir up Emily in the kitchen. Maybe there's a wee bit bacon left from the rations.'

Bessie bustled away, leaving mother and son awkwardly together. They sat either side of the fire. Sammy unbuttoned the pocket of his battledress and drew out a crumpled letter which he held out for Chrissie to read.

'I got this in France, before communications broke down.'

It was a letter from a Scottish lawyer in Calcutta, informing Sammy that his foster-father, Arthur Kennedy, had died suddenly. Sammy was the sole beneficiary named in Arthur's will. The estate consisted mostly of British stocks and shares and a quantity of personal effects and furniture listed below, presently in storage. Chrissie cast an eye swiftly down the list, which consisted of bed, dining table and chairs, a bureau and other small items. Poor Arthur. It was sad. She folded the letter and handed it to Sammy. Her own grief for her brother she kept to herself.

'What will you do, Sam?' she asked carefully.

He shrugged. 'Not much I can do with the war on. I'll write and ask for the furniture to be sold and the proceeds given to my old ayah, along with a pension from the estate. She deserves it, the kind old soul.'

Emily arrived with a loaded tray containing a heaped plate of bacon, scrambled egg and sausage amounting to one person's ration for the week. She had obviously been briefed by Bessie. She studied Sammy curiously, then smiled cheerfully.

'Eat it up while it's hot. It's dried egg, but it a' goes down the same way when you're hungry. Bessie's airing the bed for ye 'cause she ses you look dead beat. Oh, and tak' off your boots!'

'What?' Sammy showed more animation than he'd displayed so far.

'Your clarty boots. Tak' them off. They look like you've been trampin' through a midden. I'll clean them for ye,' Emily offered.

'You can't have my boots. I've got holes in my socks,' he objected.

'Oh aye? Well, I'll have your socks, an' a'.' She examined him closely as he reluctantly removed his boots and the offending socks and stretched his bare feet towards the electric fire.

'Your jaiket an' breeks could do wi' a clean. Could ye no'—?' Emily began tentatively.

'No, I jolly well couldn't!' Sammy said hastily.

Emily gave a long-suffering sigh, collected the boots and socks and whisked them off to the kitchen. Sammy sat staring after her, looking bemused.

'Who was that?'

'That was Emily McDade, our Jill-of-all-trades,' Chrissie told him.

Sammy remained with them for ten days, eating, sleeping and keeping himself to himself. He spent more time closeted with Ewan and Charlotte, or in the kitchen with Emily, than he did with Chrissie and Charles. He was scrupulously polite to his mother, but she wanted more from her son. Much more.

When Sammy was recalled to his unit he looked a new man, thanks to Emily's efforts. She was at the door to see him off, her eyes suspiciously moist.

'You take care o' yoursel', mind,' Emily ordered fiercely.

'I will, don't worry.'

The lingering warmth of his smile was for Emily; only a cool, careful handshake and polite thanks, for Chrissie. She could have wept.

War had come to Scotland early on, with attacks on the Forth Bridge and Edinburgh. In September 1940, it was

Dundee's turn for attention. A hit-and-run raider loosed a stick of bombs which straddled the city. One landed at the corner of Dalkeith Road and Nesbitt Street, uncomfortably close to Broughty Ferry.

The scare they'd had was enough to send Chrissie and the rest of the queue scuttling to the nearest air-raid shelter when the siren went some days later while queuing for potatoes in Brook Street.

'Well, fancy meetin' you here!' exclaimed Aggie Gallacher, as Chrissie sat down next to her.

Chrissie smiled at Norrie Gallacher's granny. 'How's Norrie, Mrs Gallacher? Sandra tells me he's gone to Canada to try his luck.'

The old lady looked grim. 'He's high up in a Canadian business recycling metal, he ses, but if you ask me that's just a fancy name for a scrap-yaird. You can tell Sandra he's thinkin' o' marrying a Canadian lassie.'

Aggie looked mournful for a moment. 'Mind you, I thought I would be fine pleased to see him settled, Chrissie, but to tell the truth I'm no' a' that happy aboot the match. He'll never come back tae Scotland tae bide, an' I miss that grand laddie sair,' Aggie admitted. A tear slid surreptitiously down her cheek. She took out a lace-edged hanky and blew her nose defiantly.

'Listen, there's a plane noo!' said one of the others sharing the shelter.

Chrissie could hear somebody's teeth chattering. 'Is it a Jerry?' asked a nervous voice.

Aggie Gallacher put her head to one side, ear cocked towards the ceiling. 'Naw, it's one o' ours. I can tell by the steady sound. Jerries go "wah-wah-wah" like that. You can tell a Jerry a mile aff,' she answered comfortably, and sure enough the 'all clear' went seconds later.

Comings and goings. The restless traffic never seemed to

stop. At the end of November, more unexpected visitors arrived on the doorstep at Beechyhill. It was Charles who answered the door this time, and his yell could be heard outside in the garden, where old McIntosh was digging for victory in the vegetable patch.

'Chrissie, it's Mary Rose, and wee Elizabeth!'

He hugged his step-daughter and the seven-year-old. Everyone came crowding to the door, muddy McIntosh included, and Mary Rose and her daughter were borne inside on such a wave of enthusiastic welcome, any misgivings she'd had about her reception were swept away for ever.

Chrissie was overjoyed to have her daughter and grandchild home at last. She couldn't take her eyes off the child. Black hair, eyes as blue as forget-me-nots.

Oh, Danny! she thought with a pang.

Mary Rose was talking ten to the dozen. The words spilled out as if they'd been held back a long time. She kept an arm round Elizabeth protectively as she talked.

'Roddy joined the RAF just before war was declared. He's got his wings now, and he's stationed with a fighter squadron somewhere in England. I won't say where. Careless talk costs lives! Roddy's parents want me to leave London and go to them.'

'It seems only wise, dear,' Chrissie remarked.

Mary Rose looked serious. 'You don't understand, Mum. They don't want me, they want Elizabeth. They want to possess her, to mould her into their own ways. They would send her immediately to boarding school. A little girl of seven! I don't want that, Mum, but they're strong and determined and Elizabeth will inherit the estate eventually. I couldn't fight them. So, true to form, I ran away,' she said, looking shame-faced.

There was an awkward lull. Mary Rose studied the floor. 'How's Sandra?' she asked quietly.

Chrissie answered, because Charles seemed reluctant. 'She's still in Glasgow with Harriet, working very hard in the clinic. We see very little of her.'

'Oh, I see,' said Mary Rose unhappily.

Presently she glanced up. 'Mum, would you take Elizabeth until the war's over? I'll miss her dreadfully, but I have to be near Roddy, and I know my wee girl will be safe and happy with you and Charles. I'll join the Land Army, I think, and see if I can help with farm animals and horses. I'd like that.'

Bessie clasped her old hands joyfully, and answered for all of them. 'Oh, Mary Rose, my dearie, it'll be grand to have a wee bairnie in the hoose again!'

Chrissie's smile was tinged with sadness. Her daughter would leave again soon, to live her own life. Still, there was Elizabeth, she thought with a little glow of joy.

The little girl was watching her shyly. ''Scuse me, please, but are you my new granny?' she asked.

'Yes, dear. Will I do?' Chrissie laughed.

Elizabeth examined her new granny solemnly. 'You've got a pretty brooch like a little ship, and a very nice face. I think I'm going to like you,' she decided, and smiled a wide, beaming smile that was oddly familiar and tugged at Chrissie's heartstrings.

1941 stood out afterwards in Chrissie's memory as the lowest ebb. There was the dreadful Clydeside blitz on the moonlit nights of 13th and 14th March, and three days of agonised waiting before they had news of Sandra and Harriet. The clinic had been totally destroyed and Harriet had broken a leg clambering over rubble to help victims of the raids, but Sandra was unscathed. Chrissie and Charles breathed easily again, only to be driven to black despair when Ewan reached his eighteenth birthday in April, and was called up soon after.

But there were pleasant memories and laughter, too, that year and in the ones that followed. Chrissie and Charles spent happy times congregated cosily round the wireless set with Charlotte and Elizabeth, listening to Wilfred Pickles, Cyril Fletcher's 'Odd Odes' and, of course, dear old Tommy Handley's 'ITMA'.

Elizabeth, who'd quite a talent for mimicry, danced merrily around the house intoning 'Can I do you now, sir?' like Mrs Mopp, Tommy Handley's charwoman, or imitating with gusto the woeful tones of Mona Lott. 'It's bein' so cheerful as keeps me goin'!'

Yes, there was laughter despite the war and the anxiety Chrissie felt for her children. And there was good news, too, from Chrissie's widespread family. She received a letter from her niece Georgina in Australia, the first for some considerable time.

I've had another baby, Auntie Chris! A beautiful, little boy. We have called him Thomas, to lay a ghost from my past. Do you remember Tam the shepherd? I had such a girlish crush on him. Thank goodness he married someone else, or I would never have married Bruce, had Jean-Christine and Thomas, or lived in Australia. Isn't love strange? You think you've lost it, then one day it pops up again better than ever . . .

Rationing was a sore trial, although Emily worked wonders with potatoes, stale bread and dried eggs. Jani's little shop did surprisingly well, probably because she searched diligently for off-the-ration goodies such as cinnamon sticks and locust beans when they were to be had, and kept a wee treat or two under the counter to wipe away a bairn's tears, or comfort an old body. Her husband, Hughie, sailed with the convoys, and had been remarkably fortunate so far. Sailors fell over themselves to sign on with him as he had gained an enviable reputation as a 'lucky' skipper.

But the brightest spot, perhaps, in those dark days was the arrival of Benjamin Franklin Chester's food hamper. How the American had managed to send it, Chrissie couldn't imagine. There had been no hint of his intentions in his business letters, but a large wooden crate was delivered one day to the office, and Chrissie, Charles and Maisie unpacked it with incredulous joy.

'Michty me! Tinned ham!' cried Maisie in awed tones. 'I canna mind when I last tasted tinned ham. Oh, my goad, and dates and sultanas, tinned pears and peaches! Chocolates, too!' she drooled.

Charles and Chrissie did their best to send the staff home with a gift from the hamper, and doled out goodies to some of the weavers and others who were in hospital. There wasn't much left after that, but Chrissie kept back a tin of Spam, a packet of dates and a tin of boiled sweets for themselves. The family ate these items slowly over a period of time, with tears in their eyes, savouring every unaccustomed bite.

Chrissie added a grateful postscript to her next letter to Autofibres in Detroit. 'The hamper was heavenly. God bless you, my dear Benjamin Franklin. We love you!'

And she meant every word.

It hadn't taken Ewan Rankine much longer than a stint in Maryhill Barracks to shed all romantic notions about soldiering. That hurdle surmounted, Ewan settled down grimly to endure the war and hopefully return to Dundee in one piece. He was a good, dogged infantryman with no particular desire to become an officer, although by D-Day he'd risen to the rank of corporal. Ewan was content with that. He wasn't seeking medals.

His unit crossed to Normandy on D-Day plus ten and followed Montgomery's spearhead up towards Holland. Ewan saw enough action on the way to convince him war was a daft business, but though he kept a sharp look-out for Sammy, to his disappointment he didn't meet up with his half-brother.

Ewan found something else, though. Something so incredible it excited him and fired his imagination as nothing else had done during this dangerous, miserable period of his life.

Ewan found his mother's ship. He found the *Christina K.*

Chapter 14

'What do we do in the infantry?
We march, we march, we march . . . !'

Ewan whistled the soldiers' song cheerily, because
he sat comfortably in a 15 cwt truck as the driver
breenged up the road past his marching mates. The 51st
Highland Division had the job of winkling out pockets of
resistance left behind in the main advance into Holland,
but Ewan didn't envisage any problems in the little port
of Muiden. They'd been sent to pick up spare parts for
the CO's staff car. A pleasant, cushy job.

Ewan consulted the scrawled directions he'd been
given. 'Turn right, Taffy, then straight ahead until you
reach the harbour.'

They bumped over debris and avoided shell craters
until Taffy halted the truck outside the warehouse
where Workshops platoon RASC were operating. Ewan
grinned at the Welshman.

'You won't need me to carry a cylinder head and
spark plugs, will you, Taff? I feel like a breath of
sea air.'

'Help yourself, Jock,' agreed Taffy obligingly.

It was good to be on his own for once, walking
alone instead of in a column. Ewan strolled along the
quayside. There were Dutch fishermen busy around
the little harbour, but they beamed at the lone Scottish
soldier and courteously left him to his solitude. Ewan

watched the fishing boats for a while, then headed towards the entrance to the canal.

The scene here was quite different, one of desolation and destruction. Lock gates stood wide open and had been badly damaged, probably when the countryside was deliberately flooded in an attempt to stop the Allied advance. Roofless warehouses and derelict quays added to the bleakness of the scene. Ewan hesitated, but curiosity drove him to explore.

He picked his way through the ruins and found himself in a deserted inner harbour which had become an eerie graveyard for several ships. The still water was greenish and oily, dark fringes of weed hung from mouldering mooring ropes. A dead silence lay over the abandoned vessels, broken only by a chill breeze that blew now and then and made the dark water lap lazily against the quay. A lone gull screamed indignantly at Ewan's intrusion and flew off, the harsh noise echoing between broken walls.

He cast an eye over the sad ships and shivered. Some looked quite modern, trapped in this dismal place by war, others were aged hulks. One was tall-masted, with a rusting funnel and tattered remnants of sail hanging from the yard arms. On the point of turning back, Ewan paused, struck by an odd feeling of recognition. Where had he seen those tall masts before?

He slowly paced the full length of the old ship until he reached the bows. She was in a deplorable state of neglect, and he stared stupidly for some time at the name incised on her bow before it registered with him.

The *Christina K*.

Ewan couldn't believe it. He'd found his mother's bonnie ship! She looked just like the old photographs he'd studied and the silver replica his mother always wore, but her brasses were green and tarnished, her paint flaking. He realised he was shivering uncontrollably, his eyes gritty with incredulous emotion. He'd found the *Christina K*.

Ewan came back to earth with a jolt. The keen breeze blew cold on his cheeks, and he scuffed his battledress sleeve guiltily across his eyes. He looked around wildly. Who owned the ship? What was she doing here? He had to find out.

Ewan scrambled back over the rubble and hailed an old fisherman passing by. 'Please, do you speak English?'

The old lad's face creased into a beaming smile. 'Yes. I sail many times to Aberdeen before the war. Whisky is ver' good in Aberdeen.'

Ewan explained about the ship. 'She was built in Dundee, Scotland, as a whaler, and once belonged to my mother's family. Do you know who owns her?'

The fisherman nodded thoughtfully. 'Ah yes, that one! I think she belong to a Norwegian who is trading in whale oil before the war. When Holland is invaded the Germans do not let him take the ship to Norway in case he sail to Britain instead. So your Dundee ship lie here and rot.'

Ewan heard Taffy calling in the distance. He must go, but he hated to leave the ship now he'd found her. 'What will happen to her when the war's over?' he asked.

The old man shrugged. 'Maybe the Norwegian will return. Maybe she break up and sink first. Who knows?'

'Jock! Jock, where are you?' Taffy sounded impatient.

Ewan searched desperately in his pockets and gave the old man a bar of chocolate he'd brought with him. 'Look, I must go, but when the war's over I'll be back. Please, keep an eye on her for me?'

The fisherman beamed. 'OK. I keep her afloat until you come. Maybe!'

* * *

'Oh, I'm fed up of this!' Chrissie exclaimed in annoyance as she peered through the car windscreen into pitch-blackness. The masked headlamps gave such a thin beam of light she could hardly make out the road. Driving in the black-out was positively dangerous. And all for a dozen eggs!

The mother of one of her granddaughter Elizabeth's friends had whispered to Chrissie there were fresh duck eggs to spare at their farm not far from Tealing aerodrome. 'Come in the dark,' she'd whispered, 'and for heaven's sake don't let on to a single soul, or there'll be a riot!'

Elizabeth was sitting cradling the precious box of green-blue eggs on her knee as if they were the Crown Jewels, but Chrissie was beginning to wonder if the journey had been worth all the trouble.

'Emily could make a real sponge sandwich, Gran. She can have my jam ration to spread in the middle,' Elizabeth offered generously.

Chrissie's expression softened. Maybe the nightmare journey was worth it after all to give the child a rare treat. 'Yes, it could be your birthday cake, darling,' she smiled.

'But it's not my birthday yet, Gran. I'm still only eleven!' Elizabeth protested.

'Och, who cares about a wee detail like that?'

'Oh, Gran, you are naughty!' Elizabeth giggled. She settled back, hugging the eggs, utterly content in her grandmother's company.

Elizabeth and Chrissie shared a rare rapport. Since Mary Rose had brought her little daughter to Beechyhill four years ago, Elizabeth had settled happily into the pattern of their lives. Charles doted on his step-granddaughter, and Charlotte regarded Elizabeth as a much-loved small sister. Bessie McCutcheon was a spry seventy-eight; rejuvenated now she had a youngster to care for. The nursery was a cheery place filled with laughter even in the grimmest days of war. Charlotte preferred to go to the pictures with Leon now, occupying the chummy seats in Green's Playhouse, so Bessie accompanied Elizabeth to the Kinnaird or the La Scala and sometimes to the Queen's Theatre. There they joined heartily in community singing. They sang all the popular songs with a gusto that would have made Ewan squirm.

'Mairzy doats and dozy doats, and liddle lambsy divy,' was Elizabeth's particular favourite, because it was so daft it took her mind off the war and all its misery and shortages. She started humming the tune as Chrissie negotiated Powrie Brae.

'Once upon a time,' Chrissie told her, 'from this vantage point you could see the lights of Dundee shining like a necklace of bright jewels, if the smoke from factory lums wasn't too thick.'

Elizabeth strained to see through the darkness but couldn't make out a glimmer of light anywhere. Must eat more carrots so I can see in the dark, she thought. What a wonderful sight it must be when the city was lit up. After the war, Elizabeth vowed she'd come and just stare and stare at all the lights.

She hugged the eggs. It was awfully cold in the car, and she was glad she'd obeyed her grandmother and put on a thick coat and pixie hood, because she was shivering without the benefit of a heater. Chrissie caught the small movement and glanced away from the road for an instant.

'Soon be home now, darling. It's lucky I had a gallon or two to spare from my petrol ration to make this trip, isn't it?'

Elizabeth agreed. She couldn't wait to show Emily their prize, and was out of the car and darting off towards the kitchen the moment Chrissie drew up outside the old coach-house they used as a garage. Charles came out as Chrissie was opening the doors, and something in his expression made her stop short.

'Where's Elizabeth?' he asked quietly.

'She ran into the house with the eggs. Why?'

'It's her father, Chris. It's Roddy. He was shot down on a bombing raid over Germany. There's no hope for him, I'm afraid. Mary Rose is just off the phone. She asked if we would break the news to Elizabeth.'

'Oh, Charles! When will it end, this suffering?' Chrissie cried, and he held her close. She felt his lips brush her hair, and that, more than the loss of poor Roddy, released her tears.

Charles took out a hanky and offered it to her. She mopped her eyes. 'OK now, darling?' he asked gently.

She nodded. Together, hand in hand, they went into the house to find Elizabeth.

Elizabeth wished she could feel sad, but all she felt was sort of numb. She'd sobbed dutifully when Papa Charles told her about her daddy, because she knew it was expected of her. She'd squeezed out mournful tears for the handsome, rather awe-inspiring stranger in smart RAF blue uniform, who'd come to visit her in Dundee once or twice.

She recalled there had been awkward vibrations in the air when her father and mother visited Beechyhill. Granny and Papa Charles had seemed strained and different, Bessie went around muttering and Auntie Sandra never joined the family party. Elizabeth was secretly quite relieved when her mother and father left to go south. She cried for her father now, because she remembered about those awkward visits, and was sorry.

Emily went ahead and made the un-birthday cake all the same. Emily was nice, Elizabeth thought. Emily and Charlotte gave up their sweetie rations to ice the cake with melted chocolate and sprinkle hundreds and thousands over the top. It was a lovely cake, soft, sweet and spongy. There was still one piece left when Mary Rose arrived quite unexpectedly one evening.

Sandra was there from Glasgow. She was playing Pelmanism with Elizabeth when Mary Rose walked in. Sandra stood up so abruptly the playing cards scattered all over the floor.

'You!' Sandra cried.

Mary Rose held out a hand to her sister. 'Sandra, it's over, now Roddy's dead. Please, can't we be friends?' she pleaded.

Sandra had gone pale. 'You don't understand. It's not what you did with Roddy. It's because you never let on that you two had fallen in love. I lost someone very dear to me, because of your sly ways. I sent him far away and lost him for ever. You ruined my life. That's why I'll never forgive you, Mary Rose!'

Mary Rose was devastated. She longed to make up the quarrel. It hurt her to be on bad terms with the sister she loved. The quarrel seemed futile now Roddy was dead, and Mary Rose had hoped to end it. There was a complication she hadn't suspected, though. Norrie Gallacher held the key to the bitter estrangement. Norrie had been sweet on Sandra for years, but Sandra'd had her sights set on an impossible dream.

'Oh, Sandra, it's Norrie, isn't it?' cried Mary Rose.

Sandra stared at her sister wordlessly, then made a dive for the doorway. Chrissie was making a dress for Elizabeth out of wornout curtains, and she stood up with folds of material clutched in her hands.

'Sandra! Where are you going?'

'Back to Glasgow!'

The door slammed. Nobody moved until they heard Sandra's car start and go racing down the drive. Chrissie sank into the chair, shaken by the unpleasant scene. Mary Rose would have wept if she'd any tears to spare after Roddy. Unfortunately, she'd more bad news for her poor mother.

Mary Rose went across and hugged her little daughter, who had sat frozen like a statue while all this was going on.

'Mum, I have to take Elizabeth away. I'm so sorry.'

This was a terrible blow. 'Oh, no!' Chrissie cried in anguish.

'Roddy's parents want her. They've begged me to let them care for her while I go to college. I've decided to be a vet, you see, so that I can support myself and Elizabeth now Roddy's gone.' Mary Rose stared at her mother, silently imploring Chrissie not to make a fuss.

'Oh, Mum, Elizabeth is *all* the Stirtons have now Roddy's dead. She'll inherit the estate one day, and it seems only right she should know her other grandparents, now she's older.'

Chrissie was silent. How could she argue? Mary Rose cupped her little daughter's troubled face between her hands and looked at her searchingly.

'Darling, you heard what I said to Granny Chris. I know how happy you've been here, but Gran and Grandpa Stirton need you more. They're lonely and sad, and nobody can cheer them and give them hope for the future like you can. I won't force you to go if you really hate the idea, Elizabeth, but please think very hard before you decide.'

Elizabeth thought hard. She felt scared when she thought about leaving Beechyhill and going to live with strangers. It was on the tip of her tongue to refuse point blank, then she paused and thought again.

How awful to be sad and lonely. On the other hand,

it was rather wonderful to be so badly needed. Her grandparents' need of her touched Elizabeth's generous heart. She knew she'd weep buckets if she had to leave the dear folk at Beechyhill, especially Granny Chris and Papa Charles, but Elizabeth knew instinctively what ought to be done. She stared bravely at her mother, because she knew if she looked at Granny Chris she'd weaken.

'I've thought about it, Mum, and I'll go,' Elizabeth decided.

'Och, I miss the wee soul!' Emily said mournfully a few days after Mary Rose and Elizabeth had departed for England. Emily and Charlotte were great pals. They'd been sitting in the kitchen that afternoon doing one another's hair. Their heads bristled with metal curlers, and Emily was curling shorter locks with curling tongs. Meg, the labrador who'd replaced faithful old Angus, snoozed in her basket by the stove.

'I miss Elizabeth terribly, too. If it wasn't for Leon being on leave just now, I'd be right down in the dumps,' admitted Charlotte. She brightened. 'Listen Emily, why don't you come to the Palais with us tonight? It'd cheer you up to go dancing.'

'I dinna want to be a gooseberry.'

'Nonsense. Leon wouldn't mind, and anyway you'd soon click with a lad.'

Emily turned away. 'I'm no' sure I want a click. Anyway, I've no stockings, and no coupons either.'

Charlotte frowned. The shortage of stockings didn't bother her, because she'd made herself elegant satin trousers from an old nightie to hide the caliper on her leg.

'I've no coupons left either. If you have some of that brown stain left in the bottle why not paint your legs, Emily? Nobody would know,' she suggested.

Emily was tempted. 'I suppose I could.'

'I'll draw seams up the back of your legs with my eyebrow pencil if you like,' Charlotte offered eagerly.

'Oh, thanks!' Emily sat, watching Charlotte. There was a glow about Charlotte every time she met Leon. She radiated happiness when she was with him, and he seemed very smitten too. 'Charlotte, will you and Leon get married?' she asked boldly.

Charlotte's happy glow faded. 'I don't know. He was studying to be a doctor when the Germans invaded Poland, and he wants to go back to his own country. He refuses to marry me and take me with him though. He insists it'll be dangerous and difficult living in Poland after the war, and he won't let me take the risk.'

The two young women cheered up once the curlers were removed and their freshly washed and curled hairdos were revealed. With much giggling and squealing, Emily stained her legs a beautiful pale brown and Charlotte finished off the effect with dark brown seams drawn with a steady hand.

'There. Away and slip on your dress and shoes, and let's see how it looks,' Charlotte ordered, proud of her handiwork.

Emily returned presently, dressed in a pretty shade of deep pink.

Charlotte gasped in envy. 'I thought you'd used up all your coupons. Where'd you get that new dress?'

Emily blushed. 'It was an auld sheet your mum said wasna worth the mending. I dyed it pink wi' the beetroot McIntosh brought in frae the garden, then made it into a wee frock for mysel',' Emily admitted.

Before Charlotte had recovered from a fit of laughing, the doorbell rang. Emily covered her mouth. 'Charlotte, I can't answer it dressed up like this!' There was a kerfuffle in the hallway at that point. Meg began barking and Emily eased the kitchen door open a crack. She turned as pink as the frock.

'Charlotte, it's Sammy!'

Sammy had been in two minds about taking leave. He'd been wounded in the arm. Not badly, but enough to keep him out of the thick of the fighting in the Ardennes and earn him a fortnight's recuperation leave when he came out of hospital. Should he go home? Home! That was a joke. Where was home?

Something had drawn him to Dundee. He wasn't sure what. He'd liked Charles, his mother's husband. He'd been prepared to dislike him, but who could dislike such a kind, courteous man? Standing in the hallway at Beechyhill, he shook hands awkwardly with Charles, and eyed his mother warily. She kissed him lightly on the cheek. The kitchen door burst open at that point and a friendly black dog bounded out. The animal placed its paws on Sammy's chest, tail wagging, and he fondled Meg's ears.

Looking over the dog's head, Sammy saw a vision dressed in deep pink framed in the kitchen doorway. It was the loveliest sight he'd seen for many a day. He was drawn towards her, the dog snuffling happily at his hand.

'Why, hullo, Emily!'

She smiled, speechless for once. Sammy took in the pretty dress, the shining hair-do, the long legs clad in sheer nylon stockings, and felt suddenly anxious.

'Going dancing?' he asked casually.

'Aye. Me and Charlotte and Leon are off to the Palais, but—'

Sammy interrupted with sudden and inexplicable annoyance. 'I see you have an American boyfriend.'

Emily looked bewildered. 'What are ye blethering aboot?'

He pointed. 'The nylons. Yanks are the only ones who can get nylons for their girlfriends these days.'

Charlotte had appeared at Emily's shoulder. The two young women stared at Sammy, then at each other, and burst into gales of laughter.

Emily wiped her eyes. 'They're painted on, Sammy, you gowk! I don't have a boyfriend, let alone a Yank that dishes out nylons.'

'You don't?' There was a warmth in Sammy's heart, a joyfulness. He thought he understood at last why he'd come home.

Tuesday 8th May 1945 was VE Day. Victory in Europe. The war was over, and there were crowds in the City Square, and street parties all around the city. A German submarine turned up in Dundee harbour to surrender, the young men in its crew just as relieved as everyone else to see an end to the fighting.

Chrissie felt immense gratitude that her sons and daughters had come through the ordeal safely. She mourned for poor Roddy, and thought wistfully about his little lass, Elizabeth. She had settled quite happily with the Stirtons, and was a day-girl at a girls' school. Her letters to Chrissie and Charles were full of the good friends she'd made and the fun they had. Chrissie was glad for her.

Emily and Sammy were to be married quietly after he was demobbed. There was still a gulf between Chrissie and her son which neither could bridge, but cheerful Emily had gone some way towards repairing the breach.

Sammy had decided to take a degree in civil engineering at Dundee Technical College. 'There'll be roads and bridges to be built all over the country, and I'm to have a say in it!' Sammy declared firmly.

Charles and Chrissie were very concerned about

Charlotte. Leon had gone. He'd always said he'd return to Poland, and it had been a sad day when he left Dundee with the other Polish lads who'd been made welcome in the city. Charlotte walked every day with the dog, withdrawn and lonely.

When Japan capitulated in August that year, Chrissie felt she could relax at last. Ewan was demobbed some months later, and declared his intention of entering the family business. With Chrissie safely occupied elsewhere in the house, Ewan told his father he'd found the *Christina K.*

'Dad, couldn't we buy and restore the ship, and give Mum the greatest thrill of her life?' he asked eagerly.

Charles looked troubled. 'Nothing I'd like better if we had the money, Ewan, but we don't. The war has hit Rankine's hard, and we've lost the American connection now Ben Chester's retired to his cattle ranch in Texas. In fact, the signs are the jute trade's in serious decline. I don't know if you're altogether wise seeking a future with the firm.'

'It's a challenge. If we can't spin and weave jute, then we must find something else,' Ewan declared stubbornly.

'There are man-made fibres certainly, but much remains to be done before that's a viable proposition.' Charles told him. He didn't add that he was too exhausted and weary to try out new ways and methods. The years of war had exacted a heavy toll upon Charles Rankine.

Charlotte's Polish soldier returned to her. Leon came back to Dundee with little more than the clothes he stood up in and a haunted look in his eyes. Charlotte saw Leon come hesitantly up the driveway, a little unsure of his welcome, and she gave a cry of joy. Forgetting her paralysed leg, she ran swiftly, with Meg barking and bounding by her side. She flung herself into his arms and they clung together, laughing, crying, kissing one another. The dog leaped and frisked happily round them.

Watching from the window, Charles put an arm round Chrissie and smiled. 'Another wedding on the cards, Chris, if I'm not mistaken!' He was serious for a moment. 'I'm glad that lad's come back. There'll be little joy for anyone in his sad country for years to come.'

Chrissie frowned thoughtfully. 'I've been thinking, Charles, with Sammy and Emily occupying rooms upstairs, Ewan in the attic, Bessie in the nursery wing, and Charlotte and Leon needing accommodation if they marry, why not convert the house into separate flats? It would give everyone independence, and the house is much too large for us two.'

'Good idea.' Charles nodded agreement. He returned slowly to his chair and lay back, closing his eyes wearily. 'And I won't have to climb those damned stairs to get to bed!'

He didn't see the stricken look on his wife's face. He didn't know the frantic efforts she'd made to save his failing strength, or guess at the constant fear she hid from him.

They went ahead with alterations to the big house in preparation for Charlotte and Leon's wedding. The time had come to sell old William Kennedy's house, for his former housekeeper had decided to give up keeping boarders and retire to the country. Chrissie let her family home go with many qualms, but her share of the proceeds did help to pay for the work at Beechyhill. She was sure her father would have approved.

It was to be a quiet wedding, to spare Charles too much stress and excitement. Leon had decided to continue his studies to become a doctor in Scotland,

and was more than grateful to have a roof over his head while he completed his course.

Shortly before the wedding, Chrissie inspected her wardrobe critically and made a face. 'I'm so dowdy! Everything's shabby after the war. Even poor old Dundee looks terribly down-at-heel these days. Everything could do with a fresh lick of paint.'

Charles smiled. 'You look fine to me, but why not splash out for once. Take my clothing coupons and buy yourself a nice new outfit. I don't need them. My old suit is far better than the utility rubbish they produce nowadays.'

She kissed him gratefully. 'You are a darling!'

Chrissie sallied forth next morning armed with two books of clothing coupons, more precious than gold. She browsed round the shop windows, then spotted a pretty blue dress and jacket in The Corner Shop, better known as GL Wilson's, or more affectionately, GL's. She hurried inside.

'Weel hullo, Chrissie! Still as bonnie as ever!' boomed a familiar voice, and there was big Bella, her friend of the old spinning-mill days, just as large and loud as Chrissie had remembered.

Chrissie hugged her old friend with delight. 'Bella, you haven't changed a bit!'

'Naw, still like something straight oot o' the *Beano*!' Bella roared and laughed at her own joke, slapping Chrissie playfully on the back. 'I'm retired frae the mill noo, though. Lady o' leisure, ken, that's me. Eck's retired frae the shipyard an' a'. He shook hands wi' the King an' Queen when they visited the Caledon during the war and wouldna wash his hands for a month, after. My dochter was workin' as a welder in the shipyard during the war, would ye believe? I dinna ken what lassies is comin' to these days!' Bella shook her head mournfully.

Chrissie laughed. 'My great-nephew, Jamal Kennedy, works in the Caledon too, though he's going to sea soon with Hughie, his dad. Oh, Bella, it's good to see you. Just like a tonic. I still have the bonnie blue shawl you gave me when I left the mill, you know.'

Bella sighed and wiped her eyes. 'Aye, Chris, those were the days. We worked hard, but we had a good laugh at times. You an' me will never see the likes again.'

Her daughter's wedding may be quiet, but Chrissie was determined to make it memorable. And so it was, but for quite an unexpected reason.

'It *must* be a white wedding!' Chrissie insisted. Charlotte agreed dutifully. She was in such a state of bliss she'd have agreed to marry Leon dressed in a jute sack, as Bessie had remarked.

'A white wedding! You'll no' raise enough coupons for that, Chris!' Bessie put a damper on Chrissie's enthusiasm right away, then relented as she noted Charlotte's crestfallen expression. 'There's always the ivory silk bedspread, Chris. Somebody spilt tea on the corner, but there's enough stuff left to make a braw gown.'

Chrissie could have hugged Bessie. 'Of course! The very thing. We'll need to get our skates on, though, if it's to be ready by January.' She hurried off to track down the bedspread.

Bessie shouted after her. 'And if you're considering a veil for the lassie, what aboot the bonnie net screens in the nursery?'

With a frenzied burst of activity, the wedding gown was finished by 10th January. Charlotte tried it on. It fitted perfectly. Chrissie arranged the filmy veil, setting a garland of white artificial flowers on Charlotte's fair hair. They stood back and admired their handiwork in silence. Charlotte looked ethereally beautiful.

Bessie wiped her eyes emotionally. 'They was always awfy bonnie, those screens. They set off the bedspread just perfect.'

Charlotte was delighted with the finished effect. She twisted this way and that in front of the glass, admiring the beautiful gown. 'Oh, Mum! I always dreamed about a white wedding, but I never thought I'd have one.'

'I was determined at least one of my daughters would. There's nothing to beat a nice, white wedding,' declared Chrissie smugly.

It began snowing on 12th January 1947. It started with a light flurry, then got down to it in earnest. Snow fell steadily from a slate-grey sky, with a strong north-easterly wind to whip it into drifts. In no time, the city ground to a standstill. By Charlotte's wedding day the whole country was blanketed in deep snow and ice.

'The guests!' wailed Chrissie. 'Nobody'll get here, and we've arranged drinks and a meal for fifty people at the hotel!'

'Leave it to me, darling,' said Charles. He got busy on the phone, then came back beaming. 'That's OK, Chris. I've invited forty spinners and weavers from the factory. I was giving them a half-day anyway.'

Ewan and Sammy had dug a path up the driveway for the taxi. They came in, their outfits looking decidedly the worse for wear.

'That's the two taxis now, but one's stuck at the gate. We'll all have to put on wellie boots,' they announced cheerfully.

Chrissie wondered what else could go wrong. 'Oh, I do hope Leon got to the church all right.'

Ewan grinned. 'Don't worry. We made sure of him. We put him on the snowplough.'

They all donned wellingtons and heavy coats, except the bride and her father. Chrissie kissed her daughter fondly, and so did Emily, who was a picturesque bridesmaid with wellingtons and macintosh covering her dress. Charles and Charlotte were left alone at last.

'You look very beautiful, love,' Charles told his radiant daughter.

There were tears in her eyes as she hugged him. 'Thank you, Daddy. Thank you for everything. Thank you for all the happy years,' Charlotte said softly.

The snowplough gallantly escorted the bridal car to church. Emily was waiting at the church door, dressed in pale blue with high heels and real silk stockings this time. She hissed at Charles. 'You should see the crowd in the kirk. The whole factory's turned up, the grease-monkey an' a'!'

At that moment a packed bus drew up outside the gate, and Harriet Bowers descended followed by Sandra and all the other invited guests in wedding finery. Harriet beamed merrily at Charles.

'Just in the nick of time! We decided to hire a bus to be sure of getting here, Charles. Wasn't that a good idea?'

Charles was speechless. He wondered what the hotel would say when they discovered the quiet wedding Chrissie had planned wasn't to be so quiet after all.

When spring came, Ewan returned to Muiden, in Holland. He had no hope of buying the *Christina K*, for business was too precarious in the aftermath of war. He just wanted to see her again and make sure she was still afloat.

The scene was very different this time. Industrious people, the Dutch, Ewan thought admiringly. The little port was bustling, everything neat and tidy. The broken-down warehouse had been re-roofed and repaired.

The *Christina K* was gone.

Ewan searched the wharves. He searched everywhere

for the old fisherman, but he was nowhere to be seen. His questions were met with blank stares. It was a bitter disappointment. He had found his mother's ship, only to lose her again.

The ship had become doubly important to Ewan, because it was only too evident that his father was very ill. Chrissie spent every moment she could at her husband's bedside, nursing him with a devotion that brought awkward tears to Ewan's eyes. Watching his father sinking day by day, Ewan wished with all his heart he could have given her the ship. It would have been a comfort. Little enough, perhaps, but something to cling to in the dark days ahead.

Ewan managed to persuade his mother to go to the City Square to see Lord Provost Garnet Wilson present the young Princess Elizabeth to the people of Dundee.

Chrissie was thrilled to see the daughter of the gracious lady she'd admired for years. 'She was lovely, Charles! Such a nice smile, as if she really enjoyed meeting everyone,' she told her husband.

As she spoke, she studied Charles anxiously. Did he look a little better today? She imagined he did. She took his hand, raised it to her lips and kissed it sorrowfully. He smiled without opening his eyes.

'I remember the moment I fell in love with you, Chris,' he said. 'It was at Lizzie Bowers's wedding, and you lifted your face to the sunshine and smiled. Such a small thing to capture a poor man's heart for ever.' He paused, smiling. 'You didn't like me very much.'

'Och, my head was filled with daft cantrips in those days, Charles.' She leaned closer and kissed him on the lips. 'I'll tell you one thing. I love you to distraction now, my dear sweetheart.'

Afterwards, she was always glad she'd kissed him, always glad she'd spoken up. He died quietly that night while she lay beside him holding his hand. Her kind and gentle man.

Harriet came with Sandra to the funeral, but Mary Rose did not attend. Even the death of their beloved step-father did not mend the sisters' bitter quarrel. Chrissie herself felt strangely numb and detached. Perhaps you do, when your life has lost all meaning and purpose, she thought dazedly. She dressed heavily in black. She took almost a delight in wearing deepest mourning, because she knew it drained all colour and spirit out of her delicate features.

Harriet embraced her friend, then studied her with observant eyes. She forgot her own grief for a moment in concern for Chrissie. Harriet recognised the danger in that numb detachment, that terrible, icy calm. If only Chrissie would weep. But her gaze was dry and fixed like a sleepwalker. With Harriet at her back and her children all around her, Chrissie got through the funeral in a numb, icy state. She doubted if she would feel emotion of any kind ever again.

Dear, faithful Bessie clutched her elbow. 'Come away, hen. You'll feel stronger when you've had a wee tickie o' biled ham. There's a wheen o' folk comin' back to the hoose this cauld day. The word's got roond there's tattie soup an' a drappie whisky on the go.'

So Chrissie played the hostess with dignity and grace. In ones and twos, awkward in their sincerity, the guests gradually drifted away until there were only Harriet and the members of Chrissie's family left. Sad and subdued, Chrissie's children departed to their respective flats and left Chrissie and Harriet alone together: the two women who had loved Charles Rankine. It seemed fitting.

They sat in complete silence. Harriet searched desperately for some way of breaking through the barrier

312

Chrissie had set around herself, excluding everyone. It brought tears to Harriet's eyes.

'Oh, Chrissie, don't you like me any more?' she burst out. It wasn't what she'd meant to say. It was a cry from the heart.

'What?' Chrissie was startled out of the depression into which she was slowly sinking. She saw Harriet clearly for the first time that day, noted the tears, the inconsolable grief which Harriet must bear alone. Harriet had no children, no happy memories, nobody to comfort her. Poor Harriet had nothing at all, not even her bestfriend's friendship.

Chrissie had to comfort Harriet. She must explain why their warm friendship had turned cold. She began talking agitatedly, the words spilling out. 'I was so jealous of you, Harriet. I grew to love Charles so much, you see, and the more I loved him, the more terrified I became you'd take him from me. Oh, Harriet, you're so witty and clever, all the things I'm not, and I loved him so much. That's why I've been so cold and unfriendly. Oh, Harriet, I'm sorry, I should have known you'd never act so meanly. Can you ever forgive me?'

Chrissie was weeping brokenly by the end. The healing tears poured down her cheeks. Blindly, Chrissie held out her arms to her friend, and Harriet hugged her thankfully. There was no need for words. They both knew their friendship was as strong and firm as it had ever been, and that was the way Charles Rankine would have wanted it.

'Don't you think you should stop wearing black, Mum? It's months now since Dad died,' Charlotte ventured.

'It seems like only yesterday.' Chrissie picked up a magazine and laid it down again listlessly. She couldn't settle to anything. All meaning had gone out of her

313

life. She knew her children worried about her, but she couldn't help it.

'They're planning to build a road bridge across the Tay, because the *Fifie* can't cope with the increase in traffic. Isn't that exciting now? We'll be able to drive to St Andrews in no time, and Leon is very keen on golf these days,' Charlotte added hopefully.

'That's nice, dear.' Chrissie closed her eyes wearily. She dozed a lot since Charles died. What else was there to do?

Charlotte stood looking at her mother, frustrated. They'd all agreed they must be very patient with her, but if only she'd snap out of this lethargy and take an interest in life again. She was only in her early sixties after all. Maybe it would be different when the baby arrived, Charlotte thought. But that wasn't for five months yet.

After Charlotte had gone, Chrissie picked up the unread magazine and leafed aimlessly through it. She'd just laid it down again when the doorbell rang. Frowning, she glanced at the clock. She wasn't expecting anyone to call that afternoon.

The man standing in the porch was a big man, broad-shouldered and powerful. He took off his hat respectfully when Chrissie answered the door. His hair was thick, and shone pure silver in the sunlight.

'I came whenever I heard,' he said.

'I beg your pardon?'

'I've been to the bull sales in Perth, and I heard about Charles there. I came right away.'

Chrissie was none the wiser. She'd never seen the stranger before and was wary of him. 'Well, I'm sure that's very thoughtful of you, Mr . . . er . . . but—'

He stared at her, then laughed. 'Forgive me barging

in like this. I feel I know you so well, you see, Chrissie. I forgot we never met.'

She was mystified. 'I'm sorry, but I don't—'

He held out a large hand, grinning. 'I'm Ben Chester, Mrs Rankine. Benjamin Franklin Chester, that's me!'

Chapter 15

'Ben, what a wonderful surprise!' Chrissie shook hands warmly with the American, then ushered him into the flat.

He looked appreciatively around the tastefully furnished drawing room, which had been little changed during alterations to the big house.

'This is a lovely room.'

'Yes. It was Charles's favourite.' She hadn't cried for ages, yet there were tears in her eyes which she couldn't hide.

He took her hand sympathetically. 'I'm sorry. It's been a bad time for you, I guess. Care to talk about it?'

She gently withdrew her hand. 'I'm all right, thank you. Now, would you care for tea or coffee?' she asked brightly.

He smiled. 'Tea or coffee, the British ritual! So you disappear to the kitchen for five minutes and dodge awkward questions. I'd much rather talk!'

This was such an unusual approach, Chrissie sat down and stared. He sat opposite and returned the scrutiny calmly.

'I feel we're old friends, Chrissie. I may call you Chrissie, mayn't I? I guess you know I was friendly with your brother, Ernest Kennedy, when I worked in Detroit? He has a charming wife and family, and on the wall of their apartment is a framed photo of Auntie

Chrissie. I looked at it often, and d'you know, I'll swear you smiled for me alone, and even winked at me once! Ernest's kids used to kiss your photo goodnight when they were small.'

'Did they really? I write to them all, of course, and try so hard to keep in touch with everyone.' She felt quite emotional again.

'Yes, you make the effort, Chrissie. Most people don't bother, then friends are lost, or families drift apart, but you care,' Ben said a little sadly. He smiled at Chrissie. 'Anyway, you look just like your beautiful photo, only—' he stopped awkwardly.

She was curious. 'Only what?'

'Excuse me, ma'am, but must you wear black? It's kind of sombre, and I never thought of you that way.'

Chrissie couldn't help smiling. 'Ben, do you always speak your mind?'

He grinned a little sheepishly. 'We-ell, I find it pays to speak out.'

'How long will you be staying in Scotland?' Chrissie asked, changing the subject.

'I haven't decided yet. I came over for the Festival of Britain, but wandering round London exhibitions isn't much fun on your own, and it rained all the time. So I came north in a bid to trace my ancestors. I attended the Perth bull sales, too. I don't aim to buy any stock this time around, but the Dundee link with the Matador ranch in Texas interests me. I'd intended visiting Rankine's and meeting Charles, then someone told me he'd died some time back. That's why I had to see you. Oh, I'm real sad about Charles, Chrissie!' Ben exclaimed.

'Our son, Ewan, is running the factory now, Ben. He'd be delighted to show you round and hear your views on the future of the textile industry,' Chrissie suggested eagerly. She knew Ewan was feeling his way gingerly and would welcome advice. Ewan was determined to compete in a new era of carpet design and manufacture. He was experimenting cautiously with man-made fibres and had invested heavily in broad looms, pinning his hopes on a post-war housing boom and greatly increased demand for floor-coverings.

Ben was enthusiastic. 'I'd like to hear your son's plans. It's a challenging time, Chrissie. You'll come with me, of course?'

Chrissie hadn't been near the factory since Charles had died. She'd no heart for business these days.

'Well, Ben, I think . . . perhaps—' she faltered.

He stood up, glancing at his wristwatch. 'That's settled then. I'll return to Perth, check out of my hotel and fix someplace else in Dundee. I'll pick you up tomorrow morning. Say nine-thirty, if that'll be OK with your son?'

'I'll check with Ewan,' Chrissie said weakly. She led her visitor to the front door, and found she was reluctant to let him go. 'I wish you'd stay for tea,' she said impulsively.

He paused in the doorway for a moment, looking down at her thoughtfully.

'I'm sorry, not tonight, but thanks all the same.' He took her hand in a friendly grip, then spoke softly. 'I know how it feels to be lonely, Chrissie, believe me.'

His sympathy and understanding touched Chrissie. Her family had supported her loyally since Charles's death, but this man was of her own generation, which made a difference. She was curious about his background. Why was he lonely? Didn't he have a wife and family somewhere?

She smiled warmly. 'Thanks so much for the visit. I think you're a very kind man, Mr Chester.'

'Speaking out, Mrs Rankine? Guess it must be catching,' he remarked dryly, with a twinkle in his eye.

That night, before going to bed, Chrissie hesitated as she laid out clothing for next day's outing. The black dress *did* look depressing, she admitted to herself. The thought immediately appalled her. Was she forgetting her dear husband already? She flung the dress over the back of the chair defiantly, ready for morning.

Ben Chester turned up on the dot. He carried a small parcel, which he presented to Chrissie. 'For you, ma'am.'

Wondering, she undid the wrapping and drew out a blue silk scarf. Colour rose in her cheeks. 'Oh, Ben, it's lovely, but you shouldn't!'

'Well, I don't go for unrelieved black, Chrissie, and I thought a touch of blue might suit. The scarf's Douglas tartan and I got Douglases in my ancestry, so I guess it's kinda appropriate.'

Chrissie arranged the scarf becomingly and fastened it with the silver brooch she always wore. Glancing at her reflection in the nearby mirror, she saw it worked wonders for the black dress. He bent closer to examine the little jewelled ship.

'Say, that's quite something,' he said, impressed.

She found herself telling him about the *Christina K*, and he listened with so much interest she became quite eloquent. She stopped herself with a rueful smile. 'Forgive me, I mustn't start blethering about the *Christina K*, or I'll never stop. She's gone forever, but I still have my little silver replica!'

After the factory visit, Ben decided to go in search of ancestors he'd located in the district, and begged Chrissie to join him in the hunt. She was reluctant at first, but as time wore on she became interested in the venture herself, and the pair of them thoroughly enjoyed poking around peaceful old Angus villages and forgotten cemeteries, piecing together the jigsaw of the

Chester family tree. Ben's ancestors proved to be a colourful bunch of mavericks, as he himself observed.

'There was a Douglas lived in Zoar way back, and he married a McTaggart from Jericho,' he said to Chrissie a month or so later. 'Never could work that out. Zoar and Jericho are mentioned in the Bible, y'know.'

'They're also on the outskirts of Forfar, not far from Dundee.'

He whistled. 'Well, what d'you know! Let's go, girl!'

They drove through the beautiful Strathmore valley. It was wet and misty, but Ben enthused about lush green fields and admired sleek black cattle grazing.

Steers, he called them, and Chrissie burst out laughing merrily, seeing a vision of stampeding steers rounded up by yelling cowboys on horses, just like the western epics Ewan had loved as a boy.

The echo of her own merry laughter silenced her abruptly. She hadn't laughed for a very long time, and laughter seemed a fickle betrayal of her dead husband. All the joy went out of the expedition and she became quiet and withdrawn. Ben glanced at her once or twice with a thoughtful frown, but made no comment. When he cut short the journey and returned to Beechyhill, she didn't invite him in as she usually did.

'I'm tired this evening, Ben. I . . . I think I'll go early to bed,' she said, avoiding his eye.

'Sure, you do that,' he said easily. 'I thought of driving to Pitlochry tomorrow, then on to Killiecrankie. Care to come with me, Chrissie? We could eat out if you're tired.'

'No, I'm sorry. I can't tomorrow. I – er – have an appointment,' she improvised hastily. She wasn't good at telling fibs, and her face flamed.

He studied her thoughtfully. 'I see. Well, another time, perhaps?'

'Yes, Ben. Another time.' She daren't look at him.

She hurried inside. Sinking down on the couch in the lonely room, Chrissie buried her face in her hands and burst into floods of tears.

Next day she didn't go out at all, though the sun shone for once that wet summer of 1951. The hours dragged while she pottered around the flat abstractedly, trying to sort out confused emotions. When the doorbell rang, she went wearily to answer it.

It was Ben.

'There was no appointment, was there, Chrissie? I been sitting on a bench at the foot of the hill watching your door. You didn't budge from the house all day,' he said accusingly.

She stared at him tragically. 'Oh, Ben, I'm sorry.'

'Mind if I come in?'

She led the way into the drawing room. When they were settled, he spread himself comfortably in the armchair and looked at her. 'Care to talk about it, my dear?'

She sat very straight and tense. 'When I'm with you I enjoy myself. I laugh and forget to mourn for Charles. I find it so heartless and shocking to laugh and enjoy life, now Charles is dead. I don't think we can go on seeing one another like this, Ben!'

He looked incredulous. 'Do you really believe Charles would have wanted you to stop laughing and having fun, Chrissie? Of course not! Life goes on. Why shouldn't we enjoy one another's company?'

Chrissie didn't answer. She couldn't. The problem of herself and Ben Chester was too complex to solve with a simple answer. Presently, she heard him sigh.

'And I'd set my heart on taking you over the sea to Skye! By the way, did you know Flora MacDonald emigrated to North Carolina and met up with some of my American ancestors?'

She looked at him sadly. 'Ben, I know all about

your ancestry, and nothing at all about you. Isn't there someone waiting for you at home?'

He looked at her impassively. 'You mean a wife, of course,' he said quietly. 'No wife, Chrissie. Does that make it easier?'

Chrissie couldn't answer that. In a way, his freedom complicated everything intolerably.

He reached over and gripped her hand. 'Learn to live again, Chris. Learn to laugh. Come with me to Skye?'

She dragged her hand away in panic. 'It's impossible! I couldn't!'

'Why not?'

She met his insistent gaze and caught her breath. She couldn't look away, and his eyes were forthright and honest in their demand. She knew she wasn't mistaken: he was falling in love with her. The knowledge increased her agitation, for she hadn't anticipated such a serious complication, and her own emotions were in chaos.

'Don't rush me, Ben, please!' she begged desperately.

'OK, honey. How much time d'you need to think things over about us? A week, a month, a year?'

'I don't know,' she whispered in anguish. She turned her head away to hide tears. Laughter had shocked her, but how much more shocking was her instinctive response to the touch of his hand and the longing in his eyes.

He stood up, looking determined, but cheerful. 'OK, Chrissie, so you need time to think about where all this is leading. I go along with that. I have to check out the possibility I'm related to the Wolf of Badenoch, heaven forbid! Then I head for Sutherland and the Highland clearances. I guess that'll take me away for a coupla weeks. Will that give you time to decide whether you want to see me again, or not?'

She was dazed by the speed of events and bewildered

323

by conflicting emotions. 'You go off, just like that, and I've hardly set foot outside Dundee, all my life!' Chrissie said.

'Then it's high time you did, my girl,' he said grimly.

'She's sent him away! Honestly, Charlotte, would ye credit it?' Emily declared. She planted a fist indignantly either side of her trim waist. Emily wore the 'new look': a dress with tiny waist and very full skirt reaching almost down to high-heeled, ankle-strap shoes. It was sheer luxury after the economies of war.

Charlotte, whose baby was due in a couple of months, averted her eyes enviously from Emily's waistline. 'Did they quarrel, do you know, Emmy?'

'Och, I spiered at her tactfully, but she's a fly one. She wouldna say where Mr Chester had gone or if he's comin' back!' replied Emily indignantly.

Sammy looked up from the book he was studying. 'Does it matter? The man obviously came to his senses just in time.'

The two young women rounded on him. 'Just because you have a bee in your bonnet about your ma, Sammy Murphy!' sniffed Emily.

'Sammy, I thought it was lovely; two lonely people coming together for companionship,' declared Charlotte emotionally.

'OK, have it your way.' Sammy shrugged good-humouredly. He knew when he was beaten. He closed the book and stood up. 'I'm off for a breath of fresh air, girls,' Sammy decided, leaving the flat.

'Parcel for you, Mr Murphy!' the postie called, as Sammy reached the bottom of the outside stairs. The postie opened the door of the van and took out a large, squarish parcel, rather battered. He handed it to Sammy. 'There you are, sir. All the way from India!'

India. Sammy rested the parcel on the stone balustrade and frowned at it. He'd no links with India now. He glanced upstairs, then thought better of opening the mystery parcel in front of his wife and half-sister. India was a different world, a different life. He wanted to keep it to himself.

Carefully, he undid the string, removed the wrappings and opened the thick cardboard box that was revealed. There was a neatly typed letter on top from the firm of lawyers who'd dealt with his father's legal affairs in Calcutta.

Dear Mr Murphy
According to your instructions, some time ago we sold all goods and furnishings belonging to your late foster-parents, Mr and Mrs Arthur Kennedy. We have recently been contacted by the purchaser of a large Victorian bureau which previously belonged to your foster-mother. During cleaning and restoration work, a hidden compartment was discovered within the bureau, which contained the enclosed documents. We now forward them to you, believing they may be of some sentimental value . . .

Sammy investigated. The box was filled with unopened letters addressed to himself, some quite yellowed with age. With a lurch of the heart, he recognised his mother's beautiful handwriting. He carried the box to the solitude of the summerhouse, and there amidst a clutter of old deck chairs and abandoned croquet mallets, he sat on the wooden bench and began to read.

There were unashamed tears in his eyes by the time he'd read half a dozen of Chrissie's letters to her lost little boy. They were beautiful letters, warm and funny, yet through them all shone the deep love and longing of a mother deprived of her son. There were amusing little drawings of his two sisters, Mary Rose charging a formidable obstacle on horseback and Sandra dressed up in a gown many sizes too big, staggering on high heels. Even through tears, Sammy laughed.

Other, more recent letters were unbearably poignant, for they told of Chrissie's sorrow at his rejection. She begged him to write, only a word or a line, just some small sign of recognition.

But, of course, her pleas had fallen on deaf ears. He had never seen her letters. He was bitterly angry as he thought about the woman who'd done this cruel, deliberate deed. And yet it wasn't easy to hate Lizzie Kennedy, who'd been a loving, devoted mother to him for so many years. Oh, what a mess this is, Sammy thought wretchedly.

He gathered the letters together to pore over later, and strode to Chrissie's front door, carrying the box.

It was so unusual for her son to seek her company, Chrissie was surprised. One glance at his expression intensified her apprehension.

'Why, Sammy, what's wrong?'

'Can I come in?' he asked a little unsteadily.

She stood aside, and he followed her into the study, where she'd been writing letters. Her little writing desk stood open. He laid the box down and handed her a fistful of the letters it had contained. She gasped and groped for the chair, as if her legs had suddenly given way. She examined the letters carefully, then looked up questioningly.

Sammy nodded. 'Yes, your letters to me, Mum. They were all unopened. She must have hidden each one in the old family bureau as it arrived. Whoever bought the bureau found them and sent them to my lawyer.' Anger seized him again and he clenched his fists. 'Why did she do it? She'd no right!'

'She loved you more than right or wrong, Sammy,' Chrissie said gently. To her surprise, she felt no anger, only an immense pity for poor Lizzie.

'She smothered me and wouldn't let me out of her sight!' Sammy cried angrily. 'She didn't send me to school in Scotland as other parents did, but engaged an English tutor to teach me and a few other Indian lads. But why did she try to cut me off from my own mother? Oh, it's so hard to understand.'

'Lizzie couldn't have a bairn of her own. That was her tragedy, Sam. She saved your life when you were a tiny premature baby and I was in dire straits after your father was killed. Poor Lizzie. She lived her life in constant terror I'd come and take you away from her.'

Sammy sat down, frowning heavily. He and Emily had been married four years, and there was no sign of the baby they both longed for yet. They were young, and the doctor had told Emily everything was fine and it was just a question of having patience, but what if they had been told they could never have a child? Wouldn't they clutch eagerly at any little soul who needed love and care?

In quieter mood, he found himself recalling the good things about Lizzie Kennedy. How she'd laugh and gaily ruffle his hair when he told her some corny schoolboy joke. The proud look in her eyes when he'd done something praiseworthy. He remembered the bravery she'd shown during her terrible debilitating illness, and he felt tears threaten. Life was never simply black and white, Sammy decided, it was many shades of grey.

'She wanted to tell me she'd hidden your letters,' he said suddenly. 'I'm sure she did. She couldn't speak, but when she looked at me—' Sammy glanced up at Chrissie '—it was as if she were begging for forgiveness, Mum. From both of us, perhaps. It rattled me very much at the time, I remember. I didn't understand then, but I think I do now.'

'Can you forgive her, Sammy? I can,' Chrissie said.

'Yes, I believe I can forgive her, though it was a dreadful thing to do to us.'

Chrissie sighed. 'Poor Lizzie.'

Sammy reached across and took his mother's hand, smiling at her. 'Poor us, you mean! All those lost years, Mum.'

Chrissie looked down at the strong, young hand linked tightly with hers, and uttered a silent prayer of thanks. She had found her son, at last.

'Aggie Gallacher's been awfy no' weel,' announced Bessie next day. Chrissie was sorry to hear it. 'Aye. Her grandson Norrie wrote to tell her she'd to go into a posh nursing home for her operation, but she wouldna. She went into hospital like other decent folk. Kept the ward in stitches, my pal Maggie was tellin' me. Mind you, they was in stitches onyway, after their operations!' Bessie laughed heartily at her own joke.

Chrissie decided she was duty bound to visit the old lady, now Aggie was recuperating in her own home. Black hardly seemed tactful, so she put on a soft blue suit with a silver-grey fur collar. She'd almost forgotten how nice she looked in it.

Aggie was sitting up in bed, in a purple turban and a frothy pink bedjacket, receiving guests. She graciously accepted Chrissie's offering of fruit, then giggled. 'See me, Chrissie, sittin' up here like the Queen o' Sheba in fine linen sheets! You an' me's known the best o' baith worlds, haven't we, lassie?' Aggie sighed nostalgically. 'Mind how we used to strive to keep wir washing whiter than white? We was the lucky ones in Lochee, wi' Cox's chimney stack bein' built so high. You didna get smuts frae Cox's landing on your sheets! No' likely!' She laughed and reached for a grape. 'Ye got smoke an' dirt frae a'body else's lums, mind, but no frae Cox's.'

'Those were the days,' Chrissie smiled.

'Aye, thon servant-lassies downstairs dinna ken they're livin'. They've a washing machine to dae my linen. Imagine! Mind you, you can switch aff a washing machine if ye get fed up wi' the din, which is a point in its favour. You couldna switch aff the jokin' an' blethers at the steamie.' She was silent for a minute or two, relishing the grapes, then gave Chrissie a shrewd glance.

'Norrie's comin' hame tae see if I'm deein' or no'.'

'That's nice,' said Chrissie carefully. 'When?'

'Ony day. He married a Canadian lassie, Laurette Dubois. They have French folk in Canada, ken?' The old lady paused and shook her head sadly. 'He's never said, but it's no' a success, Chrissie. The laddie's no' happy wi' the woman. I can tell.'

'I'm very sorry to hear it, Mrs Gallacher.'

Aggie smoothed the satin coverlet industriously with a hand, not looking at her visitor. 'Will ye tell Sandra Norrie's comin' hame?'

Chrissie thought about it with a frown. 'I'm not sure if I will, Mrs Gallacher.'

'Aye, that's what I thought,' Aggie Gallacher said gloomily.

Sandra's flat on the first floor of a Glasgow tenement was unpretentious, but it suited her. Once inside, with the door locked, she could shrug off the trials and tribulations of the day. They were many, for life working for Harriet Bowers was never easy. Harriet met opposition head-on, and usually triumphed, after battle. The good she'd done for the bombed, battered, down-trodden district she loved was immeasurable. Now, however, there was talk of levelling the old tenements to the ground and building new towns outside in the green belt. Harriet, who'd campaigned vigorously for years for better living conditions in the tight-knit ship-building communities, fought just as grimly against their demolition. Sandra didn't know what to think. Harriet had always been proved right in the past, yet surely it was good for these poor folk to live in new housing, in clean air outside the city?

Sandra was rinsing her hair when the door knocker rapped briskly. She sighed good-naturedly, groping for the towel. There were two days to go till pay-day. Probably her neighbour, skint as usual, seeking to borrow something. Looping the towel into a turban, she answered the summons and received the shock of her life.

'Norrie!'

Sandra could only stand gaping. Was this handsome, prosperous-looking man *really* Norrie Gallacher? Was he always so tall, or did the fact she was clad scantily in dressing-gown and bare feet make him seem taller? A trickle of chilly water ran down from her wet hair and splashed on to the linoleum.

'I was just . . . washing my hair,' she said weakly.

'Aye. So I see.' He was serious, but there was the familiar twinkle in his lively eyes.

'You'd better come in.' She led him into the living room. The flat was just a single end, with a curtained bed recess off the living room, a scullery-kitchen and toilet. She'd always found it cosy and compact; now, with Norrie in it, it suddenly became a great deal too intimate and cosy. She drew her dressing-gown tightly round her and sat down primly.

'I didn't know you were home. Nobody said,' she said accusingly.

'I don't suppose they would. It was Charlotte who

gave me your address on the sly. What a nice, friendly lassie she is!'

Sandra wished he wouldn't look at her. It made her feel weak. She studied her bare toes. 'You got married, Norrie. Congratulations.'

'You didn't, Sandra. Why not?' His voice sounded strange, almost angry.

She looked up and met his eyes. Yes, they were angry, dark and hurt, and angry. Well, she'd a right to be angry, too.

'Och, you *must* have heard. It was a good laugh in Dundee at the time. Yon stuck-up wee besom, Sandra Murphy, was ditched by her rich chap. He ran off wi' her bonnie wee sister,' she mimicked bitterly. Her mouth suddenly trembled, and she bit her lip to stop the tears. She turned her head away hurriedly and the towel fell off. She felt curiously naked, her dark hair wet and tousled, no makeup, tears on her lashes. Norrie's hand came out and caught her wrist.

'Sandra, you said you were going to marry him! I believed you. Do you think I would have left Dundee otherwise? I would never have left you if you'd given me hope.'

She shouted at him in her distress. 'I didn't know! It was all an impossible dream on my part, a bairn's make-believe. I swear to you, Norrie, I didn't know then that I . . . that I—' She almost blurted out her love for him.

His grip tightened on her wrist. 'That you *what*?'

She struggled. 'Let me go. It's not fair putting words in my mouth, and you – a married man!'

He let her go. 'Aye,' he said bitterly. 'Married. Married to a good lass I can never love because my ain true love's face is ever on my mind. Can you imagine what misery there is in that, Sandra?'

She looked at him long in silence and tears. 'Oh,

Norrie. Is it wrong to tell you now, I love you, too?' she whispered at last.

He leaned over and caressed her soft, wet cheek with his fingers. 'Aye, my dearest lassie, we've made a right mixter-maxter of our lives that should have been so blithe,' Norrie sighed wearily.

There was such sadness and finality in his tone she couldn't bear it. 'Surely it's not too late for us, Norrie? If your wife agrees, then—'

He stopped her eagerness sternly. 'Divorce is out of the question, Sandra. I would never even consider it.'

She stared at him, remembering how staunch he'd been for his kirk. She could feel her heart breaking, slowly, completely, no hope of mending. She held out her arms longingly for him.

'Then stay with me now, Norrie. Just for a little while, my love, let us be happy.'

Chapter 16

Harriet's car was parked outside the clinic when Sandra said goodbye to Norrie Gallacher next day, and strangely enough the sight of the nondescript little vehicle gave Sandra some comfort.

The day Norrie and Sandra had spent together had passed blissfully. Sandra had phoned the clinic that morning and arranged a few hours off, then they'd driven out to the Campsie Hills and walked on the fells in blinky sunshine. Hand in hand, they'd laughed and teased one another like bairns larking in Dundee streets.

'Your granny says you're worth a bob or two, Norrie Gallacher,' Sandra teased him.

He grinned. 'Are you still chasing a rich man, Sandra Murphy? Well, my gran's right, I am worth a bob or two. Mind what I told you? There's brass in rubbish, my love.'

She sighed and rested her head against his shoulder. 'To think you were my dream-man all the time and I hadn't the sense to see it.'

But mostly they'd walked in contented silence. They'd kissed, and put the confusing rights and wrongs of it aside, to be worried over later.

It had been a short-lived dream of what might have been, and now it was over. Norrie was scheduled to fly home to Canada early next morning, back to a different life, and Laurette, his wife.

Outside the clinic, he took Sandra in his arms. She buried her face against his jacket and listened to the anguished beat of his heart.

'Couldn't you write to me, Sandra?' he begged.

She shook her head. 'No, I won't write. Suppose Laurette found the letters? We agreed your wife mustn't be hurt by this, Norrie.'

He spoke urgently, for time was short. 'Listen, Sandra, my firm has this branch office in Glasgow. It's one of the reasons I'm over here, apart from checking up on my gran's health. Laurette knows I'll be making a trip to Glasgow once a year, so it's not as if I'm deceiving her on that score. Would you spend time with me just once a year, Sandra?'

She looked at him in dismay. She saw her future stretching ahead in monotonous years, lit only by Norrie's brief yearly visits. She was at a loss for words for a moment.

'I don't know. I don't know whether to make a clean break or not. I don't know what to do!'

A nearby clock boomed out the hour warningly, and he held her close. 'Please, Sandra, don't end it. I know I've no right to ask it of you, but I *love* you. Please be here when I come back?'

'I can't promise, dear. I . . . I must think about this, don't you see?' she cried tearfully.

He sighed. 'Aye, it's a difficult decision. Whatever you decide, be sure I'll bide by it. But oh, please, my dear, let me see you again!'

He gazed at her for a moment with such yearning it brought tears to her eyes, then he kissed her tenderly and hurried away. Sandra put a hand to her lips where the thrill of his kiss still lingered, then forced herself to walk into the clinic.

The surgery that evening was busy as ever. The waiting area resounded to hacking coughs and sneezes, punctuated by wails from girning bairns. Everybody's dreary expression brightened when Sandra took the part-time receptionist's place. She was popular, cheerful and efficient, and had a firm way with badly behaved youngsters. Several of the patients shouted a greeting and hard-pressed mothers smiled at her thankfully.

Harriet was assisted by another hard-working doctor, Dr Darren O'Reilly, who was prop forward for the local rugby team and commanded the considerable respect of tougher elements. The young doctor was searching for mislaid medical records when Sandra walked in, and Darren O'Reilly's harassed expression brightened considerably. With a smile, Sandra located the file for him.

'Thanks, Sandra. What would I do without you?'

'Lose yer heid, Doctor!' giggled Jessie, a retired nurse who dished out National Dried Milk, orange juice and sound advice.

'Maybe I've lost it already, Jessie,' he replied enigmatically.

The evening ended at last. Dr O'Reilly was on call that night, so he left to put his feet up while he had the chance.

Soon Sandra and Harriet were alone together in the echoing spaces of the clinic. Harriet stretched her arms above her head and yawned.

'It's on days like this I feel every bit my age, Sandra.'

Sandra's thoughts were obviously miles away and Harriet studied her young friend with keen sympathy. Something was amiss, she guessed, for Sandra looked so bewildered and lost. Normally, Harriet would never have dreamed of prying into anyone's private life, but she loved Sandra like a daughter, and she decided something must be said.

'Did you have a nice day with your friend, dear?' she ventured.

335

'I don't know, Harriet. I'm trying to work out whether it was bliss or sheer torture,' Sandra replied.

She began moving around, restlessly straightening magazines and tidying up the waiting area. Harriet waited patiently. Sandra paused, a tattered pile of magazines clutched to her chest.

'Harriet, isn't love awful.'

'But rather wonderful too, my dear.'

The pile of magazines suddenly fell unnoticed from Sandra's grasp and littered the floor. She had buried her face in her hands and was sobbing brokenly. 'Oh, I'm so unhappy, and I don't know what to do.'

Harriet was there in an instant. She gathered the weeping woman in her arms and seated her on a waiting-room bench. She listened gravely while Sandra sobbed out the whole tragic story of herself and Mary Rose, and the reason why Norrie Gallacher had gone to Canada.

'There's no question of divorce, Harriet, even though Norrie does still love me. Norrie wants us to meet once a year when he visits Glasgow, but, oh, that seems so underhand, and I don't want to hurt his poor wife.' She clutched Harriet's hand desperately. 'Should I do the sensible thing and never see him again, or should I wait for him faithfully year after year? Harriet, what should I do?'

Harriet looked away. She found it difficult to meet Sandra's pleading gaze. 'My dear, I can only tell you what I would do, and perhaps my decision would neither be sensible nor right for you. If I tell you my own story then you must make up your mind in the light of my experience.'

Sandra stared at her. 'Have . . . have you ever been in love, Harriet?'

'Been in love?' Harriet recalled the pain of loving Charles Rankine deeply and uselessly, and smiled sadly.

'My dear, I'm not beautiful like your lovely mother, I'm skinny and gawky, and too brainy for my own good, but that doesn't mean I can't fall in love.' She felt keenly the pain of being young and vulnerable again, an unattractive bridesmaid standing beside beautiful Christina Kennedy, fighting the first sharp pangs of unrequited love.

Carefully, Harriet forced herself to go on. 'The man I loved was very fond of me, I believe, and I loved him so! But he fell in love with someone else, Sandra, and loved her faithfully for the rest of his life. Mind you, she didn't encourage him at all at first, and at one time it looked as if he might marry me instead. I convinced myself he'd grow to love me if we got married. But I was fooling myself, dear.'

She paused, re-living that terrible time in her life, and momentarily she forgot to be careful. 'Charles would never have loved me. I couldn't have made him happy as Chrissie did. I can accept that, now he's gone—'

Sandra gave a muffled gasp. 'You mean it was Charles, my step-father, you were in love with?'

Harriet was forced to admit it, though she'd intended to keep names out of this. 'Yes, dear. I loved him.'

'Oh, Harriet! I never guessed,' Sandra breathed softly. Her thoughts were busy. There was a time when her mother's coolness towards Harriet had puzzled Sandra, but now she understood.

Harriet was smiling ruefully. 'So you see, dear, I know what I'm talking about, even though I'm just an old maid. My man didn't love me, but I can remember every word he said, every small caress that meant so little to him and so much to me. That's all I have to remember of the man I loved.'

She turned abruptly to face Sandra, her eyes bright with tears. 'But you could have more, if you want it.

Norrie would have married you but for a misunderstanding. He's offering you a few stolen days and a lifetime of wonderful memories, and if I were you I'd settle for that gladly.'

The two women stared at one another in silence, then Sandra sighed deeply and looked away. 'But you're not me, Harriet.'

'No, dear. I can't make up your mind for you,' agreed Harriet sadly. She wished she could give Sandra happiness, but that elusive state lay in her young friend's own hands. One thing she could do, though. Harriet leaned forward and took Sandra's hand. 'Isn't it time you forgave your sister? This feud with Mary Rose must break your mother's heart.'

Sandra's expression changed dramatically. She was outraged by the suggestion. 'No, I'll never forgive Mary Rose! She ruined two lives, mine *and* Norrie's.'

Harriet was distressed. She feared she'd made matters worse by interfering, yet she'd had to try for Chrissie's sake. She withdrew her hand and smiled fondly at Sandra, who was looking mutinous.

'Och, Sandra, don't be so sure your lives are ruined. God moves in mysterious ways, my love,' she pointed out.

The tension left Sandra. She felt a great pity for Harriet, who had suffered much and bared her soul trying to help. This decision must be her own though, and when her mind was made up she would go her own way bravely, wherever it might lead. She was Danny Murphy's daughter. She wondered what Danny's advice to her would have been. Sandra leaned forward and kissed her dear old friend's cheek gratefully.

'Thanks anyway, Harriet dear. I'll think about it,' she promised.

Benjamin Chester was no stranger to loneliness, but nothing had prepared him for the lonely moors of

Sutherland. He'd reached the croft his folk had left in despair more than a hundred years ago. The croft was just tumbled walls of weathered stone blackened by fire, with traces of runrig furrows on the moorland where hardy sheep grazed. The desolate scene brought tears to his eyes. He hadn't expected to feel forlorn here of all places, where his family roots went deep.

Ben looked wildly round the empty landscape. Where was the nearest phonebox, for heaven's sake?

He found the familiar red box some miles away in a small hamlet on the narrow, twisting road. His longing to speak to Chrissie was desperate. Fortunately, she answered right away. Ben breathed a sigh of relief, he felt better already with Chrissie on the other end of the line.

'Whose daft idea was this separation, girl?' he demanded.

She laughed softly. 'Yours, I believe.'

'It's a rotten idea. Don't you miss me?'

'Well, it's been quiet since you left,' Chrissie admitted.

He shivered. 'It's quiet here, too. I'm out on the moors. It's kind of creepy, and it's given me the shakes. Nothin' but sheep and no people.'

'Poor Ben!'

'Oh, Chris, I wish you were here,' he groaned.

Her heart beat faster, but she was determined to keep the conversation light. 'Where are you bound for?'

'Orkney's next on the itinerary, Chrissie, but I could easily—'

She broke in hastily. 'I believe the islands are beautiful this time of year. You'll love Orkney, Ben.'

'Yeah. I got Vikings in the family tree,' he growled morosely.

'Well, have a nice time and haste ye back, my dear.'

'Sure,' replied Ben miserably.

Seated behind his father's desk, Ewan Rankine was dictating a letter, a task made difficult because his mind wasn't on the job. His thoughts kept wandering across the desk to the efficient young woman who sat with pencil poised and notepad on knee.

His father's secretary for many years, Maisie, had retired, and this was Linda McLaren, Maisie's replacement.

'Would you mind reading that back, Miss McLaren?' Ewan couldn't remember what on earth he'd just said. It was those shapely, silk-clad legs which were so distracting.

She obliged. '"With reference to the spare part required for the Robertson and Orchar 1921 calendering machine . . ."' She paused and arched her brows inquiringly.

'Ahem, yes – er – well. Tell them we're fed up waiting and hereby cancel the order. We'll have it made locally. Put it as tactfully as you can, because we can't afford to fall out with them altogether.'

'Certainly, Mr Rankine.' She inscribed a few more efficient squiggles and stood up. She wasn't tall, but gave an impression of height because she carried herself so well.

Ewan had a sudden rash thought. 'Miss McLaren, I've compiled a report on recent trials spinning rayon thread. It's rather urgent. Could you stay this evening and help me finish it? We could go for a meal later,' he added hopefully.

She gave him a thoughtful look. 'I'm sorry, I can't stay. I must collect my little girl from the factory creche.'

Ewan grew hot with embarrassment. 'I didn't know you had a little girl.'

She hesitated. 'Her father and I were going to be married, but he was killed in Korea. He never saw his daughter. It's sad.'

'All wars are sad, Linda.' The name slipped out quite naturally.

She smiled. 'I could type the rayon report tomorrow morning.'

He grinned. 'OK. I'll stand you lunch!'

Ewan sat staring at the closed door after she'd gone. The sudden appearance of Sammy startled him.

'Hi, Ewan, I wanted a word. Your bonnie secretary told me to walk right in. Hope you don't mind?'

'Not a bit.' The half-brothers got on well. Sammy had been Ewan's boyhood hero, and he still admired him. Sammy knew where he was going. Ewan was more wary, weighing up the pros and cons first.

Ewan smiled. 'What can I do for you, Sam?'

Sammy settled himself in a chair. 'You know Mum and I were parted for years through no fault of her own? Well, I want to do something special to make up for the lost years. Trouble is, I don't know what. Can you suggest anything?'

'I know just the thing!' Ewan replied. 'You know Mum loved Grandpa Kennedy's old whaling ship, the *Christina K*? If we could find her and refit her as, say, a training ship for youngsters, just imagine Mum's face if she saw the *Christina K* come sailing up the Tay!'

Sammy sat up. 'Ewan, that's perfect! But where's the ship?'

Eagerly, Ewan told Sammy about his strange experience during the war and the disappointment afterwards when he'd found the ship gone.

'So she could be in Norway now?' Sammy said thoughtfully.

'Yes. I'm sure someone in Muiden could tell us where she went, but that's not the point, Sammy. Dad and

I discussed this before he died, and we decided that buying the ship and refitting her would take more money than we could scrape together.'

Sammy grinned ruefully. 'Cost did cross my mind. I'm unemployed and skint at present, having just finished my engineering degree course. Couldn't this be a family venture, involving all our relations? Once we've found the ship we could ask for contributions to buy her and finish the job. That way, we could maybe do it.'

Ewan studied his half-brother. 'Sammy, how about joining me in the firm? I warn you, it's precarious at the moment. I'm trying to adapt the factory to spin man-made fibres, and I could do with some engineering expertise. Mind you, it'll be jolly hard work. There are many problems now jute isn't an economic proposition for Rankine's. It's not easy, Sam.'

Sammy's face lit up. 'If there's one thing I enjoy more than an argument, it's a challenge. I accept your offer with gratitude, Ewan!'

They laughed, then shook hands merrily on their partnership.

Chrissie was surprised to find how much she missed Ben Chester. She'd wanted time to think about the relationship, but her mind kept avoiding the vexed question. She was dithering about this, she knew, and that wasn't like her at all. Usually, she knew her own mind.

When the phone rang, she hurried to answer it, convinced it was Ben phoning from Orkney.

'Hello, Gran, it's me, Elizabeth!'

Far from being disappointed, Chrissie was delighted. She hadn't seen her granddaughter since Mary Rose took Elizabeth away from Dundee during the war. Elizabeth was a young lady of eighteen now.

'Darling, how lovely to hear from you. Did you get my letter?'

'Yes, thanks, Gran. That . . . that's why I phoned.'

It dawned on Chrissie her young granddaughter was not her usual cheery self. 'Is anything the matter, dear?' she asked anxiously.

'Oh, Gran, Mum's getting married,' Elizabeth sounded tragic.

So that's it! thought Chrissie. She was pleased for Mary Rose's sake, but she saw it could create problems for Elizabeth. Aloud, she said brightly, 'But that's wonderful, Elizabeth! Who's the lucky man?'

'Remember I told you about Jeff Darvel who helped run the Stirton estate before my grandparents died? Well, he and Mum are getting married. Jeff will continue to run the estate, which is mine now. When they're married Mum will set up a veterinary practice in the steading.'

'That seems an excellent arrangement, love!'

'Ye-es,' Elizabeth sounded miserable. 'Look, Gran, would you mind if I stayed with you for a while?'

'Oh, Elizabeth, I'd love to have you!' Chrissie cried joyfully.

Elizabeth had grown into a lovely young woman, blessed with Danny's black, curly hair and brilliant blue eyes. Bessie's cup of happiness was full. She had Elizabeth back in the nest, and it looked as if Charlotte's baby would be arriving sooner than expected. Charlotte's blood pressure had risen recently, and the clinic was keeping a close eye on the situation. Bessie was in seventh heaven at the prospect of another wee baby to nurse.

'There's a hot water bottle in yer bed, lovie,' Bessie told Elizabeth. She'd been dotting in and out of Chrissie's flat on one pretext or another ever since Elizabeth's arrival. The old lady eyed Elizabeth's smart outfit admiringly. 'Oh, that's an awfy nice frock. That'll be the very latest frae London, is it?'

Elizabeth looked doubtful. 'Do you really like it, Bessie? I'm not sure I suit pink.'

Bessie giggled. 'Och, a'body suits pink, lassie!'

Elizabeth smiled wanly. She went to the window and looked out across the rosebeds which made brilliant splashes of colour against the green grass. 'I don't suppose it matters what I look like, anyway,' she sighed.

Chrissie and Bessie exchanged worried glances. There was something far wrong here.

In the days that followed Chrissie gave Elizabeth plenty of opportunities to talk, but the girl remained obstinately silent. Then everything was swept from Chrissie's mind by the sudden arrival of Charlotte and Leon's baby. A beautiful little girl, named Natasha.

Bessie was as thrilled and proud as anyone. 'Though why give the wee soul a foreign name like that? There's nae Natashas in Dundee!' she grumbled.

Chrissie smiled, 'It's a very pretty name, Bessie. I believe she's called after Doctor Leon's Russian great-grandmother.'

Family links with the past always delighted Chrissie. Her family had strong links with Russia, India and America now, just like the city of Dundee itself. It made her proud.

Once more Bessie had a baby to hold. She sat regally in the nursery with Natasha in her arms, her wrinkled old cheeks pink with pleasure as admiring members of the family paid homage. Charlotte had been ordered to rest after coming out of hospital, and that suited Bessie fine. She had the baby all to herself.

After Emily Murphy had seen Sammy off to his new job at Rankine's, she visited the baby and gently kissed little Natasha's soft, pink cheek. Then she ran downstairs to her mother-in-law's flat and burst into floods of tears.

They were alone fortunately; Elizabeth was helping Bessie bath Natasha.

'Oh, Chrissie, I'm sorry,' Emily gulped, mopping her eyes. 'It's just . . . she's such a lovely wee bairn, and I'd love a baby of my own, only—'

'Only what?'

Emily cast her eyes down and twisted her handkerchief round her fingers, and there was a long pause while Chrissie waited patiently. She had a feeling they were getting to the heart of the matter.

'It's because I had tuberculosis,' Emily blurted out eventually. 'The doctors say I'm cured, but what if I'm not and I pass it on to my baby? I never told anyone, Chrissie, but my mother died with TB, and that's when they discovered I had it. Oh, it . . . it was a dreadful time.'

Chrissie took her daughter-in-law in her arms and Emily clung to her like a frightened child.

Chrissie stroked her hair. 'Emily, you must trust the doctors. They've made great strides in the treatment of tuberculosis since the war, and the National Health mass X-ray campaign will catch the disease in its early stages. Maybe it'll soon be a thing of the past, who knows? Perhaps if you were to stop worrying about this you'd have a baby of your own.'

'Do you really think so?' Emily wiped her eyes.

'Yes, I do.'

Her daughter-in-law hugged her. 'Och, Chrissie, you're such a comfort. By the by, Sammy and I have decided if ever we're blessed wi' a wee lad, he's to be called Daniel.'

'Daniel Murphy,' Chrissie repeated softly. That was such a wonderful possibility it brought tears to her eyes, but she laughed. 'Ah, but what if it's a wee lass?'

'Och, that's easy. Then it's to be Christina!'

* * *

Chrissie suspected Bessie was glad to hand the demanding care of the baby over to Charlotte, who recovered quickly from the birth and was eager to attend to her baby herself. The old lady looked tired.

Chrissie was snipping some of the choicer blooms in the rose-garden when Bessie approached one sunny afternoon.

'The roses are at their best, Chrissie, I was thinking of picking a bunch for Biddy's grave. It's a wee while since I've been up to the hill.'

'I'll give you a hand, dear,' Chrissie offered.

The two worked happily in the pleasant sunshine. Presently Bessie stood up and eased her back, enjoying the fragrance of the roses. A drowsy blackbird twittered away to itself in the evergreens. It was peaceful. Bessie closed her eyes a little wearily and sighed with pure delight.

'My, how happy I've been in this hoose, Chris! Busy and merry. It's just how I imagine heaven must be, wi' a' they angels to see to and cherubs to nurse. I'm no' musical, so I'll no' be issued wi' a harp, thank goodness.'

Chrissie was touched, although she also felt perturbed by this unexpected flight of fancy. It wasn't like Bessie.

'Och, Bessie, you're a blether,' she smiled fondly.

'Here, it's no' blethers, it's true. I'm no' dotty yet!' declared Bessie indignantly. Without warning, she put her old arms round Chrissie and gave her a quick, fierce hug. 'I never thanked you proper, Chrissie, for what you did for me, but I'm down on my knees every day blessing ye, my lass. I just wanted you to know.'

She'd brought Chrissie near to tears. 'Bessie, it's me that should be blessing you for looking after me and mine so faithfully. Mind how you wakened me at half-past four and dragged me to the mill, to show me what a hard life the little mill-lass had? I never forgot that lesson, and it's stood me in good stead, I can tell you.'

'Aye, you were a wee madam in those days!' Bessie grinned. She looked at Chrissie fondly. 'But you turned out fine, Chris. A woman to be real proud o'.'

Chrissie stared hard at the beautiful bunch of roses they'd gathered. She couldn't trust herself to speak for a moment. 'I'll run you to the cemetery, Bessie.'

'Naw, ye'll no'! I'll get the tram to the terminus and it's only a wee step after that. You see to Elizabeth. That lassie's no' happy. Eighteen's an awfy sair age, Chris!'

Chrissie agreed. She could remember well how sair it was to be eighteen.

Elizabeth was in the drawing room, immersed in a book. She didn't lift her head when her grandmother joined her, so Chrissie quietly picked up her knitting and began working on baby clothes for Natasha. She wished Elizabeth would tell her what the trouble was, but she couldn't rush these things. The afternoon wore on, clouding over until the sun disappeared.

Chrissie couldn't pinpoint the precise moment a nagging worry started. She went over again in her mind Bessie's odd behaviour that afternoon, becoming more alarmed every second. Oh, she shouldn't have let Bessie go off on her own. She stood up in sudden fear, the knitting falling to the floor.

Elizabeth looked up, surprised. 'What's up, Gran?'

'It's Bessie, dear. She went to put flowers on her sister's grave, but I think I should take the car and bring her home. She's so spry and lively you forget she's an old lady now.'

Elizabeth closed the book. 'I'll come with you.'

Chrissie was too worried by now to argue. She and Elizabeth set off towards the wooded hillside on the west of the city. They didn't talk much as Chrissie drove.

Elizabeth sensed her grandmother's acute anxiety. She sat with hands tightly clasped in her lap.

There were people standing about as Chrissie parked the car, and an unusual stir going on further up the hill among the tombstones. Chrissie hung on to Elizabeth's arm as they walked, for she found her knees were shaking. They hadn't gone far before their path was blocked by one of Dundee's tall bobbies.

'I'm sorry, ma'am, you'll have to turn back for the moment.'

Chrissie's heart was pounding. 'Has there been an accident? Oh, please let us though. My friend was putting roses on her sister's grave up there. She's an elderly lady, and we've come to take her home.'

The young bobby studied her silently, then his eyes lingered for a moment on Elizabeth. He had nice brown eyes, concerned and friendly. He took out a notebook and glanced at it. 'Excuse me, but do you know a Miss Bessie McCutcheon?'

Chrissie was suddenly very frightened. 'Why yes, it's Bessie we've come for. Is . . . is anything the matter?'

He closed the notebook solemnly. 'I'm very sorry, but Miss McCutcheon was found a short time ago. She'd collapsed on the hillside.'

Elizabeth gave a low cry of distress. Chrissie turned icy cold.

'Officer, was . . . was she . . . ?'

The young bobby nodded gravely. 'I'm afraid so. A doctor attended her, but there was nothing we could do. They're just taking her away now.'

Elizabeth's mouth trembled and a tear ran down her cheek.

Hc put a hand on Chrissie's arm. 'Look, if it's any comfort, the old lady looked so peaceful. She lay there beside a beautiful bunch of roses, just as if she were asleep. There was such a happy wee

348

smile on her face, and somehow I couldn't feel sad for her.'

'Thank you, you're very kind,' Chrissie said softly.

He became businesslike. 'We'll require formal identification and that sort of thing, ma'am, but you've had a nasty shock, so that can wait till later. If you'll give me your name and address. I'll call on you this evening, if I may?' Out came the notebook, and he noted the information then studied Chrissie doubtfully. 'Are you driving, Mrs Rankine? Will you be all right?'

Elizabeth put an arm round Chrissie. 'It's OK, I'll drive my grandmother home.'

The young bobby looked at her approvingly. 'Good for you,' he said with a quiet smile.

When the policeman arrived later that evening Chrissie's family rallied round. She was still badly shaken by Bessie's sudden end, but the menfolk saw to everything that was required. All Chrissie had to do was help Elizabeth prepare tea and sandwiches for their official visitor before he went on his way. The bobby's eye brightened when Elizabeth entered with a laden tray, 'Oh, that's kind. I missed my tea, what with one thing and another.'

The others excused themselves and went off to see to various details, but the young bobby remained to eat sandwiches and enjoy a cup of tea. It was strangely comforting to sit quietly round the fire, just the three of them.

Elizabeth stole a curious glance at the young man, and caught him watching her with interest. He smiled. 'You're not from Dundee, are you? I would have noticed you before this.'

'No.' Elizabeth looked away quickly. She felt sort of breathlessly happy all of a sudden. She wondered how to explain her presence in the city.

'I lived in Dundee with Gran and Granda during the

war, and I vowed then I'd stand at the top of Powrie brae and watch Dundee shining with lights. Maybe that's why I came back, to prove to myself the war's really over.'

He was amused. 'And did you?'

'Not yet, but I'll go there one day.'

Presently the young bobby stood up and announced he must report back to the station. Elizabeth escorted him to the door. He stood looking down at her, smiling. 'We could drive to Powrie brae sometime and I'll show you Dundee shining with lights, just to prove the war's really over, Elizabeth.'

'Yes, I'd like that,' she told him simply.

Elizabeth returned thoughtfully to the drawing room. Chrissie looked at her. 'What a nice young bobby. Very kind.'

'Yes,' Elizabeth sat down and gazed into the glowing embers of the fire Ewan had lit earlier. So much had happened that eventful day. Her sadness had been comforted by a certain look in a young man's eye. She had discovered unsuspected strength as she cared for her grandmother and drove her safely home after Bessie's death. Elizabeth felt as if she'd finally grown up, all in the space of an afternoon.

'Gran, would you mind if I went home after Bessie's funeral? Mum wants me to be her bridesmaid. I said I wouldn't, but I've changed my mind.'

'I'm glad you changed your mind, dear,' Chrissie said.

Elizabeth raised her eyes and looked at her grandmother. 'I thought I was in love with Jeff Darvel, Gran. I couldn't believe it when Mum said they were getting married. Oh, I was so angry and jealous. That's why I came rushing to Dundee, but I can see now it wasn't love, only a childish fancy for a kind man I liked very much. I've been very silly, haven't I?'

Chrissie smiled, 'We all make mistakes, dear, the

secret is to learn from them. You will come back again, won't you?'

Elizabeth gave a small, secret smile. 'Oh, yes, I'll be back. There's a date I want to keep.'

Chrissie felt lost and lonely once her granddaughter had gone home. With the loss of Bessie, she sensed change taking place all round. Large houses built by jute barons were being split up into smaller flats as the industry declined, and it was rumoured the old Overgate would soon be swept away, making room for a brand new hotel and shopping centre. Chrissie shuddered at the news, for she had affectionate memories of that busy, ancient thoroughfare. She remembered buying pokes of chips and peas from the buster stalls to feed her two hungry bairns. If she closed her eyes, she could almost smell the aroma of vinegar and frying onions that had hung in the steamy atmosphere. Changes! Aye, and maybe not for the better, she thought, sighing.

It was in this nostalgic, unsettled mood that Chrissie welcomed Benjamin Chester when he phoned to announce his arrival at a Dundee hotel. She immediately invited him for tea. Scottish high tea, Ben assured her happily, would fit nicely with his plans for the evening and suited his iron digestion to a T.

He arrived on the doorstep promptly, smartly dressed, freshly shaved and smelling of aftershave. 'Oh, Chrissie love, how I've missed you!' he declared.

He gave Chrissie an exuberant bear-hug from which she tactfully extricated herself with a wildly beating heart. She intended a display of independence. She'd no intention of being swept off her feet by Mr Chester!

Chrissie had prepared a homely little repast, shepherd's pie accompanied by plenty of vegetables, followed by freshly baked scones, home-made jam and, bowing to Ben's American taste, a pot of coffee.

He ate everything with enthusiastic delight, and afterwards they relaxed in front of the fire while Chrissie told him all that had happened in the eventful weeks he had stayed away. Ben was very sad to hear about Bessie.

'I guess you must miss her very much, Chris.'

'Yes, I do. So many changes in my life, Ben. Even the town is beginning to look different, new housing estates springing up on the outskirts, old tenements coming down.' There had been a restlessness bothering her recently, and now it returned in strength. She didn't know what to do about it.

He reached over and took her hand. 'You know what? We have a lot in common. We're two lonely people, Chrissie.'

This was dangerous ground, she thought.

'Surely you're not lonely, Ben. You must have friends and family in the States?' she said lightly.

He stared down at their linked hands in silence for a minute. 'Mine is a familiar story, I guess, Chris. I enjoyed working. I was good at my job. I enjoyed making money, and made a great deal of it. I thought there'd be time to spare for my wife and two kids later.' He looked at Chrissie, and his expression was anguished. 'But my wife died just before I retired. I hadn't even noticed she was ill. My daughter and son don't want me in their lives. Guess that makes sense, since I was never there when I was wanted. It's been the loneliest few years I ever spent.' He gave her a long, level look. 'Until now, Chrissie. You make me feel happy, contented. I'm not lonely any more when I'm with you. I know you loved Charles, and maybe it's too soon, but could you—?'

'Ben—' She knew what was coming, and she must stop it. Once he'd proposed he would expect an answer, and she didn't know what answer to give. She said the first thing that came into her head, and found to her amazement she was voicing her restless thoughts. 'You told me once you didn't enjoy London on your own, so I'll come to London with you if you like, Ben, no strings attached. I've always wanted to visit London, see Buckingham Palace, maybe even watch the King and Queen drive past. Poor man, he's been so ill, did you know?'

Ben felt out-manoeuvred, but once they were together there would be plenty of other opportunities. The idea began to seem a sound one. He couldn't have thought of a better idea, himself, he decided.

'Chrissie, London looks kind of dingy and war-torn these days. I hope you won't be disappointed, girl,' he warned her.

'Don't worry, Ben. I'm sure I won't be,' she smiled.

Chapter 17

Once her mind was made up, Chrissie lost no time preparing for the journey to London. She and Ben decided to travel by train. His hired car was no bigger than a roller-skate, he declared, and he wouldn't subject his worst enemy, let alone his dear Chrissie, to a marathon journey in the darned automobile. Chrissie decided to update her wardrobe. She would never forget her love for Charles and still mourned his death, but she bundled up all the black clothing and handed the garments to the Salvation Army, where they were gratefully received.

Chrissie splashed out recklessly and bought herself a new outfit and an alluring hat which she fell in love with at first sight. Carrying her spoils home, she tried on everything nervously in front of the mirror, for it was years since she'd bought new clothes, what with clothes rationing and make do and mend. To her relief, Chrissie discovered her good taste hadn't deserted her. She arranged the hat at its most becoming angle and admired her reflection. She could imagine what Bessie would have said.

'Oh my! Twenty-one bob for a wee straw bonnet? You're jokin'!'

Chrissie smiled defiantly. Extravagant or no, she must keep her end up with posh London folk!

When Chrissie's family were told of her intentions the young folk were flabbergasted and scandalised. A few days before Chrissie's departure, Charlotte and Leon turned up one Saturday afternoon with Ewan, who was carrying his little niece Natasha. Chrissie was delighted to see them.

'I must have second sight, my dears. I've just been baking!'

She bustled around making a pot of tea to accompany the currant slices for which she was renowned, and carried the tray through to the drawing room.

'Bessie used to call these "fly cemeteries", and they're Ben's favourites. D'you fancy one?'

'Er . . . no thanks, Mum.' Ewan exchanged a significant glance with the others.

Comfortably settled on the sofa beside Leon, Chrissie reached for the baby on his knee. She held Natasha in her arms, admiring the beautiful little girl. 'She grows bonnier every day, Leon.'

'I hope you don't intend staying away too long, Mum, she grows so quickly,' said Charlotte pointedly.

Ewan chipped in. 'We all agree you deserve a holiday, but is it wise going off like this with a strange man?'

Chrissie laughed heartily. 'I've known Ben Chester for years. He's a nice, kind man and very respectable and honourable. He sent us lovely food parcels during the war, you know, and went to a lot of trouble to do it.'

'Yes, I grant you he seems a decent bloke, but . . . er . . . well—' Ewan lapsed into awkward silence.

'What are folk to think, when they hear you've gone off to London with Mr Chester?' Charlotte ventured.

Chrissie lifted the sleepy baby against her shoulder. 'They'll think the worst and say a great deal, all of it blethers. It's never bothered me what folk think, love, so long as my own conscience is clear.' The twins studied their mother in baffled silence. Chrissie tactfully refrained from laughing. She smiled kindly at the concerned young folk. 'Do help yourselves to a fly cemetery, my dears,' she urged them.

Sandra had begged her half-sister to keep her informed about their mother's expedition, and Charlotte lost no time passing on the news that Chrissie was determined to go ahead with it. At the end of their telephone conversation, Sandra replaced the receiver and sat frowning.

'Well, really! I don't know what's got into my mother!'

Harriet, working nearby, looked up with interest. Sandra explained to her the nature of the family crisis.

'I think it's an excellent idea. Chrissie could do with a holiday, and obviously it's safer travelling with a male companion,' declared Harriet staunchly.

Sandra didn't say anything. Trust that hardy generation to stick up for itself, she thought.

'By the by,' went on Harriet with studied nonchalance, 'I'm thinking of retiring. Time I gave the young ones a chance.'

Sandra sat up with a jolt. 'Retiring? But, Harriet, you'll be bored!'

'No, I won't. I'll return to Dundee and look for a worthy cause. I tire easily these days and I'm not giving of my best. Time to hang up the stethoscope, Sandra.'

'The clinic won't be the same without you,' Sandra muttered unhappily.

Harriet grinned. 'Nonsense! It might even be better.'

Later that day Sandra found herself closeted with young Dr O'Reilly in the private cubby-hole where old medical records were stored. She couldn't resist questioning him. 'Darren, did you know Harriet was thinking of retiring?'

'She did mention it.' He gave Sandra a quick glance.

'Don't dissuade her, Sandra. She's never spared herself, and it's time she took things easier. If she doesn't, then I'm afraid—' He paused eloquently.

Sandra stared unhappily at the neat stacks of folders. 'I'll miss Harriet so much. She's been like a second mother to me since I came to work for her before the war. I'd go back to Dundee myself and maybe become involved in social work, if . . . if it wasn't for – er – problems.'

She'd almost mentioned the problem of Norrie Gallacher's yearly visits, still troubling her.

'There's a man in the picture somewhere, isn't there? Care to talk about it?' Darren asked quietly.

She hesitated, then found herself telling the sympathetic young doctor all about Norrie, and the quandary she was in.

'I see. That explains a lot. I wondered why an attractive woman like you had never married.'

Sandra sighed. 'Harriet advised me to wait for Norrie and take what scraps of happiness I could find, but I'm not convinced she's right.'

'Harriet's definitely wrong for once!' Darren O'Reilly declared. 'I think this man of yours wants to have his cake and eat it. If you ask my opinion, I believe he's being selfish.' He moved closer, and she could read anger and indignation in his eyes, then his expression softened as he looked at her.

'I'm the faithful type. If . . . if I loved you, Sandra, I wouldn't marry anyone else, not ever. If you wouldn't have me, I'd die a dusty old bachelor. Norrie Gallacher only has himself to blame. He has no right to ask you to waste your life waiting for him. I would make a clean break right now if I were you.'

'Would you, Darren?'

'Yes, I would. Oh, Sandra, how I wish—' He paused and lowered his gaze unhappily to the loaded shelves.

Sandra studied his downcast expression with sudden understanding, and laid a hand kindly on his arm.

'Time rolls on. I'm a middle-aged woman and will never marry now. Perhaps I'm the faithful type, like you.'

He looked up quickly. 'So you'll wait for Norrie to come back?'

'No, I'll take your advice and end the love affair. When Norrie comes to Glasgow next year I won't be here to meet him.'

'I'm glad,' he said with quiet sincerity. He looked at her wistfully, thinking how sweet she was, how beautiful in her maturity, and knowing she would never accept anything from him, not even admiration.

'Oh, if only I were older, Sandra,' he whispered longingly.

She laughed and gently patted his cheek. 'And if only I were a young lass again, my braw young lad!'

Being an astute man, Ben Chester was well aware of opposition from Chrissie's children. Before he and Chrissie were due to leave, Ben made a point of dropping into Rankine's for a word with her two sons.

The two younger men ranged themselves behind the bulwark of Ewan's desk to receive him, Sammy standing with his back to the wall. They positively bristled with polite hostility. Ben judged this to be a time for speaking out.

'Before your mother and I go off to London together, I guess I should tell you I hope to marry her, when she feels the time is right. Meantime, I'd welcome your thoughts on the matter.'

The direct approach startled them both. Sammy, the older one, spoke first. 'It's no use asking us to put in a good word for you, Mr Chester. Mum has a mind of her own. To be honest, we wish she wouldn't go with you. We don't want her to be hurt.'

Ben's square chin set grimly. 'Let's get this straight. I would never hurt your mother. Surely you don't grudge her a pleasant vacation with a caring, undemanding companion? Because that's how it's gonna be, so help me! I would do anything, anything at all, to make your mother happy, I swear.'

The two young men looked at one another, and there was a thoughtful pause. Ben was growing worried in case he'd gone too far with the straight talk, when Ewan spoke up.

'OK, Mr Chester, we believe you. There's a favour I'd like to ask in return. Would you keep an eye open for the *Christina K* when you get back to the States?'

This took Ben by surprise. 'You mean the ship Chrissie told me about, like the cute brooch she always wears? Is it still afloat?'

'We believe it is. Sammy found out the whaler was taken to Bergen in Norway after the war and sold to an Alaskan shipping line. You see, we want to buy the *Christina K* and refit her on the quiet. The sight of that old ship sailing home to the Tay would be the best gift we could give our mother. It would be a sort of "thank you" from us for all she's done to keep the family fortunes afloat.'

A vision formed in Ben's mind, a wonderful vision of a tall-masted ship sailing in the calmer waters of the estuary, and Chrissie's face as she watched her ship coming in.

'Yeah, that surely would please her,' he breathed softly. He stood up, leaned across the desk and held out a hand. 'You can count me in on this scheme, Ewan. I'll see what I can do,' Ben promised.

Chrissie very nearly changed her mind about the trip at the very last minute. The day of departure dawned cold and dreich, but all the family turned up to see her off. They were early, so they stood shivering in the shadow of the imposing West Station, where Danny Murphy had once seen Queen Alexandra, and gained a name for his baby daughter. So many memories, Chrissie thought with a sudden rush of emotion. She was furtively dabbing her eyes when she was dealt a resounding slap between the shoulderblades, and big Bella's delighted shout froze all commerce in the street for a startled second.

'Oh, my, Chrissie! Fancy meetin' you!'

Chrissie was genuinely delighted to see her old friend from the Lochee mill. She hugged Bella's portly figure, and smiled at wee Eck, Bella's man, who lurked in the background.

'We're just awa' across on the *Fifie* tae see my sister on the Boat Brae. She's been awfy no' weel wi' shingles,' Bella volunteered. 'Me an' Eck are livin' in a prefab, but we're to get a cooncil flat when they get roond to buildin' it. My lassie's working as a weaver in thon newbuilt Taybank Works, Chris. Talk aboot swank! You should see the place, it's like a cinema frae the ootside, but it's Buckingham Palace in the weaving flat. There's nae stour floats in your tea there, I'm tellin' ye! Changed days, Chrissie,' Bella sighed.

'Aye, changed days, Bella.' Remembering, Chrissie could almost smell the peculiar, fishy odour of jute yarn on the frames. She brushed her hand automatically down her spotless skirt, expecting to find it dusty with fibrous stour.

Bella dug her slyly in the ribs and lowered her voice to what was for her, a whisper. 'They tell me you've clicked wi' another man, Chrissie. One o' the wifies at the kirk was washin' her windaes when the two of you passed, airm in airm an' awfy pally.'

So the news was getting round, Chrissie thought

ruefully. Bella stole a curious glance at Ben, who was deeply engrossed in conversation with Ewan and Sammy.

'That'll be him, the big yin in the soft hat? Aye weel, Chris, guid luck to ye, hen. One boozy wee man's enough for me!'

When Chrissie bade Bella and her man goodbye it was time to catch the London train. She was glad of Ben's steadying hand under her elbow as the express came steaming in, because she was suddenly terrified by what she was undertaking. Then came a flurry of goodbyes, hugs and hasty kisses before they climbed aboard. Emily hugged her last of all, whispering. 'Chris, have a lovely time, but please, please, come back soon!'

As the train moved off, Chrissie waved and waved to the oddly forlorn little group standing on the platform. The station and the city beyond blurred with tears, which was daft really, for she was only away for a short holiday, and she'd be back before she'd had time to miss the familiar scene and her dear ones. She stared intently from the carriage window as they reached the long bridge spanning the river. The whole city spread before her, gathered on the river's south-facing shore, and behind lay the green slopes of the sheltering peak. Danny's monument upon its summit looked starkly white against grey rainclouds. The sight brought more tears to her eyes.

Ben leant forward and squeezed her hand. 'Happy, Chrissie?'

She wondered what her reply should be, because at that moment her heart was aching. She looked into his kindly, concerned face, and was comforted. She smiled. 'Yes, thanks, Ben. Very happy, my dear.'

Harriet Bowers returned to Dundee shortly after

Chrissie left, and Sandra came with her. Sandra had arranged to occupy Chrissie's flat in the meantime while taking further training as a social worker, but Harriet's situation was more complicated. Harriet began immediately looking diligently for worthy causes. She promptly sold the family mansion and moved into a dirty, rundown tenement in a shamefully neglected area of the city. From that moment on, the other startled residents knew no peace. Harriet rolled up her sleeves and set to work.

'Hey, you! It's no' your mornin' for the stair, it's mine!' yelled Connie McPhee indignantly, when she came upon Harriet scrubbing.

Harriet removed rubber gloves and studied her wrist-watch. 'It's nearly three o'clock, Connie. Rather a late morning, wouldn't you agree?'

Connie glowered. 'I was gettin' roond tae it, after.' She went over and sniffed suspiciously at Harriet's bucket. 'What's that awfy funny smell?'

'The strongest disinfectant I could buy,' retorted Harriet.

Harriet had scrubbed her way doggedly to the mouth of the close when Sandra arrived. She grinned. 'My, Harriet, this takes me right back to bairnhood. Fancy you washing the closie!'

Harriet pushed at her fly-away grey hair. 'Come on upstairs. I'm dying for a cup of tea.'

The tiny flat had been thoroughly scrubbed and painted, its walls distempered white, new lino on the floor, a scattering of cosy rugs and a few pieces of practical furniture introduced. Harriet put the kettle on the gas and flopped in a chair. 'Any news of your mother, dear?'

'Plenty,' answered Sandra grimly. 'Just wait till you hear this!' She produced a letter written in Chrissie's beautiful, distinctive hand and began to read.

Dear Sandra

Ben was quite right about poor, old London. How war-torn and weary it looks, though re-building has started here and there. We walked along the Embankment, and I was delighted to find the old *Discovery*, Captain Scott's ship. She was built in Dundee, and I saw her once when I was a little girl. It fairly took me back over the years. She did look sad and neglected, and the sight made me feel quite sorrowful for my own bonnie ship, the *Christina K*.

It's hard to realise I've been away almost six weeks. We spent a pleasant week with Mary Rose and her nice new husband, and, of course, there has been so much of interest to see in London. I waved to the King and Queen, quite close! I wonder if she remembered meeting me once at Glamis?

I have made up my mind to a plan of action which has taken plenty of thought and organisation, dear. Ben has been so helpful there. The fact is, Sandra, I spoke to your Uncle Ernest on the telephone, and he begged me to visit him in Texas. You will remember he was very badly wounded during the Great War, and has developed painful arthritis in the bad leg, so travelling to Scotland is out of the question for him. With Ben as escort, this seemed an ideal opportunity to meet my brother and his wife and family, so I have decided to go to America.

Ben helped greatly with the documents I need. They are fussy about visitors to the States just now, but fortunately I was never a 'Red', so the authorities might let me in, Ben says. (I suspect he teases me!)

When you receive this letter, I shall have flown the Atlantic. Fancy that, at my age!

I miss you all so very much, darling. Please give Natasha a big kiss from her loving Gran, will you?

Sandra folded the letter and looked up. 'What do you make of that?'

Harriet looked thoughtful, 'I would say offhand, our Chrissie is thoroughly enjoying spreading her wings.'

'Yes.' Sandra frowned. 'Will she marry him, do you think?'

The kettle began whistling, and Harriet got to her feet. 'I wouldn't like to bet on it, love. She has a mind of her own, your mother.'

America! Chrissie could hardly believe she was actually there. It was such a far cry from the streets of Dundee. She had a dazzling impression of towering skyscrapers, and then endured another internal flight which brought home to her the vastness of the country. Ernest and his wife Geraldine had retired to the outskirts of Houston. The Texas climate suited Ernest's arthritis better than that of Detroit, apparently. Their house was only a few hundred miles from Ben's ranch, which by American standards was 'just peanuts', Ben assured her.

There had always been a special bond between Ernest and his young sister, and they were close to tears when they embraced at the airport, together again after so many years. Ernest turned emotionally to Ben. 'Thanks for bringing her, Ben. I thought I'd never see my dear little sister again.'

He was very lame and walked painfully with sticks, Chrissie noted with pity. There were those who still paid a price for that terrible war.

But Ernest's beautiful house was an eye-opener to her. 'Oh, my, it's like a film star's place, with your own swimming pool and everything!' Chrissie breathed in awe, looking round open-mouthed at the spacious apartments.

Geraldine smiled. 'Swimming is good for Ernest's leg, so I guess it's kind of medicinal, Chris.'

'Chrissie, d'you mind how we used to watch those hardy folk who always took a New Year swim in Broughty Ferry harbour? They even had to break the ice with their bare feet sometimes,' Ernest grinned.

'Yes, you mean the Amphibious Ancients Swimming Club. The Phibbies still take a New Year dook, Ernest, believe it or not!'

He shivered. 'Better them than me! To think I went dookin' in the Tay myself when I was a young lad and never even noticed the icy water. I must be growing old, Chris.'

Tactfully, Ben and Geraldine left the brother and sister alone on the porch that evening after dinner, to reminisce.

Ernest lit a cigar. The aromatic smoke scented the warm evening. He sighed softly. 'Y'know, Chris, even though I read the *Scots Magazine* from cover to cover every month, and you send the *Sunday Post* faithfully, I miss Scotland terribly. I still think of Dundee as home. I often dream about the river, and the days long ago when I was a wee lad playing chuckie stones on the Grassy Beach.'

She understood at once, for she felt the same. 'I know. I doubt if I could live happily for very long without a sight of the river. Perhaps that's what it means when the sea's in your blood, Ernest.'

He gave her a keen glance. 'Ben's very fond of you. What if you marry him?'

She became very still. 'I don't know, Ernest. I try not to think about it. I keep stalling, and he's very patient. He just keeps on waiting.'

The light was fading fast. All she could make out was

the outline of her brother's head and the glowing tip of the cigar, but she knew he watched her wistfully.

'Seeing you has been like a breath of home to me, Chris. One of my ain folk at last. I'll never see Scotland again, the doctors won't let me travel that far. I'll never walk by the banks of the Tay, but I don't mind telling you I'd be so happy if you married Ben and stayed nearby.'

'Oh, Ernest—' Tears started to her eyes, and she reached out and took his hand. She knew all about homesickness.

He squeezed her hand. 'Och, I'm a sentimental auld fool! Maybe Ben just wants help with his charity work, who knows? Maybe that's all he has in mind for you, my lassie.'

Chrissie was intrigued. 'What charity work?'

'Ah! He can tell you about that himself,' smiled Ernest mysteriously.

When Chrissie challenged Ben about his charity work, he was cagey. He grinned sheepishly and refused to tell her anything. 'I guess you'll find out soon enough when I take you for a trip to the Good Hope Ranch, Chris.'

That was all she could get out of him for the rest of the leisurely visit to Ernest's home. It wasn't until they'd waved goodbye meantime to her brother and his wife, and Ben's hired automobile was eating up the miles to the ranch, that he raised the subject.

He'd been silent for some miles, frowning thoughtfully. 'I hope you won't be too shocked when we reach the ranch, Chris. Maybe I shoulda told you. Prepared you for it, sort of—'

'Oh, I know all about ranches, Ben, Ewan was a Wild West fanatic for years. I know all about cowboys and injuns, stampeding cattle and goodies and baddies. I'm prepared for anything,' she assured him airily.

But she wasn't prepared for the scene that unfolded

367

when the car drove up the dusty track. Dozens of boys of all ages, sizes and colours were racing towards them. Ben slowed and stopped, grinning as a tide of yelling youngsters engulfed the automobile, clambering all over it. He leaned on the steering wheel and turned to Chrissie.

'My boys, Chris,' Ben said simply. 'They're outcasts and orphans mostly, foundlings, little criminals and thieves, kids from slums who never had a chance. Little devils past redemption some of 'em, decent kids, most of 'em. There were about fifty at the last count. Chrissie, meet my boys.'

He put the heel of his hand on the horn and kept it there in a blast of warning. Very slowly, they inched their way through. Excited children rode on the roof and bonnet, others jogged alongside, and at last they reached the sprawling complex of buildings that made up the Good Hope Ranch. Ben got out and cleared a path through the milling youngsters to open Chrissie's door, then helped her out. Holding her hand, he turned to the curious boys.

'I promised you kids I'd bring back something real good. Well, I have; I brought you Chrissie, a lovely, Scottish grandma. How long she stays with us is up to you an' me, I guess, so let's be good to her.' He looked down at Chrissie, and she caught her breath at the love and admiration shining in his eyes. The boys whistled and cheered and made a fiendish din until Ben held up a hand and silenced them. He seemed to exercise complete control.

'OK. Off to the cookhouse, boys. Then it's baseball practice, I guess, being Friday.'

When Ben had shown her into the comfortable ranch house, Chrissie turned to him with glowing eyes. 'Ben, it's wonderful what you're doing for these bairns.'

He shook his head modestly. 'I'd no time for my own

kids, Chrissie. I was too busy making money. Now I have much more money than I need and plenty of time on my hands, it seems only right I should spend some on these unfortunate youngsters. There's a trained staff to look after them, of course, but the kids know they can speak to me anytime.' He grinned down at her. 'Only thing missing is a beautiful, Scottish grandma. I'm offering you the job if you want it, Chris.' The grin faded, and he became quietly serious. 'No strings attached, if that's the way you want it, Chrissie, I promise,' he said softly.

Sammy Murphy and his wife Emily were having a blazing row, the worst they'd ever had all their married life. The awful thing was, it was happening when all their fondest dreams had come true at last, and their own longed-for baby boy was lying in a cot between them while they shouted furiously at one another over his little head.

They were forced to shout. Daniel Murphy was screaming at the pitch of remarkably powerful lungs. It seemed, to his weary parents, that their perfect, healthy baby had cried steadily from the moment he was born until now, only stopping when he was picked up and cuddled, or fed. Night after night without ceasing he'd roared. It became wearing.

'What's the matter with him, for heaven's sake? There must be something wrong, you're his mother, Emily, you should know. Why don't we pick him up and have some peace?' shouted Sammy desperately. The piercing howls went through his head like drills.

'Don't you dare pick him up! There's nothing wrong with him, the doctor says, just a touch of colic.' Angrily, Emily tapped the book on babycare she held in one hand. 'An' the book says you mustn't keep picking him up, Sammy Murphy! You'll spoil him. The book says let him cry. It . . . it's good for him, the book says: crying develops his lungs.'

Sammy tore his hair. 'For heaven's sake, woman! His lungs are perfectly well developed already. The Broughty foghorn couldn't do better! You shouldn't go by that blasted book, it's just a load of nonsense!'

'It isn't! It isn't!' she screamed at him. Something gave way inside Emily, despair, a deep, exhausted depression, she didn't know what. She lifted an arm and threw the book full at Sammy. It caught him on the forehead, then dropped to the floor in a sudden deathly hush. Even the yelling baby seemed stunned momentarily into silence.

Emily stared horrified at the red bruised mark she'd raised on her husband's brow, and burst into tears. 'Oh, Sam, I'm sorry! Sammy, what's happening to us? I thought we'd be so happy when the baby came, it'd be just like heaven in this house. We'd be closer than ever, loving our wee bairn, but now all we do is quarrel over him,' she wailed.

Sammy took his poor, weeping wife in his arms. He knew she was tired out and as baffled and depressed by the baby's crying as he was. It was all so new, so strange, so . . . so darned wonderful to have a son of their very own! Daniel lay quiet as a mouse. He was a fly wee lad. He knew fine when he'd overstepped the mark, young though he was. Sammy felt a little gurgle of laughter begin to rise, the first chuckle he'd had for weeks.

'I'm glad you threw that awful book away at any rate, Emmy. Pity I happened to be in the way at the time, but that's life.'

Emily stopped crying. He heard a weak answering giggle and breathed a sigh of relief. They could still laugh, which gave hope for the future. She threw her arms round his neck. 'Oh, Sam, if only your mum would come home! If Chrissie were here I'd be better able to cope with everything. I was certain she'd come for the Queen's coronation. You know how she admires the royal family, but that was ages ago, and there's still no word. She didn't even offer to be with me when Daniel was born. What's she doing out there all this time?'

Emily's tone was aggrieved, and Sammy kissed her tenderly. 'Mum's been looking after Ben's Lost Boys. Maybe they need her more than we do, Emmy, but if it cheers you up, I'll write and ask when she intends coming home to meet her new grandson. In the meantime, why not put that blasted book in the bin and pick up our son and cuddle him? He deserves it, the wee lad. He's been quiet for almost five minutes!'

Chrissie laid Sammy's letter thoughtfully beside the other one she'd received that morning. The little boy seated on her knee patted her face so that she would pay attention to him. 'Gra'ma Chrissie, sing "Bonnie Dundee" for Elmer!' he ordered.

'For the umpteenth time?' She made a comical, smiling face at the little black, Down's syndrome boy.

He held up a hand, fingers spread. 'Five time, Gra'ma Chrissie.'

She hugged him delightedly. 'Elmer, you're smart!'

So he was. He'd come on by leaps and bounds since he came blank-faced and unresponsive to the Good Hope Ranch. Ben had found kindly adoptive parents for Elmer who were prepared to love and accept him as he was. He would be leaving soon: another success story. Helping wee lads with problems every bit as severe as Elmer's kept Chrissie enthralled and dedicated. And then, of course, there was Ben himself.

Ben came into the big, airy room. One glance at his expression made Chrissie lift the little boy off her knee. She looked down kindly at Elmer. 'Mama

371

Dakota's baking biscuits, you go ask her for one, lovie.'

The little boy ran off obediently. Chrissie saw that Ben was accompanied by a young woman and a plump little boy about nine years old. Ben looked at Chrissie. He seemed decidedly ill-at-ease.

'Look who turned up out of the blue, Chris. My daughter, Miranda Steele, and my grandson, Rufus.' He laid a hand tentatively on the boy's shoulder. Rufus moved away hurriedly.

Miranda nodded vaguely towards Chrissie, then turned towards her father. Chrissie studied Ben's daughter with interest. Miranda might have been pretty if she hadn't looked so worried and washed-out. Her clothes were beautiful, though. Oh, that suit . . .

'I got custody of Rufus and the divorce went through without a hitch. I thought I'd better tell you, Dad,' Miranda was saying.

Ben smiled sadly. 'What am I supposed to do, honey, congratulate you?'

She shrugged, her mouth twisted. 'Please yourself!'

The boy tugged at her skirt. 'Mommy, I'm hungry. I'm just starved. I wanna hot dog with mustard pickle.'

She turned on him. 'Will you stop going on an' on about hot dogs? Where d'you think I'm gonna get a hot dog in the middle of Texas?'

His fat little face set in stubborn lines. 'I wanna hot dog!'

Miranda looked at her father hopelessly. 'Look at him! Just look at your grandson! He's a mess. All he likes to do is eat. His school says he's born lazy and uncooperative. His grades are an absolute disgrace, and slipping.' There were tears in her eyes as she stared at her plump, dour-faced son. 'I can't do anything with him, so I brought him to the ranch for the summer vacation.' She stared at her father with thinly veiled bitterness. 'You never did anything for me. See if you can do something for your grandson.'

Chrissie pitied Ben. The sulky little boy scowled at his grandfather. 'I wanna hot dog with mustard pickle, right now!'

Ben held out a hand. 'Come with me. I'll show you the cookhouse.'

Rufus eyed the hand suspiciously, then studied the angle of Ben's jaw. He clasped his hands firmly behind his back and went reluctantly.

The two women heard Rufus girning loudly as he followed his grandfather. 'It's gotta be mustard pickle, OK?'

Miranda flopped in a chair wearily and lit a cigarette. Eyes narrowed against the smoke, she smiled at Chrissie. She was attractive when she smiled, you could see the pretty woman she could be.

'I'm glad I've met you at last. I don't mind telling you I've been worried stiff ever since a friend wrote to tell me Dad had brought a Scottish woman to the States to live with him. I guess he's at an awkward, lonely age. I would say mostly that's his own fault, though part of the blame's mine too, I guess.'

Chrissie smiled. She couldn't help liking this frank American. Miranda had Chrissie and Ben's relationship all wrong, though.

'You don't need to worry about me, Miranda, or your father, for that matter. He keeps very busy and happy.'

Miranda drew on the cigarette thoughtfully. 'So I don't have to worry about you, hmm? What I can't figure is what you get from working in a Godforsaken place with a bunch of problem kids even worse than Rufus.'

'I like it, believe it or not. Some problems we can't solve, but most we can do something about.

That makes helping your father with the boys very worthwhile.'

Miranda was silent, studying the glowing tip of the cigarette with a frown. 'Sure, that sounds very noble, but you know what I think? I think you want to marry my father and get your hands on his dollars. You're a widow, aren't you? I don't blame you, but I have Rufus's future to think of. Dad's a very wealthy man.'

'Miranda, you're insulting! The question of marriage hasn't arisen,' Chrissie retorted icily.

Ben strode into the room. He looked angrier than Chrissie had ever seen him as he halted beside his daughter. 'Chrissie's right, Miranda. You *are* insulting, and I guess you owe us both an apology.'

For an instant, Miranda resembled her sulky son, and Chrissie was sorry for her. Then the young woman stubbed out the cigarette and stood up.

'OK. I'm sorry, Dad. I'm sorry I visited you, and I'm going now after I've said goodbye to Rufus. Where is he, by the way?'

Ben's quick anger had faded. He looked miserable. 'He's in the cookhouse eating sausages and baked beans with the other kids. You . . . you don't have to go, Miranda. I'd like it if you stayed a while.'

She glanced wryly in Chrissie's direction. 'Thanks, but two's company, three's a crowd, and anyway I've a plane to catch.' She gathered her things together and kissed her father lightly on the cheek, then gave Chrissie a quick, nervous smile. 'I'm sorry if I offended you, Chrissie. I only meant to speak the truth.'

'You made me think, Miranda my dear, and perhaps that's a good thing,' Chrissie said.

Rufus didn't fit in at the Good Hope Ranch. He lay around listening to the radio all day and refused point-blank to participate in games or expeditions. The other boys teased him unmercifully at first about

374

his bulky frame, then ignored his dour silence. Rufus girned about the plain, wholesome diet until even Ben began to lose patience.

'To think my own grandson should be one of the worst pain in the necks we've ever had to deal with, Chris. What's up with the boy?' Ben groaned.

'Give him time. He's a very intelligent little boy, and a very unhappy one.'

Ben blinked in amazement. 'Intelligent? How d'you make that out? He doesn't do anything but sit around listening to that darned awful rock an' roll on the radio.'

'Yes, but haven't you noticed what he listens to apart from rock and roll? Economics and financial programmes, Ben, what's doing with stocks and shares on Wall Street every day. He pores over the financial pages in the newspapers for hours. Rather an unusual interest for a wee boy. I've been sitting knitting and observing him, you see. He doesn't seem to mind me.'

'Wall Street, did you say?' Ben said thoughtfully. 'You think there's hope, then?'

'Yes, I'm sure there's hope for Rufus if we could only get through to him.' Chrissie hesitated. She'd been doing a great deal of thinking and planning recently, and it was time to tell Ben what her conclusions were concerning the future. He'd be upset, she knew. 'Ben, I had a letter some time ago from my niece, Georgina, in Australia. Remember I told you my brother George died recently and his widow left the farm and went to Montrose? Well, Ina's husband wants to sell the farm, so I've decided to buy it and start a venture similar to the Good Hope Ranch. I've been so impressed with the success you've had with these lads.'

He sank down in a chair and stared at her. 'But, Chris, that means you'll go back to Scotland.'

He looked so distressed it alarmed her. She went to him and took his hand. 'Yes, dear, I would have to organise everything at the farm. You know how difficult that is.'

'If you go, you'll never return,' he said heavily. The healthy colour had left his tanned cheeks, and he looked suddenly old.

'Ben, I've been thinking this over for a while. It's what I must do, and besides, I long to see my family again. If you need me, then I'll come back, I promise.'

He lifted her hand sadly to his lips. 'You know I *always* need you. Don't make promises you don't intend to keep, Chris. I couldn't bear it.'

'Oh, Ben!' She wanted to weep. She didn't know what to say to him to ease the pain of her decision, but her mind was made up. She wouldn't change it.

Ben's mind worked fast in his desperation. He clasped both her hands in his. 'Chrissie, take Rufus with you? The kid's miserable here, and if you take Rufus to Scotland, there's more chance you'll come back.'

She was startled. This was the last thing she'd expected. Though Rufus sat with her often listening to the radio, the boy ignored her presence. Still, he was patently unhappy, a poor, mixed-up, wee boy who desperately needed her help. And he was Ben's grandson.

Chrissie smiled. 'Very well, my dear, I'll take Rufus. If you can persuade him to go with me, that is.'

Chapter 18

Ben's grandson required little persuasion to visit Scotland with Chrissie. Rufus hated Good Hope Ranch and grumbled most of the time. The food was awful and the other boys made his life a misery just because he was, well, kind of plump. 'Scotland couldn't be much worse than Gran'pop's awful ranch,' Rufus declared ungraciously.

Ben had been morose and silent since Chrissie declared her intention of leaving, and she secretly mourned the end of their happy relationship. The decision upset Ernest, too, and the days before departure were clouded by deep misgivings. Chrissie busied herself checking travel arrangements and packing, and tried not to think about what she was doing to the two men she loved. After all, she would return to Texas, wouldn't she? she thought anxiously. Texas was her second home, and had comforting links with Dundee. As a small girl she could remember her father declaring investment in Texas a good spec, even for a canny Scot.

But the attitude of the two menfolk had bred doubts she couldn't banish. Lying restlessly awake at night listening to the grasses in the meadow stir and sigh in the soft night breeze, Chrissie wondered if she would ever come back. There was Rufus, of course, but Rufus's return could easily be arranged somehow.

Miranda was the only one who wholeheartedly approved the scheme. 'You mean you really want to take Rufus to Scotland?' she had gasped incredulously when Chrissie phoned. Chrissie assured her that was indeed the case.

'What does Rufus say?' his mother asked warily.

'Rufus seems keen. There's only one snag, Miranda. I'm not sure when I'll return and I wouldn't want him to miss school.'

'Don't worry about it. Rufus has been missing school since day one. He's just not interested in anything but food.'

There was a pause, then Miranda went on hesitantly. 'Chrissie, don't get me wrong. I *do* love the stubborn scamp dearly. He's all I have since my marriage failed. His father re-married when the divorce went through, and moved with a new wife and step-son to Australia without so much as goodbye to Rufus. I guess that hurt Rufus badly. He must feel so rejected, poor love. Maybe what he needs is a kindly grandma like you.'

'I'll do my best for Rufus, dear, but it's your father I worry about. Could you possibly keep an eye on him while I'm gone, Miranda?' Chrissie asked daringly, fully expecting to be told to mind her own business.

'It's funny you should say that,' Miranda replied thoughtfully. 'I have a good job in a big store, but recently it's lost its appeal. I keep remembering what you said about Dad's work being so rewarding. Maybe I will give up my job and spend more time with Dad on the ranch, so we can get to know each other.'

On the eve of departure, Chrissie walked alone along the deserted track overlooking the prairie. It was very beautiful. There was so much space all around, she felt she could walk on for ever and never reach the end. In the distance she could hear the boys singing cheerfully round a campfire, and a drift of woodsmoke mingled with the aroma of scorched hamburger came to her nostrils, making her smile. Oh, how she would miss the boys. There were tears in her eyes when she reached the seclusion of a copse of sweet-scented shrubs, where it was safe to weep a little forlornly. There were still tearstains on her cheeks when Ben tracked her down some time later. He took her hand, resisting an overwhelming desire to kiss her.

'Chris, I wish you wouldn't go. I have this fear I may never see you again.'

She laughed shakily. 'Oh, Ben, when I've bought Ina's farm I'll be back. I told you so.'

'And what if your niece won't sell?'

Chrissie smiled. 'Don't worry, she will.' She pulled him from the dangerous seclusion of the copse into full view. 'Come on, walk with me. Did you ever see such a glorious moon, Ben?'

He wanted to tell her how his heart was aching. He longed to ask her to marry him and stay with him for ever, but he hadn't the courage. She might refuse, and then he would be doubly broken-hearted. So Ben Chester walked with his loved one, enthused about the full, silver moon rising above the prairie, and remembered the glorious scene as one of the saddest moments of his whole life.

Next day, Chrissie was glad she had the wee boy to see to, or she might have broken down in Ben's arms at the airport and abandoned the trip. Not that Rufus was a demanding charge. Far from it: he spent his pocket money on a large supply of candy, and sat happily chomping his way through it on the plane taking them to New York. The steady munching set Chrissie's nerves on edge, but she endured it in silence.

On landing they checked into a hotel in preparation for the morning transatlantic flight, and Chrissie allowed Rufus to choose what he wanted for dinner. The best way to Rufus's heart was via his plump, little stomach, and Rufus expanded that evening in more ways than one. He gave Chrissie an embarrassed little kiss on the cheek when she tucked him in that night. Progress indeed, she thought, elatedly.

She had plans for Rufus tomorrow: but that could wait.

Chrissie spent a long time next morning selecting reading material from the airport kiosk. Apart from choosing a comic, Rufus was disinterested. He'd enjoyed an enormous breakfast and was feeling far from energetic. His mother would have nagged unmercifully about the breakfast, but this Scottish grandma hadn't said a cheep. He glanced at Chrissie doubtfully; when somebody didn't care how much you ate, it took all the pleasure out of eating, Rufus found.

Rufus sat staring straight ahead as the plane droned on and on endlessly. There was nothing to see out of the windows but sky and cloud, and there was nothing to do. He'd read the comic from cover to cover and worked out all the puzzles in no time at all. He was so bored he wished himself back at the ranch. He stole a cautious peep at the Scottish grandma. She was engrossed in a book but didn't seem to be enjoying it much. Catching sight of his eyes on her, she stopped her puzzled frowning and smiled at him.

'Oh, Rufus, I can't make head or tail of this.' She angled the cover to let him read.

A Simple Guide to Stocks and Shares, it said. Rufus sat up with a jerk. 'What d'you want to know?' he asked.

'We-ell, just about everything, dear! I would like to invest some spare cash in reliable stocks and shares.'

Rufus began talking excitedly. As the little boy warmed to his subject, Chrissie listened in amazed silence to the extent of his knowledge and expertise. She had not been strictly honest with Rufus, because she had a very shrewd grasp of the stock market herself. Enough to realise that the child knew what he was talking about. More than that, she thought with growing awe: Rufus was a financial wizard!

'That's very interesting, my dear,' Chrissie said, when they'd pored over the options and Rufus had handed out some sound advice. She gave him a level look. 'You're quite a mathematician, Rufus. So why don't you do well at school?'

He hung his head dourly. 'School's just boring. When the teacher writes sums on the board the correct answer just pops into my head without thinking. It's so easy I can't be bothered writing it out in my book, so I just sit an' think about interesting things while the other kids work.'

'Rufus, you know what your problem is?' He swivelled in his seat and stared at her. 'You're very smart. Much smarter than the average boy your age,' Chrissie told him. 'You should be four or five grades above the one you're in, then you wouldn't be bored. You need a challenge. You need to be stretched.'

Rufus looked extremely startled. He pondered Chrissie's words for some time in frowning concentration, then gave her an endearing grin. 'Yeah. Maybe if I was stretched some, I wouldn't be fat!'

Chrissie laughed with him. Rufus was learning to laugh at himself, and that couldn't be bad, she thought.

Sammy was waiting at Prestwick airport with his wife and young son when his mother's plane arrived. Chrissie kissed and hugged her son and daughter-in-law, then turned at last to her small grandson. This was a very special moment. They all felt it, even the wee boy Daniel, who shyly put his thumb in his mouth and stared back at her solemnly.

'Daniel Murphy. My wee Danny,' Chrissie whispered, studying the sturdy toddler's fair hair and hazel eyes. She could see no trace of Danny or herself in this wee lad, Danny's grandson. He resembled Emily very strongly, and that was as it should be, Chrissie thought.

Rufus took in every detail of the emotional little scene and crept unhappily back into his shell. He didn't belong in this united family. He didn't belong anywhere, he thought.

Emily picked up Daniel, laughing. 'He's not usually so quiet, Chrissie, he's a wee chatterbox. C'mon, son, give your gran a kiss!'

Watching Chrissie kiss the child, Rufus felt suddenly frightened and forlorn. He tugged at Chrissie's sleeve. 'I'm starving. Don't they have hamburgers in this crummy place?' he whined grumpily.

The other two grown-ups studied the fat little boy with the tight-lipped disapproval he'd come to expect from most folk, but Chrissie's expression was filled with love and compassion, just as if she understood his misery. She smoothed a tumbled lock of hair from his brow with a gentle hand.

'It's OK, Rufus dear. Don't worry.'

He hadn't got a hamburger, but Rufus felt satisfied. He trailed along behind the little family, but not once did he take his eyes off Gran'ma Chrissie's back. Somehow he felt that if ever he lost sight of her, he'd be lost indeed.

Chrissie's children had laid on a grand dinner to welcome the travellers. They were all congregated in the flat Chrissie would share with Sandra; and Chrissie looked round the family gathering proudly. How delighted Charles would have been by it, she thought with a lump in her throat. There was one dear face missing, though.

'If only Mary Rose, were here,' Chrissie said wistfully. There was a sudden hush. Sandra turned beetroot-red and looked mutinous, then everybody started talking at once with forced jollity.

Ewan proudly presented Linda, his secretary and wife, to Chrissie. They had a ready-made family already, Ewan explained laughingly, ruffling the dark hair of Linda's little daughter, Kate, who was Natasha's age. The two wee girls were obviously great pals, dancing around Chrissie merrily. Chrissie's gaze kept returning to her little granddaughter, Natasha. She'd rarely seen such a bonnie wee girl, small and very fair, with a natural grace that reminded Chrissie strongly of Charlotte before she was cruelly crippled by polio. She turned to her daughter. 'So we have another little dancer in the family. I'm so glad!'

Charlotte smiled, patting her latest black labrador, which never strayed far from her side. 'They've produced a vaccine against polio, Mum. Tashie will never suffer as I did, thank goodness!'

Rufus couldn't describe his feelings adequately when he met Natasha. She was so nimble and quick and perfect, everything he was not. He felt clumsy as an elephant just watching her dance by. A rush of muddled emotion quivered through him, a compound of resentment, jealousy, and something else so deep and hidden it made him want to disgrace himself and howl. But he never, ever cried, not even when other boys teased him cruelly. It was a point of pride with Rufus not to cry. He caught Tashie's eye as she went past, and scowled ferociously. Tashie took a stealthy glance around the adults, found them absorbed in chat, and rudely stuck out a small, pink tongue.

The door was flung open, and a beaming woman in spotless white apron appeared in the doorway.

'Your denner's on the table. Come an' sup your broth while it's hot!' she shouted above the din of conversation.

Sandra whispered in Chrissie's ear. 'That's Connie McPhee, Mum. She used to work in a buster stall, and she's one of Harriet's success stories. Connie was nearly down and out when Harriet happened to discover what a marvellous cook she is, and Connie's been with me ever since.'

'There's no' enough chairs tae go roond sic a gang, but the bairns can have a piece in the kitchen wi' me,' Connie announced.

The two little girls looked at one another, giggling. 'A piece of what, Connie?' they shouted.

Connie grinned. 'None o' your lip, or it'll be a piece o' my mind!'

Chrissie pushed Rufus forward. 'You go with Tashie, Rufus. Take her hand. You bairns will have better fun in the kitchen with Connie, I bet.'

Obediently, Rufus held Tashie's hand as Connie marched the children out. Tashie's hand felt cool and light as a feather in his hot, sweaty palm.

Chrissie took Harriet, Rufus and Natasha with her to inspect Ina's farm. The last time Chrissie had driven through the sunny vale of Strathmore had been with Ben, and she thought about him wistfully. Despite the excitement of meeting her children and grandchildren, she'd missed Ben's stimulating company so very much.

Harriet had been thoughtfully silent for a mile or so. 'Chris, would you let me look after things on the farm? It's the sort of job I've been hunting for. My old tenement will be demolished soon, and I shan't have a home to go to then.'

'Oh, Harriet, that would be perfect!' Chrissie cried with delight. 'I'll see you have all the staff you need. I visualise the place as a refuge for women and bairns who badly need a holiday or a friendly ear, and for youngsters who need time to sort themselves out in

384

peace and quiet. As a social worker, Sandra can refer needy cases to us. I think Charles would have approved of Rankine's funding this project, Harriet.'

'I'm certain he would. Charles was the most caring and generous man I ever met,' agreed Harriet quietly.

The farmhouse George and Jeannie Kennedy had inhabited for so many happy years seemed to extend a welcome to Chrissie as she walked in. It was that sort of house, homely and comfy. She could understand why her sick brother had loved the farm, and the life there had repaid him twofold; improving his frail health and giving him a long, contented life. Her eyes smarted with tears, which she impatiently brushed away. The two children had explored the house by now and were casting longing glances at the farmyard. She smiled at Rufus. 'Take Tashie outside. Look after her, mind!'

It was muddy in the yard, so Chrissie warned them to wear the wellies they'd brought. The ungainly black wellingtons made Rufus feel clumsier than ever. Tashie's wellies were bright red, they twinkled in the sunlight as she darted around exploring. A horrid sensation came over Rufus, a nasty, jealous resentment of Tashie's neat prettiness. He was so big and ugly and fat, just like an elephant. He wanted to tease her, as he had been teased so often. When she came dancing past, Rufus stuck out an arm and stopped her in her tracks.

'You have a funny name. Foreign,' he said accusingly.

The little girl pulled in her chin and straightened her back proudly. 'Natasha Zielinska. It's a very good Polish name, my daddy says.'

'So, you're a Polack!' Rufus sneered.

Natasha stamped a boot angrily in the mud. 'I am not a polecat, you horrid boy! Anyway, you're a fatty. You're a great big fatty, Rufus!'

Rufus stared at her. He couldn't deny the taunt,

because it was true. He should hate her like he hated all the other kids who took delight in baiting him, but he couldn't hate her. He couldn't hate this lovely, bright little creature. Instead, he hated himself. Oh, how he hated himself.

His lip quivered. The quivering ran right through him, spreading out from somewhere deep and dark inside. He was going to cry, Rufus thought with wonder. He'd never cried before when they teased him about being stupid and fat, but now tears just poured out of his eyes, great big fat tears.

'I don' wanna be fat! Awww . . . I hate it. They say I'm fat an' stoopid, but I'm not stoopid, Tashie. Awww . . . I'm not!' Rufus sobbed bitterly.

Tashie was greatly alarmed by the storm of tears, and her own tender little heart ached for the big boy who was sobbing as if his heart was breaking. She stretched her arms round Rufus and hugged him. Sympathetic tears ran down Tashie's cheeks. 'I know you're not stoopid, Rufus. And you're only fat 'cause you eat a lot. Connie says she'd rather keep you for a week than a fortnight.'

Rufus put his arms gingerly round the slight little figure and rested his chin on top of her head. The sobs gradually stopped racking his body so painfully and he was at peace again. He'd expected to feel thoroughly ashamed, but he didn't. Instead, Rufus felt as if the bitter tears had left him all clean and refreshed.

'Gran'ma Chrissie says I'll be OK if I'm stretched, Tashie,' he said.

She thought that was very funny. 'Oh, Rufus! Like elastic?'

He started laughing too. He couldn't ever remember laughing so freely. He didn't care so much about being fat any more. He could fix that. Tashie and Gran'ma Chrissie believed he was smart, and not stupid like everyone said. For the first time in his life, Rufus began to believe in himself. Maybe he *was* real smart, after all.

Wowweee! thought Rufus incredulously.

'Stop here a moment, Chrissie,' Harriet ordered on the way home. Wondering, Chrissie pulled into the side of the road. They were at the top of Powrie brae, with the city spread out before them. A young bobby had brought Chrissie's granddaughter Elizabeth here one romantic, starry night three years ago, and the young couple were now happily married and living in England. It was quite a magical spot.

Chrissie shaded her eyes against the westerly sun. She saw how the city was changing, spreading into the surrounding countryside. There weren't so many tall factory lums belching smoke.

Harriet tugged at her arm. 'Look, Chris!'

Chrissie followed the pointing finger with a deep sense of shock. The bronze statue of the Black Watch soldier looked so like her Danny, standing proudly on the breast of the brae. He stood quietly watching over the city of his birth, as braw and handsome as in life. Chrissie wept silently, covering her face. She was getting old, she thought. Tears came so easily these days, and the memories were so sweet and sair.

There was Harriet's comforting arm round her shoulders, two concerned little faces looked up at her, too, sharing this poignant moment.

'I thought you'd want to see the Black Watch memorial, Chris,' Harriet said softly. 'It's very fitting and impressive, very beautiful. The Queen Mother unveiled it in 1959.'

Chrissie dried her eyes and smiled at her dear friend. She took one last look at the still, strong figure of the soldier, then turned away.

'Thank you, Harriet. I can't tell you what this means to me. Danny never had a last resting place, but now I think he does. Here. Guarding his town.'

'Gran'ma Chrissie, I want to go home to America,' Rufus said a few weeks after their trip to the farm.

'Aren't you happy here, dear?' Chrissie asked anxiously. Rufus had changed quite a bit recently, for the better.

He squirmed uncomfortably. 'Sure, I'm very happy. This is the best place I've ever been, but I . . . I want to go back to school. The new semester starts in about a month and I don't want to miss any of it.'

Chrissie looked thoughtful. 'You want to be stretched. Is that it?'

He grinned. 'I sure do.'

'Rufus, I can't go with you just now. The negotiations to buy the farm from an Australian are at a complex stage. You'll have to travel alone. Can you do that?'

He looked at her gravely. 'I'm not scared. You can trust me.'

'I know that, Rufus.' She hugged him. She'd grown to love and admire this brilliant little grandson of Ben's. She'd miss him when he went, and then there was Natasha. Oh dear, Chrissie thought. Rufus and Natasha had become inseparable. Poor little Tashie would be very upset.

Ben Chester felt as if his worst fears had been confirmed when Rufus returned without Chrissie. He took it so badly it worried his daughter, and she cast around desperately for some way of distracting her father from his brooding depression.

'Dad, remember that wonderful holiday we had in Hawaii before the war when I was about Rufus's age?

Why don't you take Rufus to Hawaii with you? He's old enough to appreciate it, and I'd be delighted to keep an eye on everything for a couple of weeks while you're gone,' she suggested.

Ben remembered that holiday, in the days when he'd been on the lower rungs of the ladder to success and climbing steadily. It was the first exotic holiday he'd been able to afford for his wife and kids, and oh gosh, how they'd all enjoyed it. Maybe a holiday with his grandson would recapture a hint of that pleasure, and dispel the listless feeling Chrissie's continued absence caused in him.

He smiled at his daughter. Miranda had been a wonderful help on the ranch with the boys. He couldn't have gone on without her, and father and daughter had grown close to one another again. He knew his depression worried her, and he reckoned the poor kid deserved some encouragement for her efforts. Ben made an effort to be enthusiastic.

'Well, honey, that's a great idea! What d'you say, Rufus?'

Rufus looked up from a recent copy of the *Wall Street Journal* which he'd been studying. 'Sounds OK to me, Gran'pop.'

Miranda gave her son a thoughtful glance. There was quite an improvement in Rufus since he'd returned from Scotland. She couldn't put a finger on it exactly, because he didn't have much to say for himself these days, but it was there.

Hawaii was a bit of a disappointment, as Ben had suspected it might be. He couldn't recapture the joy of that first holiday, when the whole world had lain at his feet. Returning would have been a ghastly mistake if it hadn't been for Rufus's unfeigned delight in everything. Ben took the boy to Pearl Harbor, an emotional experience for both of them as Ben told his grandson about the sudden Japanese air attack on the naval base, in December 1941.

At Rufus's insistence they visited some of the smaller Hawaiian islands, but it was at Mauna Kea one hot afternoon that fate stepped in.

'Gran'pop, I'm real hot an' thirsty. Could we go some place for a drink of water?' Rufus suggested.

Ben looked around. They were in the harbour area, the air tangy with seasalt, a tarry, hempen smell from fishing nets drying in the sun. An unlikely area to find drinkable water, he thought, but there was a café sign nearby. Some enterprising individual had had the idea of setting out a few tables with inviting, shady parasols on the deck of a nearby ship, and Ben and Rufus headed for this oasis.

It was pleasantly cool aboard the *Aloha*. Ben relaxed and sipped a cool beer, while Rufus tackled a lemon soda. He and Rufus got along remarkably well, Ben thought. And that was odd, now he came to think about it, because Rufus used to be a real pain in the neck. Had Chrissie waved a magic wand? Ben wondered.

He studied the boy more carefully. You couldn't call Rufus a fatty now. He'd lost weight, and the leaner look suited him.

'Rufus, you've grown,' Ben observed thoughtfully. He didn't mean in height alone. There was more to it than stature, a sort of expansion of the lad's spirit.

Rufus made a suitably exuberant noise with a drinking straw in the empty glass, then grinned. 'I guess I'm stretching. Gran'ma Chrissie says I ought to be stretched, Gran'pop.'

'Ah, she does, does she?' Ben said thoughtfully.

His drink finished, Rufus leaned back in the seat and looked around with keen interest. It was an old ship, really old and exciting, but the brass fittings gleamed like gold in the sunshine. There was a ship's bell you could see your face in hanging not far away. Rufus leaned over curiously to read an inscription on the bell.

'Well, what d'you know, Gran'pop? This ship was built in Dundee!'

'What?' the glass raised to his lips, Ben almost spilt the beer. 'How can you tell?'

'It says so on the bell, anyway.' Rufus read out the inscription. '"This bell respectfully presented to Captain William Kennedy, master of the *Christina K*, on the occasion of the vessel's maiden voyage, 1st June 1895, by management and staff of Lilybank Foundry, Dundee, as a token of esteem."'

Ben stood up slowly. He stared upwards at the mizzen-mast soaring above him into the blue sky bleached with heat, trying to take in what Rufus was saying. A whaler, here in Hawaii? Well, that made some sense. He knew the huge mammals were hunted in these waters, too. But Christina Kennedy's whaler, the *Christina K*? It couldn't possibly be. The name was different for one thing. This ship was called the *Aloha*.

'Come with me!' Ben ordered Rufus. He strode to the companionway and confronted a startled waiter. 'I want to see the manager, if you please.'

The manager proved to be a young man, on the defensive because he expected some complaint. He relaxed when he discovered all Ben had in mind was information, and invited Ben and Rufus into his office below decks in a friendly manner. 'Yes, you're quite right, she was originally the *Christina K*,' he nodded. 'I bought her in Alaska for a song, from a whaling company that had gone bust. I'd been hunting for a whaler for some time. I wanted to start a small business in Hawaii, something that would reflect the local history of the islands and be a tourist attraction as well. I think you'll agree this whaling ship is an ideal solution,' he grinned.

'It could be I have a better use for her,' Ben said quietly. He leaned forward, his eyes on the younger man. 'You said you got the ship cheap, but that won't enter into our negotiations. Name your price. If it's a fair one I promise I'll pay it.'

The young owner looked taken aback, then his expression set stubbornly. 'Sorry, but she's not for sale. Price doesn't come into it. This has been my dream ever since I left high school, and I'm not likely to change my mind now I've just realised an ambition.'

Ben had a lifetime of experience in business negotiations, and he knew this man wasn't bluffing. He was a man with a vision, and as he'd said, money didn't come into it. Ben sighed. He took out his business card and jotted down the ranch phone number before handing it over.

'If you ever change your mind, contact me. Promise?'

The younger man studied Ben and decided he'd be a good man to do business with. He smiled and held out a hand. 'OK, Mr Chester, I promise to let you know if I ever contemplate selling my ship, but I hope that won't be for many years.'

When Ben and Rufus were once more on the quayside, they paused for a long time, just looking at the ship in silence. Ben put a hand on Rufus's shoulder, and the boy looked up.

'Rufus,' said Ben quietly. 'When the time comes to buy this ship, I may not be around any more. Will you promise me something? Will you use some of the money I'll leave you, to buy Gran'ma Chrissie's ship and re-fit her as a training ship for youngsters? Will you see to it that the *Christina K* returns home to Dundee one day? Will you do that for me, son?'

Rufus felt the weighty responsibility of the promise fall round him like a heavy cloak. To be entrusted with such a mission made him feel scared, yet very proud. It was the most scary, wonderful thing that had ever happened to him in all his life. He met his grandfather's eyes bravely.

'I promise. You can count on me, Gran'pop,' declared Rufus staunchly.

It took time to get the farming venture up and running once it was in Chrissie's hands. The project was greeted with suspicion, both from those they were trying to help, and from others who should have known better. Some neighbouring farmers were up in arms, declaring that Teddy Boys and other undesirables would take over the district given half a chance.

Chrissie and Harriet battled on. Based upon Ben Chester's Good Hope Ranch, the old farm steading was converted into private cubicles, a spacious living and recreation area and a spotless cookhouse. Tam, the shepherd, and his brisk, little wife agreed to stay on in the cottage, although retired from active shepherding. They formed the nucleus of the staff Chrissie hoped to employ eventually. Then there were a few sheep, dogs, cats and kittens, Donald the donkey, a small herd of goats and a flock of hens. All these had therapeutic value in the soothing of troubled minds, Harriet maintained.

But it all took time, and as the months passed Chrissie became more and more involved in the lives of her family, and more engrossed in the life of the city. Great changes were taking place, new housing estates built where the jute barons' country houses once stood, and old tenements demolished in the city. As Connie McPhee remarked grimly to Chrissie: you had to keep a close eye on your hoose, in case the bulldozers came along an' ca'd it doon when your back was turned.

Work was starting soon on a road bridge, and

the approaches to it. The obdurate thudding of the pile-drivers would be heard for many months to come, as the structure edged out across the river. It was an exciting time for a Dundonian born and bred, and little wonder Chrissie became absorbed in it. America, and her life there, seemed far away.

She was on the point of writing her regular weekly letter to Ben when she was disturbed by a frantic knocking. It was Emily, white-faced and wild-eyed with fear.

'Oh, Chrissie, come quick! There's something far wrong wi' the bairn!'

Chrissie felt her heart lurch. She was devoted to wee Daniel. He'd seemed fine yesterday, too, apart from a cold. She hurried after her daughter-in-law. 'Have you called the doctor?'

'Sammy's been trying to contact him. But Chrissie, he could be too late. The wean can't get breath!' Emily wailed frantically.

Chrissie took one look at the gasping little toddler in Sammy's arms, then turned to Emily.

'Is the water hot, really hot?'

Emily gaped at her. 'What? Yes, the immersion's been on, but—'

'Then run a bath. A scalding hot bath,' she ordered briskly.

'Chrissie—' Emily stared unhappily, then ran to do her bidding. Chrissie took the wheezing bairn gently from his father's arms and carried Daniel into the bathroom, which was rapidly filling with billowing clouds of steam. Chrissie sat on the bathroom stool, Daniel on her knee. She smiled at Emily and Sammy.

'It's a bad attack of croup, my dears. Many's the time I've let the kettle boil merrily on the gas to ease my bairns' wheezing, but this steam will do the trick just as well. See, he's breathing easier already.'

It was true. Daniel's rasping breaths had quietened dramatically in the steamy atmosphere.

Emily had collapsed with relief. 'Oh, Chrissie, what would we do without you!'

'You'd manage fine. You'd have to.' Chrissie kissed the top of Daniel's head and handed him over to Sammy. His breathing was quite normal again.

The doctor arrived soon after and confirmed Chrissie's diagnosis, but the incident left her uneasy and restless, and the future seemed unclear. Her family needed her, depended upon her. Would she return to America, as she'd promised Ben, or would she break that promise for her children's sake? Chrissie swithered unhappily, until quite unexpectedly the decision was taken out of her hands.

The phone rang, and when Chrissie answered, she was surprised to hear Miranda's voice. It was an excellent connection: Miranda sounded so close. She also sounded desperately worried.

'Chrissie, I wondered, are you planning to return to the States soon?'

Chrissie put a hand up nervously to the brooch she always wore. The replica of the ship never failed to calm her. 'I – er – haven't made any plans yet, dear.'

Miranda sounded on the verge of tears. 'It's Dad, Chrissie. I'm phoning from a callbox near Rufus's school, because Dad wouldn't let me phone you from the ranch. Dad's changed so much since you went away, apart from his wretched stubborn pride, which won't let him call you. He's lost interest in everything, even the ranch and the boys. Hank and I are running it for him now. I . . . I'm terrified if you don't come back soon he'll lose interest in life itself. Oh, it's just heart-breaking to stand by and watch him pining away and be unable to do a darned thing to help, Chris! I'm convinced only one person in the whole wide world can help him recover his strength, and . . . and that's you.' Miranda was sobbing by now, a heart-rending, desolate sound that reached out to Chrissie across the miles.

Chrissie was deeply distressed. 'Don't cry, my dear. I'd no idea Ben was in such a state. His letters are always so cheerful, to be honest I thought that – well – he didn't care about me being with him any more.'

'Care about you!' Miranda gave a gulping sob. 'If you only knew the effort those letters cost him. He's a proud man. He won't plead with you, 'cause he says you must come of your own free will, Chrissie. But I'm afraid that could be too late.'

'In that case, I'll come right away.'

When the decision was made Chrissie immediately felt better. She was in command of her life once more, going her own way. She realised her affections had been torn both ways, between all the members of her growing family and dear, lonely Ben. That's why she'd been dithering recently. In the end it was only a question of who needed her most, and Miranda had just supplied the answer.

Chapter 19

Returning to the Good Hope Ranch was quite a different homecoming. Miranda and Rufus met Chrissie when the plane touched down on Texan soil. Ben had been ill and wasn't fit to make the journey, Miranda explained. It was the first hint of change in the big American, and it left Chrissie feeling apprehensive. As it was, Chrissie had barely recovered from Rufus's miraculous transformation.

Rufus's greeting had been, 'Hi, Gran'ma Chris, see how I stretched!' And so he had. He was a full head taller. There was no trace of the fat, unhappy little boy she'd taken with her to Dundee. He had lost weight and was healthily fit and bronzed. More importantly, he walked with head held high, displaying happy, new confidence.

Miranda was driving Ben's big Cadillac, and at the same time chattered non-stop. 'Rufus is top of the class in *everything*, Chrissie, would you believe? The boys and girls in his class are three or four years older than him, too. Apparently he has this fantastic IQ which nobody suspected until recently, and he's streets ahead of other kids his age. Can you imagine my little Rufus, a genius?' his mother declared proudly.

Rufus met Chrissie's eye with a wink and the endearing grin she remembered fondly. Rufus could still laugh at himself. He would never forget he'd been cruelly labelled fat and stupid, and Chrissie hoped this experience would give him unique insight into the problems of less able people. She had high hopes for Rufus.

There were no lively boys waiting at the Good Hope Ranch this time, only a solitary figure standing on the avenue outside the porch, watching them arrive through a cloud of December dust.

'Oh, Dad,' groaned Miranda. She glanced at Chrissie. 'He shouldn't really be up.'

When they drew alongside, Chrissie was saddened by the change in the big, energetic man she'd known. His clothes hung on him, and he leaned weakly on a stick, needing its support. Had she done this to her dear Ben, unwittingly? she wondered guiltily.

Chrissie's prolonged absence had very nearly destroyed Ben Chester, but he felt on top of the world today. His eyes were suspiciously moist as Chrissie climbed from the auto. He held out his arms as she hurried to him.

'Chrissie! So you did come after all. I daren't raise my hopes too high.'

She hugged him. 'I told you I'd be back, and I always keep my word, you daft man!' She looked up at him humorously. 'Mind you, Ben Chester, your letters were so cheery, I thought you were managing fine without me. I was quite offended, and swithered whether to come back to you at all!'

'Oh, Chrissie, if you knew what I've been through without you!' he cried fervently.

Miranda paused a moment in handling Chrissie's luggage. 'He was told to take life easy, Chrissie, but, of course, he didn't. He would fret and worry about you, then drive himself hard in order to forget. A stomach ulcer that had bothered him once flared up, and he's been real ill. Oh boy, Chrissie, is he a difficult patient! I'm hoping you'll have more success with his diet. Salads are good for him, but he won't touch 'em.'

398

Ben laughed, for the first time in months. 'Gee, Miranda, greens are for jack-rabbits. You never tasted a Scottish high tea, girl. Chrissie must show you sometime. When I visited in Dundee she dished up a classy meal of pie an' peas, scones, butter an' jam, an iced cake, all washed down with two cups of strong coffee.'

'Dad! You never ate that, did you?' Health-conscious Miranda looked horrified.

'Sure I did, every crumb, and without a stomach-ache, too.'

He put an arm round Chrissie, and painfully slowly they made their way into the cool ranch-house, Miranda and Rufus following with the baggage.

Chrissie looked round the spacious apartments and sighed with pleasure. She'd forgotten how homely and welcoming the ranch-house was. Another homecoming, but very different from that in Dundee, with her children and grandchildren gathered round.

But she was needed here in Texas, and she seemed to be guided always to those whose need of her was greatest. Her gaze was drawn to Ben, who was eagerly watching her delight in the new drapes and furnishings Miranda had chosen. She smiled radiantly, and let him have hope.

'I'll walk to that copse of oleander one of these days if it kills me, boy!' declared Ben frequently on his daily walk with Rufus.

'What's so important about it, Gran'pop?' Rufus asked curiously.

'Never you mind!' grunted Ben, leaning on the growing boy's shoulder as he struggled manfully to the house, having failed yet again to reach his objective.

'Any word from the man in Hawaii?' Rufus demanded.

Ben looked crestfallen. 'No. I don't wish the poor

guy any misfortune with the *Christina K*, Rufus, but I must admit I'd expected his café to go bust long ago.' He gave his grandson a stern glance. 'Not a word to Chrissie about it, though. I don't want her hopes raised high, only to be dashed. Remember we're dealing with a guy with a vision. There's no knowing what a guy with a bee in his bonnet will do!'

With a sigh, Chrissie folded the letter that had just come from home and tucked it into the envelope. It was from Emily, containing joyful tidings, depending which way you looked at it, that is.

Emily was expecting another baby in the spring. She and Sammy were thrilled to bits, of course, but, well, Emily wondered how on earth she'd cope when the new wean arrived. Chrissie would remember what a live-wire wee Daniel was, and he was ten times worse now he was older and really inventive with the mischief! He'd nailed a whole pound of sausages to the kitchen floor in an orderly line of links, and nearly driven Bertha, the daily, crazy, trying to pick them up. Emily wished Chrissie would come home. She missed her so much, and felt really lost without her.

Poor Emily, Chrissie thought indulgently. Emily would cope, though. She'd have to. She had Charlotte to help her, and Sandra's sound common sense to fall back on. The letter was unsettling, though, particularly as Ben had been oddly preoccupied and reticent since Chrissie's arrival six weeks ago. Had he changed his mind about wanting her to stay? she wondered sadly.

Restlessly, Chrissie went outside. It was funny sort of weather, the air breathlessly still, although high thunderheads towered ominously on the horizon. Chrissie didn't know what to expect from the weather, or from Ben either. He kept her guessing. He looked so much better, but he'd kept a tight rein on his emotions since that first, revealing day.

There had been no sign of Ben since lunch and she assumed he was having a siesta in the thundery heat, but she was too restless to doze, and instead walked forlornly down the track beside the prairie. It was a lonely walk, and one of her favourites. She came here often when she needed reminding how small and petty her worries were against the wide vastness of sky.

A torrential downpour started when she'd got too far from the house to turn back. It's hardly wise for an elderly lady to sprint, so she darted into the shelter of the nearby copse.

Someone else had had the same idea apparently. She cannoned into Ben standing beneath the trees. He grinned as he steadied her. 'Well, what d'you know? I guessed my persistence would pay off sometime. There's no peace for us to speak privately up at the house, what with the boys and Rufus, and Miranda rabbiting away, so I've been coming here often since I got my strength back. I knew you'd turn up one day and I'd have you all to myself.'

She laughed breathlessly. 'Ben, what're you blethering about?'

Rain was spilling down the leaves on to her silvery hair, and he pulled her closer into the shelter of the branches.

'I'm not blethering. I've been practising, an' I'm word perfect.' He took a deep breath, looking down into her blue eyes.

'Christina, I love you very much. Would you do me the honour of becoming my lawful, wedded wife?' He broke off, grinning widely. 'There was more, Chris, romantic poetry an' that, but I guess we'll skip it. Only one thing, I hope you don't expect me to go down on one knee, 'cause I doubt if I'd get up again. Anyway,

I got the important part OK, my dear Scots lassie. Say you'll marry me, Chrissie?' he begged.

So many ways of loving, she thought. A new love for Ben and herself in their old age. Ah, well, true love grows neither old nor cold. A surge of happiness washed through Chrissie as she kissed her tall American.

'Aye, I'll marry you, Ben Chester. I thought you'd never ask.'

There was a flurry out on the track, and a golfing umbrella sprouting muddy jeans suddenly appeared. Rufus lifted a corner of the brolly and took in the two old people embracing in the shelter of the bushes. Being smarter than average, he immediately reached the correct conclusion.

'Wowee, Gran'pop! When are you two gettin' married?'

'Just as soon as Miranda can bake a wedding cake, son!' said Ben, laughing.

'Where are you goin' for a honeymoon?'

'Oh, I dunno, Rufus. I guess Paris would be nice.'

'Gran'pop, could I come to Paris with you? School will be on vacation soon, and I wouldn't be any bother, honest! I'd just love to work out on the spot how Gustave Eiffel built the Eiffel Tower, Gran'pop!'

Ben looked shocked. 'Not on your life!'

Chrissie burst out laughing. 'Oh, go on, Ben, let him. Let's be the first newly-weds to go on honeymoon with a grandson in tow! That must be a record of some sort!'

Chrissie had never been to an American wedding. Theirs was to be a quiet affair with just the family and a few neighbours, Ben assured her. That suited Chrissie, who wanted no fuss, and then she happened to glance at the guest list Miranda was preparing. She nearly collapsed.

'But there must be over two hundred names on that list!'

'Yeah, two hundred and thirty. Just a nice, quiet little wedding,' nodded Miranda, adding another four names that had just occurred to her.

'That's quiet?'

'Oh, sure. There were over a thousand at mine, and look what a mess that marriage turned out to be, apart from my dear Rufus.'

Chrissie said no more. She'd been married twice before, but was obviously a novice at the game. Miranda, with big store experience, organised everything down to the colour of stockings Chrissie would wear with the lovely pearl-grey suit and hat they'd chosen together. It was such fun choosing everything with Miranda, Chrissie thought. It almost compensated for not having her daughters there. She'd extended a warm, open invitation to all her family, but the wedding was at such short notice and so far away, none of them could make it. That made Chrissie sad, but she tried to put her disappointment out of her mind.

Ben's Lost Boys, of course, were in a ferment of excitement, because most of them had never attended a real country wedding. Ben solemnly gave each one a task to see to. Chrissie smothered a grin as he did so. With so much scope for error, the day promised to be lively!

Ben and Chrissie were married in the little white church Ben attended in the nearest small town. It seemed to Chrissie when she arrived with Miranda, her maid-of-honour, that everyone in town was packed in there. Her eyes met Ben's as he stood before the altar, and she smiled radiantly, happy for her own sake, and for this modest man who'd done so much good for the community. The local people certainly appreciated him. The ceremony over, they clapped and cheered and sang as Ben and Chrissie left the church to join the cavalcade of automobiles waiting outside.

It was as lively a reception as Chrissie had predicted. What with the younger generation vying with one another to wear the shortest mini-skirt and the older generation expressing shock and disapproval, nobody noticed when one of the boys dropped a barbecued chicken into the fruit punch.

It sure was a pity the barbecue caught fire and fused the fairy lights strung around the garden, as Ben said, but what the heck? Who needs fairy lights with a moon like that? And the firemen were real friendly guys who stayed on well after midnight to join in the fun.

Rufus was in his element, being in charge of the music relay. It had to be the Beatles, of course, played loud.

'I love you, yeah, yeah, yeah . . .' greeted Ben and Chrissie wherever they turned.

It was also Rufus who gave Chrissie the only moment of sadness she experienced all that magical day.

She'd been delighted when Ben's son Alexander turned up. Miranda had invited her brother without much hope, but Alexander had made an effort to come and meet his stepmother, and Chrissie really appreciated it. He was very smart in Marine dress uniform. Alexander had joined the army some time ago and was making it his career. Chrissie was interested, and asked about his chosen profession.

'I'm on leave from Vietnam at the moment, Chrissie. I'm stationed in Saigon meantime,' Alexander explained.

Rufus was listening wide-eyed to his uncle. 'You mean you're fighting Reds? Oh, I wish I were old enough to go!'

Alexander glanced at the growing boy with a curiously sad expression. 'Don't wish for it, boy. You will be old enough, one day.'

He looked up and met Chrissie's frightened stare,

and she saw in his eyes the same look she'd seen once in Danny's long ago, hopeless, sickened, the look of a man who must fight a lost cause whether he wants to or not. Impulsively, she laid a hand on Alexander's arm, then, stricken, she hugged her dear Rufus to her protectively.

There was so much promise and talent to be lost, just as Danny's great talents had been blown heedlessly away and lost forever. Oh, she couldn't bear it, not a second time in her life. It would kill her this time.

'Have a drink, Chrissie. A little more champagne?' urged Alexander gently, watching her with grave sympathy.

So she drank another glass of champagne and could laugh again. But the shadow of Vietnam remained at the back of her mind until she and Ben climbed into the Cadillac later that evening. Rufus clambered proudly into the rear seat, regally ignoring the gale of good-natured laughter. Ben blew the horn jauntily and they were off, a string of old shoes and tin cans clattering behind. Rufus's face beamed out cheekily, framed in the rear window above the large 'Just Married' notice somebody had pasted to the trunk.

Chrissie snuggled down beside her new husband with a contented sigh. They were an elderly couple and quite exhausted by the festivities, but oh, so happy!

'Now for the start of a new life together, Ben,' Chrissie said.

Rufus stuck his head between his grandparents. 'An' me, Gran! Don't forget about me!'

'Don't worry, Rufus, I get this feeling we won't be allowed to forget about you!' replied Ben. Then he burst out laughing. The laughter proved infectious, and still laughing uproariously the unlikely trio set out for a blissful honeymoon together, in France.

* * *

Sandra Murphy's love for Daniel, her nephew, probably had much to do with being a childless old maid, she thought, although the women fighting for women's lib would have been up in arms at the thought. Sandra had listened patiently to all the arguments. Women were free now to live their own lives, enjoy themselves without the scutter of marriage and having men and bairns to care for, they said. Most of these women had made the most awful mess of their own lives, but it didn't seem to register with them that the straight and narrow path had been made that way for jolly good reasons.

Sandra sighed. Chrissie's Farm, as it had come to be known over the years, had done sterling service with Harriet in charge, helping out the scared and despairing youngsters who were victims of the permissive society.

But that didn't solve the problem of Daniel Murphy. Even Sandra's love for the lad didn't blind her to the fact that at seventeen he was a tearaway. Of course, she loved his young brother Patrick devotedly, too, but in a more chummy, conspiratorial fashion. Patrick and Sandra often sat together over large mugs of cocoa and had a right good moan about Daniel's exploits. That's what they were doing this evening, in front of a roaring fire.

'Of course, I'm very fond of your mum, Patrick, but Emily as a disciplinarian is absolutely useless. If she'd skelped Daniel when she had the chance, he might have turned out differently,' observed Sandra grimly.

'Yes, I know.' Thirteen-year-old Patrick cradled the mug of cocoa in his hands. 'Fancy letting him have a motorbike! I mean, Daniel, on a motorbike! Can you imagine anything more lethal?'

'No, quite frankly, I can't, dear.' Sandra was desperately worried by her nephew's increased mobility. One heard such awful stories about excessive speed on motorbikes, and dreadful accidents.

'He did swear to Mum and Dad, hand on heart and hope to die, that he'd be a careful, responsible rider. There was quite a stushie before they finally gave in and bought him that second-hand bike. He's been fairly sedate ever since, actually,' said Daniel's brother loyally. Patrick had hopes of a motorbike himself when the time came, and didn't want too much drama attached to his brother's latest acquisition.

'He hasn't even passed his test yet,' said Sandra gloomily.

'Yes, that might be putting the brakes on.' Patrick took a long, thoughtful swig of cocoa. 'I thought maybe he was a reformed character because of his new bird.'

'What new bird?' Sandra sat up. Daniel was very popular with the girls, being wickedly handsome, but Sandra hadn't heard about this one.

Patrick shrugged. 'She's a bit of a mystery woman. Mum's having kittens because Dan hasn't brought this girlfriend home to pass Mummy and Daddy's inspection as per usual. He's been curiously tight-lipped too. It would seem to indicate a dark, shameful secret in the background. I haven't seen much of her myself, but the bits I have seen on the back of Dan's motorbike look first-class, I must say,' remarked Patrick appreciatively.

Sandra had an opportunity to view her nephew's mysterious new girlfriend a few days later. She heard an approaching roar as she took her usual bracing constitutional along the Broughty Esplanade, and recognised Daniel's distinctive blue machine. There was a girl perched on the pillion, but Sandra was glad to note they were both dressed sensibly in leather gear, and wore spaceman-like safety helmets.

Daniel, the rascal, swithered openly as he approached his aunt. His inclination was obviously to disappear smartly at full throttle into the distance, but he had great respect and affection for Sandra, so reluctantly he stopped the bike and put his black boots down to earth firmly, balancing the roaring monster, which grumbled away noisily at the intrusion.

'Hi, Auntie Sandra! Out sniffing up the sea breezes? You'll be taking a dook with the Phibbies any day now.'

'That'll be the day!'

Sandra pointedly eyed the girl shrouded in the helmet and waited. Daniel smiled and nodded foolishly, but no introduction was forthcoming.

'Aren't you going to introduce me to your friend, Daniel dear?' Sandra prompted frostily.

'What?' He looked round vaguely as if noticing the lissom young woman perched behind him for the first time. 'Oh yes! Well . . . this is . . . er . . . um . . . Tiger Lil, Auntie Sandra.'

'Tiger Lil?' Sandra's voice rose to a squeak.

Daniel nodded solemnly. The girl clutched Daniel and said something that was drowned by the grumbling motorbike. Sandra stared at her, but all she could see beyond the helmet's visor was a pair of laughing dark eyes and smiling lips outlined boldly in red. Tiger Lil! Oh, help! Sandra thought.

The motorbike roared impatiently and Sandra stepped back. 'Don't let me hinder you,' she remarked caustically.

'Well, we are in rather a hurry, and I promised Dad I wouldn't go over sixty miles per hour on the Kingsway, so—' Daniel shot away thankfully with a deafening roar. Tiger Lil, hanging on the back, found time to give Sandra a cheeky wave.

Sandra glared after the feckless pair. 'Well, really!'

She couldn't imagine what poor Emily would do when Daniel produced this latest girlfriend for inspection. Faint clean away on the spot, probably. Really, it was too bad of Daniel, taking up with a girl like that.

Next day, Sandra was still wondering what to do about the bad company her nephew was keeping, when the doorbell rang. She found a neatly dressed young woman standing on the doormat. Sandra studied her with surprise. She didn't know who she was, yet she had a feeling she'd seen her before someplace.

The young woman looked extremely ill-at-ease, though she smiled and held out a friendly hand. 'Hi! I'm Tiger Lil, remember?'

Sandra held the door open grimly. 'Won't you come in . . . Miss . . . er—?'

The girl smothered a laugh as she accepted Sandra's invitation.

'Oh, that Daniel Murphy!' she said. 'Fancy calling me Tiger Lil! The first thing that came into his head, he says. My real name's Lilian, Miss Murphy.'

When Sandra had settled Lilian in a chair, her young visitor stared at her worriedly. 'Miss Murphy, I . . . I don't know how you're going to take this. I'd hoped Daniel could keep it quiet about me and my family, but when we met yesterday I just knew I had to tell you all about myself.'

Sandra braced herself stoically. 'You can say anything you like to me in complete confidence, my dear. I won't be shocked.'

The girl studied her doubtfully. 'I think you will be very shocked, all the same. I didn't tell you my full name. It's Gallacher. I'm Norrie Gallacher's daughter.'

Sandra was glad she was sitting down. The room reeled and she felt herself turn pale. She stared mistily at the girl. A pretty thing, dark-eyed, with a pale, sensitive face that had somehow trapped a haunting resemblance to her father. Norrie's daughter, Sandra thought. The girl who might have been my daughter and Norrie's if Fate hadn't played cruel tricks. She felt tears sting her eyes.

Lilian flung herself down on her knees before the older woman. She chafed Sandra's cold hands.

'Oh, I've upset you, and that's the last thing I wanted,' she cried. 'You see, Dad told me all about you when I decided to study art and design at art college in Dundee. He was very frank about how he loved you and lost you, then tried to persuade you to have a clandestine affair.'

Sandra closed her eyes in pain. 'He told you about that? Oh, Lilian, I couldn't do it. I wanted to, because I loved him so, but I couldn't.'

Lilian squeezed her hand. 'I know. When he came back to Glasgow and found you'd gone it broke his heart, Dad said, but at the same time he thinks it was the saving of him. He decided to stop hankering over what might have been, and pay attention to his own marriage.'

Lilian smiled. 'I guess you could say I'm the result of his good intentions, so I've got you to thank for being here. They're very happy now, Mom and Dad, and it's a good marriage. Dad thought you might like to know how it turned out, if I met you, but . . . but I wasn't sure how you'd take it. When Daniel told me you were his aunt, that made it even worse. I swore him to secrecy, and was terrified to meet you—'

'So Daniel knows all about my sad love affair?'

'Yes, he does, I'm afraid. I had to tell him, and it worried him so. He's very fond of you, and he was scared stiff my sudden appearance in Dundee would upset you badly.' Lilian met Sandra's gaze honestly. 'Daniel's nice. The nicest boy I ever met. We sort of gravitated together when I began first term at art college and he started first year architecture. I could hardly believe it when he told me his name was Murphy.'

'Daniel is a wild rascal, you know, Lilian,' Sandra warned.

The girl's expression softened. 'No, he isn't. He's funny and imaginative and creative, and he'll be a wonderful architect one day. He just needs help and encouragement, and . . . and a little love, perhaps—'

Sandra watched Norrie Gallacher's daughter, and was filled with a strange sense of fulfilment and peace. Wouldn't it be lovely, she thought dreamily, if in the fullness of time, Daniel and Lilian—

Rufus at twenty-six was a very different character from the happy little boy who'd gone off on honeymoon with his grandparents fifteen years ago. Rufus had been stretched. Stretched almost beyond endurance, he thought bitterly, as he lay on a lumpy bed in a crummy rooming house in Boston – which was about as far away as he could get from the after affects of the Vietnam war.

As forecast by school and university, he'd turned out brilliantly; his mathematical ability soon attracting the attention of high heid yins in Government, as Chrissie called them. He'd been destined for great things in the design of armaments and guided missiles when he'd received enlistment papers. They hadn't wanted him to go, the high heid yins. They'd done everything in their power to stop him short of putting him in jail, but he'd gone anyway, just as a squaddie, in a blaze of patriotic fervour.

He still had nightmares about Nam. That's why he would never design missiles of war again, why he was working as a clerk in a shabby office overlooking the harbour, so he could watch the peaceful ebb and flow of tides and never again use his impressive brainpower to destroy innocent people.

He just wished he could be happy, that's all.

Rufus got up. Somebody had posted his mail under the door, a bill or two, and a letter from his grandfather.

Rufus sat on the bed and tore it open with the guilty feeling one has when you've failed someone very dear to you. He would like to have been a success for dear old Gran'pop's sake, but there you are. His attention quickened, however, and he sat up straighter as he read Ben's letter.

This is between us two, Rufus. I just had the results of medical tests, and the prognosis is bad. Mind you, I'm not griping about the fact I can count life in weeks, far from it. I'm a very old codger, and the past fifteen years have been the happiest of my life. I've been very fit and active until recently, and I've no complaints, son, except I'm sorry to leave Chrissie and make her sad. I haven't told her the truth, but being Chrissie, I think she knows. We're both doing an excellent job, kidding one another on that everything's fine!

I guess it's up to you to take care of the Chester empire now, Rufus, since Alexander is pretty high up in the army and not aiming to leave it. One thing would give me real pleasure though, if you could fix it: I want you to buy the *Christina K* for Chrissie. I heard from the guy in Hawaii yesterday, just a cryptic note scribbled on the back of the business card I gave him years ago:

'Are you still interested in the *Christina K*?'

It sounds hopeful, son, yet somehow it sent a shiver down my back. I want you to go to Scotland and put Chrissie's sons in the picture first, see if they'll agree to form a syndicate to buy the ship and carry out any repair work that's needed. After that, you're free to negotiate with the visionary in Hawaii. The funds to do it are all made available to you, and you have probate. I know I can leave things safely in your hands, Rufus, and that makes

your ever loving Gran'pop real happy and content.
God bless you.

Tears ran down Rufus's unshaven cheeks, sorrowful,
unashamed tears. He cried for a long time, then washed
and shaved and reached for a clean shirt. He packed a
case and looked around the crummy, little room for the
last time, then he closed the door quietly upon another
chapter of his life.

'And a one, and a two, and a three, and a four – that's
good! That's splendid, Mr Simpson!' Natasha Zielinska
beamed at the octogenarian performing wonders in her
Dundee Pensioners' Keep-Fit class.

Natasha had forty senior citizens in various states of
fitness under her care. Maggie Carmichael, a large lady,
fanned herself weakly.

'Och, lassie, I'm fair melted. Could we no' hae a wee
break?'

'I'm pechin' an' a',' admitted the redoubtable Mr
Simpson.

Natasha, delectably trim in purple leotard with a
white belt clasped around her narrow waist, smiled
and relented. 'Oh, very well. Ten minutes for a tea
break, then back to work!'

She smiled to herself. She knew the old folk enjoyed
blethering during the tea break as much as they enjoyed
the simple dance movements she gave them to catchy
old tunes.

When the gymnasium emptied, Tashie arched her
small feet and twirled up on her toes and performed
two grand jettés to the last few bars of recorded music.
Every movement was a graceful pleasure to watch,
from the poise of her head to her slender arms and
expressive hands. Natasha could have gone far in the
world of ballet if she'd wanted to, but instead she'd

chosen to help the large and clumsy, the unskilled and uncoordinated to experience the joy of movement. She didn't know why she'd turned down the chance of fame when it was offered, but she knew there was a reason hidden somewhere in the past. It would come to her one day, she thought.

But she did love helping people, particularly mentally handicapped patients or those with cerebral palsy. Yes, she thought, those people above all rewarded her efforts. She sank down in a deep curtsey on the dusty floor in a grand finale of dying chords. She'd thought she was alone, and a sudden burst of clapping startled her.

A young man stood in the doorway, applauding enthusiastically. Tashie scrambled up, her face hot. He moved towards her, smiling.

'That was great!'

'Oh – er – thanks.' She squinted up at him curiously. He was tall and lean and very handsome: a complete stranger. 'Were you looking for someone?' she asked.

He grinned. 'Yes. You, Tashie. I wanted to renew our acquaintance.'

She frowned, bewildered. 'But we've never met, have we?' Tashie studied him. If they'd met she would *certainly* have remembered him.

He laughed. 'We met years ago. I cried on your shoulder, and you were kind to me. Don't you remember Rufus?'

Tashie's jaw dropped. 'Rufus? The fat boy?' A confused memory came rushing back. A muddy farmyard, and a big, clumsy, ugly boy crying in her arms as if his heart would break. She looked speechlessly at the amused, tall man.

Rufus nodded. 'I know, it takes some getting used to. I stretched like elastic, I guess.'

They laughed at that. Tashie felt herself relax, and a

little burst of happiness exploded inside her. 'Talk about the frog and the prince, Rufus! What a transformation!' she laughed.

'Yeah, and you only held me in your arms. Who knows what a kiss might do?' Rufus said. He moved closer. The big empty gym suddenly seemed small and intimate. Tashie hastily skipped backwards.

'Rufus, I better tell you. I'm engaged to be married.' She held out a hand to display the sparkling ring Mark had placed on her finger not so long ago.

Rufus didn't seem unduly perturbed. He studied the gem. 'Yeah, I figured there might be someone. Only natural, with a beauty like you.' He looked at her, and Tashie felt her head spin. He had such unusual, compelling eyes, so warm and sympathetic. They made her feel weak.

'Don't marry him, Tashie,' said Rufus quietly.

She suddenly felt like crying, angry and confused. 'You've got a nerve!' she cried. 'I hardly know you, and Mark and I have known one another for years. It's always been understood we'd marry one day. Our parents were delighted when we announced the engagement!'

He just kept looking at her. Tashie wished he wouldn't. She was mesmerised, and couldn't look away. He put a hand on the graceful curve of her neck, a touch that was electric, thrilling her. 'Rufus, don't—' she whispered with tears in her eyes, pleading with him to stop the pain and confusion.

'Don't marry him, Tashie,' Rufus repeated. 'Look, I have no time left to court you, I just have this warm memory of a little girl in red wellies who once changed my life, so I decided to find her. Then I saw you just now, and I know I want to see you again and again. But I must leave Dundee tomorrow. I have a . . . well . . . a mission, if you like. I don't know how long it will

415

take, but you can be sure I'll be back, Tashie. I swear I'll come back.'

His hand moved gently down the long line of her neck and rested on her shoulder. 'Tashie, please don't marry him?'

'Hey, Tashie, so *that's* why we got our tea-break early. Just so's you two could canoodle?' Mr Simpson's jocular tones cut across Natasha's thoughts. The pensioners had come crowding back, ready for more effort. They were standing round grinning and nudging one another delightedly. Nothing her elderly friends liked better than a hint of romance, Tashie knew.

But oh, if only they knew the muddle she was in.

A widow once more. Chrissie could hardly bear the sorrow of her new state, although six weeks had dragged by since Ben died peacefully. She was an old lady now, her fair hair faded to the beautiful, soft sheen of old silver, but at eighty-five Chrissie still walked erect, without the aid of a stick. She inspected the bunkhouse and cookhouse every day and listened sympathetically to any gripes and grumbles the boys and staff might have, just as Ben had done to the end of his long life.

Chrissie moved to the ranch-house window which looked out across the porch towards the pool. It was so hot today all the lads were congregated around the pool. Hank, Miranda's husband, had organised a swimming gala, and the youngsters swam races under his vigilant eye, making a joyful, unholy din. It was a scene of youth and boundless energy, and she was old now, and had no part in it.

If only Rufus would come, Chrissie thought longingly, but she had lost Rufus years ago. It seemed she was fated to lose those she loved most of all. Rufus had gone to Vietnam, and three years of her life had been spent in constant terror for his life. Well, he'd been sparcd, and yet she'd lost her bright and brilliant laddie as surely as if he'd fallen with those other dear lads in dark, green jungles. Rufus never came to see her now, never even attended the funeral of his beloved gran'pop.

She'd had a letter from him though, a long loving letter, postmarked Hawaii, but he obviously hadn't thought it worthwhile breaking his holiday to see her. He'd just written that he was taking control of all Ben's complex business affairs, and not to worry about a thing, he was a mathematical genius, remember?

She turned away heavily from the window. All very well to tell her not to worry, but she *did* worry. She worried about all of them. All her dear, scattered family.

Miranda was sitting watching her. Chrissie had almost forgotten her presence, she sat so quietly. They smiled at one another, a smile of complete trust and understanding. They'd grown very close over the past fifteen years, like a real mother and daughter.

'Chrissie, you're not happy, are you?' Miranda asked abruptly.

'Dear, how could I be, with Ben gone?'

Miranda frowned. 'No, apart from missing Dad. I miss him terribly too, but that just makes me all the more determined to carry on his work. Hank feels the same, but . . . but I don't think you want to stay on the ranch any more.'

Chrissie stared at her. 'But the ranch is my home, Miranda!'

'Is it?'

Miranda rose and walked towards her stepmother. She stood studying Chrissie sadly. Even in old age, it was still such a lovely face, full of character and humour, the mouth still firm and determined. Miranda didn't often weep, but tears threatened now.

'I've watched you stand often by the window with a far-away look, Chrissie, and I know you've gone from

417

us, away home to Scotland. I don't know what to do about it. I don't know how to make you happy,' she cried tearfully.

Chrissie hugged her. She forced a laugh. 'My dear, I'm an old widow, well over eighty. Do you think I'd go flying home to Dundee, at my age?'

Home. That evocative word. It had just slipped out, but they both realised the significance. Miranda sighed and dabbed her eyes.

'What has age to do with it if you feel like that?'

Chrissie gripped Miranda's arms. 'Miranda, tell me what I ought to do,' she begged.

The younger woman stared at her for some time in silence, then wearily shook her head. 'I can't tell you what to do, Chrissie. You'll make up your own mind. You always have,' said Miranda sadly.

Chapter 20

Miranda was right. After some heart-searching, Chrissie did make up her mind: old woman or not, she must go home to Dundee.

Once the decision was made it seemed the only possible one. The two men who had given purpose to her life in Texas had gone. First, Ernest at a ripe old age, and now her dear husband, Ben.

Miranda bowed bravely to the inevitable, and she and Hank, Ben's trusted foreman, did everything they could to make Chrissie's departure smooth and painless. Ben's Lost Boys were dismayed when they heard the news, and protested loudly at the loss of their adopted grandma.

'Don't worry, lads,' Miranda told them. 'There's an applicant right here for job of resident grandma. See the grey hairs I got from looking after you lot? I guess I qualify for the job!'

And Miranda was voted unanimously into the vacant position.

While her stepdaughter was arranging a trouble-free departure, Chrissie was giving anxious thought to her arrival on the other side of the ocean. She knew her decision to return would be causing concern, if not consternation, amongst her children, who were faced with the care of an aging mother.

Chrissie couldn't help grinning. Little did they know how spry she was for a woman in her eighties, and how fiercely independent. Sandra, at the other end of a transatlantic line, had generously offered tender care in the Beechyhill flat which had once been Chrissie's, but was now occupied by Sandra. Chrissie had accepted the offer sweetly in the meantime, but could see trouble ahead. Two strong-willed women occupying the same kitchen? That was a recipe for disaster!

After some deliberation, Chrissie sat down and wrote two letters. Miranda, observing her stepmother through the open window, wondered what Chrissie was up to. As she wrote, Chrissie wore the harmless-old-lady smile usually reserved for little tough guys. Miranda knew that deceptively innocent look well. Chrissie was definitely planning mischief!

The days flew, and soon it was time to leave. Chrissie had secretly hoped Rufus would turn up to see her off, but as she stood in the airport with Miranda and Hank, she knew it to be a forlorn hope. She had lost Rufus, her bright and brilliant boy. They were calling her flight, and Rufus hadn't come.

Chrissie blinked back tears. There were enough tears already, pouring down Miranda's cheeks.

'Oh, Chrissie love! Will I ever see you again?' Miranda sobbed.

Chrissie wasn't having any of that depressing talk. 'Don't be daft, of course you will!' She hugged Miranda fondly. 'I won't be far away, love, just across the pond, and the world gets smaller every day.'

Hank put an arm round his wife as they watched the spry, little figure hurry away. Turning, Chrissie smiled and waved gaily.

'Oh, Hank! How can I bear it, if we never see that dear old soul again?' Miranda whispered.

He grinned. 'You heard what the little lady said, honey. Somehow, I don't think we've seen the last of Gran'ma Chrissie.'

* * *

Sandra was a bag of nerves, waiting for her mother's plane to arrive. She didn't know what state her dear mother would be in after the marathon journey. Would she need a wheelchair, a doctor, a swig of brandy, or what? Would the flat be cosy enough in this chilly weather, after the heat of Texas? Would her mother survive the car journey to Dundee? Would she manage to climb the steps outside the flat? Oh, dearie me, what a worry it was!

Sandra huddled in a corner of the airport and pretended to be absorbed in a magazine. She'd been all at sixes and sevens since her mother had announced she was returning home. Chrissie's unexpected decision had taken the whole family by surprise but they were all absolutely delighted and looking forward eagerly to Chrissie's arrival.

It was OK for the others, though, Sandra thought, feeling hard done by.

The onus of caring for their mother in her declining years fell squarely on Sandra as the unmarried daughter. She knew her mother was a strong-willed character who liked to have her own way, and that meant an assault upon Sandra's cherished independence. Oh dear, thought Sandra, suddenly feeling isolated, if only she hadn't quarrelled so bitterly with Mary Rose, her sister might have helped out.

Sandra realised the plane had landed and passengers were disembarking and crowding into the concourse. She hastily bundled the magazine into her bag and rushed forward, nervously scanning faces.

There she was. For a moment Sandra forgot all her apprehension in the pure joy of seeing her mother again. Sandra stood motionless, breathlessly studying the elegant, elderly woman who stood patiently waiting, a little apart from the others.

She had style. She was an elderly lady now, of course,

yet somehow not old. There was something everlastingly youthful about the interested poise of the head with its shining crown of lovely pure-white hair. Joyful emotions of love and happiness washed away Sandra's misgivings. Her dear old mum was home.

'Mum! Mum, here I am. I love you!' she shouted and waved. She began pushing her way through the crowd, but another figure darted forward and reached Chrissie first, hugging her delightedly.

'Oh, how lovely to see you! How absolutely wonderful—'

Sandra's jaw dropped. 'Mary Rose!' she yelled indignantly.

Her sister whirled and went white with shock. 'Sandra! What are you doing here?'

'Meeting Mum, of course!'

'But so am I! Mum wrote and said you couldn't meet her, so she asked if I could do it!'

'She wrote to me and said I must be sure to meet her, because nobody else could come! Oh, Mary Rose, I don't understand this!'

The two sisters looked at one another with a dawning suspicion, then turned and stared hard at their mother.

Chrissie smiled sweetly at the accusing faces.

'Dearie me, what a mixter-maxter! I must have written to you both, my dears. Fancy making a silly mistake like that. I must be going quite dotty in my old age. Mind you, it's nice to see you two speaking again. High time all that nonsense was finished and done with!'

The two sisters stood motionless, gaping at her, then Sandra began to laugh helplessly. She couldn't stop once she started, and presently Mary Rose joined in. Neither of them had laughed so much for years. Weakly, Mary Rose flung her arms round her sister and they clung together, laughing and crying at the same time. Chrissie looked on with a smug wee smile.

Sandra wiped her eyes. 'Oh, Mum, what a rascal you are!'

Mary Rose touched her sister's arm hesitantly. 'Sandra, it breaks my heart to think I ruined your life, running off with Roderick like that. I'm so sorry, love. Won't you forgive me?'

Sandra was silent. A cutting retort rose to her lips, and then she paused, thinking about her worthwhile job as a social worker and all those she'd helped and comforted in grief and distress. She remembered the folk she'd helped during the Glasgow blitz, and the despairing youngsters in Dundee for whom she'd patiently built a happy and challenging future. Sandra thought about Norrie Gallacher, now living happily with his wife because of Sandra's sacrifice, and her thoughts turned to the years ahead, safe in the hands of Lilian Gallacher and Daniel Murphy. She'd never been a wife and mother, but her life had been rich indeed, all because Mary Rose and poor, brave Roderick had fallen in love. It was a humbling thought.

Sandra kissed her sister's cheek contritely. 'There's nothing to forgive, dear. You didn't ruin my life, Mary Rose. I've only just realised how much I owe you.' A tear ran down her cheek, and she went on with a misty, far-away expression. 'Besides, I never met a man that measured up to our dear dad, Mary Rose. I never met anyone to match Danny Murphy.'

The busy airport was hardly the place for such an emotional reunion. Mary Rose agreed to follow Sandra and Chrissie to Dundee, where the sisters vowed they'd catch up on the lost years and have a good long blether.

It was an eye-opener to Chrissie, returning after fifteen years to the city she loved.

'They've done away with the Overgate, Mum,' Sandra said.

'Never!' Chrissie was shocked. She couldn't imagine Dundee city centre without the ancient narrow thoroughfare, dirty and tumbledown though it had been. No more Saturday markets and buster stalls in the Mid Kirk Style. The thought unsettled her. Didn't they value age and tradition nowadays? she wondered.

'That's not all,' Sandra went on. 'The Wellgate Steps have gone, and the lovely old gaslamp we used to call the "bobby's helmet". They're building a shopping centre where the Wellgate used to be. All the shops will be under cover, with a fountain playing all day long.'

'That'll be to remind folk of the rain pouring outside,' remarked Chrissie dryly. She gave a shriek. 'Sandra, just look at the skyscrapers!'

Sandra laughed indulgently. 'Those are multi-storey flats, Mum dear. Big Bella and wee Eck live in that one, on the tenth floor. She says the view's grand, but you can't throw a jammy piece down to your grandchildren when they're playing in the court, like you could in the old tenements. She tried, and the gulls got it halfway.'

Chrissie liked the road bridge across the Tay, although she mourned the passing of the busy little fifies. The bridge opened up great possibilities though. The Kingdom of Fife lay waiting to be explored.

'The Queen Mother opened the bridge officially in 1966,' Sandra informed her. 'Pity you weren't here, Mum. You would have enjoyed it.'

By this time they had reached the gates of Beechyhill, and Chrissie breathed a sigh. She was home, and she didn't know whether to laugh or cry.

'Why, the lodge is empty!' she noted with disappointment as they drove past. She'd been looking forward to meeting her nephew, Hughie, and his lovely Indian wife.

'Yes. Jani sold the shop ages ago to her cousin from

424

Pakistan. Hughie and Jani have retired across the water to Tayport, but Jamal keeps the Kennedy sea-faring tradition alive and is chief engineer on an oil tanker. Jamal's young lad, William, is following in his dad's footsteps too.'

Chrissie fingered the little silver ship pinned to her blouse. 'Just imagine, Sandra, another William Kennedy at sea. How proud your grandfather would have been, bless him!'

The frustrations Rufus had faced during the past months in Hawaii would have finished a lesser man, but Rufus had more than his fair share of determination, so he hung in there. The *Christina K* was still berthed in Mauna Kea, older and grubbier, a little more paint flaking and wood crumbling. She was still named *Aloha* and dispensed food and drink to passing tourists. Miki, the little Hawaiian chef in charge of the restaurant, said sure, she was for sale. The only trouble was, how do you buy a ship when there's no sign of the owner?

Rufus knew the owner's name by now. It was Michael Faraday. He had systematically combed the islands, and everyone he asked beamed and said sure, they knew Michael Faraday well. But nobody had any idea where he was. He'd disappeared completely as if he'd vanished into thin air.

And months were passing. Sitting aimlessly on the beach watching the timeless sea, Rufus was acutely aware of the relentless passage of time. Old women didn't get any younger, and his beloved Gran'ma Chrissie had had another birthday, her eighty-sixth. What if he couldn't keep his promise to Gran'pop and buy the ship for her in time? What if she never saw the *Christina K* come sailing up the Tay, because it came too late, for her? Grown man though he was, Rufus felt tears threaten, and not only because his grandmother was growing old. As time dragged by on his wild goose chase, would Natasha wait? And why the heck should she, just because a complete stranger begged her to? Months had passed since he'd seen her, watched her dance, and fallen deeply in love. The memory of Tashie never left him. He could see her dancing now if he closed his eyes, dancing along the shimmering curve of the sandy bay. Oh, would Tashie wait?

'Ahemmm?'

Rufus looked up, startled. Miki, the little fat chef from the *Christina K*, squatted beside him on the sand.

'I remember something about Michael Faraday. Quite suddenly it come to me. I think he go whaling!'

Rufus's brows shot up. 'Whaling! No. He's not the type, Miki.'

'Not killing whales, saving them. I remember he tell me about whales one day, how they are intelligent and care for their families and little ones, and how they are still cruelly hunted and someone must stop it. He said he would go fight for the whales if this rich man would buy his ship, but he'd had no reply. He said I could lease the ship, and he would maybe go anyway, for he was sick watching people eat while children starve.'

Rufus was jubilant. This was the breakthrough he'd been hoping for. 'You think he's gone to save the whales?'

Miki nodded solemnly. 'It is possible. He is a good man, a fine man, but a little . . . you know?' Miki tapped his head significantly.

'Now your grandmother has settled down in Dundee, how about fixing a date for your wedding, Tashie?' asked her mother hopefully.

Tashie's heart lurched sickeningly. She didn't understand why, but it did. 'Maybe in a year or two?' she suggested tentatively.

Frowning, Charlotte sat down and studied her daughter. Tashie was very quiet and preoccupied these days. It wasn't like her. 'Darling, why wait so long? Don't you want to get married?' Charlotte asked.

'Yes, of course! But—' Tashie turned away, biting her lip.

Why must she remember Rufus? Not even the handsome, dazzling stranger who was Rufus, but Rufus the fat, ugly, weeping boy she'd held in her arms, Rufus who'd touched a little girl's tender heart years ago. She understood now why she'd given up her ballet career in order to help others to dance. It was because of Rufus, fat and ungainly and desperately unhappy. Rufus, miraculously transformed but still in need of her help, had begged her to wait for him. But he took so long! Oh, why didn't Rufus come?

Charlotte levered herself up and limped across to kiss her daughter. 'Tashie, it's just an attack of nerves, darling. I understand, of course, but I'm sure you'll feel more confident if you and Mark name the day, and soon.'

Tashie smiled vaguely but didn't answer. Nobody understood. How could they? There was only one person who knew Rufus and loved him. One person who might tell her what to do. Her grandmother, and his.

'Mum, what were you up to this morning, creeping about at that unearthly hour?' frowned Sandra.

'It was six-thirty, love, and I was only making myself a cup of tea in the kitchen,' replied Chrissie mildly.

Sandra sighed. 'But you can make tea in your own room and have it in bed. Why didn't you?'

'Because I wanted to be up and doing, that's why!' retorted Chrissie with a flash of spirit.

With difficulty Sandra choked down an angry retort.

She loved looking after her mother, when she was given the chance, that is. It was Chrissie's defiant gestures of independence Sandra found most irksome. What with Harriet refusing to hand over the reins of Chrissie's Farm to a younger person, and Chrissie asserting her independence, Sandra felt almost at the end of her tether.

'I wish Harriet would return to Dundee. I'm terrified she will fall and break her hip again. She's still lame and needs care,' Sandra complained worriedly.

Chrissie took a sip of tea. 'I've been giving that some thought too, Sandra. Why don't Harriet and I move into the lodge? We could look after one another then, and you could keep an eye on us both.' Chrissie's lively eyes sparkled. 'It would be rather fun!'

'Fun!' Sandra stared. 'But it's cold and damp, and hasn't been painted for years!'

'It's amazing what a lick of paint will do, and we'll install central heating. It's a dear wee house. Harriet would love it.'

Sandra bit thoughtfully into a slice of toast. It was a solution. In fact, the more she thought about it, the more attractive the idea became. It would give her mother independence with discreet supervision from the family, and solve the problem of dear, old stubborn Harriet at a stroke.

'OK, Mum. I'll drive out to the farm this morning and put it to Harriet,' Sandra agreed, feeling a good deal happier.

Natasha found Chrissie on her own when she called later that day. Chrissie was delighted to see her lovely granddaughter.

'Come into the kitchen, Tashie. I'm baking scones. I don't get a chance when Sandra's around. She treats me like fragile old china!'

428

Tashie perched on a kitchen stool, watching the old lady work.

'Gran, you know Rufus well, don't you?' she ventured.

Chrissie's happy expression faded. 'Yes, I suppose I know Rufus better than anyone, dear.'

Tashie took a deep breath and told her grandmother all about her last meeting with Rufus. 'You see, I felt somehow, as if there was a strong bond between us, something so strong I couldn't possibly ignore it. I wanted so much to wait for him, to help him and know him. But . . . but he hasn't come back. Should I marry Mark, or should I wait for my dear little frog who's turned into a prince? Can I trust Rufus, Gran?'

Slowly, Chrissie dusted flour off her fingers. Oh, it would have given her such joy to watch Rufus and Natasha fall in love, to see them marry. But Rufus was too fickle to be trusted with Tashie's happiness. His recent conduct showed total disregard for those he professed to love. He mustn't be allowed to break this lovely young woman's heart.

'No, Natasha, you mustn't trust Rufus,' Chrissie warned. 'He's brilliantly clever and I love him very dearly, but somewhere along the line Rufus took a wrong turning. He designed complex weapons, then saw the weapons he'd designed used in Vietnam against civilians. It broke him, Tashie, changed him. Rufus can't be trusted any more.'

She took the sad young woman's hands gently in her own floury ones. 'If you want my advice, forget about Rufus, my love. Set a date for your wedding, and marry Mark.'

Charlotte was delighted by her daughter's decision to marry Mark in September. It didn't give much time to organise a big wedding, but time enough. Charlotte decided to make the bridal gown herself. She was a skilled seamstress, and could see the gown already in her imagination, based on the beautiful paintings of ballerinas by Degas. Perfect.

Tashie was amenable to all her mother's excited plans. She had become oddly docile, almost listless, once the decision to marry had been taken. Pre-wedding nerves, Charlotte thought tenderly, and pressed on with the gown.

By the end of August it was almost finished, and Charlotte had Tashie stand on a table for a final fitting and adjustment of the hem. How beautiful her daughter looked, Charlotte thought emotionally, like a little lost ballerina, wistful and sad? Charlotte paused abruptly in her pinning and studied her daughter intently for the first time. What was wrong? Oh, dear, something was very far wrong, she thought anxiously. Why hadn't she noticed before?

At that point Connie McPhee burst in. Connie always entered with a clatter, a quirk from days spent serving in the buster stalls, but today her entry seemed louder and more significant than usual.

'There's a man chappin' on the door, asking for Tashie. A Yank by the sound o' him. Wi' a funny name: Rufus!' Connie announced.

Natasha felt her whole being light up with joy. Her body seemed to lift from the table without effort, fly through the air and land lightly, poised on her toes. Then she was running as she'd never run before.

Rufus saw her come flying to him like a vision straight out of his dreams. He opened his arms, and she flew straight into them.

'Oh, Rufus! What took you so long? You were very nearly too late!' She looked up into his face, her eyes shadowed with sadness. 'Rufus, Gran said you weren't to be trusted. I didn't know what to do, so—'

He laughed and kissed her for the first time. 'I guess

Gran'ma Chrissie doesn't know the whole story, darling, and I can't tell her yet. But I promise you can trust me, Tashie, with your life.'

He held her close, his eyes so honest and sincere, all Tashie's doubts melted away.

'I know that, Rufus,' Tashie said.

'Tashie, I have to find this man. He could be in Japan, Norway, anywhere, for he's a man with a mission. First I had to reach you before it was too late, because crazy as it must seem to you, I love you and want to marry you. I've loved you ever since you were a little girl. I hoped we could go find this man together. Would you go with me, my love?'

Tashie didn't hesitate. She knew she'd had a lucky escape. She'd tried to please her parents and very nearly married her friend instead of her own true love. Now she must please herself and follow her heart. She slipped poor Mark's engagement ring off her finger and laid it gently on the hallstand. She felt free then to make another promise.

'Yes, Rufus, I'll go with you anywhere, always,' she said.

Once the stushie occasioned by Natasha's change of heart had died down and Tashie and Rufus had been married quietly with only the close family present, Chrissie and her old friend Harriet settled down to life in the lodge.

'This works fine, Chrissie!' Harriet enthused after a cautious start. 'I hate cooking, and you love it, so you're welcome to rule in the kitchen. We both like pottering around the house and garden, so that's OK. We agree to differ on some things, but otherwise we're a perfect old pair, dear,' the old lady grinned.

In the course of a year or two, Harriet collected one

abandoned small dog and three stray cats, and was happy as Larry.

Chrissie's family found the lodge a small haven of peace and comfort, the two old ladies a constant source of amusement and wisdom. Chrissie's sons, Ewan and Sammy, were now elder statesmen in the textile trade, and Rankine's had long since amalgamated with a larger consortium.

'It was the only way forward once the jute trade declined, Mum,' Ewan explained. 'We're spinning polypropelyne now. It's a strong man-made fibre, used to make bulk containers for chemicals and suchlike and foundations for roads and seawalls.'

'What would your father have thought?' Chrissie wondered. 'So many changes. Even the coinage has gone decimal. They did away with the good old tanner and threepenny bit while I was in Texas. Oh, and I do miss the dear old half-crown piece and ten-bob note.'

Ewan laughed and reached for another piece of delicious shortie.

'Well, dear, it's an ill wind, as they say. Decimalisation meant new cash registers, and that boosted Dundee's reputation in the field of new technology and the micro-chip. Anyway, Linda and I are delighted young Charles has decided to join the firm when he leaves school. One day there'll be another Charles Rankine heading a new technological age in the city.'

In the summer of 1986 Rufus received a cryptic cable from Miki in Hawaii. It consisted of two words.

'He's back!'

'What on earth does that mean?' Natasha wondered, as she nursed three-month-old Leonora, while four-year-old Benjamin played on the floor of the Good Hope ranch-house.

'If it means what I think it does, we've found the man

we've been hunting for, my love!' said Rufus jubilantly. He bent to kiss his wife. 'Tashie, I'm sorry to break our holiday, but I must leave for Hawaii at once. You know how crucial time is, don't you?'

She met his eyes gravely. 'Yes, darling. I know.'

Rufus was heartened by thoughts of his wife and two lovely children as he strode along the dockside at Mauna Kea, because he had no idea what he would find when he reached the *Christina K*. He hadn't seen her for over ten years. A long time in the lifetime of an old ship and a very old lady.

He saw her three masts first, towering above the quay, and breathed a sigh of relief to find she was still afloat at least. He walked on, and found himself staring at a scene of shabby dereliction. There was a lanky old greybeard leaning over the after rail, staring soulfully at the sea, and Rufus mounted the gangplank and approached him.

'What happened to Miki?' Rufus asked.

The man turned and leaned his back on the rail, surveying Rufus.

'Miki went bust.' He looked ruefully along the deck littered with rubbish, and at the blistered, peeling paint. 'Poor old lady. It's a mess, isn't it?'

'It could be fixed, with plenty of dollars and goodwill,' Rufus said.

The greybeard gave a bark of laughter. 'Who are you? Santa Claus?'

'I might be.'

The man narrowed his keen, blue eyes. 'Good heavens. You're serious. I believe you really are serious!'

'Did you save the whales, Mr Faraday?' Rufus asked quietly.

Michael Faraday threw back his head and laughed. 'You're the guy who's been hunting me from pillar to post, aren't you? And to think I've been dodging you! Sure, we saved the whales. There was legislation passed in 1982, protecting them, but it still requires constant vigilance. Maybe I saved the whales, for now, but am I too late to save the ship?'

'What has to be done to make her seaworthy?'

Michael Faraday started along the deck, Rufus by his side. 'Her hull's sound, so far as I can tell, it's very strong, built to withstand crushing by the ice, but part of the stern, the counter and the lower mizzen-mast would have to be renewed, her auxiliary engine completely overhauled, the rigging and sails replaced. It would take some time and cost a small fortune.'

'The funds are available, but time is not on our side,' Rufus said sadly. He explained about Gran'ma Chrissie, still hale and hearty at ninety-five, but a very old lady.

'Let me get this straight,' frowned Michael. 'Gran'ma Chrissie's family intend to refit the *Christina K*, then bring the ship by way of the Arctic Ocean and the fearsome hazards of Baffin Bay, to the east coast of Scotland and the river that gave my ship her birth, all to please an old, old lady.' He paused for a long moment and stared in silence at Rufus. 'You must love your Gran'ma Chrissie about as much as I love this ship.'

'We do,' Rufus said simply. He gripped the older man's arm. 'Michael, if I give you ample money and authority, will you see to the complete restoration of the *Christina K*? Would you be her skipper and sail her to the Tay when you think she's ready?'

'I would need a good crew. The best,' the greybeard pointed out cannily.

Rufus grinned. 'Don't worry. You'll have as fine a crew as you can muster when the time comes, and as many willing young lads to train as you can handle,' he promised.

* * *

'Wonderful old lady, the Queen Mother. Just fancy, ninety years old!' remarked Sammy Murphy as the car drew to a halt, patiently negotiating a snarl-up in Dundee's traffic. Chrissie, although in total agreement, couldn't resist a little friendly rivalry.

'Och, she's just a chicken. I can give her ten years!' She sniffed complacently.

Emily, seated beside her husband in the car, twisted round to look at the regal old dear in the back. 'Chrissie, you'll have to give some thought to your hundredth birthday, coming up. It'll cause quite a stir in the town, you know, especially with celebrations on the go for Dundee's eight-hundredth birthday.'

'The Hogmanay street party was grand, with merry-go-rounds and buster stalls in the streets again,' recalled Chrissie with relish. 'It was just like the good old days in the Greenmarket, though Sandra would only let me have one poke of chips and wouldn't let me go on anything.'

'Well, you'll have to be prepared for your own great day, dear.'

Chrissie heaved a sigh. 'Sometimes I'm glad dear Harriet was spared all the fuss of living to be a hundred. She'd have had something to say, I've no doubt!' She missed her friend, though Sandra had moved into the lodge now, and mother and daughter got along very well, now they were both so elderly.

'Anyway, I'll have my hair done and maybe stand myself a new outfit for the Lord Provost coming with the Queen's telegram. Oh, and I'll make some shortie for his cup of tea. I'll maybe have a wee glass of whisky and lemonade for once. That'll be enough celebration for me,' Chrissie chuckled.

Sammy and Emily exchanged a look. Chrissie's eyesight was still keen, and that secretive glance upset her. She'd caught that look so often from members of

435

her family, and it never failed to puzzle and sadden her. She was still a perceptive woman, and she knew her loved ones kept something from her. Deep in her heart she knew it, and their secrecy hurt. As fiercely proud as ever, Chrissie scorned to spier an answer from any of them.

The car was on the move again along the riverfront. Passing by the dock gates, Chrissie caught a glimpse of the masts and rigging of Captain Scott's *Discovery*, and as always the sight gave her a queer feeling of sadness and regret. In 1986 she'd gone with Sandra to watch the *Discovery* come home to Dundee from the Thames, and the event had been so emotional it had made Chrissie cry. Of course, it was wonderful to watch that other historic vessel take its place beside the ancient man-o'-war, *Unicorn*, in the dock, but it had made her think about her own dear ship, and wonder where its poor old bones lay rotting.

When the great day arrived at last, Chrissie thoroughly enjoyed playing hostess to the distinguished guests who crowded into the cosy living-room of the lodge to celebrate her hundredth birthday. Of course, they asked her what the secret of her long life was, and she thought about it seriously.

'Well, I could say it's because I sup porridge every morning, or maybe because I had the good fortune to be happily married three times,' Chrissie answered with a grin. Then she looked at her three daughters, her two fine sons, all elderly themselves now and very dear to her.

Her eyes misted. 'But I think it's the love my family gives me that keeps me going. Their love for me has been as steadfast as the river flowing out there. They grew from wee bairns to men and women with lives and bairns of their own, but their love grows strong as I grow weak and old. It carries me along until I reach great old age, aye, just as the bonnie river gathers strength and flows, until it joins the sea.'

Her head nodded drowsily, and her guests tactfully took their leave, leaving Chrissie to catnap until Ewan gently woke her some time later.

Chrissie grinned at him. 'My, Ewan, what a grand party that was. They fairly scoffed my shortie. That was the best birthday party I ever had. And to think we have Dundee's eight-hundredth birthday to come yet, on the first of June. There's to be a grand parade and sideshows in the street, and a fireworks display at night. Oh, I do love fireworks!' she declared with relish.

'Your own birthday party's not over yet, Mum. Put on your coat. Wrap up well. It's a wee bit chilly out.'

'We're going out?' she asked wonderingly.

Sandra piled so many woollies and scarves on Chrissie she protested she could hardly waddle, but she was glad of the extra warmth when she felt the chill air of the April afternoon. Ewan tucked his mother tenderly in the front seat of the car. Everyone seemed to have turned a little deaf, for nobody answered when Chrissie plaintively demanded to know where on earth they were going.

Ewan headed for the Grassy Beach, past the spot where the Kennedys' house once stood, a row of neat, small houses now occupying that prime site. Chrissie smiled mistily, remembering a small, excited girl on a birthday many years ago, tugging at her father's sleeve.

'Oh, Papa! There's my ship!'

When she closed her eyes, she could almost hear her own excited, childish voice, hear her dear papa's deep, delighted laughter, and Ernest's awed whisper as the *Christina K* came sailing majestically past the window.

'Papa, she's beautiful!'

'Mum, we're here!' Chrissie opened her eyes with a start. Ewan had driven the car close to the shoreline, and Chrissie stared in surprise.

'My, Ewan, what a crowd of folk! What's going on? Is it the Phibbies swimming across the Tay?' she asked.

Ewan laughed. 'Come and see.' He helped her from the car then tucked her arm firmly through his and guided her faltering footsteps down the rough path on to the beach where once she'd played at chuckie-stones and met a poor, despairing mill-lassie.

It wasn't the Phibbies Bathing Club, though. The crowd standing on the shore turned and cheered as Chrissie approached, and she hung back, confused and startled by the unexpected noise and laughter. Ewan smiled and urged her on. When her eyes became accustomed to the brighter light, Chrissie saw with a sudden lift of the heart that she knew everyone gathered on the shore. This was her beloved family, come from near and far to be with her on her special day. From the oldest to the youngest little babe in arms, they had come here just to greet her.

What a magnificent gesture, what a wonderful surprise.

Rufus and Tashie came forward to kiss her, and Hank and Miranda rushed to follow suit. Dear Miranda weeping buckets, as usual. Chrissie surveyed her large family, her heart very full, and gradually a hush fell as they waited breathlessly for her to speak.

She wondered why they'd chosen the Grassy Beach of all places to hold the reunion, and hoped anxiously they wouldn't catch their death of cold. She felt suddenly full of high spirits, and her eyes twinkled.

'Aye, well, if you're expecting me to take a dook at my age, you're in for a sair disappointment, all of you!'

A gale of laughter greeted the remark. Her family's

love wrapped round and warmed her like a shawl. She felt herself borne up by their love, brought almost to the edge of the silvery water which rose high on a spring tide, lapping at her feet.

Rufus's arm was around her shoulders.

'Look, Gran'ma Chrissie, look! Here she comes!' he shouted, pointing towards the estuary, his strong voice vibrant with joy and excitement.

Wondering, Chrissie looked where he pointed, shading her eyes with a hand. Past the Fairway and Lady and Newcome buoys, the markers that had safely guided whalers to harbour long ago, past Broughty Castle on its rocky promontory, Chrissie saw a ship come sailing. A graceful, yet sturdy ship with three tall masts, creamy furled sails rigged on the mizzen-mast, flags flying bravely in the breeze. A drift of smoke from the tall funnel was dark against the pale April sky, as the *Christina K* went by.

Chrissie stared, and thought her old eyes were playing daft tricks, but then she saw the young lads lining the rails waving furiously, and a drift of cheering came to her across the water like remembered echoes of laddies' voices singing round a campfire: Ben's Lost Boys!

'Rufus, it's the *Christina K*,' she whispered. She looked up at him, afraid to trust her senses. 'It is the *Christina K* isn't it, Rufus?'

He nodded. Emotion choked him and he couldn't speak. A wonderful, joyous glow lit his grandmother's old face so that she seemed like a bonnie wee girl again. It made worthwhile all the work and worry of the past few years, and the dangers faced by Michael Faraday and his young crew as they battled to bring the old ship home.

There were tears in Chrissie's eyes as she watched the last Dundee whaler sail past. She rejoiced not only for herself, but for her father and other brave men who'd faced hardship and danger on icy seas, trusting in Dundee-built ships. The *Active* and the *Balaena*, the *Windward* and the *Diana* and the *Polar Star*, and so many more grand ships, all gone. But Chrissie's ship, the *Christina K*, sailed on towards harbour. It made her feel proud and very humble. She understood now why her loved ones had guarded their secret so well. She turned to Rufus and her family, who had crowded round to watch her delight.

'How can I ever thank you? Oh, why did you do this wonderful thing for an old Dundee woman like me?' she cried with deep humility.

Rufus bent and kissed her cheek, spokesman for them all. 'Because we love you, Chrissie, and we love your ancient city and bonnie ship. We want the *Christina K* to go on sailing for years, training young lads in skills the old Dundee sailors knew. Can you think of a better reason?'

She couldn't. She just stood smiling at them all, her eyes bright with happy tears. Presently, they brought a tiny baby to her, dear Ernest's great-granddaughter. The proud mother eased the shawl away from the baby's face to let Chrissie see the bonnie wee girl better. 'Look, Gran'ma Chrissie, she's another Christina Kennedy, another Christina K!'

Chrissie looked down at the wee bairn named after her, sleeping peacefully in her mother's arms, and many memories flashed through her mind, some happy, some sad, all mingling to make a rich, rewarding fabric. Fumbling a little, Chrissie unfastened the silver replica of the *Christina K* from her blouse and pinned it to the baby's shawl.

'There, wee Christina Kennedy, this is yours now. I don't need it any more. My own bonnie ship is safely home to the river,' Chrissie said.

JOSEPHINE COX

ALLEY URCHIN

In the grand tradition of Catherine Cookson

'A classic is born'
LANCASHIRE EVENING TELEGRAPH

By 1870 Emma Grady has spent seven years of servitude as a convict in Australia. Now, having earned her ticket of leave, she is still bound by chains of honour and friendship. Yet Emma lives for the day when she will return to England, to face those who cheated and betrayed her. And to Marlow Tanner, the man she loves – and whose tragic child she had borne and then lost.

Emma struggles to make something of her life in Australia despite the sinister presence of her employer's evil son Foster. His determination to 'have' Emma leads to dark and terrifying consequences.

As Emma battles against adversity, she is unaware that in England the child she has given up for dead is being lovingly raised by Marlow's sister Old Sal. Emma's daughter Molly grows up to be an expert pickpocket, but her fierce loyalty to her partner in crime Old Sal earns her the admiration of all who come to know her.

Will Emma ever be reunited with Marlow? Even if she finds him, will he still love her? And what of the child lost to them both? Emma is plagued with fears but her love for Marlow never weakens – and can never be forgotten...

FICTION/SAGA   0 7472 4076 0

A selection of bestsellers from Headline

LONDON'S CHILD	Philip Boast	£5.99 □
THE GIRL FROM COTTON LANE	Harry Bowling	£5.99 □
THE HERRON HERITAGE	Janice Young Brooks	£4.99 □
DANGEROUS LADY	Martina Cole	£4.99 □
VAGABONDS	Josephine Cox	£4.99 □
STAR QUALITY	Pamela Evans	£4.99 □
MARY MADDISON	Sheila Jansen	£4.99 □
CANNONBERRY CHASE	Roberta Latow	£5.99 □
THERE IS A SEASON	Elizabeth Murphy	£4.99 □
THE PALACE AFFAIR	Una-Mary Parker	£4.99 □
BLESSINGS AND SORROWS	Christine Thomas	£4.99 □
WYCHWOOD	E V Thompson	£4.99 □
HALLMARK	Elizabeth Walker	£5.99 □
AN IMPOSSIBLE DREAM	Elizabeth Warne	£5.99 □
POLLY OF PENN'S PLACE	Dee Williams	£4.99 □

All Headline books are available at your local bookshop or newsagent, or can be ordered direct from the publisher. Just tick the titles you want and fill in the form below. Prices and availability subject to change without notice.

Headline Book Publishing PLC, Cash Sales Department, Bookpoint, 39 Milton Park, Abingdon, OXON, OX14 4TD, UK. If you have a credit card you may order by telephone — 0235 831700.

Please enclose a cheque or postal order made payable to Bookpoint Ltd to the value of the cover price and allow the following for postage and packing:

UK & BFPO: £1.00 for the first book, 50p for the second book and 30p for each additional book ordered up to a maximum charge of £3.00.

OVERSEAS & EIRE: £2.00 for the first book, £1.00 for the second book and 50p for each additional book.

Name ....

Address ....

....

....

If you would prefer to pay by credit card, please complete:
Please debit my Visa/Access/Diner's Card/American Express (delete as applicable) card no:

Signature ....Expiry Date ....